I0614276

To request permissions, contact the publisher at ScharaReevesPress@gmail.com

Paperback: 978-1-7362987-6-3

First paperback edition April 2025.

Edited by Alyson Montione
Proofread by ScribeCat (ScribeCat.ca)
Cover art by Jake Bartok
Cover text by The Modern Jane

Schara Reeves Press

ScharaReevesPress.com

ACKNOWLEDGEMENTS

Editor:

Alyson Montione

Proofreader:

ScribeCat (ScribeCat.ca)

Cover Artist:

Jake Bartok

Cover Text Artist:

The Modern Jane

General Support:

Jesus Christ

Family

Friends

Schoharie Library Writing Club

Beta readers:

Rebecca Schmid

PRONUNCIATIONS

Alenor (AL•eh•nor)

Alkemar (AL•keh•mahr)

Astra (AS•trah)

Atlys (AT•lis)

Baey Tihali Mornaro (BAY teh•HAHL•ee moor•NAR•oh)

Baeno (BAY•no)

Bethyn (BETH•ehn)

Bethynese (BETH•eh•neez)

Ckaknimaen (KAK•neh•mayn)

Cyl (SILL)

Darbeshay (DAR•beh•shay)

Dyress (DIE•ress)

Eknemar (ECK•neh•mar)

Emarian (eh•MAYR•ee•in)

Esmer (EZ•mer)

Estasia (es•TAY•zha)

Eugene Atarah (YOU•jeen ah•TAR•uh)

Grenedil (GREN•uh•dill)

Hytat (HY•tat)

Illan(il•OHN)

Jaythos (JAY•thohs)

Kaedna (KAYD•nuh)
Kaedovarna (KAY•doh•VAR•nuh)
Kassander Knyte (CAS•and•dur NIGHT)
Kearn (KEE•urn)
Kovo (KOH•voh)

Maeko Kuto (MAY•koh COO•Toh)

Ovok (OH•vok)

Patelayna (pah•tuh•LAY•nuh)

Rhioa (rye•OH•uh)
Rugo (ROO•go)

Sefen Kalaesia (SEH•fehn Kel•AE•shee•uh)
Skayla (SKAY•luh)
Syvil (SIV•uhl)

Tanner Pardaya Armon (TAN•er par•DAY•uh ar•MOHN)
Thackeray (THAK•er•ay)

Tirzah (TEER•zah)
Tyron (TIE•ron)

Veka (VEHK•uh)

Xyrilcylduin (zy•rill•SILL•doo•inn)

Summary of To Take a World: The Living Stone

After reuniting with Sven's mother—The Crafter—in Alkemar, Baey and her friends embark on a new challenge: to find The Living Stone so that The Crafter can repair Moira's watch. However, this requires the group to split up. Sven, Baey, and Estasia remain in Alkemar while Tanner, Maeko, Jaythos, Sefen, and Syvil head off to Rugo.

While their friends are absent, Baey trains under Sven to hone both her fighting skills and her ability to use his ring. Meanwhile, Estasia makes contact with an ally in her network of spies, and soon, she discovers that they aren't the only ones fighting against Skayla after all. New friends appear in the form of Atlys, Darbeshay, and Thakeray, who are running a secret underground city full of refugees who have escaped Skayla's MindHold.

Now with more access to information and resources, the group investigates the portal site where the Drogans first arrived. There, Sven stumbles upon his sister, Moira—or rather, her ghostly figure trapped outside of time. They later return to the site with Alenor so that she can try to dismantle the machines that are meant to force the portal open. But Skayla finds them and Sven faces off against her. A stranger appears through the portal in the middle of the battle, and Sven uses his newly revealed ability to warp reality in order to whisk them away to safety—but not before destroying Skayla's armband, the source of her power.

Meanwhile in Rugo, Tanner struggles with his deteriorating mind as his group sets off to find The Living Stone. They make a new ally named Marion, a Drogan who narrowly avoided being put in Skayla's MindHold and has been hiding ever since. She reveals Lord Kovo is none other than Ovok, and that he has been much more involved in Skayla's actions than people have believed. It is also discovered Jaythos's brother, Kearn, is stationed in the city they arrived in and that he is determined to seize them by any means necessary.

Eventually, they are captured and Tanner is forced to use his abilities as a Memory Keeper to lead Ovok and Kearn to The Living Stone. In a final attempt to keep him from it, Syvil attacks Ovok and the two take to the sky in battle over The Living Stone. The ensuing clash on the ground leaves Jaythos mortally wounded. A very injured Syvil is later discovered by Baey on the shore of Alkemar. Before he dies of his wounds, he informs her Ovok has taken possession of The Living Stone.

For Luna

TO TAKE A WORLD:

THE LAST ESMER

A DAUGHTER'S RANSOM: BOOK VI

BY NIAMH SCHMID

THE LAST ESMER

When time is unwound and fate is undone,
When the heart of the world hides away from the sun
And chaos befalls the order that was,
Then will this prophecy come.

When the labyrinth crumbles, its hiding place torn,
And the oaths of the guardians three are foresworn
And the light of the worlds is taken by one,
Then will this prophecy come.

Then will the child of the wind and rain
Rise up to triumph as darkness's bane.
For the one with wings shall take back the Heart
Of the world when this prophecy comes.

Then rise the daughter of human and elf,
The healer of hurts done beyond themself,
Shall take up chaos's Mind to undo
The harm when this prophecy comes.

Then the one molded new must die to the old
In order to live as he takes up the Soul.
Ransomed and price come together at last,
Redeemed when this prophecy comes.

Then conduit Soul, the Heart, and Mind,
Shall shatter the worlds as together they bind.
The called must follow eternity's voice
To prevail when this prophecy comes.

THE LAST ESMER

PROLOGUE:

Ovok:

I clutch Rhioa's body close, desperate to feel her life and afraid that, at any moment, it might disappear for good. She's dying. She's *dying*, and she's the only good thing that's ever happened to me.

"Cyl—Cyl, *please!* I'll do whatever you ask—just help me save her!" I gasp between the choking sobs. I am no longer above begging. All I feel is panic and a fear I have not felt in a hundred years. "We'll just use The Living Stone and then put it right back—I'll rescind guardianship of Eatris—I'll even step down as lord of the Myrandi. *Please!* I can't lose her!"

Cyl—once someone I called friend—stands across from me, eyes cold and unforgiving in his pompous, self-appointed role as god. "You brought this upon yourself, Ovok. I can't help you, nor do I care to trust you."

I would squeeze my fists until they bled if not for the fear it would only hurt the limp form of my daughter, still cradled in my arms. "You won't regret it, I promise. I swear on her life I will make this worth your time—I won't try anything. You can take the lead and talk to the Baenians. I won't even touch The Living Stone myself—I'll even stay here and you can bring Rhioa to them. I just need her alive. I—I'll go away and never come back. *ANYTHING!*" My voice cracks as I search for any reaction from Cyl.

"From what I hear, it was a fair consequence. The Eatrisians shouldn't have been meddling with the Miadoris, and Rhioa shouldn't have gotten involved. We've closed the Door and it will remain that way. Consider this…a lesson learned. For the Eatrisians *and* you. Be thankful you still have one daughter who hasn't succumbed to the blood on her hands." Nothing in Cyl's tone betrays even a hint of emotion. No empathy. No acknowledgement that I am holding my dying daughter in my arms.

My mistake. I was weak. I thought Rhioa would be happier gone. I thought I could fix myself, and then she and her husband would come back willingly, and that maybe…just maybe we could have tried a different way of doing things. So naively I'd believed I could show Tirzah and Rhioa the love they'd deserved and been the father they so wanted.

But it would seem I was too late.

"A lesson learned," I repeat Cyl's words, resignation and rage mixing together. A thousand plans already swirl in my head, each one worse than the last. "I'll save her, myself."

Rhioa will hate me for this, but I don't need her to forgive me. I need her to live.

I have taken Rhioa to the world-between-worlds and put her in the Amaranthine Axis, where she will remain in a state of stasis; alive but barely. Of course, I made sure to put her in a cell safely away from the…other problems I store there.

Cyl is probably dead where I left him, and the cursed Myrandi blade, Ckaknimaen, is strapped to my belt—the blade I'd sworn never to touch again after I'd let Rhioa leave with her husband. Now, it giggles gleefully, visions of violence playing in my mind's eye as I try and judge for myself how to proceed in Baeno. My ears are roaring almost as loudly as the hum of the blade at my side. I just need to talk to the leaders on Baeno. I just have to borrow The Living Stone—only for a moment.

Let's have some fun. I'm thirsty.

Baeno is just as prejudiced as every other forsaken world. After over two years disguised as Lord Kovo, I see now there will be no bartering. I can wait no longer. Now, the Myrandi are with me. None of them know exactly what is happening, but when I'd returned to Eatris, I'd grabbed anyone who was there and left with them—just in case I'd need to get The Living Stone by force.

Well, I'd grabbed *most* of them. I did not tell Tirzah, who had been away when I'd arrived. I've made her do enough dirty work, and if all goes well, it should only be a short time before I'm back with Rhioa. Then, hopefully, she will understand.

In the meantime, I have enough of the other Myrandi to help me. All they know is that we are attempting to find a safer place to live. Which perhaps is not completely incorrect. After what Eatris did to Rhioa, leaving for Baeno is the best option.

At least, that's what I'd thought. The Baenians' guardians—The Watchers—now prove a challenge. When I'd first arrived on Baeno in disguise, I had worried they were too young to be responsible for an entire world. Now was the first time I'd officially met them and, as I'd feared, it took only moments to confirm that the oldest one, Moira, is too dangerous; the youngest, Sven, too naive and inexperienced in the ways of politics; and the middle, the only one with an open enough mind for me to even consider explaining my true mission. It took me a few days to see how Moira uses time to go back and talk circles around me, and now I know if I tell her of my reasons for being here, she will act against me and I won't even know.

Please. This is so boring. I want to taste blood, not listen to your pathetic whining—the sword's whispers in my ear are constant and make it quite difficult to think.

Panic is my constant companion as of late, and things are only growing worse. The portal won't reopen. I can't get back to Rhioa—I can't get off-world even if I *do* find The Living Stone, and all I can think of is being trapped here forever, one daughter abandoned on Eatris and the other doomed to remain frozen in time for an eternity in the Amaranthine Axis, grasping forever at life, just out of reach.

At least Skayla has agreed to help…but her fear is keeping her from what needs to be done. She's a lot like I was, when I was young.

—*Young and stupid. Stupid to think Cyl was a friend*—Ckaknimaen laughs. —*Fear is for the foolish. Fear is for prey.*

Yes. For once, the sword is onto something, and it gives me an idea. Skayla needs to use that wonderful little persuasion on herself, perhaps. She needs to purge herself of fear. Just like me.

This is all wrong. I have so much blood on my hands. *So* much blood. Not even I could have predicted that Skayla putting herself in a MindHold would break her mind as much as it has, but now not only has she murdered Henry Mara—the person we *needed* in order to get The Living Stone—but she's gone on a killing spree like some deranged animal. Her laughs now match those of Ckaknimaen, and they are both attempting to drive me insane with the infernal sound. All I can do is focus the energy into what I need. I can't control Skayla, that is clear, but I can at least steer her in the direction I need—not that it's helping. We've been looking *everywhere*. Country after country has fallen and still, I can't find it. I know Rhioa will never forgive me now. This *has* to be worth it. I can't let this much violence go for nothing. I am drowning in blood and I can't get out....

It has been years. *Years*. Years of guilt and anguish, and years of sinking further into this wretched pit of blood. Years of going further from who I'd vowed I would be after Rhioa left with Tyron.

But I cannot go back, it's too late. Now, the plan is not only to save Rhioa, but then to rid all the worlds of these powerful relics; to be rid of the Miadoris, Living Stone, and the Ithys that resides on the world of Kryso. To destroy Ckaknimaen and any other Myrandi blade I can find. All they bring is power and corruption. Yes, I must purge the world of these and of anything that can cause this much pain and suffering—so that nothing like this can happen again. No one will be able to abuse power because no one will have it. The deaths such a task might cause will pale in comparison to those it will save; I must believe that. I have no hope of redemption at this point, anyway…there is just so much blood. Every step of the way I see Rhioa's eyes pleading with me to stop. This was *never* supposed to happen.

We've taken the last stronghold of Baeno, and *still* it isn't here. Duke Emarian held no knowledge of The Living Stone's whereabouts, no matter how Skayla scoured his mind.

To make matters worse, Sven has escaped, the poor fool. Skayla had turned him into her plaything like some cat toying with a mouse. Killing him would have been more merciful, and apparently the smarter decision. Now he's made off with Moira's watch, which had been what was helping Skayla remain so powerful. Without it, I worry Skayla won't be able to continue holding the number of minds captive that she does. What if others begin to slip through the cracks?

I cannot dwell on that possibility right now. First, at least I know where Sven is going: Valdon. And thanks to the leak from Valdon, we will soon know for sure when he has arrived. All we have to do is get there before Sven leaves. Then we'll have Sven *and* the key to wherever The Living Stone is. Certainly it must be there.

It has to be.

I stand on the shore of Patelayna, the pulsing green stone resting in both my hands, the gears inside it whirring and clicking. I have it. Blood still splatters the stone in a few places, marking the struggle with Syvil, and it only reminds me of the crimson ocean I have created on this planet. Ckaknimaen has gorged itself on the blood of my own kind, taunting me.

But I have it.

I could almost laugh in relief. I'll save Rhioa, and then I'll get rid of this and anything else powerful enough to cause so much suffering.

All I have to do now is get the portal open, and with The Living Stone, I should be able to have enough power to push open The Doorway by force. Cyl is at the root of that, I'm sure. That selfish coward survived his wounds. This destruction is just as much on his hands as it is mine. If only he'd looked past his own self-righteousness for once and helped me, then none of this would have happened.

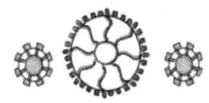

"What have you *done?!*" I scream into the void of the ravine. The place is in ruins—and the soldiers are still cleaning up the upheaval of dirt and metal as well as the casualties. What has me in utter shock is the displacement of…everything. There is a house from the city now in the middle of the clearing, as well as a lamppost sticking half out of the ground as if the world has been folded up and spliced together. Rubble hovers strangely in the air, gravity itself changed. I have been informed that Sven Mara is behind this. How had I underestimated him so much? These are no illusions.

But worse? Skayla's relic has been destroyed, leaving her catatonic, and those in MindHolds are slipping out daily. This means the Myrandi that I'd had Skayla keep under her influence are also abandoning ship…panicking and trying to disappear among the populous of Baeno. Resources will start to dwindle and my time is running short.

Still, there is further ill news.

The portal is gone. Not closed; *gone*. In the displacement of matter, it seems Sven Mara has also managed to displace the portal as well.

I'm somehow *still* stranded. So close to saving Rhioa, and now so pitifully far.

I am done playing games.

CHAPTER I: More Strangers

<u>Baey:</u>

My eyes snapped open, the muffled hub of The Underground filtering through my tent. Right. Morning. I got up, shaking my wings awake as I rubbed life into my extremities. It was always colder down here: cold and damp, far different from the cozy warmth Alenor's manor held.

I grabbed a set of cleanish clothes—yet another new set after an unexpected growth spurt—taking only a few moments to get dressed before exiting my tent. I made a stop over to Alenor's only to find it unoccupied. Of course. That meant she was either at Sven's bedside, or already at the portal with Grenedil.

I knew it wasn't her scheduled time to be watching over Sven, but I still gave myself the excuse she might be there in order to pop over to the tent that had been set up beside Darby and Thackeray's. It had needed to be a bit bigger to accommodate the devices meant to help him in his coma.

It only took me a minute to get over there, and I wasted no time ducking inside, hoping somehow, I would see a different sight than had greeted me for weeks.

Darby was beside him, as per rotation, sitting and reading aloud from some book Alenor had brought down from the manor.

"Still nothing?" I asked, forcing myself to look at Sven, lying unconscious on the cot, surrounded by a strange set of machines that helped nourish him. Alenor had built them—she'd had enough scraps to make two; one for Sven, and one for the main hospital of The Underground to use.

Darby, who had paused her reading upon me entering, shook her head.

"Alenor isn't here then?" I asked further, trying to stick to my pretense for checking in.

"No. She and Grenedil are monitoring the portal."

It was hard to look away, let alone acknowledge that Sven would someday just fade away completely, leaving me angry and sad; angry that he'd survived so much just to go like this—still so unsure he had done any good in his life—and sad that he would leave us without knowing how much he was loved.

"She's been at the portal a while. I think she was gone even when I took the shift here this morning." Darby's gentle prodding reminded me there were a million other things to worry about right now, and Sven wouldn't have wanted me to sit here blubbering over him being gone. Even if I had to remind myself of that every day that I checked on him.

"Right," I shook myself, a few feathers fluttering away and onto the ground. "I'll go to the portal next, then." With that, I peeled myself away from where I wished I could be, and returned my attention instead to where I had to be—for Sven and for everyone.

The portal. The other thing Sven had apparently brought with us when he'd miraculously transported us all from the original portal site back into The Underground and away from Skayla. Only, "miraculously" might not be the best word to describe it. I knew Sven would have had some blunter terms for it, at least. It turned out that he hadn't just *bent* reality, but instead torn it and sewn it back together, leaving bits of Alkemar spliced into place like a bad attempt at forcing jigsaw puzzles into spots they didn't belong. The portal site was a mess, the landscape marred with even gravity altered, according to our sources. We'd been surprised to discover that Moira's "ghost" had somehow been one of the few things to remain at the ravine—surprised, and maybe a little disappointed. Meanwhile, the city of Alkemar had been…"reordered"… as well, and some of it had been put together down *here*. Entire buildings had appeared. Some were upright and complete; others were slanted or half buried under the ground or even in the cave ceiling. It was as if I had tried and failed to cast an illusion of a city down here. Only they weren't fake.

Neither were the deaths it had left behind.

As I made my way through the streets—now a mixture of the rough stone from The Underground and lighter cobblestone from the surface city—it was hard to smile and remain normal for the civilians around me. Syvil's death had been a week ago, and every day Sven didn't wake up made it ever more likely he never would. There was also now a *huge* target on our backs; the portal that Skayla had been guarding so vehemently for years was now here, in the center of our one sanctuary. We'd been sending scouts out for weeks now, trying to find somewhere we could move the civilians to so they wouldn't all be taken down should Skayla find us, but even Atlys had explained just how difficult it would be to hide the quantity of people like The Underground had. The population had grown in number since the battle at the ravine; there were now over nine hundred people down here.

Still, I kept my smile as long as I was in the main part of the city, nodding to those that greeted me and trying to appear as if everything was under control. It was strange being so recognized, even if it did make sense. The wings sort of gave me away pretty quickly. I suppose the truly weird thing was the respect that seemed to come with the recognition now.

At last, I arrived at the barricade, which Darby had ordered be built to keep the general populous away from the portal and allow Grenedil and Alenor to study it in peace. There was enough unrest and scrutiny: They didn't need more.

"Baey, they'll be happy to see you," The guard at the entrance to the barricade smiled and stood aside.

"Thanks, Tarca," I managed a smile back, nodding to the woman as I crossed over the threshold and into the small circle of isolation. The hum of energy resounded all around the wall of wood and debris, the power of the portal palpable.

"Aha, there you are," Grenedil commented as he looked briefly up from the machine gauges he was fussing with. It was hard to get an understanding of this near stranger, even after the few weeks he'd been here. I would have been more wary if not for Alenor vouching for him.

"I hope you got some rest—I told Grenedil you needed it," Alenor chimed in, pausing mid-turn with her wrench to give me a much more vibrant smile.

"Yes, thank you," I replied, watching the pair as they continued to tinker with the machinery around the portal area.

I couldn't quite understand the two. Alenor, whose son was in a coma and quite possibly never coming out of it, was livelier and more upbeat than this quiet stranger, Grenedil. Sure, he'd told us quite a bit about the world he'd come from; about the Drogan—or well, Myrandi, as he said they were called—Mitheau, and the two called Louko and Astra. But I still didn't really see *him*. He reminded me a little of Estasia, the way he dodged everything, and yet…unlike Estasia, it didn't seem like he did it on purpose. Instead, it was more as if he didn't want to think too much about anything or didn't have time. While it appeared more because of the fact he was jumping from crisis to crisis on different worlds, I still didn't like the knowledge that he was so scattered. It made me a little apprehensive about trusting him, even if Alenor had apparently met him years ago. In fact, Alenor was who had given me most of the other information on Grenedil and his position as The Merchant—collector and protector of magical artifacts—which had been stolen by his brother. She'd said they'd met briefly when her children were quite young, when Grenedil had still been training under some interworld guardian named Cyl in order to be this "Merchant."

It had been more information than Grenedil had cared to share with us. The moment he'd found out what a mess Baeno was, he hadn't been much good for giving us any details besides the fact that he had to find Cyl and that this Cyl would know how to help. This had just led to him being mostly obsessed with the portal and monitoring the various readings from the machines that surrounded it. I, in the meantime, was left wondering why this Cyl hadn't shown up years ago if he was so helpful. To me, it could either mean this guardian was dead, or perhaps not as benevolent as Grenedil was trying to lead us to believe.

"How's the pressure look on that measurement now, Grenedil?" Alenor called over, taking her wrench from the bolt she'd been adjusting.

I walked up behind Grenedil just in time to see him tap the glass on the gauge that measured the energy of the Maze door. "Still a little high…" I could hear the concern in his tone.

There was a sudden clang and I jumped in the air, caught off guard by how Alenor had struck the portal machine with her wrench.

She grinned shamelessly. "Apologies." Yes. She hid the pain well behind the smile lines of her face, but I saw it even now. Briefly. The acceptance that she was once again alone with no family, and the acknowledgement that Sven would never wake up. Alenor had said it was a danger any Gifter faced when they over-extended themselves to the degree he had, and that almost no one had ever woken up after being out for this long.

"Uh, Alenor…It's…that did not help." Grenedil worry became even more evident, and I fluttered back to the ground so I could take a look over his shoulder again. He was right, but I didn't even really need to look at any of the meters to understand that. The portal machine was shaking now.

"Get back!" Grenedil grabbed my arm, pulling me back before I could even think of getting out of the way myself. An explosion of glorious blue light radiated from the machinery as we took shelter at the far end of the barricade, watching as the light flooded everything in sight.

"Grenedil! What in the worlds are you doing meddling with The Doorway at such a precarious time!?" The voice thundered through the space, the source of it coming from this newest figure that had appeared through the mysterious portal. He struck an intimidating shadow, standing in the clearing and wearing the strangest clothing. Something like a long, thin cravat was tied around the neck of a clean, buttoned up white shirt visible from beneath the shortest suit coat I'd ever seen, not even reaching past the top of his waist.

Yet another stranger from another world. I was at least slightly less confused than when Grenedil had appeared, and yet something in my bones told me I should be a lot more wary of this visitor. Maybe it was the instant hostility in his tone, or maybe it was the fear-filled awe I felt from the numerous scars running down his face.

"Cyl!" Grenedil jumped up and ran up to the man almost the instant the stranger had spoken. "*Finally*, I thought you were *dead!* I went to the portal and you weren't there so I was sure—" He stopped awkwardly just short of the man. "Where have you been? Things are bad, Ovok is—"

"Going for The Living Stone, I know," Cyl cut in coldly. "I was trying to seal one of the other tears in The Maze and must have missed you coming through. I've been *trying* to keep The Doorway sealed so he could not get out, should he obtain The Living Stone. I thought it was secure enough for me to seal the other tears…but then you decided to reopen it. I wrongly presumed you were past the need to be babysat." The glare he gave Grenedil was impossible to miss.

So Cyl wasn't dead, then.

"Cyl, thank the worlds you've arrived." It was Alenor, now, having followed Grenedil up to the man, I knew a less-than-subtle redirection when I saw one.

But I was still in shock, trying to process this newest player. Cyl. The Guardian of the Doorway. Grenedil's friend. Only, he didn't seem very friendly....

I stayed awkwardly behind, clutching the broken timepiece, unwilling to take a step closer to the man. Or wait, Drog—Myrandi. Grenedil had said he was another Myrandi. That he'd been Ovok's friend, long ago before Ovok had changed.

Maybe that's why I was hesitant.

"Alenor, how in the three worlds did you get a Door opening to move?" Cyl's eyes locked on the woman.

"I...my son. You remember my youngest? Sven? He...He can bend reality. He was trying to keep us safe." Her voice faltered for the first time.

"He tampered with *reality?* Why are Baenians so foolish—you realize what that could have done? If The Doorway had split in the process—"

"He saved our *lives* and possibly the world!" I interjected when both Alenor and Grenedil were scolded into silence. Some stubbornness in me fought against the awe Cyl's presence had originally inspired. Maybe it was the promise I'd given to the unconscious Sven. The promise to be strong enough; to push past the fear and take care of his mother. "Where were you, anyway?" The words left before I could think twice, and the way Grenedil swiveled around and stared at me wide-eyed told me they were probably unwise. But I found I didn't care.

"As I said. I was keeping the portals closed. I was *trying* to stop Ovok from returning to Eatris, which I would hope you have also been trying to avoid," Cyl replied coolly, looking completely unaffected.

Before I could open my mouth for further interrogation, Grenedil interjected.

"Yes." I didn't miss the pointed look in my direction. "Alenor and Sven had been in the process of destroying the portal machines when I appeared and Skayla showed up to try and get through." His finger tapped nervously at his side. "Skayla's been helping Ovok."

Cyl seemed a mixture of irritated and confused. The look he gave Grenedil was again that of disappointment, and I didn't like the way Grenedil seemed to silently shrivel under it. "And why did you feel the need to jump head first through an entrance after knowing Ovok had nearly killed me trying to open one?"

Again, Grenedil only barely beat me to replying, "I…because I was trying to find you. You just disappeared and I didn't know if you were dead, Cyl. Eatris is having issues and the new Guardian there surfaced but Ovok's son-in-law is hunting her and—"

Cyl brought his hand up to his scarred brow and rubbed the bridge of his nose. "And where is your brother?"

"Havirax is still missing—I haven't seen him since Ovok left." Grenedil's voice cracked a bit.

"So you have yet to find your brother, and then you abandoned this supposed new Guardian on Eatris just so you could come reopen the Door here and Ovok could get through? How do I know you aren't really helping Ovok? Maybe you're a little more like your brother than you let on."

"Who do you think you are that you can just show up and start insulting people?" I was finally able to get a word in, and oh, did I have words. I could only hope I was channeling my best Estasia impression. "Aren't *you* the Guardian of the Doorway? Not Grenedil. Well, *Guardian*, we have been trying to survive for the last decade because *you* let Ovok get through in the first place. You don't get to ignore us for years and then show up telling us we're doing it all wrong. At least Grenedil was trying to help us."

"Baey," Alenor whispered. "Careful."

Cyl regarded me with a heated stare, and again, I was reminded that this *guardian* of worlds was someone I wasn't supposed to mess with. Yet I was finding him more irritating than scary.

"I suppose she isn't wrong," Cyl said simply. "Things are complicated. We all make decisions we regret." He bowed his head, then turned back to Grenedil with a little less irritation. "For now, I need you to update me on *everything*, and quickly. I have sealed all the tears in The Maze for now, but Ovok must not get The Living Stone."

Grenedil's wince was all too visible. "It seems…we are possibly a bit too late for that."

"What?" The one word was like one of Alenor's hammers striking against the anvil, and just like that all the new patience that had entered Cyl's demeanor vanished again.

"According to…to the dying breath of a friendly Myrandi, Ovok has gotten possession of The Living Stone," Alenor replied, putting a hand on Grenedil's shoulder as she spoke.

"Ovok's taken all of Baeno, Cyl. It's gone. He…He's destroyed it all," Grenedil added, voice choked up. "Do you have any idea why?"

Something flinched in Cyl's expression, but I wasn't completely sure what. Whatever it had been was too quickly hidden, but he was definitely hiding it for a reason. "He wishes for the same thing he always has: control. His lack of trust drove him too far and then he capitalized on other's trust. I assume that is how he took your world? He came here and told you all to trust him?"

My eyes narrowed.

"I…yes." Alenor's eyes fell.

"Alright, well maybe in the future let's not trust strangers." The tone was patronizing. It reminded me of when one of the warriors of Valdon would try and chide me like some infant incapable of knowing the simplest right from wrong.

It wasn't a pleasant memory.

"Noted." I found myself once more speaking without any care to this supposed guardian of worlds. "I suppose that rules out me trusting you, then?"

Alenor looked more proud than aghast. Grenedil settled for the aghast part. I, however, couldn't care less, busy at the moment fighting the irritation boiling in my stomach with the "I am dealing with a child" expression Cyl was now throwing at me. That look I was all too familiar with. Familiar with and tired of.

"Well, I would hope Grenedil and Alenor's word would help you to see I am no stranger."

"I like to form my own opinions of people," I replied.

Grenedil groaned and placed his head in his hands, making me feel only a little bad.

"Hm," Cyl gave the noncommittal noise before stating, "I need to talk to the remaining Watchers immediately."

Everyone looked at me, the sorrow deep in Alenor's expression.

"Yes. Well, that would be me," I again spoke up, crossing my arms and looking defiantly at the Myrandi.

"I think I would prefer Moira…or Sven, seeing as he was the one who moved the portal down here." Cyl's tone betrayed his fraying patience.

I simply replied, "Moira's stuck in time, and Sven's in a coma. I'm the only option you have."

"The Creator did choose her, Cyl." Alenor's voice filtered quietly through the tension. "To replace the failure of my family. She's the guardian of Baeno now."

I bit my tongue at the last bit. She and Sven were far from failures.

"Of course you are," Cyl showed a little bit of annoyance as he addressed me. "Then why don't we have a chat somewhere a little more private than…this?" He gestured around to the barricaded area, a twisted look of bewilderment rippling across his face as he turned around.

I did not back down. "This is pretty much the only option unless you want to surrender to Ovok and Skayla's soldiers on the surface. But I'm sure we can use Darby's tent."

Having yet another stranger showing up through the portal was quite a shock for Darby—who had only just gotten off of her watch with Sven. But, as usual, she took it in stride, allowing us in the tent and remaining calm as she awaited an explanation.

"This is—uh—Cyl. As I've told you previously, he's the Guardian of the Door between Worlds and he was the one that Ovok fought to get to Baeno." Grenedil wrung his hands nervously and turned back to Cyl. "I was worried you were dead—I came looking for you from Eatris because of Astra; she's being hunted for her ability to apparently tap into The Maze. She must be Ovok's replaceme—"

"Yes, you said as much. But what warranted leaving for me?" Cyl interrupted, towering form taking up quite a bit of space in the tent.

Grenedil's face was flushed as he stuttered, "I-I, uh, I thought if you could allow her to use The Doorway, she could protect her family and stop the madman who's chasing her. I know you've had The Maze sealed off, but if you just let her have access to it—she's smart. She'll use it wisely and stop someone terrible from getting access to The Maze."

I tried to keep things on track. "And why is Ovok here? Did he come here just for The Living Stone, then?" As much as I also wanted to help Grenedil's friends, we needed help first, and that started with Cyl answering some of our questions first. I was still worried about the rest of our friends. Maybe Cyl could help.... We hadn't heard from Tanner and the rest—not since Syvil. Atlys had sent a messenger with one of his merchant airships to Rugo in order to contact Estasia's informant there. As much as I hoped they'd heard anything, or maybe knew where they were, I was so afraid of what we'd hear back.

"Ovok is after The Living Stone for his own gains. Not even I can fathom his mind or his pretended persecution." As much as I appreciated Cyl at least acknowledging my question, part of me was rather annoyed with how easily he had ignored Grenedil and his own pleas for help. He went on, seemingly unbothered by any of what Grenedil had shared. "I fear, however, he plans to take it off-world, which we must, above all else, avoid. If it leaves Baeno, your world will again begin to tear at the seams as it did in the days of old."

I was glad to not be the only one looking utterly puzzled. Darby looked confused as well. Alenor and Grenedil seemed to understand, though, and I decided that in the list of questions I had, wanting to know whatever the days of old entailed wasn't at the top. It seemed enough to know it would be bad. "So you're going to help us get it back, then?" I asked. "And help Astra?" Grenedil added on.

Cyl's face twisted a bit but soon settled into the impassive state it seemed characterized by, and he nodded. "I will do everything in my power to keep Ovok from leaving this world and taking The Living Stone with him…but I need to fully understand the situation. Please?" He turned to Alenor, *again* ignoring Grenedil.

I bit my tongue only for now. That's not exactly what I'd asked. I'd asked for *help*. Help for our friends…help for us.

Alenor stepped up, briefly explaining everything from Skayla's turn to the present, including Henry's death. I couldn't understand how she remained so composed through it all—having to just explain how her whole family had been torn from her, one by one. But it wasn't unfeeling; not like Cyl. It was clear that behind the composure, every memory brought her agony.

"So you *led* Ovok to The Living Stone?" Cyl again sounded deeply displeased. I was getting rather tired of the constant judgement.

Cheeks flushed; I was just about to say my piece when Darby beat me to it. "You're telling me he wouldn't have found it eventually once he found us? Getting Moira back and having the Mistress of Time on our side was the best chance at combating him, don't you think?"

Cyl gave a huff. "Well, it appears your gamble didn't pay off. Now, not only do you *not* have the Mistress of Time, but you also do not have The Living Stone, either." He then turned to me. "And you. You can manipulate The Living Stone itself?"

"I can manipulate the relics, that's all we know," I replied, a little baffled at the question but refusing to appear shaken in front of this self-important stranger. Could I control more than *just* the relics? I'd never felt any connection like I had to Sven's ring or the watch.

Sighing as if dealing with infants, Cyl again rubbed his temples. "I would hazard a guess that you can manipulate more than just their Gifts, given some actual, *proper* training. But I digress."

My wings bristled. He had no right to claim Sven a lesser teacher.

"As for you," Cyl turned to Grenedil. "I do not see how opening this Astra's access to The Maze will do anything but cause more chaos."

"But Cyl. Astra was practically dead when I left her—if she dies, then…what happens with the new Guard? She has nowhere to run and for all I know she could already—" Grenedil choked back something. "Already be dead."

He hadn't whispered a word about *this* to us. He'd spoken so fondly of Astra and her friends—only stating they had been in danger. I felt a bit of guilt at having so selfishly taken the attention away from helping them, even if I knew logically, Cyl helping us would make us able to help Grenedil's friends. All the same, the anguish in Grenedil's plea was real to me. It echoed around in my own brain day in and day out as I wondered if Sefen, Maeko, Jaythos, and Tanner were alive. If the goodbye all those weeks ago in Alenor's house had really been the last one.

Grenedil continued, "Just grant her alone access to it. You can trust her, Cyl. There's a reason she was chosen to replace Ovok, and she's already saved my life and the life of a young Myrandi when it did nothing but cost her. Please. It will allow her to be safe."

Cyl shifted, pressing his lips firmly together in thought. It took a great deal of my own discipline not to yell at him for even hesitating. Maybe I was clouding my judgment—maybe it was because if I had a chance to help Tanner, no matter the risk, I would immediately have jumped on it.

"Alright, I will give her access to it. But only to get into The Maze. If she is able to reach that, I can locate her and make sure she remains safe." Cyl's shoulders settled a bit from their tense position as he spoke.

"Thank you," Grenedil breathed, then looked around the room. "But we really do need to figure out how to help the Baenians, Cyl. It's not...it's not great."

"Yes, perhaps you could help by also opening a portal to Rugo?" I suggested. "We have some—"

"—Absolutely *not*," Cyl growled. "Allowing this Astra to tap into something she can already use is an entirely different matter from using The Doorway here. If I use the portal in this city, it will do nothing but attract Ovok. He has The Living Stone—any use of The Doorway on this world will be picked up by it, and he will find us. Then we'll all be dead. Your friends are better off finding their own way home."

My heart sank, but I didn't voice the fear that whispered at the answer. He said they were better off finding their way home on their own...but what if they were trapped? What if they weren't even alive anymore?

THE LAST ESMER

CHAPTER II: When Dying isn't Fatal

<u>Tanner:</u>

"He's still breathing! There has to be a way we can help him!" I latched my one hand around Jaythos's arm, my other hand clutching the shard of green Syvil had dropped. As soon as I grabbed hold of Jaythos, all of his pain ran through my mind and seared itself into my memory, but I was falling apart anyway. Nothing mattered anymore. I just let it hurt.

"There's…nothing…nothing we can do." The small voice of the once-confident Kearn sifted through the thick, dusty air. "…Nothing…" he feverishly repeated as he held his brother's hand.

Life flashed before my eyes, but it wasn't mine; it was Jaythos's. Him and Kearn playing as children. The tearful goodbye. The years of second-guessing. The grief and regret as the sword plunged—

"Tanner! What is that in your hand?!" Marion's voice was harsh and desperate as it cut through the tumult of the collapsing cave.

Tanner? I didn't know why she was looking at me as she called a stranger's name, but for some reason, I looked down at my hand, but it was the one holding Jaythos's arm.

Without another word, Marion lurched at me, but I was so paralyzed by the pain and shock that I didn't move as she grabbed my *other* hand and pried it open. I just stared at the small glowing bit of stone. Right. I'd grabbed the shard when Syvil had dropped it.

"It's probably the only reason he isn't dead already!" Marion yelled above all of the commotion, now pressing the green bit of stone against Jaythos's chest.

Jaythos coughed—the first sign of life besides the shaking—and groaned, but nothing else happened.

"We need to stop the bleeding *now*," Marion ordered, looking at everyone with a fire in her eyes.

Everyone—Bethynese or otherwise—began tearing off pieces of their shirts, handing them to her as quickly as they could manage.

But still I couldn't move.

I'd gotten Sefen killed…probably Syvil, too. Now, Jaythos was on his way to join them…. I could hardly remember I wasn't him, let alone who I really was or what was going on. One minute, I would see Jaythos's body, gurgling and groaning as Marion and Kearn desperately tried to stop the bleeding, and the next moment, I would see Rhioa, her body still on the bed as I came face-to-face with my worst mistake. It was as if all of the agony I had collected in my mind finally came out at once, leaving me utterly undone as the room shook around us. Was it the room? Was it just me?

"We need to get out of here. Is the entrance still unblocked?"

"W-w-will we be able to move him?"

"We'll have to. He's stayed alive this long. I'd rather him die being moved than by being squashed by a rock."

As if on cue, another rumble echoed about the crumbling chamber, shaking me to life.

"The entrance is clear enough, but if we don't hurry, it might not be for long." It was one of the Bethynese soldiers, panting as he came back over. There was a bit of blood trickling down the side of his head, and I only vaguely registered the debris falling left and right.

"Well, come on, then! Let's move him." Marion was the one who answered.

"Get the rest of our comrades and head for the entrance! Quick, don't leave anyone behind!"

Kearn. He had to hate himself. What had I done? It would have been more merciful to shoot him rather make him not only witness my death but also the—

SHUT UP!

"Tanner, come on, get up!" A hand was on my shoulder, and I opened my eyes—the eyes I hadn't realized I'd closed—to find Marion already trying to hoist me up. Maeko and some of the other Bethynese soldiers were carrying Jaythos now. Why weren't we fighting anymore?

I didn't even register that I was walking—or running, rather, Marion pulling me by my hand. Nothing felt real as dreams mixed with nightmares, pouring over my brain in an endless rush of water threatening to drown me. But they weren't nightmares; they were real. They were the worst moments of everyone's lives playing out inside my head. Was I drowning in water? Or was it blood?

Get out. Get out and leave me alone! It was like I could hear the audible tearing of my sanity ripping at the seams.

"Stay. Here," Marion ordered as she grabbed both my shoulders and placed me against a wall. We had gone back into the long hall before the chamber. The ground was rumbling, but no debris was falling here, yet.

I couldn't make myself move even if I'd wanted to, and so I stood there, the commotion from the collapsing chamber muffled as I screamed in the dark. My hands went to my ears, and this time I did register my eyes squeezing shut.

Panic is my constant companion as of late, and things are only growing worse. The portal won't reopen. I can't get back to Rhioa—I can't get off-world even if I do find The Living Stone, and all I can think of is being trapped here forever, one daughter abandoned on Eatris and the other doomed to remain frozen in time for an eternity in the Amaranthine Axis, grasping forever at life, just out of reach.

"I'm drowning," I whispered. "I am drowning in blood and I can't get out..."

"Tanner!" I was being shaken again, held by both shoulders.

"What has happened to him?"

"What do you *think* happened? The stress broke his already fragmenting mind—keep going with Jaythos, we need to get out of here!"

"Yelsi, run ahead and tell the others what is going on. We need to get him on a horse and back to the city as soon as possible." Kearn. It was Kearn's voice, so scared and vulnerable. I hadn't heard him like that since....

"Jay—no—Jay, you're not leaving, are you? You're turning the position down—you have to!" Kearn's eyes brim with tears, fists white with tension as I face him. I've brought him for a walk by the water, hoping our favorite spot would be more private. I knew he would hate the news, and I'd wanted the reaction to be away from our parents. They wouldn't take kindly to such weakness. I need to show them Kearn was capable— to somehow convince them that going overseas with me will be valuable and that he can learn more with me than staying back for basic training. Deep inside, however, I know it is fruitless. I'd always known I would be left with the choice to make my escape; to use this station with the Bethynese Embassador as my chance for freedom from the cruel and loveless land of Bethyn—or to stay with my brother. To stay and have both of us trapped.

"I…I can't really, Kearn. It's a great honor, after all. Not many my age are ever asked to go on such a high-profile attachment." It was true. I had trained hard…for survival. For chances like these. I couldn't stand the Bethynese way. Many of us couldn't, and yet it was always how it was done, wasn't it? The Council of Generals and those in authority told us it was the only way to survive. That the other countries would strike at the first sign of weakness and laugh at any who tried to seek sympathy.

"No! I don't care! You can't—I don't want to—" Kearn's eyes are floodgates now, doing a poor job at holding back the tears streaming down his cheeks. "I thought we said we weren't going to be soldiers. I thought we were going to be sailors. We were going to explore and leave one day, you promised!"

33

"I know—I know what I said. We will, Kearn. I promise, I just…I have to find a way. I will find a way, don't worry." Guilt gnaws like a termite at rotting wood, and again, I tell myself I will figure it out. I'll make a plan; maybe I could sneak him on board? "We might be apart for a while, but remember, it's not forever, Kearn. You have to be strong. We'll find a way."

But we never did, and I abandoned him to the mercy of the country I'd fought so hard to get away from.

"This is chaos." It was Kearn's voice again, older and bitter. Tired, too. "What happened?"

"Their eyes…their calls—I-I think Skayla's losing her power."

I blinked, my own eyes feeling dry and my entire body sore. Light filtered in from the room, and I found myself sitting in a chair. In a house, with some sort of loud, mob-like chaos going on outside. Kearn was over by one of the windows, hand above the frame as he peered out of it.

"Tanner!" The voice startled me, and I jerked a bit. "You—are you in there?" It was Marion, she was sitting in a chair nearby and her gaze was now fixated on me. She moved, slowly kneeling before me and touching my hand. "Say something. Tanner?"

Her voice triggered so many memories. Her always getting into trouble. The look she gave when I tried to talk her out of it. The evening flights, the afternoon *fights*. The terror of being without her when Skayla had taken my mind. The years of fire and—

"No, no, please, not you, too, don't go again. Tanner, stay here, child."

34

I shivered, but slowly faded back into the present, desperately clawing to keep a hold of my name. Tanner. I was Tanner. Tanner the orphan. Tanner the Memory Keeper. Tanner, the only friend Baey had. The Tanner who had gotten Sefen killed.

Sefen....

"Kearn, get me the water by the pitcher, please?" Marion asked quietly.

"W-wait...he's on our side now?" I managed to ask limply. He'd let Sefen be killed. Why?

"Yes, Tanner. He's helping. Jaythos is still alive. Syvil is—Syvil is back. Just breathe."

"Just breathe, feel the wind around you. Don't be so afraid of falling, Rhy. I'll catch you." I let out a deep rumbling laugh, unable to hide my amusement at Rhioa's small, golden form flapping helplessly in the breeze.

"Tanner?"

Jumping up in a panic I pushed back on the woman in front of me. Where was I?

"Tanner, *please* I—Ah!" The woman touched my arm and withdrew when I kicked at her, panic seeping deep. A dungeon. I'd been captured.

"Get away!" I screamed as I backed up, desperately searching for anything I could use as a weapon. My eyes landed on a knife on the table next to a plate of food. It seemed the Bethynese soldier also in the room had realized my intentions, and we both leapt into action, diving for the knife. I had to get out of here—had to get free before I told them something. Before they broke me.

"Kid, stop it!" The soldier yelled as his hand landed only just before mine, sparking a full out wrestling match between us as I fought for the knife. I tore at his viselike grip on the small weapon, a small part of me confused at him labeling me a child even as the rest of me surged with the primal instinct to survive.

All of a sudden, the man gave out a shout of surprise, and his grip loosened. Right as I was about to liberate the knife from his fist, however, someone grabbed me from around the waist and hoisted me off of Kearn, causing us both to topple backwards on the floor.

It was…it was Syvil?

"Tanner please stop!" The voice cracked out a desperate plea.

I broke down and sobbed, dropping the butter knife and putting both hands over my ears as I wept. "Go away, please, go away!" I cried over and over again as I realized with a sudden and cruel clarity just what was going on.

I was broken. I'd finally done it and my mind was in shambles, reliving the life of everyone I had ever touched.

Tanner was gone.

Kearn:

I gasped; the sudden vision having rooted me to the ground. "He…is he done, now?" I asked hoarsely as I tried to regain my senses. I didn't know what I had just seen, but the intense flow of emotions had been impossible to ignore; the hatred, fear, the need to survive—the inner scream of agony.

I looked over to find that the person who had saved me from the butter knife–wielding child was not Marion, but in fact, our other companion in the room. It was the one who had fought Ovok at the mountain. He'd reappeared very suddenly beside Marion a few days ago. She'd said he'd apparently…died fighting Ovok? According to her, Drogans got two lives, apparently. What I wouldn't give for a second life to start over with.

This other Drogan—Syvil—was now sitting beside the boy, looking about as much of a mess as the child was. I still wasn't used to the reality of Drogans being shapeshifters, let alone the fact Ovok and Kovo were the same person.

Marion rushed over from where she had been knocked over in the fray. "Syvil, thank The Creator—here let me take that." She discreetly picked up the knife from the floor and tucked it into her belt. "Lesson learned. No butter until further notice," she murmured to herself, eyes darting from the pair on the floor to me. "Are you alright? What happened?"

One hand clasped firmly around the hilt of my sheathed sword, I replied, "Whatever his memory issues are seemed to have bled out when I touched him." A shudder ran through me as I couldn't help but think of how many nightmares had to be floating around in that head of his. I'd only gotten a taste. "But I'm fine." I squared my shoulders, having enough nightmares of my own to deal with without someone else adding to them.

I still had enough to deal with for turning traitor as it was. Part of me wondered what in the world I was thinking, but when even the rest of those under my command had agreed to desert the army in favor of Jaythos's crew, I'd been a little caught up in the moment. The ragtag group with my brother had saved our lives getting us out of that tunnel, and Jaythos's stupid act of bravery had earned the respect of my soldiers. Jaythos's friends had even helped rescue several of my group who had been trapped during the cave-in.

It had earned me a lifetime of guilt, and the knowledge that I could never, *ever* again be on that side of the sword against Jaythos. All of that had led to this: desertion.

We were all traitors now. But that was the thing…Bethynese soldiers didn't commit treason. Jaythos had been an anomaly that had earned me scrutiny for years. Now…it seemed the scrutiny was rightly given.

"Wait, he…he gave you a memory?" Marion's question reminded me of what we'd been discussing. The woman was an intimidating figure, I would give her that. But I was beginning to wonder if it was a Drogan thing.

I shook myself and said, "Yes. At least I got something that I assume was a memory."

Tanner, who had been rocking back and forth with his knees up to his chin, slowly calmed, eyes opening and peering from me to Marion, to Syvil. "What happened?" he croaked.

I prepared for another fight. The kid had been catatonic since we'd gotten out of that tomb of a mountain, and I had not exactly expected him to do…this. Marion had simply said his Gift had overtaken him.

"Tanner, we're safe. Syvil—Syvil is back, and Jaythos is getting better. I need you to concentrate, can you do that?" It was amazing how her tone was instantly transformed from stern and commanding to tender and comforting in a matter of moments. It showed where her trust lay. I only heard her like that regarding Syvil and Tanner.

I dared not take a step further, instead looking nervously out the window I had stood by before the whole butter knife disaster. The riots were getting worse, and it didn't matter whose side we were on, we had to get out of the city. Yelsi and the others had already left the city to retrieve the airship Maeko had directed us to, and would wait to depart for Patelayna until Jaythos was well enough to travel.

I couldn't stop wondering how long it would be until the riots weren't just in this city. Perhaps turning traitor would protect my soldiers in the long run. After all, if the riots truly turned into overthrowing Skayla, there wouldn't be much ability for us to hide. We were Bethynese soldiers, hated no matter who we helped. Hated, and yet somehow everyone had been shocked when we'd joined Skayla—not that the people of Bethyn had been given a choice on what side they fought for. Not everyone had been as lucky as Jaythos, yet I wouldn't exactly call him lucky. Just on a different end of a stick.

But then, apparently, my side of the stick hadn't even been what I thought. We weren't working for Skayla. I had long known Kovo was the real one making the decisions—well, a lot of them, anyway. Skayla, at the end of the day, had her own whim and little discipline to ignore it—but I had not realized that all these years we had been working for a Drogan. That they had been walking among us without our knowledge. I felt like a puppet; the strings, orders—and I unaware of who pulled them. I didn't want to be like that anymore.

I shook my head, again trying to concentrate. Whatever that kid had done to me had really put my brain in a fog. I wasn't used to the lack of ability to focus.

"That's it, just breathe," Marion whispered, talking to the boy. "Relax, and we'll find a way to get those memories out of you. Don't worry."

I realized I had definitely missed something from the conversations happening around me.

"It's not working," Tanner whispered. "I thought you said you would help."

"It might take time, Tanner. But we can do it together, alright? Just breathe and relax. We'll try again when you've had more rest."

The boy's breath hitched, but he nodded, folding his hands and looking like he was trying desperately to hang on and stay in one piece.

Just like me the day my brother left.

The brother that I wasn't allowed to see, right now. Maeko had been very clear about that.

"Good," Marion replied, getting to her feet and turning to her other Drogan friend, Syvil. "We're going to be alright."

What a group this was. I only hoped the rest of their party was a little more organized. What had I gotten myself into?

Jaythos:

The first thing I heard besides the ringing in my own ears was the chaos. Shouts, screams—vague representations of human voices all around me hummed with a clamor of feet against cobblestone.

"What in Baeno is going on?" A vaguely familiar voice echoed somewhere close by.

The pain felt like a bolt to the chest, and some unfitting noise escaped me as I became more aware of the agony I was in. I also somehow registered that I was on a horse, or at least that's what the constant excruciating movement made me think. Not that I could think beyond the pain.

"We just have to get him to Runin's." It was Marion this time, I could tell. Vainly, I tried to focus my eyes on where the voice was coming from, but I could see nothing but glaring light.

"Sir, the whole city is in riot. What do we do?"

"Seeing as we are being insubordinate as it is, I say ignore it until we find somewhere safer. Then we will discuss."

I passed out once more.

When I woke again, it was with a jolt, sitting up straight and freezing from the flurry of misery it created.

"Woah!" There was a startled sound from next to me.

A bed. I was in a bed. What in Baeno was going on? I shouldn't be alive.

My vision at last returned to me and I found myself staring at a decrepit, wallpapered ceiling.

"Don't scare me like that, you are going to kill yourself." The voice was Maeko. He was standing over me, rubbing the back of his neck and

looking very displeased as he addressed me in Rugonian. *"Are you alright? Does it hurt?"*

That seemed like a stupid question if ever there was one. I shook my head anyway and then, vaguely registering the clamoring filtering in through the nearby open window, I asked, *"What happened?"* My voice was irritatingly gravelly, but I managed to get the words out. It also hurt to speak, and I looked down to see my chest heavily bandaged, but no blood peeked through. How long had I been out?

"Syvil. He dropped a piece of The Living Stone." Maeko grunted. *"Marion kept it with you all the way back—it kept you from dying and has helped your recovery. But maybe...maybe moving is not a good idea."* He tapped the base of his neck, making me aware for the first time that there was, indeed, something fastened around mine. Gingerly, I touched it—some sort of shard with twine wrapped around it.

Maeko gently took hold of my shoulder as if to encourage me to lie down again, but I didn't budge, ignoring the pain that shot down my neck and back as I shook my head. Why did that hurt? Did everything need the back in order to move? I groaned, even more loathe now to lay back down and feel anything touch my back. *"What about..."* I trailed off, partly to catch my breath and partly unable to bring myself to ask.

Maeko's face actually betrayed a little bit of displeasure as he sat back down. *"Your brother decided to help us get you here. The rest of the Bethynese soldiers seemed displeased that Ovok abandoned them to a collapsing mountain."* Disdain was evident in every syllable the Rugonian uttered. *"They now see you as more honorable."*

The relief I felt was, for once, more powerful than the pain still pulsing through me and I closed my eyes for a moment. Kearn was alright. *"Where is he now?"*

Another huff from my friend. *"Downstairs with Marion. But please, sit back. You are still very ill. Here—"* He moved behind me and adjusted the pillows so that they were more a wall to lean against. *"Please."* The legitimate desperation in his voice was something I hadn't heard from Maeko since Serafina's death.

Guilt burned my cheeks as I realized what I had put my friend through again, all because I couldn't pull the trigger. But Kearn was alive, Maeko was alive...we were all alive. Well, all except Sefen. I swallowed hard.

Silently, I allowed Maeko to help me lean back, feeling pathetic as I winced from the unpredictable spikes of pain. But even with the discomfort, I couldn't help but wonder why Kearn stayed downstairs.

"I'm going to fetch Runin so he can have a better look at you—he and Marion are the only other reason you're alive besides The Living Stone," Maeko said as he made his way towards the door. *"Please stay put?"* were his last words before he disappeared behind the door too quickly for me to ask him to maybe fetch Kearn too.

Now alone, I tried to strain my vision to the window, aggravated at how little I could see from where the bed was. At least I could still hear the shouts from the streets below. They were indistinguishable, except for one name:

Skayla.

The urge to get up grew almost as much as the shouts outside, and no discomfort could stop me. With agonizing slowness, I sat completely up once more, careful to take my time. Next, I swung my legs slowly around so that they hung on the side of the bed. So close.

Maeko could yell at me all he liked later; I needed to know what was going on outside. As if on cue, the door opened, revealing a cherry-faced Maeko and a very amused Runin.

"Pity. I was sure you would have gotten further," the older museum curator said with a shake of his head.

I just looked unimpressed and continued to try and work through the process of getting up even as they came up on either side.

"You need to lie back down, you imbecile," Maeko grumbled as he came quickly up beside me, grabbing my shoulder much more firmly than earlier.

"I can't waste away in this bed while the world is ending," came my retort through a clenched jaw. The more my ears abated from their roaring and the more I could hear the tumult outside, the more desperately I needed to know what was going on. Were we even safe? Why was no one else concerned? Also…how had we gotten back into the city? Kearn or no Kearn, there was no way we should have been able to without being found out.

Runin rolled his eyes at both of us, motioning to my bandaged wound as if asking permission.

I gave him a stare.

Runin simply replied with, *"If I don't look, you can't get up. I'll be quick."*

"He's not getting up," Maeko protested.

"Right, because he isn't going to try the moment we leave. Might as well let him see while we're here to catch him when he faints, rather than pick up the mess if he does it by himself." I was sure I saw Runin wink at me as he spoke. The curator was a puzzle, that was for sure, but I wouldn't complain about him being on my side of the argument.

True to his word, the older man was quick, with surprisingly nimble hands as he inspected the wound. I couldn't believe how it had healed. The stitches were quite evident, and the area around them still a garish blue and purple, but it was actually healing. All the same, it made me a little ill looking at it, much to my irritation. I'd had my fair share of cuts and close calls…but somehow seeing how all that had kept this hole through me together was a good set of needles and some thread made my stomach curl a little. Or maybe it was just that the healing wound was such an unnatural look—one usually saw this sort of thing on a dead man.

"Now, would you like some help getting up?" Runin eyed me like some parent facing down his petulant child as he finished rewrapping my chest.

"That would be lovely," I whispered back, turning my gaze to Maeko.

"Alright, here we go; take my arm," Runin interrupted my uncharacteristically wandering thoughts as he held out an arm. I took it and was surprised by the steadiness it greeted me with. Maeko gave me his, and together, we managed to get me on my shaky legs.

Slowly, we made our way to the window, having at least three occasions where I would have fallen on my face had it not been for their support. As we grew closer and closer, the noise became louder, and my eyes began to focus on what was beyond the glass. People were in the streets—droves and droves of people shouting and throwing things and generally making a huge disturbance.

"What…?" My question died away as we finally made it and Runin left my side to open the window a bit further. The noise erupted as it opened and a thousand shouts flew in to meet me.

"Kill Skayla!"

"No more!"

"Down with Skayla!"

Voice after voice screamed and called before disappearing again among the crowd.

My heart stopped. Long had been the day since I ever really thought something like this would happen. I found myself unable to breathe, dizziness kicking in from the sheer weight of what I was witnessing. What had happened? Was I dreaming?

"Imbecile. You should go back to bed…" Maeko's voice was one of worry as he gripped my arm.

"No," I whispered, suddenly firm. "I want to watch." This wasn't a dream.

Finally, after a few minutes of the unearthly sight, my senses returned, and I allowed Maeko and Runin to carry me away and back to the bed, where I sat down. "What happened?" I asked slowly. "Did we get The Living Stone?" Surely that still would not have caused this much of a stir….

"No." Maeko rubbed his bald head, his body stiff. "Ovok has it."

My heart plummeted. "Then what is going on?"

Sighing, Runin cut in, *"We do not know exactly, but we know something happened with Skayla back in Alkemar, and now many are no longer in a MindHold. But if Ovok truly has The Living Stone, that may change. Skayla will be more powerful if she has it in her possession."*

"We need to get back to Alkemar." I looked earnestly at Maeko. This *had* to be something regarding the others. We needed to leave as soon as possible, and I wasn't waiting around to heal any longer.

"Estasia had already sent a message. We will be leaving when you can walk." Maeko shifted his position, seeming uncomfortable with having to be the one relaying all the information. *"It did not say much, other than checking that we were still alive. But you are correct, we must leave soon. Your...brother..."* Displeasure washed briefly over his face before moving on quickly. *"...And those under his command have done nothing to put the city back in check, those that were with us in the caves, at least, refuse to do anything more for Ovok. The other Bethynese who had been overseeing the city have apparently left,"* he continued to explain as I recovered my breath. *"Your brother wants to help."* He didn't sound particularly thrilled about this. *"They are going to return with us to Alkemar. But your brother plans to act as a spy under Ovok. No one but those loyal to Kearn were witness to him helping us, and no one is exactly paying attention to us now."*

My heart throbbed in my chest—a very unpleasant sensation at the moment—as I processed everything; Kearn helping, the MindHold crumbling...Ovok with The Living Stone. I laid back on my pillows, closing my eyes as exhaustion overcame me once more. Was this a dream or nightmare? It seemed a little bit of both, and only time would tell which won out in the end.

THE LAST ESMER

CHAPTER III: Allies, Enemies, and Sometimes Both

Jaythos:

Walking was frustratingly difficult, and the chaos in the streets did little to help.

"Careful now." I didn't know if Marion was talking to me, Syvil, or Tanner. We were quite a group as we made our way through Veka's labyrinth roadways.

Before we'd left, Marion had come to visit my room and get me further up to date. Apparently, Syvil had died—killed by Ovok. The scar barely peeking above his shirt collar on the side of his neck, though freshly inflicted, looked decades old even if his shock was fresh. The Drogan had hardly said two words together, and every noise seemed to startle him, meaning the streets full of rioters weren't exactly the best environment for him right now. Marion said it would take him time to adjust, but the look in his eyes was hard to bear. Looking into his eyes, I didn't see someone who had come back from the dead, but instead, someone who was still actively dying…. I didn't like it. I'd been there way too recently.

Then there was Tanner, quiet in a very different way. Marion said she had been trying to coach him on getting his overcrowded memories back into the shard of The Living Stone or even other objects, but it took him actually bringing them up coherently enough to do so. Apparently, his mind had finally cracked a little too much. It was hard to swallow the guilt in the part I'd played leading him here.

So yes, we were quite a dismal group, indeed. But now wasn't the time for guilt. Now, I had to focus on staying upright as we swam through the crowded streets, Maeko helping me walk as well as shielding me from the uproar around us as people shoved and shouted and ran about on every side. Occasionally, I would see a listless, violet-eyed person walking in seeming oblivion, but very rarely, and usually they were quickly grabbed and taken away. Would people have sympathy after having been in Skayla's hypnotic state as well? Or would they turn on each other like Maeko had done with Sven?

I shuddered.

At last we made it to the docks. The plan was to board the airship Kearn had commandeered and brought back from where he'd been hiding it with our invisible one—apparently everyone had been worried keeping it at Veka's dock for so many days would lead to it being burned by rioters or taken by those fleeing the insanity. Kearn had brought the ship back about an hour ago, so we'd need to be quick about boarding and setting off. Meanwhile, the invisible airship would be launching from its hiding spot and heading separately to Patelayna.

"Send word as you can," Runin said as he stepped back from Syvil. The older man had come with us to the docks, but would not be accompanying us to Patelayna, claiming his desire to try and protect as many of the artifacts in the museum as possible from the riots.

Marion hesitated and went over to talk to the museum curator, leaving the rest of us standing on the docks, waiting. I gave Syvil another glance and was glad to see at least a small sign of nervous fidgeting. He hadn't shown any emotion since yesterday at least. Tanner, however, was mumbling something under his breath, rocking back and forth with his eyes closed.

"Tanner?" Even as I dared address the boy, I felt Maeko stiffen from where he was supporting me.

The boy didn't so much as open his eyes, just shook his head and said, "Leave me alone."

I winced at the well-deserved cold shoulder.

"He is likely talking to the memories, Jay. Not you," Maeko whispered in my ear.

He said that like it was supposed to make me feel better. It didn't.

"He is very glad you are alive."

I still remembered the kid screaming as Sefen's body fell to the ground, lifeless, in front of us. I hadn't been much help even in that regard, had I? Another failure to add to my list.

I was distracted by the sound of footsteps coming down the gangplank of the ship, and gingerly turned around to find myself face-to-face with my brother, at last. I'd been disappointed when he had continued to avoid me as I recovered.

His face was hard to read—a storm, really, changing and unknowable. "You made it." The way he said the words made it clear he meant more than just to the airship.

I only stared, wanting to deck him as well as wrap him in the fierce hug I had been dying to give for a decade. But perhaps a hug wouldn't be a good idea right now.

"How are you feeling?" He gave a sideways glance at Maeko before continuing, appearing calm outwardly but clearly on edge. I realized suddenly that Maeko must have forbidden him to see me. Of course. I couldn't help but feel a little annoyed at the prospect. It was something I was going to have to try and not be bitter about.

"Better."

"I thought I had killed you." Kearn's voice cracked a little.

I flinched. "Yes. You kind of did."

Now *he* flinched, arms restless at his side.

Thankfully, Marion returned now. "Is everything set to leave?" she addressed Kearn with a stern eye. "We really should be setting off as soon as possible."

He nodded and stepped to the side, making an elegant motion for us to board. Then he turned his gaze directly at me and offered an arm on the side Maeko wasn't already supporting, expression earnest.

If only because I knew I would fall with the rocking of the boat, I slowly took it, allowing him to help me as we made our way up the gangplank and onto the unsteady boat. I ignored Maeko's clear displeasure with this arrangement.

Finally on board, I found we were surrounded on all sides by people busy at work on the vessel, none in Bethynese garb. Best not to alert the city rioters to the presence of the ones they hated. The thought was a sour one, but a reality I was also fairly used to. It never mattered what side we were on, the Bethynese were always pariahs. If we made it out of this mess alive, maybe people would be more sympathetic to understanding forced service. Or maybe they'd just hate us more and care even less about us. We'd seen how well Maeko had taken to Sven…would anything ever change?

"Alright, cast off!" Kearn's command rang about the ship and caused a moment of lull in the work as everyone realized we were now on board. This was then replaced with cheers and frantic scurrying as the anchor was let and the boat began to rise higher into the air, slowly leaving the dock and rocking as it cut through Rugo's warm wind.

The first real bump landed me almost flat on the deck, and even with Kearn and Maeko, I was hardly able to keep upright.

"Why don't we get you down below where you can sit and rest?" Marion suggested. "You look tired again."

As refreshing as the smell of the sea was, it was also nauseating, so I didn't argue with Marion's suggestion. Below deck, however, was no less sickening, and I found the stifling air almost worse than outside.

Marion helped Syvil over to a hammock where he almost immediately fell asleep, while Tanner went as far into the corner as possible and remained there quietly, leaving me to be led by Maeko and Kearn to a place carved out from the wall. Both of my human crutches looked equally unpleasant in each other's company, and both seemed full of things they wanted to say.

"I need to make sure the heading is right and no one is getting us killed." Kearn tapped his sword and looked at me. "I'll be back to check on you in a moment." His gaze then flitted to Maeko as if waiting for an argument. Maeko's entire expression looked like he was ready to give one, too, but now in my presence, he seemed to know better than to interfere.

I became painfully aware that I didn't want Kearn to leave. Every time I saw him, it hurt. But at the same time...it was like a dream I'd thought would never come true. Just him saying he had to leave—even only to go above deck—was a reminder that I had left him. Hopefully, I would do well with this second chance.

I watched as he slowly left, wishing to call him back. I just wanted to talk...to apologize...to ask so many questions.

"You act as if he isn't the one who impaled you only a few weeks ago," Maeko commented irritably as he helped me to lay down against the only slightly comfortable alcove bed.

"Unlike you, I am a little more willing to give second chances." I raised an eyebrow, not having intended to bring up the grudge he'd been holding with Sven. Maeko winced. I, however, added, *"You of all people should understand my reasoning. I've told you what Bethyn is like...I left him to that. Survival was all that mattered, but he wants to help now. That's enough for me."* I'd left Kearn to that...to be forced to conform or be sent off to the Isle of Curr to die like all those who were traitors or too weak to serve the Bethynese empire. Yes, all our arguments still stood from when he had held us captive...but I could see it in Kearn's eyes now. He would never raise a hand to harm me again, and that extended to those I called friend.

Maeko merely gave a grunt and got up, mumbling something about helping up on the deck and giving me an eye that clearly ordered me not to move. I nodded in surrender, and soon, I was left alone with my thoughts.

That did not last for long, however. Marion left where she'd been checking on Tanner and came over to me.

"How are they?" I asked as she pinched the bridge of her nose in clear stress. I was still wrapping my head around the fact that *she* was alive. I'd barely gotten time to let that sink in before, well, before I'd almost died, myself.

"It will be hard to tell with Tanner until I can get him to start releasing memories. Even then, how much his mind will recuperate isn't exactly something I can know, easily." She sighed.

I swallowed hard. "And Syvil?" The Drogan had saved our lives too many times now. He'd fought the person he feared most—Ovok—not once, but twice, and it had cost him a life…and his wings.

Another sigh from Marion. "Trying to recuperate. When I lost my form…it wasn't like that. It was quick; nothing personal." I watched her expression as it changed. The way she held such ancient expressions was unnatural on a face that looked not much older than my own. "Syvil is such a gentle soul—at least, he was. And he was always so terrified of…." She closed her eyes a moment. "And then, he was in his Dragon form so long he almost forgot how to be Human again. Now he's stuck being one forever...but he did so love to fly."

"I'm sorry." Honestly, I had *no idea* how else to deal with what she was saying. "He made a difficult sacrifice. Hopefully, we can pay it back."

"Hopefully, the bit of Living Stone he dropped is enough to repair Moira's watch," she replied, looking pointedly at the thing around my neck.

"Hopefully." So much hope. I had given up on such a silly thing years ago. It was so odd to revert to it now. "But now we'll have Ovok and Skayla with The Living Stone to deal with." I laid back down, staring at the very close ceiling.

"We don't know. Tanner said he found something, but Tanner is...well, you've seen him. He couldn't finish the thought beyond something about Ovok's dead daughter, Rhioa. And Xyrilcylduin."

I blinked and turned my head to once more face her. "Who?"

She just shrugged. "The last Guardian of the Doorway between worlds. Xyrilcylduin was one of the few Myrandi who still held to The Creator's call to protect the worlds and tried to stop Ovok when he forced himself and all of us through."

"And Ovok's daughter?" I tried to sound less confused than I was. "How did she die? Why could it be important?"

"I...don't know. She'd been killed by a power on the world of Eatris in some experiment gone wrong. Before Rhioa married and left us, she and her sister were a terrible force who did the bidding of their father. We feared them...but no one really knew *what* they did. We allowed ourselves to believe they kept us safe...but I wonder...." She trailed off, fingers fussing with her sleeve. "But her death was likely what drove Ovok here."

Some of the names of the worlds were vaguely familiar, but only from stories told as a child or legends from a book, and a few of the ones she or Syvil had tried to tell us previously.

"But Tanner keeps saying something about it being for Rhioa...about something going wrong. He's even cried for Cyl—which I think was

Xyrilcylduin's nickname. But I dare not press him to relive the rest of the memory." Marion shrugged in a way that made her shoulders seem like they weighed a thousand times what they should. "Anyway. There's nothing we can do but wait and watch. And for you, rest. Please, sleep. You need it," she said as she got up, giving a stern glare that I dared not argue with.

"Thank you," I felt obligated to say—but not *only* obligated. We hadn't known her for long, and in that time, she had given us the key to The Living Stone, fallen twice from a cliff, and saved my sorry life. The least I could say was thank you, and I realized I hadn't really said it in the days I'd been awake. Both she and Syvil had risked their lives so many times for us that I began to realize just how similar the Drogans were to the Bethynese. Not the leaders…the *people*. Hated and judged because of the crimes of others, when many of them hadn't had much choice in the wars they fought.

There was a slightly amused smile and she replied, "You're welcome," before disappearing above deck.

"I will try and get in to see Ovok when we arrive." Kearn was standing in front of me, arms crossed.

I didn't like that idea at all. "Right, because that won't be suspicious at all." I wasn't sure if it was my wound or the panic swelling in my chest that made it hard to breathe. This was such a bad idea; Kearn wasn't a spy, he was a soldier. Spying and treason were two things Bethynese soldiers were horrible at—because doing one or the other immediately got you killed in horrible, horrible ways, so no one ever dared to try. His whole group was being incredibly stupid, in my opinion. I didn't want them to spy; I wanted them safe.

This was the opposite of safe.

It didn't help when Kearn gave that smile. I hadn't seen him smile in a long time, and somehow it only made things worse. It had always meant he was about to do something he *knew* was incredibly brainless, and knowing I was against it only made him more determined to follow through.

"Oh come, it will be fun," he said.

"Fun? Like impaling me was fun?" I snapped back, images rising unbidden in my mind of it being him next time, and on Ovok's blade.

His smile turned bitter as he replied, "Fun like you leaving?"

I threw up my hands in surrender, a gesture that apparently had not been in my best interest. I hid the wince that accompanied the sharp twinge of pain, instead saying, "It's still a moronic idea. How won't he catch onto you? Unless you *are* just leading us into a trap." I'd meant it in jest, but I knew part of me wondered. Like a fool, I had to doubt.

"If I was loyal, I would have let you bleed out, and then killed the rest of your insufferable friends, Jay." Kearn didn't hold onto the fake pretense of a joke. "I'm not so sure about them, and I am painfully aware they would much prefer to throw me *and* those under my command overboard, but I'm not about to stand on the other side of the blade that kills you. Not again." He stared at me. "Not again," he repeated.

The fact Kearn was so willing to now throw away everything and follow people he didn't even trust—just so he wouldn't hurt me again—spoke volumes. I knew how scared he was. It was how scared I'd been when trying to save him and Maeko from each other.

Clearing my throat, I said, "They're quite capable, don't you worry. Sven Mara alone is quite the force." And, admittedly, Estasia had proven herself to be quite a capable ally, herself. Her network hadn't failed us yet.

"Oh, it's not the fighting I'm skeptical of," Kearn's laugh held plenty of emotion in it, but it wasn't humor. "It's who's allowed to be free after Skayla and Ovok are taken down. No one liked Bethyn, and that was before we allied with Skayla. I don't want to think of how they'll treat us after. No one cares who wanted to fight in this war, just like no one cared how Bethyn treated their citizens before it."

A pit formed in my stomach. I couldn't deny the point. "They're not all like that. Maybe you'll see." Admittedly, many were *just* like that. But not everyone—not Sven, not Baey, not Tanner. "Maeko accepted me."

"Yes, clearly. He loves me so much as well." My brother made a flailing hand gesture.

"You let one of his friends get impaled and then sort of did it yourself to his only other remaining friend," I couldn't help but point out, flinching as I did so. "I don't think you can really blame him. He was still upset all those years ago when you didn't come after I wrote to you, and he didn't even know you then."

Kearn's face contorted a bit, and he turned around a moment, running his hand through his hair as his shoulders rolled back. "You know I couldn't have gotten out. No one leaves that place unless it's on orders or banished to Curr. Besides, the world was falling apart. Jay…" He turned back. "It was supposed to be just the one year of mandatory service. Then the Council of Generals overruled that law when they allied with Skayla, and we all found ourselves in a lifetime of the Bethynese *dream*." The last bit dripped of a resentment I understood.

Bethyn; where you were killed or sent to the Isle of Curr if you couldn't survive the week of initial training. Where you were flogged if you placed last in the monthly tournaments. Where you were ordered to let your children starve to get used to battlefront conditions. Where the mere hint of reluctance got you punished. This only made me acknowledge just how high the stakes were for Kearn and the others in his group helping us. Traitors were unheard of in Bethyn. *Unheard of.* It just wasn't something you did. The worst you could be was a spy or traitor, and any punishment they could think up wasn't enough. Bad offenses got you sent to Curr or executed. This…this wasn't even something that had an official punishment. They let the imagination run wild with what would happen. Kearn wasn't just gambling under Ovok. He was about to gamble around his superior officers, and if they got a sniff of his changed loyalties, it would be a fate worse than death.

"Kearn please, this…this is a really terrible idea." I found myself more desperate by the moment.

Kearn set his jaw, looking only out onto the waves "I've trained and served under General Reth, and he's been stationed at Alkemar for the last five years now. He trusts me. I'll be fine. Besides, it's not really up to you, Jay. I am quite capable of making my own decisions."

"And look at your track record!" I waved my arms and ignored the surge of pain it caused. "You got my friend killed, you nearly got me killed, and now you're going to get *yourself* killed!"

"And then will you be happy? It'll make us even—maybe it'll prove I'm sorry." Kearn's tone remained completely controlled, yet somehow that only made it feel worse.

And then silence.

At last, I found my voice. "I didn't mean it like that, Kearn. I just…I have made enough mistakes of my own. I don't want you to make them, too. I don't want you to leave me like I left you. Because if I could do it again, that is the only thing I would change. I would have brought you with me."

"I know." He took a deep breath, whispering, "And I think…I can forgive you for that now. But this is my decision, Jay, and I'm not changing my mind. You wanted me to do something besides be the good, little, mindless soldier, so here I am. But I'm doing it my way, and my way means no one is going to give me orders. Not Ovok, not Skayla, but not you either."

I swallowed hard. "Even if that means getting caught for something you don't even know you believe in?"

Now he just shrugged. "Guess I won't get caught, then. But I'm not doing this for a cause, Jay. I want that to be very clear." He looked me right in the eye. "I know your 'friends' would let all of Bethyn burn if they could. I'm doing it for you, and you need to promise to make it. I'm not burying you."

Something in me broke, and I was barely able to find the words to speak as I replied, "Then you had better promise me the same thing, because I can't bury you either."

Baey:

I shifted uncomfortably as I stood in the storage building, the scent of the ocean wafting in through the large opening into the bay. It was one of Atlys's unloading warehouses right by the docks, kept immaculate and meticulous—unlike his own house. This was...not an ideal way to go about this, but the note had said Jaythos was still too injured to make the journey to the lagoon—where they'd dropped off the invisible airship for now—and if this ship didn't enter into an official port, it could raise red flags for their new allies. Because apparently...they had found some. I clutched the ring hanging once more by the chain around my neck. I'd borrowed it so we wouldn't be seen. Sven would be fine without it for a few hours—I'd had to use it before while he was unconscious—but I still hated the thought of him being without it when it seemed one of the only things keeping him with us, even if only slightly.

"And here I thought you were getting better at not fidgeting." Estasia's tone held a smile even as she remained outwardly expressionless.

"Yes, well, today is a little out of the ordinary," I countered, still wishing I was better at witty replies.

Estasia made no remarks, having already reassured me multiple times this would go smoothly. Yes, the city was currently distracted. Yes, the soldiers running through the streets were busy trying to stop the riots, but we'd gotten word only a few days ago that Ovok was back. Well, Kovo. But apparently, they were one and the same.

And then there was Cyl. The older Myrandi was very different from Syvil. Cold, commanding…and a bit irritating. We had to keep Estasia and him separate half the time, with the former having little patience for the dismissiveness of the latter.

In fact, that was part of the reason she was accompanying me today. The other reason being that she was now in charge of all correspondence and information along with Atlys. Temorn had been forced into seeking shelter in The Underground after the whole…upheaval of the city and the sewer patrols that had followed it.

Estasia let out an impatient breath and fiddled with the knife at her side. I still found it strange how she kept the gift from Temorn. She'd said it was from when they were children, and yet for as much as she hated him now, she still kept it. I imagined it might be to try and keep the memories of the camaraderie, but not even I could fathom her motivations sometimes.

"Now who's acting all uneasy?" Unlike her, I didn't hide my smug expression. In truth, we both knew we were on edge; it was just easier to jab at each other over it rather than sit and wallow in the tension. After all, we hadn't gotten much information when those at Rugo sent word back on one of Atlys's ships. Just that Sefen was dead. It was weird—being so used to people leaving and never coming back—but it didn't make me feel any less empty. I tried my best to focus on the news that Jaythos, while injured, was going to be alright at least, and that Tanner was alive as well. The note had said Jaythos just needed to recover, but that they would be on the airship with someone called Captain Kearn. They'd already followed through on their promise to return the invisible vessel to the lagoon, where it had arrived a day ago. The soldiers manning it quickly disappeared, only leaving behind the fact that this Captain Kearn and the others would be arriving at Alkemar's docks shortly after their arrival at the lagoon. I wondered why a Bethynese captain and his soldiers were helping us, and both Estasia and Atlys had been wary of the strange addition.

But they had given the call sign Estasia had provided. Everything was in order, though if Estasia had taught me anything, it was to be prepared for the worst. Which was why I carried Sven's sword at my side, even if it hurt knowing it was likely now mine forever.

The commotion of workers around us was an unwelcome distraction, but I knew none of them could see our true appearances. To them, we simply looked like two of Atlys's higher ranking dock inspectors. Even so, all of Atlys's workers were carefully vetted. Like Illan, they owed him in some form or other, and they still didn't know much. Fortunately, Estasia didn't even need illusions—just a borrowed uniform from Atlys. After all, no one knew her face.

Then came the announcement of arrival, and the ship lowered from the sky, docking lower than most airships did. That's when I saw them coming down the gangplank. Tears threatened as, for the first time in months, I saw my friends. Even if only some of them.

Maeko was hard to miss, standing taller than the others. Someone was using his arm for support, and it took me a moment to realize it was

Jaythos. It wasn't so much the disguise he was wearing—along with the other non-Bethynese soldiers—so much as how much frailer he looked.

I allowed the illusion of my disguise to drop so that our friends could see my true form, while keeping it up for the workers around us. It took a great deal of extra concentration, but I'd been practicing a lot with the ring since Sven had gone comatose.

"Welcome. We will make sure your guests are shown a proper place to stay. We will be taking over the inspection of the airship on behalf of Lord Atlys." Estasia stepped forward, hands folded behind her back as she addressed the Bethynese captain who had taken up the front spot in the group.

I forced myself to mimic Estasia's composure, desperately trying to keep myself from gawking at my friends. I could have choked, but I didn't. I didn't react; Syvil's dying form had prepared me for the worst. It didn't matter that Grenedil had explained Syvil would come back. He'd said we couldn't even know to whom or where, if even on this planet, he would appear. But more than that, it didn't matter because Syvil had still died in my arms. I'd still tried desperately to wash the blood from my hands, and in that moment, I had buried all of my friends, thinking they'd all died.

Anyone who came home now was a miracle.

And now? Now it was so hard not to stare at Syvil, standing there, alive. Alive, and coming up behind Maeko and Jaythos with a stranger. I could hardly believe it—still having not dared hope in Grenedil's reassurances of Myrandi having two lives.

Focus. You're out in the open parading as an inspector, have a little more discipline.

65

"I need to check in with my superiors. I trust you have no further need of me?" the Bethynese captain asked, watching us with almost as much distrust as Estasia's own looks were throwing back at him.

"Actually, I would prefer you not leave this warehouse until we have debriefed our companions and clear you. We hear there were some riots in Rugo, and we would like to know if any of the goods were damaged, as well as understanding your part in securing said goods. Forgive us if we lack faith. I don't believe I've dealt with you before, and Lord Atlys is very nervous." It was incredible how clearly Estasia could get her point across while still remaining completely in character and discrete.

"He's clean, trust me," Jaythos's voice was startlingly thin.

"I'm sure he is," I jumped in, perhaps not the best decision, seeing as my covert skills were still a bit lacking. But I was hoping I would have a little more tact. "But we need to vet everyone. Lord Atlys's request." I tried to make it clear we needed to be covert about this discussion out in the open but wasn't really sure it was coming across. Jaythos wasn't exactly known for his subtlety.

"But he's—"

"—I don't care who he is," I interrupted, having gotten the sense that he was about to say something very stupid and obvious that could draw attention. "I would like to hear his part in things just to confirm and clear him to leave. Please, come into the office so we can do so privately." I gestured to the little office on the left wall of the large warehouse.

"It should only take a moment if everything is in order," Estasia's tone was a lot colder than mine, and I knew it was only partially an act. While she had definitely warmed up a lot to both me and the others in The

Underground, she still had not been long with the rest of those from Valdon, and Jaythos's lack of tact was undoubtedly trying on her very tenuous patience. "The captain may wait here and see to the rest of his soldiers. I'm sure he wants to make sure they are all doing well."

The Bethynese captain did not appear pleased at this but gave no argument.

A few moments later, we were safely tucked behind the doors of the office, everyone fortunately having enough room inside with still a little to spare. At least I didn't need to keep my visual disguise in here—the office fortunately had no windows.

For the first time, I felt as if I was able to actually take in the fact that my friends were here. Well, and one more; the woman with Syvil, helping him. Estasia had been eyeing her like a hawk, but she seemed to trust Syvil's judgement a little more than Jaythos's, and had allowed the strange woman inside.

It was probably the fact Syvil had died for us. I, at least, felt it earned our trust a thousand times over.

But the rest of our troop...they looked awful. Tanner wasn't even reacting, other than mumbling some inaudible gibberish under his breath and occasionally closing his eyes. Jaythos, meanwhile, was pale and sickly, straining against Maeko's arm in an attempt to stand upright, while Syvil flinched at every little sound.

"I'm so glad to see you," I spoke up, wanting to say *something* other than business.

"It is good to see you as well, Little Baey," Maeko said gently. "Where's Skinny?"

I'd almost forgotten that's what he always called Sven. Having to explain Sven's condition was not exactly something I looked forward to doing. It was a fact that almost a month had made the news old, but it didn't make my heart hurt any less. No one back in The Underground said it out loud, but Alenor's defeated manner the last few days wasn't just from Cyl. Sure, Sven was still technically alive, but no one had any hope of him waking up anymore. I wondered suddenly if Maeko would even care. Or if...if he'd be glad. The realization hurt.

"Locked in a death sleep, thanks for asking." Estasia's tone was even less civil than before. I forgot how much she disliked Maeko.

His brow furrowed in a strange show of unbridled concern, looking from Estasia to me, but now wasn't the time for details.

Not that Estasia allowed any further time for it. "Now who is that captain and why are you all just trusting a Bethynese soldier?"

"I'm Bethynese," Jaythos rasped, glaring at her.

"Yes, and I don't trust you."

I elbowed her, giving her a glare of my own that told her to behave. "Who is he?" I asked. "And why is he helping, then?"

Jaythos looked suddenly sheepish, replying, "He's my brother."

"What?" I tried to take the information in stride. Jaythos had never been one to say...well, anything about his past. I hadn't really thought of the very obvious possibility that he had a family.

"He was never able to leave Bethyn. I left him behind, but he saved us from the avalanche. He wants to help.... He wants..." Jaythos winced. "...to spy for you."

Estasia just scoffed. "A Bethynese soldier? Spying for us? Why should I believe you when last time you trusted someone, she turned out to be working for Skayla?"

The reminder of Namaya was unpleasant, especially with the way it drew attention to Sefen's glaring absence. The note they had sent ahead had said he was dead, but it was still hard to grasp the reality of it.

"For someone who embraced The GhostMaker so willingly regardless of his past, you seem very reluctant to ever think that maybe he isn't the only one that didn't do things willingly," Jaythos spat back, some of his old strength seeming to return in the moment.

Estasia sighed, rubbing her forehead. "Fine. But I need a legitimate reason why I should trust him."

"You seem well acquainted with Bethynese." Jaythos's tone was still bitter. "You know we don't play spy. We don't do tricks. If he was still loyal to Skayla or the Bethynese Council of Generals, he wouldn't be pretending to help us. He would simply have killed us. That should be proof enough."

"He's right," I said, knowing Estasia knew it as well. "We don't even need to give any further information to him right now. Just let him go and have Atlys and Illan keep an eye out. Tell him one of your code words in case we decide to make further contact, and then where to expect a message if we decide to contact him, and then he will know nothing more than what we want him to."

Giving a small chuckle, Estasia returned her hands to her side. "Alright, Birdie." Then she turned to Syvil and the mysterious lady next to him. "And her?"

"I am Marion," the stranger replied.

"S-she is a friend. Another Myrandi. One who was killed when Ovok tried to trick us into Skayla's MindHold," Syvil explained, trying to smile when he met my eyes.

"She saved our lives multiple times," Jaythos once more jumped in.

Estasia let out a long breath, then turned to me.

We shared a silent look before I addressed everyone. "You all look like you could use some rest. We'll return you to Alenor's Manor, and then you can rest and give us a full explanation. A lot has happened since you left."

"Before you do, Tanner said...that someone named Alenor would want these back," Marion reached into her pocket, pulling out the case for Henry's spectacles. I'd almost forgotten all about them—Tanner had taken them in order to use their memories to lead them to The Living Stone.

Stepping forward, I gave a nod of thanks as I gingerly took the box. "Thank you. I'll make sure she gets these."

"Great, now let's get out of this place. I don't like us being so out in the open," Estasia announced.

As we prepared to leave, I turned my attention once more to Tanner, wishing I could just throw decorum to the wind and give him a gigantic hug. But his eyes...it was like they weren't even his. It was like...the only friend I'd had growing up was gone.

CHAPTER IV: Therapy, and a Good Old Punch to the Face

<u>Estasia:</u>

"I still do not like the idea of a Bethynese captain involved in this," Atlys said with a huff as he looked out into the streets from his very broken window. This part of the city was still quiet and deserted as ever—there was plenty of fighting going on in the more populated areas.

"Neither do I." I didn't bother hiding my own displeasure. After we'd gotten to Alenor's house, Maeko had given a full explanation; Tanner's deteriorating health and the whole...Kearn situation. The gaping hole healing in Jaythos's chest was enough to give me pause, but at the same time, Jaythos's point had been a valid one, and it made it unlikely to be a ploy. Besides, even if, for some outlandish reason, the Bethynese soldier was willing to deceive us—as Baey had pointed out—there was no way Ovok could have communicated such a complicated idea to Kearn during a fight, when originally there wasn't supposed to have ever been a fight. And if he *had* been loyal to Ovok, surely, he would have immediately made off with The Living Stone shard Syvil had managed to give the others. Instead, he'd brought it here—to us.

And that was the biggest surprise, wasn't it? The shard. The stupid trip to Rugo hadn't been a complete disaster after all. While they hadn't gotten the entire Living Stone, they had at least gotten enough to fix the watch, Alenor had said. Cyl had begrudgingly given the mission that much.

But oh, that Drogan was getting on my nerves. I didn't like the way he acted as if he was running this whole operation now after sitting on the sidelines for at least a decade, keeping the portal closed all this time instead of helping anyone. Had there *really* been nothing he could do? He reminded me of all those nobles and highborn egotists I despised. Not like Atlys or Sven, but all the others who thought they knew better when they didn't have a clue. The ones that shook their heads at the needy and cried into their golden goblets as if they couldn't help. It didn't exactly make me like Grenedil, the way he kept trying to play peacekeeper. I didn't care how old the crusty Drogan was—age didn't make wisdom, it made people, and I wasn't seeing a very good one in Cyl.

"So then I am to use Illan to make indirect contact with him during my visit to the palace?" Atlys asked when it was clear I would make no further comment on the matter.

I set my other worries aside for the moment, focusing on the stupid Bethynese-sized problem at hand. "Yes. Keep an eye on him and see if anything he does will be actually useful…maybe he could help us find Skayla." Baey was right, of course. Kearn could be a valuable ally. Atlys still had no idea what was up with Skayla's absence—or the sudden freeing from the MindHold so many had experienced—but a Bethynese soldier close to "Lord Kovo" would be privy to all sorts of sensitive information.

"I will see to it. Lord Kovo—" there was an angry light in his eyes as Atlys said the name, having only just learned the man's true identity. "He is calling a meeting with the other nobles in the city. It will include Lord Atarah. His parents were recently executed for allowing a rebellion to fester in the city walls, but they were previously in charge of the overall city." He choked in disgust.

I froze. "Lord Atarah?"

"Yes. Why?" Atlys's brow furrowed.

"Is he a possible ally?" What was wrong with me?

Face twisting in an unpleasant expression, Atlys gave a garbled laugh. "Oh no. I'm pretty sure he was the one who brought his parents forward to Ovok. He's out for power, and I am hearing whispers that he is to be the new head of Alkemar. So no, I do not think he will be anything but a problem. What in Baeno would possess you to ask? You know none of the other nobles are to be trusted."

"Nothing, forget I asked," I muttered, quick to hide my slip in discipline. I was being weak. Yet part of me still couldn't imagine Eugene like that. Betraying his own parents? He'd never struck me as power hungry. Then again, I never would have pinned myself as a freedom fighter…so. I blamed Baey for the impulsiveness. Or maybe Sven…and we'd all seen where that had gotten him. I wondered if I was the reason Eugene had changed. Had Temorn's betrayal and abandonment hardened him that much?

"In fact, he's anything *but* an ally. He's been a pain in my rear for the last five or six years, constantly snooping around my business. And here

I thought you weren't much for aristocracy." Atlys's mouth twitched in amusement even as his eyes narrowed.

I was eager to move on from the subject, and didn't bother to hide it as I replied quickly, "It's none of your concern. Tell me what you find out and what you think of the captain. And please don't do anything stupid."

Atlys made an exaggerated bow. "But of course. Just remember, I don't work for you." He smiled humorlessly at the last bit. "And I am allowed to ask questions should I feel you might make an unwise move and endanger what I've managed to save of this forsaken world."

"I'll leave the 'unwise moves' to everyone else, thank you. I have enough to clean up from others." He was right, of course, but who was I to admit that? I still wasn't used to someone matching my pace, let alone actually holding the same level of cynicism as I did. Part of it was refreshing, but the other part was just downright irritating.

"Speaking of cleaning up messes…" Atlys trailed off a moment walking over to one of the mildew-ridden sofas and collapsing onto it, staring up at the ceiling. "I still have not been able to find anywhere safer than the current location. Not unless we risk splitting the city up and smuggling them on my airships, which as I have said before, is an extremely stupid idea. Even with the invisible ship your friends returned with, it would still be a logistical nightmare. It would help if we could at least find a secure enough location." Even the invisible airship risked being bumped into with the number of trips it would need to make. While there definitely seemed to be fewer Drogans in the air, there were *still* Drogans. The real problem, of course, was that it was only *one* invisible ship, and would take multiple trips to move people. Baey had been practicing with Sven's ring, but cloaking multiple airships was still a bit too complicated for her.

I allowed myself to sit on the arm of one of the other dilapidated chairs. It was a good vantage point to view the streets from, however quiet the ones here were. "Moving this many people in general is going to be a problem, but our newest off-world guest has said we need to speed up the search." I sighed at having to bring up Cyl. This had actually been something I agreed with, but the problem was that it was one of the *only* things I agreed with.

"That friend doesn't seem to be very helpful with finding a solution, so far," Atlys replied coyly.

He wasn't wrong…. The proposition had been brought up to maybe use the portal to hide the civilians of The Underground, but Cyl had said opening it would only attract Ovok and he refused. When we'd suggested hiding *in* the portal, he'd simply claimed this world-between-worlds—The Maze, he called it—was very different and too dangerous.

I sighed. "No, he really isn't, but for now, we tolerate it." Key phrase being *for now.*

Atlys folded his hands over his chest and continued to stare at the ceiling. "Well, unless they want to try and hide the people among the chaos of the streets here, I am not finding anything with enough space to accommodate as well as something that wouldn't draw attention…unless…." Sitting up, Atlys looked in my direction, that spark of mischief lighting his eyes. I was growing to admire the way this man thought. If I hadn't known he was once a great lord, I would have pegged him as a con artist or some other master manipulator. Either way, it was clear how he had not only survived under Skayla, but hidden an entire city right under her nose for so many years. He was cunning. "They just pulled out the soldiers from the portal site. With nothing to guard anymore, they were told to return and report for managing the city."

It was a thought.... I scowled. "But wasn't it quite...uprooted from the battle? There are some anomalies and such that are still left over from what Sven did."

"Yes, but that could help ward off anyone coming to look there," Atlys pointed out.

While a better option than what we had otherwise—which was nothing—I still wasn't a huge fan of the idea. "Even so, the area is very exposed, and what tents we have underground are not exactly meant for that much exposure to the elements. Maybe it could work if our bird friend could potentially manage to put an illusion to ward off passing Drogan patrols, but still...keep looking. Using the ring for something of that large a space could be difficult for her. I don't know if she has tried something quite that extensive yet. She doesn't have...guidance at the moment, after all." She had made leaps and bounds in her abilities without Sven, but there was only so much you could self-learn. That being said...she might be able to. Sven had been able to place simple illusions and leave them even when he wasn't actively keeping them—like the cave where we hid after escaping the Kovian Fortress or hiding the airship we stole in Hytat. While she still hadn't figured out how to do it over anything that needed to move—such as an airship—she had put some small, stationary illusions in the tunnels to ward off patrols from finding the entrance to The Underground.

"Very well. I've sent some riders up West, but we begin to wander into further terrain issues that way. Less water, and then you run into the sand pits." Atlys replied. "But I will inform you if the search is somehow fruitful. In the meantime, still no word on how *he* is?" His voice grew quiet as he brought up Sven.

"It is looking unlikely." It was harder to say than I wished.

It was rare you saw Atlys's genuine expressions, and yet there was no mistaking the pain in it, now. "Stupid boy," he murmured.

I could second that statement. It was easier to be angry at Sven than face the reality that was becoming more inevitable by the day—that he wouldn't wake up—that after all his pain and sacrifice, he'd be a fool and get himself killed. Yes, it was easier to be angry, because the only other option hurt too much.

The sewers were quieter than usual, and my best guess was that the arrival of Kearn had diverted most of the troops to the surface, where riots were a lot more likely. But I knew it wouldn't last, and it was only a matter of time before we were found. I mulled over the newest evacuation suggestion by Atlys, wondering how feasible it really was. The portal site was so exposed, and Baey was still having difficulty with making long-lasting, large-scale illusions. Even beyond that, shelter would be difficult and there were no trees to break the sun or rain that could come our way, let alone the wind that would make its way into the ravine. But the problem was…no other possible solution we came up with yielded more favorable odds.

Nothing was turning out how we wanted. Nothing…and no one. I found myself rubbing the hilt of that stupid knife as I again entered The Underground, still battling with the logical bit of me. I didn't want to believe Eugene would have become the ladder-climbing, ruthless aristocrat Atlys was making him out to be, but Atlys had been nothing but an accurate source of information, and there was no real reason for me to doubt him.

But I wanted to. I wanted to hang onto that image of the kid who'd painted me that funny little picture on slate. I wanted the kid who had wanted nothing to do with his parents' life. I didn't want to face the fact that while I had grown out of only looking out for myself, he had grown into it.

"Well, you're back at last," Temorn's rotting smile was as unwelcome as his greeting as he practically sprung out from the shadows to meet me. He'd clearly been waiting—I was hardly even two steps onto the beaten path considered the main street.

"And you have no reason to care. What do you want?" I growled, quickly moving my hand away from the knife. I hated how I clung to it; but whether from Temorn or not, it was one of the only possessions I could call mine. Not something I stole; but something that had been given by the oldest friend I'd had.

Even if that friend was the reason that I'd avoided making any new ones for years.

"Come from Atlys?" he asked, trotting up and matching my pace as I brushed past him.

I was not in the mood to deal with this. "It is no concern of yours, Temorn."

"Oh come on, I'm so *bored*, Esa." He tried to put an arm around my shoulder, but I put a quick stop to that by quickly stepping just out of reach.

The streets became livelier as we walked further into the heart of The Underground, but unfortunately, he kept pace with me instead of letting me be for once in my life. "I don't care if you're bored. You should be thankful you are among good people like Darbeshay and Atlys. If I was the one making the decision of whether to bring you here to hide, I would have let you rot."

Now he looked hurt. Honestly, I couldn't care less. In fact, I was glad. Good. See just how much he had thrown away with that stupid, greedy decision all those years ago.

"Really? You're still sore over that? After I turned out to be right?" He grabbed my arm, eliciting a hiss from me as I, in turn, grabbed his tattered coat collar.

"Let. Go."

He obeyed, palms up in surrender as he said, "Fine. I don't get you. You're still pining over a stupid aristocrat who was just as narrow-minded and selfish as the rest of them."

"He was your *friend*." It took every ounce of discipline not to scream the words. "He was nothing but nice to you and you got *jealous* because all you care about is yourself."

"But here I am, helping refugees in these stupid sewers, risking life and limb to try and help a bunch of washed-up optimists rotting in the filth of the city I grew up in. Meanwhile, a little bird told me *he's* up there living in luxury and getting a promotion. We weren't his friends, Esa. We were the pastime for a bored, rich brat! I—"

I had punched a few people over the years, but I think this was the first time I'd ever found it therapeutic.

"What in Baeno!" Temorn cried as he stumbled back, grabbing his nose as blood dripped from both it and his mouth.

"I think you lost another tooth," I said tersely, ignoring the throbbing pain in my knuckles.

Looking down at the dirt, Temorn's eyes suddenly caught onto what I'd meant. That stupid gold tooth, laying in the grime of The Underground. It probably hadn't been in his mouth very well, guessing by the fact he wasn't friends with very many doctors.

The way in which he completely dropped to all fours and grappled for the pathetic little thing made me completely forget about my aching hand.

Without another word, I left him there, groveling in the dust like the coward he was. He wasn't helping these people out of the goodness of his heart—he never had been. All he cared about was survival and being in control, and he knew he would lose both if he ever aligned with Skayla.

But no matter how satisfying that punch had been, it couldn't make me forget his words. It couldn't make me forget that the one real friend I'd had might not even have been so genuine after all. What if Temorn was right? What if it wasn't that Eugene had changed, but that he'd never been the person I thought he was from the start. Was I that bad at making friends? No. Baey was different. Darby was different. Sven was most certainly different. But it was little comfort to know that at least now I was better at friends when they just kept getting themselves killed.

THE LAST ESMER

CHAPTER V: A Useful Maggot

<u>Ovok:</u>

"Has there been any change?" I asked, evaluating the catatonic woman before me. I had foolishly thought Skayla couldn't possibly test my patience any further than she already had these past years, but it seemed I had been wrong. Apparently, my concern over leaving her to deal with her brother had been more than simple paranoia, and now everything was falling apart; now I couldn't get back to Rhioa.

"Still nothing, sir," the Bethynese General Reth replied from behind me.

Pathetic. She's pathetic—

"Useless," I murmured, glaring at the burn scar on her arm where her armlet used to be. Completely obliterated. Sven Mara had completely obliterated an item created with The Living Stone. I didn't like the dread that revelation brought with it.

Skayla continued to sit completely still, not so much as flinching from my touch. Under most other circumstances, I would have revelled in the absence of her incessant mumblings and crazed laughter, but now her current state only made things worse. This also proved Sven Mara was a great deal more powerful than I had given him credit for. If I had known what he was capable of, I would have killed him with or without Skayla's approval.

See? Told you. You should have let me taste his blood—

Too late now. Yet another mistake. I was so prone to them, these days. Desperation made me weak.

Yes. Weak and pathetic, just like her. Ha!

Somehow Ckaknimaen's voice was more irritating than Skayla's. Maybe because I feared it was right. Every time I ignored it, lately, things went wrong. But why did I still pretend as if I wasn't already drenched in blood? Maybe I should stop acting like one more body on my list would make a difference.

—List? Cute. Adorable. We have a book, my friend. A whole chronicle to your name and my prey.

Its prey, not mine. I reminded myself of the lie. It was the sword that so willingly took lives. I simply did what was necessary, and if this was the price I had to pay for Rhioa, then I would gladly pay it.

And that was why after this...I would make sure the option was no longer there for anyone. I would make sure no one could be tempted like this again.

I turned to General Reth. "Continue to keep her here for now. Monitor her condition. Do not, under any circumstances, tell anyone of this posting, and keep the same rotation of guards. Understood?" Skayla was currently being held in the dungeons, far away from where anyone would see her, but I wasn't sure how long I wanted her so far from where I was, in the higher realms of the palace. Everything was falling to pieces.

For you, Rhy. I have undone myself for you, and you would be horrified.

General Reth followed me out the door, locking it behind me and giving some silent command to the two watching the door. But his doubt was palpable. I knew that, without Skayla, it would be only a matter of time before her allies began to fall away.

"In the meantime, get these riots under control and focus on locating where the rebels are hiding—if the upheaved ground in the city and ravine is anything to go by, I would say they are in the sewers somewhere," I instructed as we walked away from Skayla's cell. I still couldn't figure out how in the worlds Sven had created such a mess of the city. He had moved an entire Maze entrance. Such a feat was nearly incomprehensible, and it made even me nervous.

Nervous and frustrated.

"My lord...I have very little personal guard left. The attack on the ravine ended with heavy casualties, and the riots in the city have left my remaining captains with little to spare for time."

"Then use what you have, General. Bethynese are resourceful."

"I barely have enough for the patrols of the sewers I've already been running, Lord Kovo. Without her, there is little hope of keeping the—"

"I did not ask you for your opinion, General," I spat. He was right. At this rate, there was very little hope of keeping any of this going for too much longer. But I didn't care about that. I needed the portal—and for that, I needed them to keep the riots under control just long enough so we could find it. All I needed was a little more time—always a little more time.

"I will do my best, Lord Kovo." General Reth clasped his hand to his chest and bowed before departing, leaving me to find my way back up to the higher levels of the palace and my room.

So many problems to solve. I had always guessed Sven's Gift of illusion was some form of matter displacement. It reminded me of the sort of display glitches you would find on the computers in Kryso, and I now theorized if illusions were what he had without his relic, then his true Gift with his ring was more akin to actual change in matter, perhaps even the time and space around him.

We should have gotten rid of him with his sister, but of course, Skayla had been convinced he'd known where their mother was. After she had up and *killed* Henry Mara, the one we needed. If she hadn't gone so incredibly insane and killed her own father, then maybe I would already be back with Rhy right now. Maybe so many people wouldn't have died. Why could nothing ever go right?

It made it feel foolish to hope that the strange quiet after the ravine meant that perhaps Sven had overused his ability and thus at least eliminated one problem off of my ever-growing list. Surely, if he was normally capable of this much destruction, he wouldn't have stopped at the ravine. It had been over a month now and still no further signs of his handiwork. If I was lucky, he was dead. He'd moved a Door between worlds, after all.

Oh Rhy. Don't look at me now. I was refusing to think of how I would explain this to her.

Stop whining. You knew what the risks were—

The blade was right. I just…I'd thought maybe I could have avoided it. I was a fool.

Yes. You are a fool. Thinking you would leave me to starve—

After living on this insufferable planet for over a decade, I'd realized just how true my fears had been. Two of the three worlds now had shown me just how badly they reacted to power. If I hadn't pushed Skayla over the edge, Moira surely would have gotten there soon enough. I had done nothing that wouldn't already happen. Even Eatris, for all my meddling and attempts to keep the world from cannibalizing itself, desired nothing more than to abuse their Gift. Kryso was little better, treating their own as animals to be caged and experimented on. No one could be trusted with the Gifts we'd once been given, and now…saving Rhioa would just be the beginning. I knew what I had to do.

So self-righteous. No better than the rest of them—

The sword's giggles echoed, but I accepted them. I was no better, that was the point. Not even I could be trusted with power. In the end, everyone had something they were willing to bend the rules for.

I reached my room at last, unlocking it and entering as quickly as I could to find the safe where I kept The Living Stone. Upon taking it out of the small, locked vault, I was overwhelmed with the ancient pulse of energy as I ran my hands along the moving gears and breathing stone. I needed to find Havirax if I was going to make this portable. Grenedil's self-serving younger brother was the best shot at having a device to safely store it and, as much as I despised the charlatan, I had manipulated him into the position of The Merchant for a reason: He was easily used.

Yes. Let's find the idiot. He's always good for a laugh—

Perhaps Ckaknimaen thought so, but the man disgusted me more than anything. Still, it was time I made him work for a living.

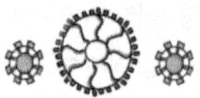

It was all too typical for the fool to be using the old Ostinar's coastal mansion for his own pleasure. It was revolting, but of course, he didn't care. Havirax was rather like a maggot, feeding off the ruins of the dead.

Even so, I had to admit: He was a useful maggot.

Maggot. Ha, a good one. You're a maggot, too, aren't you—

"Havirax!" I called as I stood in the surprisingly intact vestibule of the mansion, wondering if Havirax paid for some wretch to take care of the place, or if he'd actually kept the place himself. More than likely he'd once more abused several of the relics he was supposed to protect, using some magical item or other to keep the manor tidy and up to date.

When I did not receive an immediate response, I added, "Get down here before I feed you to Dyress!" I at last heard a scuffling from upstairs as if he was scrambling to get out of bed. It was early afternoon but, while he wasn't exactly an early riser, he knew better than to keep me waiting.

My grip tightened on The Living Stone, held firmly even as my mind was turning through all of the various scenarios that might or might not play out. I had to get out of this forsaken world—and hope Sven Mara was indeed dead—before the youngest of the Watchers got his hands on The Living Stone. Somehow, I had a feeling that the amplified power would make him a nearly unstoppable force, much like the watch had amplified Skayla's Gifting.

A head popped out into view from the second story banister, and a very disgruntled, yet wary, Havirax appeared. He was not unlike his older brother in appearance—dark haired and dark eyed—yet he and Grenedil couldn't be more different in personality. Or morals.

"Ovok? What pleasure do I owe to such a visit?" I smiled at the nervousness in his tone even as he played the careless fool.

"You owe me many things," I reminded him coolly, allowing him to come to me. I would not be left staring up at him.

It didn't take long for the disheveled Havirax to slide down the stair banister and arrive before me, wearing a simple night shirt, hastily put on breeches, and a housecoat he had clearly stolen from the closet.

Maybe maggot was too kind a word to describe him. I didn't bother hiding my disdain even as Ckaknimaen laughed at it all.

"At home as usual, I see," I commented as I looked him up and down, pleased to see the way he squirmed at my scrutiny.

"Well, *they* certainly weren't going to need the place anymore." Havirax gave an attempt at a laugh. Its echo was empty against the walls of the haunted mansion.

"They are dead," I replied calmly. He sobered, looking around me as if expecting someone else to appear.

"Oh don't worry. She isn't with me…right now." And I wasn't referring to Skayla. I knew my earlier threat had gotten him on edge. Rhioa wasn't the only one being held in the Amaranthine Axis. Among many mistakes, I had imprisoned the previous owner of Ckaknimaen as well. The one who'd given me the cursed blade. The Myrandi killer: my wife.

Another strangled laugh. "But really, what do you want now, Ovok? I thought we had a deal. I got you the things you needed for the portal and you would leave me alone."

"Are you implying your usefulness is ending?" I tilted my head to one side, keeping nice, long eye contact.

That's more like it. I so love playing with our food—

Havirax recoiled but gave that insufferable grin and replied, "Alright, but I am beginning to wonder who needs who more."

I chuckled. "Oh, I could certainly manage without you just fine. You should have seen the last person to stand between me and this." I gestured to The Living Stone even as young Syvil's broken body plummeting into the ocean burned again in my mind. A little bile rose in my throat, but nothing I wasn't used to. It was too late to go back. It got the desired effect in Havirax, and that is all that mattered. Rhioa was all that mattered.

Still squeamish, I see? Dyress would have basked in it. Weak—

With a nervous cough, Havirax shoved both hands in his house coat. "So what can I do for you, my lord?"

"I need you to get me something that contains this. It's unwieldy as is."

"I see." Havirax's tone turned uncharacteristically somber, his eyes widening as he stared at The Living Stone, likely fully realizing what it was for the first time.

I had lived too long to have any more time to fawn over the ancient powers. They had caused nothing but power struggles and heartache.

"Will you get me what I need?" I asked curtly.

Clearing his throat one last time, Havirax bowed low and nodded. "Of course, my lord. Ever at your command."

Kearn:

I placed my fist to my chest and bowed low, ears ringing as I stood before Ovok—well, "Kovo." My mind still couldn't believe it. I hadn't had time to process the revelation when Jaythos's group had exposed his true identity in the mountains, but now I couldn't help but see just how much it made sense. Kovo had always been the brains behind Skayla's brawn.

That being said, would Ovok let me live now that I and those under my command knew the secret? Would he even need to suspect our treason to have an excuse to kill us? I hadn't pinned him as one to be *that* fickle but, then again, he'd had no hesitation in killing Jaythos's friend.

Perhaps this really had been a bad idea. Too late, I realized I'd once again jumped into something headfirst before fully weighing the consequences.

"Glad to see you made it, Captain," Ovok's menacing tone rang through the space as he came up to me, having been standing in front of one of the large floor-to-ceiling windows lining the throne room of the new palace. "I feared the worst with the cave collapsing. How *did* you get back?"

I felt the hair on the back of my neck rise. It was as if the very room buzzed with a dangerous energy, but I reminded myself everything was fine; I just needed to say exactly what I'd rehearsed.

"It was a close call. The cave-in was fortunately not bad enough that we couldn't get out. When we didn't return within the day, the rest of my soldiers came to find us. They helped dig us out. I killed...I killed my brother...and the Rugonian. The boy and the woman were crushed by the rocks." I swallowed hard, allowing my guilt to show in full force. I needed Ovok to believe I had killed Jaythos—and the best way to do that was to show the genuine pain *almost* killing him had caused.

"You killed your own brother?" I felt the danger, thinly veiled behind the question.

I forced myself to meet his eyes, and my voice cracked as I replied, "Yes. It-it was an accident. He—" I gritted my teeth. "He got in the way."

Ovok's eyes narrowed, but he said nothing more.

I took it as my cue to continue my report. Time to see how smart Ovok thought I was. Or how dumb I was for trying to lie to him.

I cleared my throat. "After we returned to the city, we found it overrun by riots. The commanding officers had already fled, so we took one of the last airships out as soon as possible. We had to wait until those among my company who had been wounded were well enough to travel, so that is partly why we were delayed so long in returning."

Ovok betrayed no reaction as he watched me closely, hands folded neatly behind his back as he soaked up every detail. The Drogan made me more nervous than even the highest ranking Bethynese General, and those were fierce enough as it was. Again, I wondered if maybe I should have listened to Jay. This whole idea had seemed so much better in my head.

"How did you stay in the city so long without being spotted?" Ovok's question was simple.

"We stayed at one of the abandoned factories," I replied without hesitation, even as I found it increasingly difficult to breathe. "Fortunately, it seemed most of the crowds were busy trying to break into the governor's mansion."

The continued scrutiny under the ageless gaze was unnerving, to say the least, yet I didn't dare so much as twitch as he tested the resolve of my half lies.

"I see. Report to General Reth and make him aware of your return. You are, however, to report to me first with all things and not him, do you understand?" Ovok took a step closer to me.

I frowned; the chain of command was a sacred thing in the Bethynese military. Even Skayla had long abided by it. In fact, so had Ovok.

He pounced on my hesitation like some animal of prey, face suddenly inches from mine. "You know more than I would prefer, and if I get even the slightest suspicion that you have shared my true identity with anyone—*anyone*—I will make sure the rumor is eradicated. Do you understand?"

Every inch of my body rebelled against the need to remain calm, and I shrunk under Ovok's looming shadow, the instinct to run pricking the soles of my feet. "I understand, my lord," I whispered, frustrated at the slight tremor in my tone.

Just as quickly as he had grown close, the Drogan retreated back a distance, completely composed and expression neutral, as if the threatening moment had never happened. "Good. You shall report to me daily. I need you and those under your command searching the sewer system. The…change in terrain in the city suggests that the sewers are where the troublemakers fled, and I think that may be where the last of those who escaped Valdon are hiding. I need you to locate them as soon as possible so we can get this over with."

Clearing my throat in an attempt to swallow the lump that had lodged itself inside of it, I replied, "Yes, sir."

"You are dismissed. I have already made arrangements so that those under your command remain that way and no one is transferred. Keep them close." The air felt inexplicably cold with the comment.

This wasn't just me at stake. It was those under me, as well. I should have left them in Rugo…but they had refused to hide or run. We were all going to get ourselves killed, weren't we?

"Yes, sir," I replied, my voice steadier this time.

"You are to talk to no one besides General Reth and Lord Eugene Atarah. I have given Atarah charge over the city and will fill him in regarding your arrival and orders. He will give you proper schematics of the city above ground and below." Another long silence with that impenetrable stare. Then, at last, he said, "You are dismissed."

Relief didn't exactly wash over me as I gave a bow and turned to leave, but then again, I'd lived with dread every day for the last decade: I'd grown used to it. Yet, somehow, Ovok's parting words for me left a pit in my stomach deeper than any I'd experienced before.

"Be careful, Captain."

I marched down the hallway, hand clenching the hilt of my blade as if it was the only thing keeping me grounded on Baeno. I wondered why Ovok hadn't killed me then and there. Somehow, I doubted it was mercy.

As I turned a corner, I nearly ran right into some Patelaynian noble, the run-in anything but random. In fact, I sidestepped far enough so that he couldn't pull me to the side like he had clearly been intending.

"You just returned from Rugo, is that so, Captain?" The man was only a few years older than myself and not much taller, but he attempted to tower above me in some show of intimidation. It was an almost amusing sight after having been in the legitimately terrifying presence of Ovok. This stranger held little weight. It was more irritating than anything, the arrogance paired with the disdain I saw in his eyes, as if he were somehow better than a Bethynese soldier. As if we weren't all answering to the same person.

"You can discuss with Lord—Kovo, if you would like information." I quickly caught myself before giving Ovok's true name.

The man's eyes hardened. "We have not heard any news from Rugo since General Riran withdrew from Veka and sent word through. I can and will take it up with Lord Kovo *or* Lord Atlys, I just wanted to avoid the bureaucracy of it all."

I could care less about this man and his own problems, and part of me suddenly wondered if this was some convoluted test by Ovok. "I am not permitted to give out information to just anyone," I replied with a scowl.

He straightened, smoothing the already immaculately steamed cream-colored jacket. "I am Lord Atarah, and Lord Kovo has appointed me to the command of the city, as I'm sure you have been made aware—given you are leaving a meeting with him? So then what was the news on Rugo, *Captain?*" I hated the open hostility. Naturally, the Bethynese were still the dirt of Baeno, because the Bethynese who had joined the winning side were somehow worse than nobility like him, who had done...the same thing. How ironic. With how well-groomed and calm this man was, I highly doubted he was under duress, so he didn't even have the excuse several of the other nobility could use.

"I do not appreciate the tone, Lord Atarah," I kept eye contact, a much easier feat than keeping Ovok's. "I do believe we are to be working together in the future, and I do not think Lord Kovo would take kindly to the way you are addressing me for simply being cautious. You should appreciate my hesitance to share any information without proper introduction."

The man's jaw worked back and forth for a minute, and he looked out one of the windows lining the hallway as if they somehow held the key to his composure. Then, with a deep breath, he turned back, the fire in his eyes only slightly dampened. "My...apologies, Captain. If you could be so kind, I need any information you carried with you from Rugo. I am happy to go through proper channels, I would just prefer efficiency over democracy—and I know you are all about efficiency."

I narrowed my eyes at the less than subtle dig but knew this was the chance to get on the man's good side. Whether I liked it or not, I was on thin ice with Ovok as it was, and I didn't need to make any more enemies. "The city of Veka is rioting, and our troops have pulled out. We didn't have quite the manpower you have here in Alkemar, and I returned to the city too late. Something happened to those in a MindHold, and it seems from the little I've seen that Alkemar is not much better. The Governor of Veka did not get out of the city fast enough, however, and the rioters were getting close to penetrating his home when I left." I had little sympathy for the governor. He'd been one of Queen Serafina's advisors and had happily leaked the information that had led to her assassination. "That is all I know. They were fortunately busy enough with that, so we were able to leave the city." We had, of course, also not been in Bethynese uniform.

Lord Atarah's lips drew into a tight line, and he took a deep breath. "I see."

He looked about to take his leave when I added, "But if I may, Lord Atarah, you have saved me the trouble of having to find you. Lord Kovo has requested you supply me with all the maps of the city and the sewers so I can hunt the rebels and Skayla's rogue assassin. I believe Lord Kovo summoned you here to inform you of such. I am happy to wait until after you meet with him, but I will be stopping by your manor this afternoon."

The mention of Kovo seemed to instantly put the man on edge, but he hid it well. "I see. I can't say I look forward to working with you, but I hope you prove yourself capable. I do not deal well with incompetency."

The phrase was rather humorous, coming from someone who had clearly never tasted Bethynese discipline. I barely bit back a retort, tired of jabs given by a man who was hardly in a place to judge me. He seemed all too comfortable in his tailored suit to be anything but eager to serve Skayla and Ovok.

I gave a humorless smile. "Of course."

Lord Atarah swiveled around to continue his way to the throne room where Ovok was. "Until next time, Captain." With that, he disappeared down the hall, leaving me somehow even more frustrated than before. Dealing with him was going to make this all an even bigger pain.

I didn't make it far before I was again stopped, this time by none other than General Reth.

I quickly put my fist to my chest, straightening to attention under my superior.

"Captain Kearn, I am glad to find you safely returned," the general said, giving a nod and hand motion for me to return at ease. "I expect a full report of the situation in Veka on my desk by the evening."

"Of course, General." I nodded, folding my hands behind my back and relaxing only a little.

"Are you alright?" The general's question was...out of place. Reth was considered to take better care of his soldiers than some other high-ranking officers, he still generally didn't show such care openly. "Several under my command had been asking about you after we heard you had docked here." It was a small thing, but a reminder that when I'd been one of his attending officers, I had felt a relative sense of belonging.

"I..." I realized I had to choose my next words very carefully. On the one hand, I had no desire to risk lying to one of the highest-ranking officers in the Bethynese military—especially General Reth. On the other hand, I was far more scared of Ovok, at the moment. Besides, this was a chance to keep the narrative of Jaythos going in order to convince everyone of my loyalty. "I am alright, General. Simply disappointed in my brother. He was in Veka."

"Ah. I see." Reth's eyes searched me intently. He had been the first to look past my kinship with a traitor at the time. I had always been grateful to the general for giving me a chance, but now I wondered what he would think of me for joining Jaythos.

"What became of him?" the general asked.

Weakness was punished, so I kept my voice steady this time when I replied, "I did what was required. He is no longer a disgrace. We shall hear of him no more."

Was I insane? Did Reth wince? My mind had to be playing tricks on me—it had already been a very long day.

"Very well. Please report to me everything…before anyone else. I want to keep a close eye on things." The general gave an order that unfortunately, I would not be carrying out.

"Yes, General," I again put my fist to my chest, giving a small bow.

"You are dismissed. I will await your formal report, Captain."

I gave one more nod and then continued on my way, baffled by the encounter. My instincts were all mixed up, and now it felt as if I was hoping to see doubt on the general's expression. I wanted so badly not to be the only Bethynese willing to abandon our country. Perhaps even more, I wanted the one Bethynese general who had ever shown me a shred of civility to be more than what we were forced to be, even as I knew General Reth would waste no time in dealing swift and brutal justice should he discover my treachery.

Mentally exhausted, I made it back to my quarters in the barracks of the palace, at last. But I was not able to rest yet. After explaining to Yelsi, Gvar, and the others what the next step was—not daring to say anything

but the need for silence and discretion in regards to Ovok's true identity—
I was then shown to the officers' portion of the barracks and given a
private room, where my things had already been brought up by one of
the countless slaves, no doubt. I opened up the lone case that held my
clothes and as I went to put them in their proper place, found a scrap of
paper tucked inside my shirt.

*Await further instructions. Use the space behind the 14th brick in the
fifth row of the southern cellar to drop any necessary updates.*

Well…that hadn't been exactly enlightening, had it? I sighed and
used the nearby gaslight to burn the shred of paper. I really had gone
and done it this time. I wasn't a hero…. I just wanted my brother to stay
safe. What in Baeno was I thinking? Bethynese didn't defect, and they
didn't play spy. I still hadn't even figured out *how* I would play double
agent for Jaythos or what would happen if I ended up finding The
Underground, and this mysterious message hadn't exactly helped. What
if this Eugene Atarah was there as well? Would I have to kill him? How
long should I keep the guise of following Ovok and how would I benefit
from it?

And where was Skayla?

CHAPTER VI: Alone with My Responsibilities

<u>Baey:</u>

I hated how little I sat by Sven's bed these days. I'd agreed to take fewer shifts watching over him but couldn't help feeling guilty for it. There was just too much to do, and I knew the last thing he'd want was me sulking over his unconscious body.

Now it was even harder to spend any time at his bedside, what with Tanner and Jaythos also needing attention. They were at Alenor's house—it was a better place for them, especially with how overstimulated both Syvil and Tanner seemed to get. Jaythos hadn't been required to stay at the manor, but he'd insisted on finishing his recovery there. He'd said he wanted to be near Tanner. I was helping Marion with Jaythos's continued progress and, more importantly, forcing him to rest properly. Now that Alenor had taken The Living Stone shard to fix the watch, his recovery would be that of a normal person trying to heal, which was not exactly something Jaythos was accepting.

On top of all that, I was trying so hard to break through to Tanner and get him to say…anything. Marion was busy enough as it was between Jaythos and Syvil—the latter of which needed a lot of assimilating after the trauma of, well…dying—but she had still made time to try and coach Tanner into releasing memories.

It hadn't been working.

While I had been able to glean quite a bit more information from the healers from The Underground, not even Namaya had given me any idea on how to deal with something like what Tanner was experiencing.

And then, of course, there was Cyl. Marion had mentioned Tanner had even called his name a few times—but it made sense when the Guardian of the Doorway had once been acquainted with Ovok. Maybe I just wanted a reason not to trust Cyl, but something just didn't sit right about the whole situation surrounding his story or motivation. That stupid, puffed up prick was always talking over Darby and Estasia, acting as if he knew best just because he was however many years old, and did nothing but weigh everyone as assets. Not people—assets. Grenedil had been of little help, bowing his head and accepting any blame thrown his way by Cyl. Until now, I would have pegged Grenedil as a halfway decent judge of character. It made me wonder about the other friends he was always talking about. Were they as bad as this?

All this led to me being at Alenor's manor, on an errand for her and, honestly, grateful for the break away from dealing with Cyl. Granted, this trip was always on my schedule in the mornings, but I was a little more eager to take it today. Alenor's forge had been unceremoniously transported to The Underground due to Sven's "reorganizing" of the city and surrounding area. Her manor was still intact and invisible to the city people, but the room where her forge had once been was now a strange twisted mass of tree and sewer brick. It was beautiful, but meant Alenor was stuck running back and forth between The Underground and the manor for supplies while trying to fix the watch.

As I always did, I went upstairs to check in on Tanner first, again hoping continual interaction with him might help with his state.

Knocking on the door produced no response, as usual, so I entered the room, careful to make enough noise so as not to startle him. He was sitting stiffly on his bed and gave no acknowledgement of me having entered.

"How are you feeling?" I asked, sitting on the mattress beside my friend.

He only stared blankly at a wall, and I'd never felt further away from him. Somehow being just out of reach hurt so much more than him being an ocean away, but I'd learned quickly that touching him was an even worse idea.

"Have you practiced with Marion today?" I asked, knowing the answer but just trying to get him to talk. "I'm going to grab some things for Alenor while I'm here. Would you like to come help?"

"Did Moira misplace something again?" Tanner asked weakly, breaking the long silence that had settled in the room.

"We're fixing her watch, remember? Things just got…a little messed up while you were gone." I tried my best to remain calm and not show my worry. Once again, he wasn't Tanner. He didn't really know who he was…constantly jumping from person to person, memory to memory.

Tanner winced. "It broke? Oh, right. It broke."

There was a knock on the door, and Marion opened it slowly. Tanner's eyes shot up from where he was staring, instead locking onto her like a lost child clinging to their only family. It hurt a bit, but I reminded myself she was the person who'd been there for the breakdowns—the one who'd been helping him through this. I was thankful Tanner hadn't been entirely alone, at least.

"Are you ready for some morning practice, Tanner?" Her tone was gentle, as it always was with him. Like a mother, almost.

"I think...Baey needed help." Tanner looked over at me then back to Marion. I managed a smile, wings flicking a bit at the small bit of familiarity.

Marion also looked pleased. "Alright. I'll be back in a short while, then. Jaythos is still complaining about the exercises you gave him," she added, turning to me.

I rolled my eyes, hiding the painful memory of who had taught them to me. Namaya's healing skills were still going to good use, at least. "He complains about everything. We'll just be going down to grab something for Alenor. Shouldn't be long." Then I really had to go. After all those years of being pent up in Valdon, it was somehow equally as hard never being able to stay in one place. I couldn't just be here for my friend—I had to trust someone else to help him. I couldn't personally oversee Jaythos's recovery, couldn't be at Sven's bedside, and hardly ever saw Estasia unless we were in a meeting planning and sharing information— what with her having to be so involved with Atlys trying to find a new place to evacuate those in The Underground. Even in my free time, all I did was practice. My hand went almost unconsciously to the ring once more hanging around my neck. I missed Sven.

With a sigh, I stood up, smiling at Tanner and waiting for him to follow me to the door. Only barely did I remember not to offer my hand to him.

It took a moment, but Tanner stood limply up from the bed, eyes ever wandering, his expression that of constant perplexion. Marion said he just had way too many people in his mind. She said until they could get some of them out, anything that would help Tanner cling to his actual identity was helpful. Only now I realized...I didn't even know what that might be.

"Alright, ready?" I kept my tone as chipper as possible.

He nodded, and we left the room to go downstairs and find what had once been Alenor's forge.

It was quiet except for our footsteps, and while I wanted to find something to say, I wasn't sure what.

"Sefen's dead."

I swallowed, almost stopping in the middle of the hall from the abrupt statement. "Yeah, I know."

"He and Namaya. They had kids. Two of them. Namaya just...she didn't want us to end up like their kids. That's why she sold out. She thought if we surrendered, they would at least let us live."

Kids? I swallowed hard. Marion had said to try and keep Tanner away from rabbit holes, so I refused to ask further, instead going, "Have you been down here yet? To Alenor's forge, that is. I mean, it's not really a forge anymore, but it does look quite...unique." I really wasn't good at changing subjects. Sven was the best at that.

"Did you hear me?" Tanner's voice grew harsh, and he grabbed my arm. I turned around and tore away from him, beginning to instinctively reach for the knife at my belt before I stopped myself.

He was shaking with frustration. "Does anybody even listen to me? Does anyone *care* what I see?"

"Tanner," I spoke his name firmly, looking into his desperate, confused eyes. "I do care. That's why I brought you out of that stuffy room so you could do something other than think about what they put in your head." All I wanted to say was sorry; sorry that he'd devolved into this; sorry that I'd never even thought about the repercussions of what his Gift could do.

"What, you don't need me to try and check something? Isn't there some item you need from Alenor that you'll need me to search and find out some stupid thing or other?"

"No," I replied firmly. "There isn't."

The laugh that followed was brittle. Tanner threw up his hands. "Sure. I'm sure. It's never that easy—there's always something. Someone you all don't trust or something you are too lazy to figure out yourself. And you wonder why Skayla turned out how she did!"

My eyes widened and I found myself hissing his name. "Tanner. Don't say that. You aren't going to turn into Skayla. I just—I thought we were friends."

"Friends? I—" He seemed to choke on his own words, and suddenly his eyes were squeezed shut and his hands went to his ears. I took a step forward, uncertain if I should get Marion. But then, as quickly as Tanner's outburst had come, it left. His eyes shot open and his hands, still shaking, fell to his side. "Yes. We're friends. You and me, Baey. Sorry."

THE LAST ESMER

"It's alright." My lips pressed firmly together before adding, "I really did just want to get you out of that room for a bit."

"I know." The smile was weak. "Let's go."

He'll get better. Marion said they'd figure it out. The fact he was able to pull himself back like that should be proof, and yet it just made me think of Sven, and how he hadn't gotten better. Instead he was unconscious, possibly forever, alone and fading away.

"Here we are," I announced as we came to the door. "Be prepared to be confused." I tried to slide a sly little grin, but it was difficult after what had transpired in the hall.

Tanner raised an eyebrow. "Ominous."

My grin became a bit more genuine as I winked and opened the door, revealing the beautiful chaos within.

One of the walls had been removed, and in its place was an earthen tangle of dirt, rock, and shrubbery. A few bricks peeked through here, spliced unnaturally to make up the one wall, while the floor now created a patchwork mesh of forest and sewer along the ground, with swatches of greenery and grass littered over the now dirty brick floor. Then, of course, there was the entire tree that took up the center of the room, growing up and disappearing into the ceiling. I wondered how long until the thing would die, and how exactly Alenor would even deal with it when it happened. Certainly it couldn't continue to survive here, all cut up and spliced together like old rope. Unless Sven's Gifting changed much more about reality than even I could have guessed.

"Woah. It's...beautiful," Tanner whispered as he stepped into the room.

I quickly walked over to one of the shelves that had not been transported into The Underground, looking for the cup of old glass pellets Alenor had been asking for. It wasn't exactly easy to try and go through shelves that had branches now.

"Sven did...all this?" Tanner asked hesitantly. He hadn't been to The Underground to see *that* mess, and he had hardly been paying attention to his surroundings when we'd first brought him and the others back to Alenor's house, so he didn't even know the half of it.

"Yeah." My reply rang hollow around the room at the reminder that all the evidence of Sven was here...but no actual Sven, and that even if he did wake up, explaining this all to him wouldn't exactly be pleasant. He had enough blood on his hands already. I didn't want to tell him about the fact that now everyone hated him even more for the chaos he'd caused—even though it had been the only way to stop Skayla from getting all of us. Even though it had allowed hundreds—maybe thousands—of people to break free of her MindHold, he would still beat himself up for it, wondering if there could have been another way.

I wondered if Sven had even known something like this could happen. His mind hadn't exactly been in great shape.

"It's...it's incredible." Tanner walked slowly around the room; eyes riveted on the tree. "It's a good thing Skayla didn't know about this when she caught him.... He always had suspicions, you know."

My hands rested on a promising looking jar, but I paused. "What do you mean?"

"Sven. He never told anyone about the Reality thing, because he worried what Moira and Skayla would want him to do. He was always a little afraid of them."

I turned around, jar in hand and a perplexed expression on my face. "Why would he be afraid?"

"I don't know. He just worried. Worried about the power changing him…and how it changed them. I—he always got this weird feeling whenever he thought about telling them his true abilities." Tanner was frowning too. Then his eyes grew dim.

Right. Don't let him go down the rabbit hole. I looked down at the jar in my hand and then gave it a tentative shake. "Well, I found the glass pellets Alenor wanted. Weird looking, aren't they?" I held them up so the light from a nearby window—which hadn't been there originally, mind you—would catch on the jar. The glass prismed and left sparkles of light dancing around the room.

"Yeah."

And we were back to one-word answers…. I chided the pessimistic thought, reminding myself just how much he'd actually opened up, comparatively. He was making progress.

The journey back to his room was a quiet one, and soon I found myself alone in the hallway, Marion having just gone in as I'd left.

"How is he?" The question was almost as startling as the fact that I found myself staring at Jaythos, awkwardly standing there and disobeying about half the instructions he'd been given about resting.

I bit my lip, looking over to Maeko, who was further back, leaning against the wall. He shrugged in a clear show of frustration. No one could make Jaythos listen.

"Not…great. How are you feeling?" I turned the question back on him. "You should be resting."

"I feel fine. That shard worked wonders—do you think I could see him?" he pressed.

"I…" I looked back at the closed door for a moment. "I don't know that's a good idea, right now. Ask Marion." I knew he was likely talking to me because he *had* asked Marion. "When he's a little better, maybe. When you're *both* a little better."

The frustration was evident, but what was more subtle was the guilt I saw behind it. "Listen, Baey I-I'm…I don't want him to just feel like we don't care. I don't want to abandon another friend."

"You're not." Why did my insistence sound weak?

"I'm…I'm sorry, Baey." The sincerity and the apology coming from Jaythos startled me. "We were warriors. We were never great friends, let alone family. I rationalized it by just telling myself we weren't supposed to be. But I could have been. I could have been a friend, and I'm sorry." He paused, frowning in seeming bewilderment—like he was surprised he'd actually said any of that out loud. "I just don't want to sit by and accept orders when it means watching people I care about get hurt. I can't pretend it doesn't bother me anymore."

I swallowed hard. "Then show it. Right now actions speak louder than words. Show Tanner you care—ask Marion how you can help him. And for me…maybe try listening to my instructions? Like resting. I know what I'm doing, Jaythos."

"I know," he replied without breaking eye contact.

Those two words somehow meant more to me coming from him than the whole apology had. The acknowledgement that I was capable.

I bowed my head, feeling painfully aware that Maeko was also present for this. "Now, do those exercises like I told you, and rest. Ask Marion if maybe you can bring Tanner his dinner tonight or something. Maeko will tell her you spoke with me."

"Thank you." I couldn't think of the last time I'd heard Jaythos say those words, let alone to me. "And…Baey, one more thing."

I stopped, having been about to head back downstairs. "Yes?"

"Kearn…my brother. Please, keep him safe? I know if you make a promise, you'll keep it."

Estasia had been quite unhappy with Kearn's addition. I, on the other hand, had remained baffled that Jaythos had a brother I'd never known about. But I didn't need to look hard now to know how much he cared for him.

"I promise," I replied. "I will do whatever is in my power to keep him safe—to keep everyone safe."

No more words passed between us, only a quiet gratefulness and understanding, and that silent acknowledgement followed by his words. The acknowledgement of who I was, now. Someone to depend on…and that recognition settled deep in my heart.

I made the journey home in silence, using Sven's ring to hide me from the numerous patrols now wading around in the sewers.

After being let back into The Underground, I started down to Alenor's forge, only to be almost run over by Darby, breathless and wide-eyed. "Baey! The guards said you were back! It's Sven—he's awake!"

CHAPTER VII: Reunions and Redheads

<u>**Sven:**</u>

The quiet was unexpectedly refreshing. No nightmares, no screams. Just...silence. I hadn't been prepared for how desperate I was for it, and I felt as if I'd been trapped in a desert of noise and terror only to finally be given a drink. For the first time in a long while, I could breathe.

I wasn't really sure how long I'd been here, in this place of stars and silence, but I didn't want to leave; I wanted to get closer to this peace. Time passed in blissful quiet, and I noticed there was something in the distance—a door standing in the reflection of the stars. Somehow, I knew it was the source of this tranquility I was experiencing. I was drawn to the door, but just as I began making my way towards it, something happened.

Sounds. Voices I swore I knew—they were calling my name. I tried to ignore them, continuing closer to this door in the distance, but it felt as if the voices behind me were trying to tell me something. They would fade in and out, indiscernible and faraway...until they weren't. As the days— or however time came and went here—continued, the voices grew louder...more distinguishable. They were asking me to come back, to wake up. Wake up? I was asleep? Sleep hadn't felt this blissful for an eternity....

I didn't want to leave. Part of me wanted to finish my journey to that doorway, wherever it led. Something told me going back would make me lose this—this feeling of rest. But the voices grew more desperate. The voices of my mother...of Baey...of Darby.

I knew in my heart I couldn't ignore them any longer.

"Go. It is not your time." I did not recognize this voice, but it rang more clearly than the others. It was almost as if it came from the stars.

The peace remained, but the desire for the door—now only a little ways in front of me—diminished. I knew I couldn't rest when my friends—my family—were in such danger. I turned around and, looking back at the nothingness behind me, closed my eyes, taking a deep breath as I tried to listen to the sounds of my friends calling for me.

I gasped awake, my lungs feeling strange and almost unused as my senses were quickly bombarded by noises, smells, and the colors and shapes around me. I couldn't breathe...I...I couldn't breathe; there was something in my throat.

"Sven! Sven, you're awake! Calm down, it's alright—someone find Darbeshay and Baey!" A hand reached out and took hold of my shoulder. Instinct took over. I grabbed the arm with a free hand and wrenched it away from me. I became acutely aware of the fact I was attached to something in several places, and all I could think of was how I needed to get whatever was choking me out of my throat.

The cry of pain from my mother shocked me into releasing the arm and recoiling further back. I tried to speak, but my throat again closed around the strange tube in my throat.

"Shhh, it's alright, darlin'. I'm okay—please lie still. I'll take the tube out, but you'll hurt yourself." Mum again put a hand on my shoulder.

I flinched, forcing every survival instinct back down as I surrendered. I couldn't breathe. I couldn't....

"It's alright. Relax. It's alright, you can breathe. Just lay back and I'll have you out in a moment," she continued to walk me through instructions I could hardly process, explaining everything she was doing as I tried as best as I could to stay still and calm.

At last, what was apparently some form of nutritional tube was removed, then shortly after, the numerous other strange things I had been hooked up to. Everything felt...sore. My throat, my stomach....

"Are you...are you alright? I'm sorry I didn't mean to..." Talking hurt my throat, but that wasn't the worst of it. I felt violently overstimulated, my chest tightening as breathing once more became difficult. Everything was rushing in on me at once. Except...except even more so than usual. Memories crashed in and made it difficult to concentrate, even as I tried so hard to keep my head above this invisible ocean.

It didn't even matter if they were bad memories or good ones; it was too much.

"Just sit back. I'm alright, don't w—" Her own words were cut off as she frowned and leaned forward.

I remained frozen, eyes glued to her as I tried to focus on something—anything. There weren't just screams in my head; there was music and dancing and arguments and laughter. Everything at once.

"Sven y-your eyes are—never mind, what do you last remember? Only speak if it doesn't hurt too much, though. Can you hear me, darlin'? A nod is fine."

I could manage a nod. But what did I last remember? There was so much. Years and years of my life were tumbling over me like an endless wave, but at last, it clicked. "The...portal site—is everyone alright?" My eyes widened as I recalled the battle.

Mum's eyes darkened, but she nodded, stammering, "Y-yes, everyone is safe."

"SVEN!" I was suddenly and unceremoniously smothered in a pile of feathers as Baey tackled me with a fierce hug, causing me to almost fall completely back on my bed. "Sven, you're awake. I can't believe you're— I mean—what in Baeno were you *thinking?!*" She stood back and looked at me, a mixture of relief and anger warring in her expression.

How had I missed them coming inside the tent? I felt small; small and confused.

"Sven, do you...remember us?" It was a third voice. Darby.

I locked eyes with her and her breath caught, confusion rippling across her face as she tilted her head ever so slightly to the side. "Y-your eyes."

"W-what? They aren't...they aren't..." Skayla's again? What was so horrible about them? I suddenly wanted to throw up.

"No, no, they're—" Darby gave a soft smile to go with her suddenly far-off expression. "They just have their color back. They're that beautiful gold."

I was too distracted to completely care. "What happened?" I continued to ignore the hoarseness of my own voice as well as the pain speaking brought. Skayla...her armlet...I'd broken it, hadn't I?

"It's been a while, Sven," Darby stammered. "Once Baey looks you over, we can talk you through it."

I felt so…lost.

"Does anything hurt, Sven?" I heard Baey ask quietly.

I shook my head instinctively, frowning as I desperately attempted to process everything. I wanted to relax—to get even the slightest bit closer to the feeling of peace I'd had only moments ago, so blissfully unaware of what I'd left everyone to.

We were in Thackeray and Darby's tent now, and they had finally finished catching me up on the apparent month I had missed. I could hardly figure out what to think, let alone what to say. Somehow, waking up had been a worse nightmare than I'd ever had when asleep.

"How many?" I whispered.

"No," Baey said firmly. "Don't ask that and don't think that. If you hadn't gotten us out of there, it would have been everyone."

But she didn't know that, and now I had even more blood on my hands. Had there been children? I couldn't stop from conjuring countless horrible scenarios. I'd split reality apart and left the world a mess. Again, I'd made things worse and gotten people killed.

"Sven, please." Darby took a step forward and put a hand on my arm. I tried not to flinch, instead looking away.

"What's next, then?" I couldn't make myself look up at my mother as I asked, "The watch will be finished soon?"

"Yes. Baey and I are almost done with its forging," Mum said quietly. "And then we might be able to get Moira back."

I felt a strange tension in the air, but chose to cling to the good news. "And the portal?"

Baey let out a strange, frustrated laugh as Darby replied, "Well, Grenedil and—erm—Cyl have been taking watch over it, mostly. Cyl showed up, as we explained, just a week or so ago. He's been helping us understand Ovok and is watching over the portal to make sure no one else can get through."

Again, that sense of tension. I'd caught onto it when this Cyl had been mentioned earlier. Darby looked particularly perturbed.

"What is Estasia's opinion of Cyl?" I asked.

Darby's sarcastic snort was unexpected. "Oh, she says one wrong move and she'll punch him even harder than she did Temorn. The only reason she hasn't already is because Baey has convinced her he's necessary, for now."

I turned to Baey, frowning. Why had Estasia punched Temorn?

Baey quickly jumped in to explain, misinterpreting what exactly I was confused about. "Cyl can control the portal. If we need to make a quick evacuation of The Underground for any reason, he's the only way we could potentially do that. Cyl has made it clear that now that Ovok has The Living Stone, he is going to want to get off of Baeno—and Cyl is the only thing standing in his way. Him, and the people of The Underground, until Atlys and Estasia find a safe place to bring them. Right now, we are still having difficulty finding somewhere safe."

I felt overwhelmed and useless. It seemed as if they had this more under control without me, and now what had I done? Killed potentially hundreds of people by accidentally bending reality too far and putting lives directly in the line of fire for Ovok. I'd done exactly what I had always feared; crossed the line for the "greater good." There had to have been another way.

"I suppose you should have this back, though," Baey gingerly removed a chain from around her neck and took the ring from it.

I didn't want to take it, but suddenly every memory of when I'd given it away came to mind; every one of them a bad decision. Quietly, I took the cursed object and slipped it back on my finger, giving a nod of thanks.

"Oh. Uh. And this?" She went to take my old sword from her belt.

"No," I said all too quickly. "You...you probably will use it much more wisely. Keep it."

She frowned, biting her lip before asking, "Are you sure?"

Setting my resolve, I gave a firm nod. "Yes. Moira gave it to me as a way to protect others. I can't see it that way anymore, but I think with you, it might be able to be that again. You've done well protecting everyone so far."

Her wings twitched, shimmering blue for a moment before returning to their more neutral greyish-white. "Alright." But even if she hid the emotion from her wings, I saw how much this meant to her. I knew she'd make a better name for that blade, and maybe even redeem it.

"So, how do we clean up my mess?" I asked, turning back to the problem at hand.

"Sven, it's not your mess. Without you, the portal would be in Ovok's hands right now, and he'd be gone with The Living Stone already. Atlys and Estasia's reports say that Ovok arrived back and was very perturbed at the portal being gone, and Cyl said…" Darby gagged a little. "Cyl said it was definitely a blessing in disguise, in the grand scheme of things. We'd have lost if you hadn't done what you did."

"Don't call that a blessing," I snapped. "The death of innocent people is never a blessing. It is the curse of war and greed." And I would never forgive myself for it.

Everyone in the room visibly winced, but for once, I didn't apologize. There were many things I should be groveling for right now, but that one rule—that one rule I could never place aside, and I could never forgive myself for breaking it. Even by accident. I should have known better.

"You really should rest, Sven," Mum whispered. "Maybe take a moment. You must be extremely overwhelmed."

I clenched my jaw, shaking my head firmly as I replied, "I'm fine. I think a month of doing nothing is enough rest. I'll catch up." In all honesty, I was feeling…remarkably more coherent. I hadn't realized just how much work it had been to physically function until now. Even moving seemed easier, and as overwhelming as every sense was…I felt much more alert. There was also something else different—something about my mind that felt easier to maneuver and more my own. I had more memories than before. Memories of my childhood—of moments with Darby and Sera and others before I'd become The GhostMaker. Memories I'd been unable to recall before.

"Sven?" I missed who had called my name, but shook myself back into the here and now.

"May I see the portal?" I asked, again feeling out of place. I had to try and make myself useful again—somehow. So far, the only thing that changed when I was around was the body count.

"Of course. Alenor, do you need me with you today?" Baey turned to Mum and asked.

"No. I think I am almost done, actually. The last bit I must do myself—if you brought back the necessary supplies this morning." She gave me a weak smile.

"Yes. Here—" Baey handed her a jar of glass pellets. "If I'm not needed, then, why don't I show Sven the portal? I still have to check in with them today, anyway." Baey flicked her wings and straightened her back, so much transformed from when I had last seen her. It was unsettling. To me, it was like I'd only seen her yesterday, and yet she looked so different; taller, her hair longer, and face somehow older—not that those were the things that caught me off guard. It was the boldness and this new sense of authority. Had I only been holding her back? I had tried so hard to help her with her confidence, but it seemed as if all she'd needed was for me to be gone.

"I am still waiting on Thackeray to return from unloading the supplies from Atlys, so I will remain. Estasia is also supposed to be stopping in to report," Darby added, giving me a small smile. "I will see you soon, though."

Mum followed us as far as her forge, which had apparently been one of the things slammed into The Underground after my mistake. I couldn't stop staring at the mess of a place, all mixed up like some strange dream bleeding into reality. The forge was just placed here like a room dropped with no ceiling, the walls from her manor still visible even as they held up nothing but air. But her workshop wasn't the only evidence of my missteps. As Baey and I continued on in The Underground, I saw the strange interspersing of what was supposed to be road from the surface city. It was hard to ignore the occasional building half sticking out of the ground.

"So, I've been practicing—maybe I could show you how I've been doing later?" Baey chirped on, cheery even with the new weight that she seemed to carry on her shoulders.

"Yes," I managed to get the word out, my mind still trying to catch up on everything. Ovok had The Living Stone…we were losing. He just had to find us down here, and we would be doomed. But why had Skayla disappeared? Had something happened when I'd broken her armlet? Was that why my mind felt so much clearer? Had she still locked some of my mind away even after Hytat?

"Are you feeling alright? I mean, you were unconscious for…a while. Are you sure you're up to this?"

I winced and said, "I am used to it." A month was nothing compared to almost a decade. At least I still had my brain intact.

Baey's wings darkened. "Right."

Any further conversation was cut off as we arrived at a strange barricade in the square with two guards at the entrance. But I was more distracted by the raised voices from inside the makeshift blockade.

Every muscle in my body tensed and I looked at Baey, wondering if that was normal.

There was a mixture of frustration and confusion that made it hard to tell. "Is everything alright?" Baey asked one of the guards.

The woman shook her head. "I don't know. It just started, but it's getting pretty bad." Her eyes—like that of her companion—wandered to me, widening ever so slightly and then hardening. But she didn't say anything, and I decided it was best to not make further eye contact.

Baey just sighed. "Alright, let us through." There was an undertone of urgency in the order.

"SHE COULD DIE!"

The hair on the back of my neck raised at the words, and I looked at Baey once more, every alarm bell going off at the crystal-clear phrase screamed from just beyond our sight.

Baey pushed through without another word, and soon, we found two men arguing by the mess of my mother's machinery.

"Get it through your thick skull that there is more at stake than a single life, and if she brings Tyron through, there could be *far* bigger repercussions, Grenedil!" The strangely dressed man littered with scars growled back.

"But if she's trying to get through into The Maze, there has to be a reason—I told you she would never do something to endanger others!" Grenedil shouted back. Grenedil...I did remember him, barely.

"What in Baeno is going on?" Baey joined in on the yelling, gaining their attention.

Both Grenedil and the other man—Cyl—turned to face Baey.

"Sven! You're awake!"

I blinked, confused by the whiplash of just having seen Grenedil shouting to save someone and now addressing me so…positively.

"And you just continue to allow him to possess his relic?" Cyl's eyebrow shot up as his gaze landed on my finger. "An unwise decision in my—" Suddenly he stopped, head jerking behind him as if he had heard something.

My hand went to the sword that was not by my side. Right.

"That idiot child—she is going to tear the whole thing open—" Cyl backed up into the area between the machines and disappeared in a flash of blue.

"Cyl, no!—Gah!" Grenedil threw up his hands and then ran them both through his hair.

Was I awake? I was starting to wonder if perhaps I was actually still unconscious and this was all a strange dream….

"Grenedil, what is going on—where did he go? I thought he said we *weren't* supposed to use the portal," Baey said, taking a step forward. One hand was on her sword.

"I don't even know anymore! He had better not be going to shut Astra out and trap her with that mad—"

I was so incredibly lost in the situation. Astra? Who was Astra?

Before Grenedil could even finish his sentence, the portal flashed again and we all stepped back as Cyl entered into the clearing, holding a small, redheaded girl by the shoulder. She instantly pulled away, falling to the ground from the effort.

"Do you have any idea what you almost just did?" Cyl growled as he reached for the girl, who had been trying to scramble away. Her wild, unnaturally blue eyes were quite literally emanating sparks, and she looked around frantically, pulling a knife out and brandishing it at Cyl.

I stood frozen, the terror in the gaze of this stranger so penetrating that I had the sudden urge to run forward and separate her from Cyl—Guardian of the Doorway or not.

"Stay away from me," the girl hissed. My breath hitched as her short, red hair whipped back to reveal a horribly precise scar running in a crescent shape around one side of her face. That sort of mark never came from the battlefield.

And then she turned to look at Baey, Grenedil, and me. Something inside me tore in on itself as I even more acutely felt the anguish in this child's every being, because that's all she was—a child; hardly older than Baey, if I were to guess.

Just as I was about to step in and try to calm her down, the girl's expression suddenly changed away from fear and instead to open confusion as she said, "...Grenedil?" She got to her feet, still holding the knife and looking like a cornered animal.

"Yes—Astra, it's alright—you're alright. I'm sorry, please just...just put the knife down." Grenedil came forward, both hands in the air.

"Alright? Things are anything *but* alright—your ignorant decisions could have unimaginable consequences for the TetraWorlds." Cyl made little effort to hide his displeasure, looking as if he wanted to make another move for the girl.

"Stop it!" I had no idea where I found the strength to speak, let alone so loudly, but somehow, I managed it. Cyl looked baffled, but I couldn't care less what this stranger thought right now. I'd seen the way he'd handled this child so callously.

"Grenedil, wh-wh-where is Tyron—where is he? I have to get him to Ent. That's the only way to contain him—I have to—" The girl was cut off by none other than Cyl.

"You will be doing no such thing. How could you let a madman like that into The Maze? How could you be so *careless?* Now Ovok could be alerted to the use of the Door, and for all I know, you could have doomed us all."

"I need to go back! He—where is Tyron?!" The girl's eyes were wide with panic, and a strange, nearly electric feeling grew all too present in the air.

"Cyl, you're not helping." Now it was Baey. I was pretty sure we had established that Cyl was being extremely *un*helpful. "Astra? Grenedil has told us a lot about you. Are you alright?"

But I knew the look on Astra's face all too well; she wasn't listening. She was in full blown panic as she begged Grenedil. "Please, you saw what Tyron did to us—I don't know where he is now—wh-where I am. I can't let him hurt—he's going to *kill* them! I can't—" I could almost hear her lungs squeeze shut with the way her last sentence splintered off into oblivion.

"I could not grab both him and you. I do not know where he is, but it is likely he is…" Cyl sighed. "He is either in The Maze, or now on Kryso or Eatris. With the way the moons were aligned, the former is more likely."

"Then take me back." The words were hard. "Take me back, *now*."

"Certainly not," Cyl said with an indignant snort. "You've already done enough damage. The last thing I need is for you to further alert Ovok to our presence here."

It all happened in a moment. I felt the way the energy bubbled up even before the blue light flooded the clearing inside the barricade—the same strange blue that made up the color of this girl's eyes. One fear crossed my mind: that the pulse would kill everyone in the vicinity. So, in that second before the blue enveloped us all, I made a few decisions. One was to use the ground to push everyone back, altering reality to allow Baey, Grenedil, and Cyl all to phase through the barricade that had kept the portal secure. The next was to create the same safe space I had made so often with Baey—so that whatever damage this girl's blue energy was about to do would do no damage to the actual world. I left her and myself alone in the invisible dome, making sure no one would be allowed in just as no energy would be allowed out.

And oh, the energy tried. I had never felt such raw power—blinded as the light coming from the girl flooded the surrounding area for minutes on end, tearing up the earth and pieces of the barricade and even setting fire to my coat with a strange blue flame.

"Astra, you need to stop, please!" I called out above the roar of chaos happening in this protected space, hoping I had correctly remembered the name Grenedil had used earlier to address the girl.

I just heard her screaming; a tortured sound that reverberated deep in my soul. Slowly, ignoring the searing heat and pain from the pulses of primal power, I crept towards her, gravity itself bending to her will even as I tried to make it bend to mine. It was a tricky thing to battle this incredible foreign surge of energy and get it to obey me. I could only get enough of a grasp for it to allow me to pass on and reach the girl in one piece. She was on her knees, hands over her ears and tears streaming down her face, illuminated by the intense light coming from not only her eyes but her scars as well.

And the one on her face was not the only scar.

I knelt down, putting out the fire that touched my coat for the hundredth time and whispering, "Astra, I will do anything I can to help you, but I need you to stop, please."

"I can't, I can't stop. I can't—he might—I can't." Her words were as haggard as her breathing as she gasped through the sobs.

Closing my eyes, the recollection of when Skayla had first lost control of her abilities and had been unable to get out of everyone else's heads came to my mind unbidden. "Breathe with the power, Astra. Everything has a heartbeat. It's okay if you can't stop it yet, just breathe with it. In and out. In and out," I instructed, even as I matched my words with the waves of energy obliterating the ground around us. I could hardly see anything besides Astra in the blue haze, but I kept my focus on the energy. Astra appeared to obey, and soon the uncontrollable pulses of power began subsiding like a receding ocean tide.

"Good," I encouraged. "Just keep breathing. Don't worry about anything else, just match the breathing with the waves. You're doing wonderfully." I hated the sound of my own voice, but right now, I needed to focus on Astra.

Eventually, the blue faded back into her eyes alone even as her sobbing continued, and she collapsed into a heap on the ground, her knees brought up to her chin as she whispered, "I'm sorry…I'm so sorry. I'm sorry."

"It's alright, don't worry." I didn't dare touch her—getting the feeling that, by the look of her visible scars, unexpected contact would be unwelcome. Instead, I just sat down on the upheaved ground next to her, daring to look around at the complete decimation she had caused. What I saw beyond it, however, was a very, *very* unhappy Baey sitting just beyond the invisible barrier I had created. Behind her were Grenedil and an irate Cyl, though the latter I couldn't care less about.

Dread filled the pit of my stomach as the full realization of what I'd done hit me like one of Astra's waves of energy. I'd used my power. Again. So instinctively and so *carelessly*, mere hours after learning how doing so before had caused the death of so many people. I was no better than Skayla. I…

…I needed to concentrate on Astra. I turned back to the little heap next to me on the ground and whispered, "It's alright. You didn't hurt anything—I made sure of it. Everyone is fine. Are you alright?"

"I…he could have them. I failed. I promised Ent." She wasn't crying anymore, but somehow, I knew it wasn't for lack of trying. She was clearly exhausted.

A while longer passed before she slowly sat up, looking around at the carnage with an empty-eyed look I could understand.

"Don't worry. It will all disappear when I bring the barrier down. You have done no harm." I tried to hide the sudden and oppressive emptiness as I realized that while I could promise her that, I couldn't promise *I* hadn't done something.

"I failed," she said, void of all emotion. "I might have just killed my entire family."

CHAPTER VIII: Nothing is Ever Simple

<u>Estasia:</u>

"What in the *world* were you thinking, Sven?!" I didn't care if I raised my voice, I was furious. "You just wake up and decide, 'You know what? Let's go do *exactly* what put me in a coma for over a month'!"

Sven's dead expression was not helping. "I'm sorry." The words were as empty as he seemed. Darbeshay and Baey had caught me up on the disaster surrounding the *third* person to come through the portal.

"You have done this, what, five times, now? I don't even know if I can keep count anymore! You need to stop that stupid impulse telling you to jump into every suicide scenario, because none of us want to pick you up off the floor after it!" The words were coming out all wrong, and yet the image of him lying unconscious week after week would be burned in my brain for the rest of my life.

"Then stop trying to pick me back up!" Sven's vehement words cut the space and left even me momentarily speechless.

"Listen," I spoke at last through grit teeth. "As nice as that sounds, that's not exactly something I am willing to do."

"Why not?" Sven threw up his hands. "I can't do it—I clearly can't think enough to stop myself, and all I keep doing is getting people killed. I was gone for a month, you say? Baey's been able to use my ring to keep you all hidden just fine without me. She's more than capable of keeping you safe without the danger of going off the rails and breaking *reality itself*. You have an entire network between you and Atlys feeding us information and supplies. What do you *need* me for, Estasia? I got you out of the Kovian Fortress—I got you Moira's watch and since then, all I've done is waste your resources with you all trying to keep me safe and alive. Whatever you did to keep me alive this last month, I am sure it would have been far better to use it on others who were hurt by what destruction I left in my wake. I thought—I thought at least all the friends I'd killed hadn't been out of choice. I'd been in a MindHold. But no, I have no excuse now and somehow, I still got people killed. So why? Just don't wake me up next time and you'll all be much better for it!"

"Because you're my friend, Sven! Would you shut up and stop talking about dying—because if there is one thing that needs to happen, it's that you need to live." I didn't wait for anyone else to speak, although I had clearly only barely stopped Darbeshay from doing so. "I need you to prove me wrong—I need you to show me good people can survive in this forsaken world, and if you just go get yourself killed, then I will be proven right and—" my breath caught unexpectedly—"I don't want to lose the first friend I've had in over a decade. So shut up and stop giving us all a heart attack. Whether you like it or not, you have people who care about you, and maybe…just maybe, they're worth staying alive for. Sometimes that's a bigger sacrifice than getting yourself killed, you big oaf."

No one said a word for a long time, although I wasn't sure who wanted to disappear from the tent more: Sven…or me. He looked down at the ground, his golden eyes sparkling in the lamplight as they seemed to struggle with the very concept that he was worth something.

"I'm sorry. I will try not to be a—" He cut himself off, wincing as if he realized whatever stupid thing he was about to say would have only made me more upset. Which, judging by how that sentence was going, he would have been right. "I will try."

Clearing my throat awkwardly, I had no idea what else to do other than pretend that the entire thing had never happened. The way everyone was still gawking made that difficult, but seeing as I was very good at ignoring other people, I just turned to Darby and asked, "So what about this Tyron person the girl was trying to trap?"

"The son-in-law of Ovok, and a very dangerous man who Astra attempted to allow to waltz into The Maze." Cyl was ever-so-thoughtful as to interject before Darby could answer my question.

It had been a long day. I was beginning to wonder if punching him would be as satisfying as punching Temorn had been.

Apparently, Cyl wanted to push his luck. "Astra has proven herself very dangerous, especially when enabled by Grenedil." He didn't have to look at Grenedil to make known his displeasure. Not that I gave a rat's rotting carcass for his opinion. "She apparently has little control of her Gifting, and because of it, she is going to draw Ovok right here—if her opening The Doorway hasn't already. My people are extremely sensitive to her Eatrisian Gifting. It will be like a beacon for him. We should send her as far away as possible, or lock her up somewhere that will lead him on a wild chase. At the very least, I cannot *stand* the headache she is giving me and would kindly like her removed from any sort of close proximity to me."

"Out of the question. We're not just sending her away." Sven had reentered the present, it seemed, naturally way more willing to defend someone other than himself.

Honestly, at this point, I was for anything that got under Cyl's skin. Even if I was a bit reticent at the idea of adding yet another stranger into this mess.

Fortunately, as I suspected, Baey already had a plan. She stepped in, pretending Cyl hadn't even opened his mouth. "Alenor is with the girl for now. I was thinking it might be a good idea for Sven to be the one to keep tabs on her. If her powers were to surface like that again, I think Sven is probably best suited to keep things from—er—exploding, and he could hide her Gifting from Ovok."

I arched my eyebrow as the irony was not lost on me. "You mean he should do the thing I just yelled at him for doing?"

Sven did not say a word, only keeping eye contact with Cyl much better than he did with anyone else. That really said something about Cyl, and I was pretty certain it was not flattering.

"Yes. Just...carefully." Baey's cheeks reddened a bit. "And making sure to get out of the way if she were to have another episode instead of, well, going towards her and nearly incinerating yourself." She turned to address Sven with this. "Would you be able to hide the presence of her Gifting, by any chance?"

He winced but nodded. "Yes, I can do that. But we need to find out about her family." Sven was addressing Cyl. "She will calm down if she knows they're safe. Can you please check?"

"Absolutely not. Have you not been li—right. You haven't been, because you were too busy turning the world inside out. As I have explained to your companions, any time I use The Door, it will alert Ovok and bring him closer to knowing where the location is. If we're lucky, he may only have a general idea of where we are now, but still have a big enough radius that he doesn't know where for sure we're hidden. If I use it again, he will be that much more likely to be able to pin down the exact placement of the portal door." He explained everything like we were children.

I couldn't help but roll my eyes.

"But there has to be something—her family. She's afraid she kill— she's afraid they're dead. Or in danger." Sven's persistence was not unexpected, but the feverishness of it was more of a surprise. "If we don't get her some form of answer, then she will continue to break down. There *must* be something you can do."

The self-righteous sigh of perseverance from Cyl was enough to make me gag. "Fine. I stand by my statement. I cannot go in. But…perhaps if I am able to concentrate enough, I can feel The Maze— just as I felt her opening The Door to it. I might be able to tell what world Tyron has fallen into. That will help her know if her family is in any danger."

This was enough to satisfy Sven for the moment, and he replied with, "Thank you."

Personally, I wouldn't have thanked the Drogan yet. Or at all, even if he was successful. Better not to give any of that ego a boost.

"I will be able to properly do it once you hide her Gifting signature and take her out of The Underground." Cyl waved a dismissive hand. "Her Gifting is too loud, right now. Which means I also suggest you do that sooner rather than later, for the sake of avoiding Ovok."

Sven gave a deep look of concentration, then said, "I have put a mask to the best of my ability over Astra's energy signature. It will work better when I am with her, but it should stop Myrandi from outside The Underground from sensing it."

Cyl nodded in begrudging approval. I assumed that also meant it had worked, as he would have definitely stated if he was still annoyed by the headache her Gifting had been giving him.

"I don't suppose you could hide the portal the same way...." Baey asked hesitantly.

"Not possible." Again, Cyl decided to answer for someone. "While your Sven Mara might be able to sense the power of The Doorway and The Maze that lives behind it, no one can block its presence. It is like trying to stifle the Gifting of all three worlds all at once, and clearly hiding just that girl's Gifting is quite a burden."

I jumped in, annoyed at the way he so quickly put Sven down. "Noted. Then let's turn to what I was originally calling this meeting for." It had been meant to talk about my meeting with Atlys...before I had been informed of Sven's whole debacle with this girl. "I was going to talk to Baey about possibly being able to help use your ring, Sven, to organize an evacuation of the people here to the old portal site. Perhaps you and Baey could do it?" I moved the conversation on as quickly as possible. "No bending reality. Only illusions," I added to clarify.

Darby sighed. "But that would still hold a great deal of risk and...and there's no infrastructure. How would it be sustainable? And how would they get food and water? How would we even get everyone there? The census we carried had the number over nine hundred and fifty. And then there are still the gravitation anomalies, are there not?" She said the last bit hesitantly, clearly trying to avoid Sven taking on yet another thing being his fault.

"Honestly, this is still not the most ideal plan. I'm just trying to weigh our options—I'm hoping maybe Atlys's scouts find something better. In the meantime, Atlys said there is a larger creek nearby the ravine that would provide water, if we were to use the purification system you all have been using down here. I know we'd prefer a larger source of water, but that is still better than nothing. If Sven did an illusion around the space, then we would be able to have small fires without too much attention drawn to it. We could still use the beach on the cliffside for Atlys to provide us with supplies using the invisible ship that Sven had helped us steal so long ago. We'd just need to be able to transport them after that, and of course, we'd need to work out how to hide our tracks—maybe Sven and Baey could make an invisible route of sorts? There is admittedly…still a lot we would need to work out, but I want to at least have one plan set—even if it isn't ideal—in case something happens and we have to move unexpectedly. If Cyl is right about Ovok getting closer because of Astra coming through, we really are running out of time."

"Would Skayla possibly be able to sense us using the ring to move people, wouldn't she?" Darbeshay asked.

I shook my head. "No one has heard heads or tails of her since…" Looking over at Sven, I finished, "…you broke her armlet. Atlys is planning on seeing what Kearn might be able to glean on that front. But seeing as those in a MindHold have been for a large part freed…I think Ovok is the more impending threat."

I did not miss the way Sven's brow furrowed, but whether in confusion or thought I wasn't sure.

"If we are going to move everyone out there, though, perhaps we could use the portal to do so?" Baey suggested. "Since then everyone would be out of harm's way when Ovok arrived here in the city."

I didn't need to look at Cyl to know his face was turning red; his voice showed that clearly enough. "I am getting tired of repeating myself. It's not about the people inside the city. It's about stopping him from getting the portal at all. We need a plan to *stop* him. Not evacuate."

The silence was eerie as Cyl once again confirmed just where he stood on helping us. He was exactly the sort of person I despised.

"Well," Darby said, awkwardly moving on for now. I caught her look, though. We would figure out the other logistics for an evacuation, and Cyl could deal with what we came up with. "I think since we're on the subject of the portal site, there is another matter of business. Alenor informed me the watch was finished. So if Baey can figure out how to use it, then we might be able to get Moira back."

This should be a good thing, and yet the way Darby always brought up Moira seemed like she was a little afraid of her. Was it just a reverence for the Watchers, or was there something more? Surely, she would not have wanted her freed if she wasn't on our side, but I didn't like it. Darby always seemed to have a knack for judging a person's character.

Sven's head shot up as if some spell had been broken, and all of a sudden, he was very present in the conversation.

I shifted uncomfortably. "So then the plan is for Baey to practice using the watch, and then we organize a party to go out and inspect the site?"

"Yes. We can discuss who will be accompanying the party later, but for now, I think we need to finish the matter at hand. Sven, you should go up to Alenor's manor with—what was her name?"

"Astra," Sven whispered.

Of course, he remembered her name. I wondered if, with his memories back, that would be the next issue to tackle. First, it was that he couldn't even remember his own name, but after knowing him for the past few months, I got the feeling he was the kind of annoying person who never forgot a name or whatever sob story laid behind it.

We finished the meeting and Sven quietly went with Baey to relieve Alenor from the post of watching over this Astra. I, in the meantime, found myself running my hands over my face and wishing I could take back half the words I'd blurted out in the last half hour.

"Are you alright?" Darby asked, the only one still remaining inside of the tent.

"Just fine, thanks." The words came out much more like a groan than I'd intended. "It would be nice for something to go our way, though."

"Yes. I suppose it would. I think Baey will have little trouble in picking up the watch, at least. With time on our side…well, that is quite the ally."

The topic allowed me to seize the opportunity, the despair of a moment ago lifting. "And Moira?" It had been rare for Darby and me to have a moment alone; between me running back and forth from Illan and Atlys, and then Darby trying to keep the entire Underground in one piece while keeping everyone from wanting to tear Cyl to pieces—yes, I still wanted to do that.

The look in Darby's eyes was conflicted. I didn't like it. Again, if we were about to free Moira—who was supposedly the most powerful of the three Watchers—I would rather there was a little more enthusiasm behind the realization. Was that too much to ask?

"I trust she will do what is needed to keep us safe." Darby's reply was vague. Not exactly what I wanted.

"What? What aren't you telling me? If we're about to try a jailbreak, I think I have a right to know the pros and cons of this. You're making her sound like another Skayla, and I don't care if Moira is Sven's sister or Alenor's daughter—I do not want another Skayla." All the reservations about the Watchers I once had came bubbling up to the surface. With how different Sven Mara and Alenor had been from what I'd always expected, it was easy to forget my own dread over the amount of power the Mara family held.

"Sorry. She's not another Skayla. She's just..." Darby made a face that looked somewhere between apprehensive and pained. "She was very powerful. I always felt uncomfortable knowing someone could go back in time and I would never know. Everyone always just had a healthy fear of her. There's a reason Skayla knocked her off the list first when the bloodbath began."

Still not exactly helping my confidence. "Darby," I kept my tone even. "If you have *any* reservations about this plan, I need you to tell me. Moira may be Sven's sister, but so was Skayla. I don't want playing favorites to get us killed."

I didn't like the way Darby struggled to keep eye contact. "She's the best shot we have. She kept entire wars from happening. She'll give us time to think."

"Darby, stop side-stepping." I refused to let this go. "What are you not telling me?"

Throwing her hands up in exasperation, Darby replied, "Nothing! That's the problem. Nothing. Under Moira we saw peace like we hadn't seen in years. But the thing was, sometimes I didn't understand how we got there. She always kept Sven out of things—like she was afraid he wouldn't agree with her methods or something. I do not doubt she will be on our side, but I doubt her methods. I wondered how many times she would run a scenario until it got the solution she wanted…. And talking to her felt very much like you were talking to some entity rather than a person. Like she was simply observing and passing judgment. I don't know. I have nothing but a gut feeling to give me hesitance. I just…there was always something that left everyone a little scared of her."

"Great," I gave a huff. "Well then, I will make sure to keep an eye on my back, and I feel Baey needs to know this too. Seeing as your gut feeling has helped keep you alive so far, I really am confused why you'd want to dismiss it now."

The glare I received was worth it. "Because we need her if we're going to win. Just because I don't like Moira doesn't mean she warrants this much doubt."

I scoffed. "Everyone warrants doubt, Darby. I wouldn't still be alive otherwise."

"Perhaps. But it sounds lonely. I don't think I could live that way."

Unable to stand dancing around subjects any longer, I replied, "Well, living and surviving are two different things, and right now, this world is impossible to live in, so I'll settle for surviving, thank you." And with that I left the tent, really not in the mood for some further retort on friendship or camaraderie. I'd already spent all my energy on Sven, and I didn't want to admit Darby was right.

Maybe I wasn't alright with just surviving anymore.

Kearn:

Working with Lord Atarah was proving to be difficult. In all my years, I had always loathed the way those outside of Bethyn looked down on my people, yet this man seemed to hold a special kind of hatred every time he was forced to see me.

Unfortunately, that was quite often, as time was showing. It had been a pain to even get the various charts of the city from his manor, as he'd taken over two hours sorting through the tomes and scrolls that littered his quite extensive library. While stalling was technically beneficial for my situation, I somehow still found myself frustrated by the lack of discipline.

Perhaps I should have been more thankful for his inability to keep things organized because, now that I actually had them, I had to figure out what to *do* with the charts. Certainly I couldn't conveniently *lose* them, as at that point, I might as well just turn myself over as a traitor, or at the least be strung up by General Reth or Ovok for being utterly incompetent. I was supposed to take over General Reth's sewer searches, and I had already dawdled for too long. I wondered why I was even taking over for the general, and what more important things he could possibly have to do.

"Captain?" Yelsi intruded into my room as well as my thoughts, and I quickly folded one of the maps I'd been pretending to look at.

"Yes?" I didn't like the pale look on Yelsi's face.

Clearing his throat, he put his arm to his chest and said, "Lord Kovo has called an urgent meeting. In the grand hall."

The grand hall meant there would be other people…. This wasn't any simple update request—which there had been plenty of.

"Thank you," was all I managed to say aloud to Yelsi before turning around and collecting myself. The streets were rioting, and I had used that as an excuse to stave off searching the sewers, but how long would I be able to use that? General Reth had seemed to accept the excuse, but Ovok was extremely impatient. It was becoming clear that the last thing Ovok cared about was the state of Baeno, and there had still been no sign of Skayla.

What had happened, and where was she hiding?

"Sir?" Yelsi had, apparently, not left.

With another deep breath, I replied, "That will be all, thank you. Do nothing outside of what we have discussed." Which really meant practically nothing. They were to keep an ear out for whispers of where Skayla was, and if there were any other Bethynese soldiers bold enough to voice their displeasure with the way things were; that was all. While I knew the common Bethynese soldier was far from content with serving the beck and call of the imperious Bethynese Council of Generals, very few ever let that cross their lips. I was the best example of that, and I still wasn't exactly going around announcing it to anyone.

Yelsi gave one more nod and then left, leaving me alone to try and prepare for whatever disaster this meeting was going to be. Why had I ever agreed to this? As if unbidden, the image of Jaythos's pale and bloody body rushed to the forefront of my mind, and I couldn't help but let out a bitter scoff. That dolt was not just going to get himself killed, but me along with him.

Still. There was something more…something I had not seen. The fact his friends had accepted our help even when Jaythos was not there to convince them. The way the Rugonian—while as furious as he was—had trusted us enough to aid in Jaythos's rescue. For years, it had been drilled into our heads that no one outside Bethyn would ever accept us. I'd known for a fact that even if one of us defected, it was to a life of isolation and abuse because of the name our country had made for ourselves. A name that was only because of those who ruled over us, forcing farmers to become soldiers and bakers, killers. It was to embrace the life of a soldier or die, and those that could not prove their worth in the military were left to do just that on the Isle of Curr. However, maybe I was done being someone else's puppet. Maybe I was done just taking orders. Was I only leaving one master for another, though? Was I just blindly following these rebels—who still hated me and my people—doing whatever it took to help Jaythos survive, just as I'd done whatever it took for me to survive in Bethyn before?

All these thoughts boiled unpleasantly in my head as I quickly made my way down to the grand hall, hating how I'd somehow allowed my mind to again have room to breathe. It was better not to think. Things were easier that way; easier but not better. I was beginning to think I no longer wanted things to be easy.

When I arrived at the grand doors that led to the hall, I was unpleasantly surprised to see that the others had already arrived. There were a dozen or so nobles, one of whom was, unfortunately, Eugene Atarah. Two other Bethynese captains stood not far away, and I also noted General Reth's presence as well—or rather, he noted mine, meeting my eyes until I was uncomfortable. I reminded myself there was no way he could know I had betrayed them all. Still, I did not dare turn my gaze away until he gave a slight nod.

"Ah, the last to arrive? Do you love being in Lord Kovo's good graces so much you dare keep him waiting?" Lord Atarah had apparently spotted me, making his way over with a very unpleasant smile.

I didn't like the way he said it louder than it needed to be, and I certainly did not appreciate the sideways glances.

"Have you been able to figure out the charts yet?" His tone remained hostile.

I resisted the urge to square my shoulders, knowing any change in posture would do nothing but show weakness.

There was no more room for discussion, thankfully, as the doors to the hall swung inward, and we were ushered inside to find Ovok waiting in the center of the room.

All was eerily quiet after the doors closed.

Then, at last, Ovok spoke. "Please, enlighten me as to why I am forced to send for Grand General Brahj in order to try and get this city under control because you buffoons cannot manage a simple riot?" The words echoed like an angry drum, and I only barely held in a wince. Many of the others in the room were not so stoic.

A noble was foolish enough to try and offer a reply. "My lord, we are trying, but if we could see Lady Skayla—"

"ENOUGH!" I had always wondered how such a lesser noble who had been mostly unknown was able to command such a space. Now knowing Ovok's true identity, it did not surprise me, but neither did it stop the way my soul wished to shrivel back inside me when he raised his voice.

"Are you going to sit here and give excuses, or do we need to start with public executions?" The words, suddenly so calm, sent a shiver down my spine. "General Reth? You said you would get the riots under control if you didn't have to also search the sewers. I have provided a solution for that, and still the riots remain."

It was impressive the way the general remained calm, but I would have expected no less from such a high-ranking officer of the Bethynese army. That being said, was that a small sigh of frustration? Or was I once more projecting my own feelings onto other people?

"I said I would be better able to assess the situation, my lord. You must have already sent for Grand General Brahj before relieving me from the sewer patrols, so even you know the riots are too out of control."

The glare he received from Ovok was nothing short of venomous. "You're right. I had little faith in you."

I had expected to see fear, but all I saw from General Reth was further frustration. "I will appreciate the reinforcements, my lord. After all, those under my command were decimated from the attack on the ravine—"

"—Due to your inability to realize there was a rebellion under your very feet! Be glad I didn't execute you along with Lord and Lady Atarah!"

Reth moved his jaw back and forth before replying, "You do not hold any rank in the Bethynese army. Do not threaten me, Lord Kovo."

"It was a statement, General. Not a threat." The words made my blood run cold.

"Lord Atarah!"

The suddenness of the shout made my stomach jump, even as I was able to remain outwardly collected. The same could not be said for most of the others in the room—General Reth being an exception.

"My lord?" Lord Atarah's response was calm—I might have been impressed if I didn't hate the man so much already. He was clearly out for Ovok's ear and all the benefits that came with it.

"You have wasted my time enough. Now, you will either get in those sewers yourself tomorrow and start searching with Captain Kearn, or I will find someone else more afraid of losing their heads. Isn't that right, Atlys?" Ovok spun his head to face one of the very pale, trembling lords in the back.

The man said nothing intelligible, stammering apologies under his breath.

Then Lord Atarah replied, "Certainly, my lord. I trust the captain was just about to tell me he had finished with the notes I gave him. We can begin tonight, if you wish."

The way he diverted blame to me without offering excuses was both impressive and utterly infuriating.

Ovok's eyes locked on mine, and I stood there unable to break from the gaze of a millennium. Knowing who he was only made it so much more terrifying.

Ovok spoke at last. "Yes. There was a disturbance in the northeastern district, and I believe it was from the rebels you all so conveniently forgot to tell Lady Skayla and me about. Grand General Brahj will be handling public executions as soon as he arrives if the riots do not immediately respond to him. I don't care who. Atlys." He again swerved around to the shaking man in the corner. "Cut off supplies to the city. Any food and medicine are to be brought here to the palace and not distributed until the riots stop. If I hear of *anyone* feeding the people in the city, I will feed *your family* to the nearest Drogan. Or did you forget about them so easily?" The smile...it was like some rabid animal. Ovok was desperate, and that was far more frightening than if he had control over the situation.

"Y-yes, my lord. Right away. The next shipment is due in two days. I will have it brought here promptly."

"Now, you are all dismissed! Except you, captain. You stay." Ovok's eyes again caught me, and I found it suddenly difficult to breathe.

I'd never seen a room clear out so quickly, and never had I so badly wanted to leave with the rest of the cowards.

"You as well, Reth." Ovok didn't even bother using his title this time.

I hadn't realized the general was still there. "I prefer that you speak to those under my jurisdiction with me present, Lord Kovo." The tone was even.

"He will soon be under Grand General Brahj's jurisdiction, if I am not mistaken. Until then, I believe there are much more pressing issues for you to be keeping watch over if you don't want to be court-martialed when he arrives. I do believe your people hate incompetence, and you're showing a great deal of that right now." While it was no surprise that Ovok would so openly threaten a Bethynese general, it was much more surprising that "Lord Kovo" would. Ovok didn't even seem to be trying to hide that much anymore, regardless of all his warning for me to remain silent. He and Skayla had always respected the Bethynese hierarchy of command until now.

"You are not nearly as frightening as she was." Reth matched Ovok's dangerous tone.

The ancient Drogan narrowed his eyes. "Oh. But I am much more dangerous than your superior officers. Remember that, and be careful, General. Now leave before I show you what I mean."

General Reth gave no salute or any other show of acknowledgement to Ovok. He simply looked at me, gave a short nod, and left, hand gripping the pommel of his sword.

I had never seen a general so openly slandered like that. I'd never been worried for a general like that before, either.

"Are you playing games with me, Kearn?" The words were like the tip of a blade pressed against my throat, threatening murder.

I bowed deeply. "No, I would never. I…I've seen what happens."

Ovok drew close, leering over me like a vulture, though he didn't wait for you to die. He struck whenever he pleased. Without warning, I was grabbed by the throat and hoisted into the air as I found myself unable to breathe.

"I need a little more proof besides words, Captain. You will give me results by the end of the week, or General Reth will wonder what happened to your *body*." With the last word, he dropped me, and I landed hard on the floor, choking for air as I rubbed my neck.

"Understood…" I gasped, looking up and trying to keep from letting my fear show so clearly. Did he know? Was he suspicious already? Or had Atarah's words taken root?

That braggart.

"I don't want *words*. Get me the people I need, or I will find someone who will. They are in the northeastern part of the sewers, so *find* them. I am tired of delays. Get out of my sight."

I obeyed as quickly as I could, stumbling to my feet and trying not to choke as I left the grand hall, terror much more potent than I wanted to admit.

The walls felt like they were closing in around me, much like Ovok's fingers around my throat, and it took all my self-control not to race down the palace halls back to my room.

And that's when a hand grabbed me and pulled me further into the shadow of a corner in the hallway. In the same moment they did it, the assailant found themselves a breath away from having their throat slit by my knife.

"*Gyt Tov,*" the figure hissed as his grip on me tightened. "And we only have five minutes before the next guard round is due down this hall, so listen."

Gyt tov...that had been the phrase the people at the dock had said meant *friend*. I did not move my knife from the stranger's neck, but I didn't make any further threat, at least. My heart was pounding too loudly in my chest to allow for me to relax, and with or without the stupid phrase I'd been told to watch for, I wasn't going to just let my guard down for a stranger shoving me in a corner. Not after my interaction with Ovok.

"What did Kovo want with you?" the stranger whispered urgently.

I was about to reply when suddenly just enough light from a nearby bioluminescent lantern illuminated the face of my assailant.

It was Lord Atlys. *He* was working with them? It did make more sense now why it was so easy to evade any suspicion when arriving in his dock at Alkemar.... I withdrew my knife and returned it to my belt.

"I thought I was only supposed to receive notes." I kept my voice barely audible as I looked around warily. Had more than a minute gone by? We didn't have much time left. Then why in the world was I wasting time asking about this?

"What did Kovo want? What happened to your neck?" His eyes widened and he leaned forward, squinting.

Instinctively, I put my hand to my throat and realized just how tender it still was. There had to be a bruise forming by the reaction I'd garnered. "He wants results by the end of the week. From the sewers. I'm trying to keep Atarah off the scent, but I don't even know where to avoid. As you heard, Kovo somehow knows you're somewhere in the northeastern part of the sewers. He seemed sure of the fact just now." Frustration boiled together with the fear.

Atlys's clear concern did not help at all. "Listen. Do what you have to in order to remain in Kovo's good favor. That is still quite a bit of sewer system to work with. You don't know where to avoid, so you won't show partiality. Just be *careful*. Atarah is out for power and has killed his own family to get it. Do not anger him."

I gave a hoarse laugh that unexpectedly hurt my throat. "Thanks. A little late for that warning."

Atlys groaned. "Listen. We need to know where Skayla is. That's what matters. Do your best to follow the orders of searching the sewers and we'll take care of the rest. Understood?"

I didn't like taking orders from strangers, let alone some puffed up noble. Once more, I wondered if I was just trading one master for another. "I think I should be more worried about you, seeing Kovo's leverage over you."

The smile Atlys gave in return looked even more crazy with how the light from the hall bounced off of it. Not quite Skayla's level, but still close enough to make me shiver. "He has nothing. Worry about yourself, Captain, and keep your ears open. And for pity's sake, be careful. Now leave."

Nothing more? Just be careful and leave? How charming. But I knew I didn't have time to voice my opinions on the matter, as there could only be two or three minutes left before the next patrol came by. If he was right, that was. So with a hard glare at the practical stranger, I straightened my officer's coat and stepped back into the light of the hallway, turning and resuming my walk back to my room as if nothing had ever happened.

But Ovok's threat echoed repeatedly in my ears, and I couldn't help but wonder why Atlys had risked a meeting. Was it because I was marked as a dead man? There seemed no way out of this unless I delivered Jaythos's friends, and yet even if I knew where they were, there was no way I was doing that now.

Again, I rubbed my sore neck. Find Skayla. I had to try while I was still breathing.

THE LAST ESMER

CHAPTER IX: Everyone Needs a Shower

Baey:

I'd been trying since yesterday to figure out how this stupid watch worked and still nothing. For something I'd had around my neck since Valdon, it clearly did not have nearly the connection to me that Sven's ring had always possessed. Maybe that was because I'd worn his relic for almost a decade, while the watch had only been with me for several months…or maybe it was because I couldn't figure out how to even think of Moira's Gift.

"Staring at it doesn't seem to help, if nothing else," Grenedil piped up from where he sat. We were practicing by the portal, waiting for Cyl to find out where this Tyron person was. He said he'd needed to concentrate, and so in the meantime, Grenedil needed another person to guard the portal with him. Alenor and I had been happy to oblige today, as Estasia was gone to touch base with Atlys and see what he knew about the heightened searches into the sewers that had apparently started last night. I wondered if we would hear anything about Jaythos's brother.

"Sorry, I guess I am just…not very focused." I was beginning to wonder if that was the problem. There were a million things constantly going wrong, and I'd been unable to shake off Sven's words from yesterday. Well, or everything that had come before…but for the moment, at least, it was mostly the words. The way he'd woken up and just seemed to immediately declare he was no longer needed. That I didn't need him—the person I'd so naturally considered family.

Now he wasn't even here to help me figure out this stupid contraption. I'd thought…I'd thought when he woke up that maybe we could resume training, but instead we'd had to send him up to Alenor's manor with Astra for the time being. We needed to make sure Astra was, well, stable, and we didn't need her triggering the portal or destroying half The Underground.

But I still felt lost…and in a very different way from when he'd been lying there unconscious.

"Baey, did you hear me?" Now it was Alenor.

Ugh. "No, sorry. Could you say that again?" I looked up from where I had been aimlessly staring at the watch in my hand.

Alenor pressed her lips closely together for a moment before quietly replying, "Which part?"

I wanted to throw my hands up in exasperation. I thought Sven waking up would somehow make things better, but it hadn't. It had just made me more confused.

Focus, Baey! I shoved the watch in my pocket and rubbed my forehead. "Sorry. I don't think I am in a great mindset for this, right now."

"I mean, I'd be surprised if you were," Alenor said with a sigh. "But I really need you to try, Baey. We don't have time."

I nodded. She was right, of course. I was the only hope her daughter had.

"But you know, if you do figure it out, theoretically, you'll have all the time in the world, then," Grenedil offered a weak attempt at humor. He'd been fairly quiet since Astra had arrived but still seemed eager to help as ever.

"Yeah." I tried to laugh for his sake, hoping he still didn't understand my wings and how my emotions were reflected in them. They did not show humor, right now. "He is safe with her, right?" I couldn't help but ask, knowing I needed just a small break. Maybe getting just one or two things out of my head would help. "She almost vaporized him yesterday."

Grenedil winced, rubbing the back of his neck and breaking eye contact. "I'd never seen her lose control like that but...I mean...I admittedly only knew her a little while. She would do anything to help people. And if Cyl hadn't—" he cut himself off, but I caught the sudden anger in the last sentence. "She's had her whole world ripped out from under her, but from what I know about her, she's resilient. Sven will be fine—as long as Cyl brings us some good news, anyway."

"How long did you know her, exactly?" I asked.

With a sheepish look, Grenedil shrugged and replied, "Um. I don't know. A few days."

If Estasia were here she would probably scream. Honestly, I couldn't help but look a little incredulous. Seeing how Cyl was turning out, was I really supposed to trust Grenedil's first impressions—however well intentioned?

"A few *days?*" Alenor beat me to it, sounding as distressed as I felt.

"And in those few days, she almost killed herself trying to save my friend and me—who she had only known for about an hour before deciding to help us." Grenedil was suddenly indignant, sitting up straighter as he spoke. "Then swore to protect Mitheau even though it was going to get her friends and her in great trouble. She will do anything for the innocent."

I relaxed only a little. "You also said Cyl was an ally, and he's the one that apparently ruined Astra's plan."

"I didn't know she'd have enough power over The Maze to start tearing holes. Any guard should be able to open a pre-existing door, but she was able to create one herself."

I frowned. "Wait...does that mean I should be able to?"

"Eventually if you were taught...but not without Cyl coaching you. I had been trying to convince him to perhaps teach you, but he was against that even before Astra pulled Tyron into The Maze. He said you can't be practicing anything with Ovok so close to the portal."

I decided it was best not to press that issue with Cyl for now. Not wanting me to experiment with the portal Ovok was after was actually a reasonable ask, as much as I didn't want to admit it. But at the same time, I didn't like how we had to rely so much on Cyl for the portal. It would be nice to be able to use it ourselves, if needed.

With a sigh, Grenedil added, "Cyl is complicated. I don't understand his reasoning at times, but he's the Guardian of The Door.... He's the only Myrandi that stuck with it, and things haven't exactly gone his way."

Alenor scoffed, "He's no Kassander, that's for sure."

Grenedil crossed his arms. "Well, I didn't know Kassander, and all I know is he's dead, so you get the guard that's left."

This had been a very lengthy conversation weeks ago, where I'd found out that Alenor had apparently been friends with one of the other guardians—Kassander Knyte, who had also apparently been a Myrandi.

I guess she'd only known him as a protector and cultural cultivator of Baeno, until he'd disappeared. She'd also apparently met Cyl very, very briefly once, but with only the knowledge he had been a friend to this Kassander.

Much of this had also been over a hundred years ago. Alenor had explained that because she and Henry had kept The Living Stone with them, it had prolonged their lives, which made sense with the way even just a shard had helped save Jaythos. Still, I wasn't sure I understood it all.

"All I know is that Cyl seems to care very little for collateral damage," I mumbled, taking the watch back out and closing my eyes. It had that same feeling of longing as Sven's ring did, but something I disliked a lot more: anxiety. It was almost like it was terrified—grasping desperately for control—and when I tried to draw closer to that feeling it would explode into a roaring panic.

I gasped, opening my eyes and trying to take deep breaths. "I don't like where I think I have to go."

"Moira had an intense personality. It makes sense that it will take you time." Alenor dipped her head.

Again, I remembered it was up to me if she would ever see her daughter again. Not exactly a warm and fuzzy feeling.

But what I really hated about the emotions from Moira's watch were perhaps how familiar they were to me. Now that it was fixed, I could find myself relating all too keenly to the anxiety and that horrible whisper of helplessness.

I closed my eyes again, but it wasn't long before my concentration was once more broken, this time by Grenedil.

"Cyl! Were you able to find out which door he'd gone through?"

Snapping my eyes open and swiveling around, I found Cyl standing at the entrance of the barricade.

The heavily scarred Myrandi looked around with a mixture of his usual condescending aloofness and constant state of irritation, eyeing Grenedil in his usual patronizing way. "He is not in The Maze any longer. I felt a Doorway to Kryso open. He must be there now."

For a moment, I thought Grenedil might collapse with relief. Based on what he'd told us of Astra's situation, I didn't blame him.

But I was beginning to grow very tired of Cyl. He wasn't like Marion or Syvil—he reminded me more of how I thought Ovok would be. He was more concerned with the end rather than the means one took to get there. It didn't matter how he kept the worlds safe, only that they were—and what was even more confusing was that somehow that meant the worlds themselves, not necessarily the people *in* them.

That didn't sit well with me.

"The last thing we need is poor judgment leading to another explosion like what happened yesterday," Cyl added, still addressing Grenedil. "So I suggest you stop running around giving advice on matters you have no business interfering with."

"Of course." Grenedil's tone was that of surrender, even if it conflicted with the tension in his jaw.

Wait, was Cyl seriously blaming Grenedil for Astra?

160

That's when I noticed how Cyl was staring at the watch in my hand, and I quickly stowed it around my neck and away from prying eyes.

"Are we almost ready to collect the remaining Watcher?"

I tried to keep the frustration out of my voice as I replied, "Almost." Realizing Cyl was about to do some reprimanding about being low on time, I quickly added, "I am going to find Sven and Astra and inform them of the news that Astra's family is safe." Well, probably safe. I wondered if Cyl would even tell the truth…. Would he even have told us if Astra's family was in harm's way, seeing the way he so adamantly just said no one was to use the portal?

"Is that safe? Aren't they searching the tunnels?" Cyl squinted skeptically.

Squaring my shoulders, I refused to break eye contact as I said, "I have enough skills at my disposal to get where I need to, and I think Sven's insight with the watch would be useful."

Cyl's expression soured. Oh yes, he also didn't like Sven. Another reason I wasn't exactly in Cyl's corner. He had been quick to judge Sven as too broken to be of use—I'd seen it in his eyes even if he didn't say it plainly for others to know.

"I do not think that is wise, young one." I hated the way Cyl infantilized pretty much everyone, but especially me.

"Well, fortunately for me, you don't give the orders around here. You merely offer advice, and I think I am going to ignore it this time." For a minute, I didn't recognize my own voice, feeling more as if Estasia had transported here instead to give Cyl the what-for.

I had clearly wounded Cyl's pride. "Very well, but remember that when you beg me for help in the next emergency."

"Cyl, please, we're all on the same side, here." Grenedil's plea was almost inaudible, but the way Cyl jerked his head to glare right at him showed it wasn't *quite* inaudible enough.

Grenedil shrunk back where he sat.

"Stop it, all of you. We need to get along. Grenedil…why don't you go with her? Maybe Astra will appreciate a familiar face." Alenor was always the one to step in, gracious even as pale and worn out as she looked recently.

Cyl's look of displeasure grew and, to be honest, I wasn't exactly thrilled that Grenedil would be coming with either, but I had a feeling Alenor wanted him away from Cyl.

"Yes, that works for me," I blurted out before the Myrandi could give any further argument on the subject. Part of me really felt like this was a bad idea, seeing as I just had planned to use my wings to shield me— now that Sven had the ring—but that made hiding Grenedil a little more difficult.

I decided it was best to leave before Cyl had a chance to think of anything to say, so Grenedil and I quickly made our way to the sewer entrance as I began formulating our route in my head. The sewers had completely reordered, and I had managed to throw in a couple extra roadblocks using Sven's ring while he'd been unconscious. Still, the searches in the sewer system had suddenly increased last night, and Cyl conjectured that it was likely due to Astra's arrival helping Ovok narrow down the area of where we were. So as much as the sewers were different from any schematics they had on hand, even blind mice could find cheese once in a while.

"Follow me, and don't make any noise," I said to Grenedil after we'd passed the man and woman guarding the entrance tunnel to The Underground. "If you hear something, just tap my shoulder, understood?"

"Right," Grenedil murmured.

I realized he hadn't left The Underground since he'd first showed up during the battle at the ravine. Why was I bringing him again? I hoped Alenor knew what she was doing, because after Cyl had shown up, I'd lost a bit of faith in Grenedil.

We arrived at the final door that led into the sewers, and after using the key I possessed, we entered into the signature aromas of Alkemar's sewers.

No amount of going through these would ever get me used to the pungent smell, and Grenedil's retching told me it was likely a universal feeling.

I was on high alert the entire time, glad to see there were no patrols too close to where The Underground was. But the further into the heart of the sewers we went, the worse it got. Voices echoed around every corner, and lantern light licked at our heels wherever we went. It would be difficult for my wings to be able to hide both Grenedil and me, so I had to resort to the little closet-like rooms that Estasia had shown me—several of which I had now put illusions over so as to be available for hiding without fear of being discovered.

But I couldn't help but worry about The Underground. There was an illusion over the door, and with the way Sven's reality bending had reordered the tunnel, no one would think twice about the dead end. Yet even so, it was only a matter of time before someone found us.

We were just about to reach a fork in the tunnels when an unexpected glow of lantern light appeared ahead of us. There was nowhere to hide, now, and I shoved Grenedil down, hissing, "On your knees—*duck!*"

Trying not to gag as I followed suit, I quickly spread my wings over us, hoping we were low enough with the murky water and my wings were large enough that we wouldn't be seen. And that was, of course, if the patrol behind the lantern didn't turn down this way. My wings ached from how far open I stretched and contorted them to cover us.

I heard footsteps sloshing through the muck and then come to a halt. I could only hope it was them deciding which way to go. If Grenedil wasn't here, this would have been remarkably easier....

It sounded as if it was only one person—ahead of the rest of their group, perhaps—and I pressed my hand against the hilt of my blade as I heard them stop in the middle of the fork in the paths, clearly now in view of us. I could practically feel the light of their lantern's bioluminescent glow, and held my breath so as not to have any movement in my wings. Grenedil stared up at me, eyes wide and every muscle unmoving as stone.

"I think we're going in circles! Let's backtrack and take the other way!" The strong voice called from an uncomfortably short distance away.

The abrupt change...suddenly, I wondered if Jaythos's brother was in the tunnels. There was no other reasoning for the sudden change in direction unless this person had seen us...and chosen to look the other way.

Of course, the other possibility was a trap, and as the footsteps retreated and the sounds of patrol became fainter, I made a note that we would be exiting the sewers away from Alenor's house in case.

After another two minutes, I straightened; my back incredibly sore from the way I had been hunched over Grenedil.

"I think I might be ill," Grenedil gave a very weak smile as he accepted my hand up, going to brush himself off, but instead just twisting his face in disgust.

"Don't worry, we can clean up at Alenor's mansion. But we need to go to the surface first. There's an exit this way. Follow me." I didn't dare explain further, knowing if this really had been a trap, they'd be listening in. But I was using one of Temorn's escape tunnels, and we'd make sure no one was following us back to The Underground first. Guess I would be once more testing just how well my wings' camouflage worked out in the open.

Sven:

Astra hadn't spoken much since we'd arrived here at my mother's mansion. Marion hadn't been able to get her to eat a single bite, and I'd even tried eating with her to coax her into taking any sort of sustenance. I could understand what she was going through—finding herself unsure if any of her family or friends were alive, having possibly left them to a horrible fate. I could only hope she had better luck than I did.

The only break in her otherwise unreadable behavior was her clear curiosity with my mother's inventions, and at the moment, her eyes were riveted on the miniature train making its way through every room from the tracks suspended near the ceiling. It seemed to come around every day once in the morning, once at noon, and again in the evening; and I wondered to myself what sort of complicated contraption Mum must have come up with in order to get it to run at such a consistent schedule.

"Believe it or not, it moves without Gifting," I said. My memories…they were so much clearer now. I could remember Mum and Da's explanations whenever we'd helped in their shop. But I remembered lots of other things, too; the good right alongside the bad. I remembered the night when I'd been forced to hunt down Darby and Thackeray—when I'd been unable to stop myself from hurting Thackeray but then, at last, able to break through to stop from killing them both. I also now acutely remembered that sense of suffocation as Skayla strangled my mind to death.

I then realized I'd been talking to Astra and hadn't explained further about the train like I'd intended. I was supposed to be helping her stay away from her thoughts, and here I was unable to even get out of my own head.

"It's a mixture of gears and using…I…" I frowned, looking up to where the train had disappeared into a tunnel leading out of the living room. "I suppose you'd have to ask Mum what exactly she used. It might be steam powered, but I wonder what she has to get it hot enough." She wouldn't have very easy access to coal, that was for sure. Plus, how was it staying running even while she wasn't here to refill its fuel? I'd have to ask her about it sometime. It was nice, at the very least, to have this connection with my parents back. I'd always loved working with them, and now to be able to remember what they'd once taught me left me a little comfort, perhaps.

Astra said nothing from where she stood by the window, turning back to watch outside. My pathetic attempt at distraction seemed to have done little to distract her from her hypervigilance. I recognized the way she checked every entry and exit point.

I contemplated trying my luck again at conversation when the bell signaling someone was in mum's tunnel rang.

Astra jumped and I felt a surge of her energy crackle throughout the room.

"It's just the bell. Someone is probably here with an update," I said, unmoving from my chair. Above all things, I felt it important to remain calm when Astra's powers began to boil like this. From what I could tell, she was so afraid of her abilities that anyone else being so would send her into a cannibalizing spiral of panic.

All the same, I quietly tried to push against the pulse of energy, feeling the way it interacted with the surroundings. It was almost as if her power was an entity in itself, and the turmoil inside it was enough to give me a headache.

"We're alright. Marion is getting the door." My stupid, hoarse voice was probably the furthest thing you could get from comforting, but I still tried my best to sound reassuring.

Astra returned to her unmoving state, and the fizzling energy died away for the most part. Then her hand went to her other scarred wrist, rubbing it anxiously as we waited.

Marion's footsteps were heard on the stairs and down the hall, and even from the living room we could hear her opening the door. She was now the one in possession of the key to the door, but I had chanced a little bit of reality bending to also install a peephole so that one could see who pulled the rope to the bell before opening the door. We didn't want anyone coming in uninvited, and with the increased patrols, it was far more likely than before someone could potentially stumble upon the tunnel to the manor. Without a key, it would take a great deal of explosives or Gifting to open that door from the tunnel's side.

"Oh…you both…don't you go near Jaythos until you've had a bath…. Oh…oh, stay here, I'm grabbing you each a towel—oh, you smell so bad." Marion's gagging could be heard from down the hall.

I sat up a bit straighter. It sounded like someone had a nasty time with the sewers…but Marion didn't sound concerned—at least, not beyond the filth.

I felt another wave of sizzling energy coming from Astra, but this time more subdued.

"Don't worry. Most people have to go through the tunnels, and as you've seen they are…" I trailed off, making a slight face and tapping the side of my nose slightly. "A bit unpleasant."

Astra, staring now at the open doorway to the hall, said nothing, only nodded.

Just then, Marion came by looking a bit flustered, announcing, "Baey's here with Grenedil," as she went upstairs, clearly getting some clean towels from the closet.

As much as I wanted to jump up and immediately go see Baey, I forced myself instead to calmly stand and straighten my coat. "I should—"

"—Don't go near them until they've cleaned up!" Marion called from upstairs. "They'll get us all sick!" The exasperation in her tone was hard to miss, but perhaps the way she stomped back down the stairs with an armful of cloths was the bigger indicator.

"Do you need assistance?" I asked, hesitant as she rushed back down the hallway. Either she hadn't heard me or she didn't care. I turned back to Astra and felt the need to do *something*—anything that could help the child relax. But all I did was make some sort of helpless shrug and try a small smile.

Astra did not return it.

I heard Marion's steps as she once more went up the stairs, and there were a few minutes of tense silence before she came traipsing back down, entering the room as she declared, "They are both fine, but I ordered them to wash before they come near anyone. The last thing Jaythos needs is that kind of contamination." She shook her head, looking from me to Astra. "Speaking of, I should go make sure no one upstairs is too disturbed from the commotion. Maeko might not be able to handle all three at once."

I again stepped forward. "Astra and I can check on Tanner. Really, it's no trouble." Astra had resumed fidgeting with her wrist, and I had a feeling keeping her busy was a good idea.

Looking skeptical, Marion at last acquiesced. "Alright, but be careful. You've seen how he is."

I had been up to see the kid after Astra and I had gotten here, but at the time, I hadn't wanted Astra anywhere near strangers. Fortunately, she was much calmer now, and hopefully Baey was bringing *good* news to calm her down even more. The fact she'd brought Grenedil meant that it was likely she was bringing some sort of update regarding Astra's family and the portal.

Marion disappeared back up the stairs, and I turned quickly to make sure Astra was ready to follow me. She seemed hesitant.

"It's alright. He won't say much, just follow my lead." I beckoned for her, then turned and walked into the hallway that led to the stairs. The soft footsteps behind me proved Astra had obeyed, sticking close behind.

She didn't say a word but, somehow, I could tell exactly what was going through her head. As we climbed the stairs, I said quietly, "You won't make things worse, don't worry. Tanner has just…had too many people in his head. He has a difficult time remembering who he is, and Marion is still working with him."

"People in his head?" Out of all the things that had gotten her to actually speak, Tanner's condition was not what I had expected.

"He is a Memory Keeper. He took too many memories from others." I winced as we arrived at his door. Sefen had made him carry too much— he had used the boy as a weapon at the same time he had treated Baey as a porcelain doll. Even with the tragic end of the man, I found it difficult not to remain bitter over it.

I turned to face Astra as I put my hand on the latch to Tanner's door. Her otherworldly eyes stared at me in some strange form of understanding. I turned back and opened the door.

Tanner was standing in the middle of the room, eyes wide and fists clenched.

"Who are you? I don't know you." It was rare he was so talkative, but his gaze was fixed on Astra.

"Astra. I'm…"

"—She's a friend of Baey's, Tanner. Are you alright?" I closed the door behind us and took another step forward. Tanner mirrored me by taking one backwards.

"Who's Baey?" His breathing grew more rapid.

"Well, she's a friend of mine, then. Baey's your friend, too, but it's alright if you don't remember." One would think I would be better at handling someone with issues that were not so different from ones I'd struggled with not long ago, but I still felt helpless.

Tanner's laugh was brittle, and he took another step away from me. "Friend? You kept Rhioa from me. What exactly makes us friends?"

Astra's breath hitched.

"Tanner, I am not keeping anything from you." I decided the best course of action was to repeat his name and try to remind him he wasn't whoever he thought he was.

"Then why does she have Rhioa's eyes? Those…cursed eyes." Tanner's gaze was now riveted on Astra.

Well, apparently this *had* been a bad idea, and not understanding what in the world was going on definitely did not help. I stepped in front of Astra so she was out of view. "Tanner, snap out of it. Who are you right now?"

"I...I don't know...I don't know, who am I?" The change was instantaneous as Tanner grabbed his head with both hands, almost clawing at it.

"It's alright, calm down, Tanner," I leapt forward and grabbed one wrist gently, putting my other hand behind his shoulder. "It's alright." The kid cried a moment against my coat before going still, slowly backing away.

That's when I felt the rise of energy, and I swiftly poured more of my attention back on Astra's Gift as it tried to pervade the room. Meanwhile, Tanner remained quiet, shrinking back into the corner of the room where his bed was and sitting back on that, keeping his head in his hands and breathing slower.

I turned back to see Astra frozen, staring at Tanner in something similar to panic. Who was Rhioa, and how could Tanner possibly have a memory Astra would also know of?

"Why won't you just all shut up?" Tanner murmured to himself, letting his hands fall limply next to him, leaning his head now against the wall and looking at the ceiling blankly.

As empty as those eyes seemed, they did seem to be *his* eyes. While they didn't change, you could tell the shift in personality, and the ones he'd worn moments ago had been so full of darkness.

"H-how do you know of Rhioa?" Astra's question was quiet, contrasting with the harsh bursts of Gifting I was only barely keeping from breaking through into the room. Even just bending reality like this made me nervous after what I'd done to the city.

Tanner did not look away from the ceiling. "She's who I'm doing—she's...she's who *Ovok* is doing this for. He wants to save her with The Living Stone." He shuddered. "He killed Sefen for her. Killed so many people...so many deaths just because...."

"Tanner, it's alright, come back." I had no idea what was going on, but whatever connection this had with Astra wasn't worth sinking this poor kid back into another's brain—let alone Ovok's.

Letting out one last shiver, Tanner closed his eyes, once more going silent.

There was a knock at the door, and Tanner was the only one who wasn't fazed, somehow.

"Yes?" I was the one who called out, and a moment later, Jaythos entered, narrowing his eyes at Astra before turning to me. "I can watch him. Baey is ready."

Jaythos had been making much better progress than Tanner and even Syvil, the latter of whom had refused to be around Astra—stating she was "loud" and unpleasant to be around. I was able to mask her signature, but every once in a while, one of her larger fluctuations could take a second for me to contain. Marion seemed to have more patience for it than Syvil. She said it was likely due to his recent...trauma. With him readjusting after coming back from, well, the dead, he was more sensitive to everything right now.

"Thank you." I looked at Astra, who was even paler than before. "Ready?"

She hardly even nodded but followed me out nonetheless.

Once in the hall, I dared ask, "Who is Rhioa?"

"Tyron's wife," Astra whispered. "Which means…he was right. She must have appeared to Ovok….Ovok took her and was trying to save her…."

My brow furrowed as we went back down the stairs. What had Tanner said? That he needed The Living Stone for Rhioa…that's what it was for? Everyone had been so busy trying to stop Ovok that no one had really asked why he wanted The Living Stone. Until recently, we'd all assumed it was Skayla who really wanted it—to amplify her powers much like she'd used Moira's watch to do—but now it seemed more and more like Ovok was the real one in charge even from the beginning.

"Are you…alright?" I asked Astra as I worked on subduing the large waves of her Gifting emanating from her.

"Sorry," was all she said.

"Hopefully Baey will have some good news," I tried to steer the conversation away from what was clearly upsetting Astra, although I knew I would need to relay all of what had happened with Tanner to Baey.

CHAPTER X: Advice and Adversaries

<u>Baey:</u>

While I did appreciate the nice hot shower, it still wasn't enough to release the tension in my back or wings from the last few days. After drying off a bit and getting dressed, I had quite a job of gathering up the molted feathers plastered everywhere in the shower, folding them up in a towel so they could be used later for a blanket liner or something for The Underground. It had been a weird concept at first, but they were so short of common necessities down there that anything that might help was worth it...even if it was my feathers.

Refreshed and relieved to not reek of the sewers, I made my way down the hallway, making a quick deviation to check on Tanner instead of immediately going downstairs. Grenedil still had to clean up, and I didn't want to give the news to Astra without him. Something told me a familiar face was best for relaying anything to Astra regarding her family, even if it was fairly good news.

I gave a knock at Tanner's door, and Jaythos was the one who responded to enter.

I went in to find Tanner staring at the ceiling while Jaythos looked helplessly from where he sat in a nearby chair.

"He had a bit of an episode with Sven and the girl," Jaythos explained briefly, suspicion in his voice as he mentioned Astra.

I gave him a brief look of acknowledgement before addressing my other friend gently. "Tanner? I just wanted to see how you and Jaythos are doing."

My wings sagged when I did not receive any reply.

"I was going to give Sven an update on our situation, if you wanted to come listen?" I offered.

"No. I scared her." Tanner's quick reply contrasted his earlier silence.

He what? Did he mean Astra? I knew better than to ask questions. If he'd had an outburst, then asking about it was the last thing I needed to do. Sven would be able to explain.

"Alright. Well, if you want me, I'll be just downstairs. I miss you, you know."

Again, silence. No acknowledgement he'd even heard me.

"Thank you for watching him," I addressed Jaythos. Nothing else was said, but knowing he was stepping up—knowing he was actually trying to make right the mistakes of the past—made me feel strangely grateful.

It was with mixed emotions I left the room, wondering what exactly Tanner had done to frighten Astra, but glad he at least had Jaythos for company now. I'd barely entered back into the hallway when I came upon Marion leading an anxious Syvil towards me.

"He wanted to see you," she murmured.

Syvil still looked very different from before his first death. Quiet, and small, more similar to how he'd been on the airship right after Hytat and his first encounter with Ovok. But now, he gave a small, hesitant smile, and that, at least, was encouraging. It was better than the memory of his pale, bloodied face when he'd died in my arms.

"I wanted to know how your flying practice was going," he whispered. Marion winced.

"I…I have been trying some things on my own—the exercises you taught me. But I'm probably not very good."

"…I could…I'll come back with you, perhaps. I could coach you more on your flying, maybe?" He stumbled over the words, especially "flying." It hurt to remember he would never be able to do that again.

I wasn't the only one who looked surprised—Marion looked quite startled, herself.

"Syvil, wouldn't you rather stay here and rest?" she asked.

I saw the flicker of determination on his face. "I…I want to help."

I remembered his protests from what seemed so long ago. The insistence that he was not a fighter, and the way he'd been so afraid. He'd literally *died* for us and he still wanted to help. I wondered really how much we deserved it, after how I'd viewed the Myrandi for so long.

"Alright, that would be nice…only if you want to, though." If it would help him, then I would do it. I would also be lying if I said I couldn't use the help. But that wasn't really the reason. I just wanted to see him better—to see anything but this shell that we'd made of him.

Syvil gave another nod, then said, "Just come find me before you leave. I'll have my things ready by then."

My smile turned more genuine. "Sounds like a good plan. I'll make sure to."

I turned to Marion, who gave a helpless sort of shrug and said, "It's settled then, I suppose."

Syvil looked surprisingly brighter now. "I should go make sure I have my things," he said softly before turning and leaving.

Marion, however, stayed in the hallway with me, looking uncertain. "I don't...I don't know if it's such a good idea."

"I know," I replied. "But maybe it will help to get his mind off of things."

She sighed. "Yes. That cursed blade...."

I frowned, vaguely remembering Syvil saying something after Hytat. "The one Ovok carries?"

Marion's expression was grave. "Ah. He told you of it already?"

With a shrug of my wings, I replied, "Not really. He just mentioned it briefly after his first fight with Ovok at Hytat."

"Ckaknimaen. One of the nine blades. I have heard its voice as well." She shuddered.

"Voice?" I asked, only willing to dawdle here because Grenedil was still washing up.

"Yes. These blades...they were made by the Myrandi. Thousands of years ago. They were forged with Ithinian Gasper from Kryso and were meant to imprint upon their owner. The Myrandi made them as gifts to the most powerful and wise of the TetraWorlds to help keep peace." Her frustration was all too clear in her words. "But the swords...they amplified both the good and the bad. Some of those who received a sword were not as righteous as they appeared—or well, not strong-willed enough to balance out the blade's voice. Ckaknimaen's original owner was Eatrisian, actually. Like Astra. Not many would know of him nowadays, but he was called the Scourge of Eatris. He became twisted, and hungry for conquest, and was only at last killed by Eknemar and his brother, Alkemar."

Before I could say anything, she smiled sadly and nodded. "Yes. Their battle took them off-world and here to Baeno. They were twins and fought valiantly. Alkemar was killed, supposedly on the spot this city's foundation was laid. It is one of the oldest still-inhabited cities on Baeno, along with its other pair, Eknemar, which is a city south of here in Patelayna."

"Huh." I wondered what other histories of old were so intertwined between worlds. It was still so strange to think of the fact that there were others, that I couldn't even comprehend how connected they might once have been.

"Not all nine blades are accounted for. Some had noble owners, some have changed ownership enough to the point they no longer reflect their original wielders. It was rumored that Ovok's wife, Dyress, gave Ckaknimaen to Ovok, and he has worn it for as long as I have been alive." Again, she looked uncomfortable. "But they speak. Usually just to their wielder. But…not Ckaknimaen. It likes to speak to its prey."

I felt suddenly cold. Prey. Marion had been Ckaknimaen's prey too, once, hadn't she?

"That blade is probably only exacerbating Ovok's already impossibly mixed-up moral compass." Grenedil surprised us both as he came up behind me. I had been so engrossed in Marion's tale that I hadn't realized he had finished and come to join us. "It is also made of a great deal of Gifting and rare metals that would counteract quite a lot of healing, so it's best to try and steer clear of the sharp edge of it."

That made sense, seeing how even Syvil's more minor wounds had not healed when he'd landed on the shore, contradicting the way he had healed so quickly when we'd first met him at the Crafter's ruins.

"Noted," I shivered, then decided it was best not to keep Astra waiting. "Shall we?"

"Right. Astra's downstairs?" Grenedil asked, looking eager to share the news from Cyl.

Marion gave a nod. "Yes. I shall go make sure Syvil doesn't need any help."

It was quiet when we entered the living room. Sven sat in a chair while Astra stood by the window, visibly nervous. Neither moved much when we entered, but Sven was the one who broke the silence with, "Run into trouble?"

I rolled my eyes. "A little. Mostly sewage."

He gave both of us a good look up and down before replying, "So Marion said."

Was that a hint of humor? Or was that glint just from his golden eyes reflecting the light? I still wasn't used to them having any sort of color, let alone the unnatural gold I had only seen when I was a child.

"Yes, well, we got our tongue-lashing and are sufficiently sorry. It was better than being discovered by a patrol, though. We got close." Too close. Maybe it had been a bad idea not to just go by myself.

And now you're going to bring Syvil back, I reminded myself. Maybe I should have thought a little longer before agreeing to that….

Sven's brow furrowed in worry, but he said nothing.

I didn't miss the way Astra fidgeted with her sleeve, watching us closely and acting as if she wanted to say something.

"Astra? Grenedil has an update for you—good news. Right, Grenedil?"

Grenedil rubbed the back of his head awkwardly and winced. "Yes, uh, Cyl has found out that Tyron went to Kryso, not Eatris." I didn't miss the way he changed Cyl's words ever so slightly. Cyl had admittedly left it a lot more open-ended, and yet, in this moment, I understood the small tarnishing of the truth. It was that or have Astra possibly try and blow up the whole house.

Astra immediately stiffened—if she could have been any more rigid—the fidgeting with her scarred wrists stilled. "H-how is he sure?"

"The alignment of the planets. The way that Cyl…interrupted you both in The Maze would have sent Tyron on the path to Kryso's Doorway, and Cyl was able to sense it open. Tyron has likely already been brought into custody on Kryso. They, uh, usually have their act together pretty well on that planet, so Tyron won't be able to harm anyone else, don't worry."

"But what if he—"

"Trust me, Astra. He can't hurt your family. Louko and everyone else will be alright." I caught the way Grenedil's fists clenched by his side and didn't miss the conviction in his tone. But I wasn't prepared for the tears I saw tracing Astra's cheeks when I looked over to see her reaction.

"You don't understand. I can't be too late again—I can't lose anyone else. Keeshiff is already dead because I didn't get there in time. If Tyron reaches my family before I do, I'll lose *everyone*."

Something inside me twisted, the raw emotions in her plea to Grenedil sounding all too familiar. My eyes flitted ever so briefly to Sven before I could stop myself.

He was as still as stone and unreadable except for his gaze, which was so much more intense now.

"Wait—Keeshiff is dead?" Grenedil's voice cracked. "N-no, I was just there—Louko's uncle, he got them out of the tower. He was a little beat up but fine. Astra, he was safe."

My gut began to sink with apprehension. Maybe it was how close this felt after so many deaths. After Sefen didn't come back.

Astra cradled herself, taking deep, shaking breaths. But no more tears came. "He was. But then Merimeethia declared war and he...he tried to stop it. We split up. There was a spy. I was too late to save him."

The last sentence was empty. Empty like Sven was. The kind of numb that wished it could force more tears.

The room was silent for a while, Grenedil looking on in shock and Astra staring down at the floor. I found myself unsure exactly what to do. Only Sven seemed at ease, sitting in his chair as he watched Astra intently. I saw the understanding in his eyes, and thought how I'd rarely seen him look right at someone that long and that comfortably in a while.

Meanwhile, I realized with quiet relief that the room hadn't blown up, so that was a good thing...right? I wondered suddenly if that was the other reason Sven was so closely watching Astra. Was she fighting back another power surge—whatever it was?

"I…I'm sorry," Grenedil spoke at last as he slowly went over and took a seat on the couch, looking deeply troubled as he processed the death of this Keeshiff. A part of me worried for him—realizing he really never showed much of himself to anybody. If not for his clear earnestness, such avoidance would have made me suspicious, but instead it just made me wonder if he really had ever had anybody stick around long besides Cyl. After all, he'd said he only knew Astra a few days, and he'd never mentioned anybody else besides her, his friend Mitheau, and his brother—who had taken his position as The Merchant and left him. And now he seemed shaken, taken aback by the death of Keeshiff, who he'd also have only known a few days by the sound of it.

Astra's eyes were glued to the floor, face impassive in a way that showed she felt too much. "He…" She swallowed. "He's home now. I hope there is no more war wherever he is."

Home. Was that where Sefen was? Home? I preferred that. It was better than just saying they were gone—like we would never see them again.

Astra looked up at Grenedil. "Promise me that I will not go back to bury anyone else."

"We'll get you back—we'll get you back to Louko, and everyone will be alright—I swear it, Astra. Even if I have to steamroll over Cyl, myself." The last bit seemed like it had been meant as a joke, but Grenedil didn't laugh.

Astra took a shuddering breath but nodded. "When can I go?" Grenedil wasn't the only one to grimace at the hopeful question. In fact, Sven was the only one that didn't.

"I...we have to stop Ovok, first. It's...rather like a Tyron situation, Astra. But Ovok seems to want to get back to Eatris, and if you leave and go back, it's too likely he'll find the portal and follow you. Then everyone on Eatris could suffer a fate like Baeno." Grenedil's explanation was not exactly enthusiastic.

I decided to try and help. "As it stands, Ovok seems to be too close to our location. We were almost caught. If Ovok leaves with The Living Stone—our world could die. Cyl says it would slowly fade?"

"Yes. Time and reality would slowly crumble until nothing remained. It's like the old stories before the time of The Living Stone, when the fabric of this world tore apart and left holes of nothingness," Sven added, still watching Astra carefully. "We just have to get The Living Stone back...and if we get Moira, then we have the advantage we need." The last statement found me now the recipient of Sven's golden stare.

I was still not used to Sven...knowing things; things like stories and legends; things he would have known before being The GhostMaker. It was nice.

I was distracted, however, by the mention of Moira. With a wince, I said, "I'm...I'm trying. I just can't seem to connect with her relic the way I did with yours." I suddenly wondered if we really should be saying any of this in front of Astra, but after forcing her to remain stranded here, I couldn't bring myself to keep it from her. At the very least, the power she possessed could come in handy against Ovok...and while I knew Estasia wouldn't approve of me being so open in front of a practical stranger, my instinct told me to trust her. I was learning to trust that more.

Now, if I could just figure out exactly what my instincts were telling me about Cyl….

"How did you connect with my relic?" Sven asked, shifting forward in his chair in interest.

"I…I, uh…" I quickly stowed away my embarrassment, keeping my wings from covering me and instead tucking them neatly behind me. "I just thought about the night we met."

Tilting his head a bit, he asked, "What about it?"

"I focused on details. What you said and then your sword. I focused on that and it would help me feel less alone. Then after you showed up to Valdon, I felt it calling for you, I guess. I…I felt your loneliness. And then the illusion of your sword was suddenly in front of me."

Sven folded his hands and broke eye contact at last, taking a deep breath. "And does the watch call to you? Do you feel anything from that?"

I frowned. "It's…it's hard because it calls to your ring, too. I don't know. It's harder to tell…."

"Wait. Before, you said you didn't like where you had to go. Clearly you must have felt something more?" Grenedil interjected himself back into the conversation.

It made Sven look back from the window and give a little smile—a *smile*. It was quick, but held some humor. "Oh, did she?"

My cheeks burned a little, as did my wings. "Alright, so I keep feeling…panic. Helpless. Like I need to be in control, and if I don't figure it out then everything will be for nothing. But I don't know if it's even the watch or just…" I sighed. "Just me thinking of the stakes."

"You'll get it." Sven's encouragement should have helped, but somehow it made me more frustrated.

"But what if I don't? I was only able to use your ring by *accident*. We have no reason to believe I can even use the watch—only because I can sense the bond in the relic. People aren't supposed to be able to use the relics besides the owners, right? I'm not Moira—I could always tell between my feelings and your ring's—but I can't figure out if I'm even feeling the watch at all or if it's just my own stupid head."

"It's Moira." Sven hesitated a moment, then continued, "Perhaps you are a little like her. I remember seeing that anxiety. I…sometimes I worried she went back too much—she needed everything to work out perfectly. She never talked about how often she would use the watch, but you'd see it in her eyes. Sometimes I was too afraid to ask." There it was; that emptiness I'd heard earlier in Astra. "Go back to how you sensed my ring. What did you do when you felt…it?" He stumbled only a moment.

"I just. I don't know." Frowning, I tried to go back to that place. It felt so long ago; those years in Valdon all alone even when surrounded by those who loved me. The loneliness I hid and the helplessness I tried to run from. The frustration that had built to a head when Sven had shown up as Feyn Cavo. That constant draw to him that I could see now was the ring—the need to follow and try to be brave. Try to help. Try to… "I just wanted to be like you." I couldn't help it, I looked right at him, desperate to see his reaction. That's all I'd ever wanted; to be as brave as he always was…as willing to throw away his life for others. To brave that loneliness and accept the pain just to help someone.

His expression was almost unreadable. Almost. He was looking at me, a measure of disbelief as if he couldn't fathom anyone ever wanting to follow in his footsteps. But I saw the little spark, the look in his eyes that wanted so desperately to believe that maybe he was worth looking up to. That he wasn't what his sister had tried to make him: He wasn't a monster.

Clearing his throat abruptly, he spoke at last, "Well, I think then maybe you need to stop running from your fear of failure, Baey." Breathing in deeply, he rubbed his temple and closed his eyes. "You wanted to be like me, but I think maybe you're running from the watch because it's time for you to be you. It's time to be alright with that."

I just stood there, trying to process everything he'd just said. Sure, I'd heard him…but I fought to understand. Or maybe I was fighting to accept he was right. I was fighting the watch because it was too much like me— too much of my own fears and insecurities. His ring had only ever made me want to step up, but the watch had brought back that feeling of helplessness I'd buried at Valdon. The feeling I'd buried with Sefen.

But he was right. Sven really *was* right, and suddenly I realized I'd let a tear escape. "Well," I wiped it away quickly, attempting a pathetic laugh with it. "When you put it that way, it sounds so simple."

Sven laughed too. "Oh it's not easy. Why do you think I hate using my ring?"

He'd laughed—and not the dry humorless sort of laugh, either. No, this was an older laugh—a laugh that changed his whole expression for a moment and made him smile again, and for a moment, I imagined I was seeing a glimpse into the past; into the Sven that Darby always talked about; the one before his entire world had crashed down on him. As short as it was, it was a laugh that somehow made the whole room feel brighter and more inviting.

"Thank you, Sven," I said, pouring all my energy to make the words sound as sincere as I felt.

He nodded, not saying another word as understanding passed between us.

<u>Kearn:</u>

Panic was a constant companion, these days. A bit ironic after I'd sworn the day Jay had defected: I would never let myself be so vulnerable again. Nevertheless, here we were. I was in way over my head. What had I gotten all of my soldiers into?

I stared at the outline of some form in the sewers, heart hammering against my chest like the thud of being repeatedly stabbed. Someone was there—someone who didn't want to be seen.

"I think we're going in circles! Let's backtrack and take the other way!" I called back to the others in the tunnel with me. Lord Atarah was present with his own band of mercenaries, but many in our group were from my command: Gvar insisted on staying close to me in case something happened. Paylos, Assin, and Laros had also given me no choice in being among those who came, not that I would have denied them.

I had to commit to my lie, and walked back away from the fork in the tunnels to where they were catching up. I'd purposefully made a habit of running ahead—in case something like this happened—and quickly put on a very genuinely exasperated expression as I nearly ran back into Atarah, who was looking equally perturbed.

"We've gone in another circle. We need to back track to that fork in the path and take a left instead," I reiterated, only briefly making eye contact with Gvar, who was standing near the front.

The glow of the unearthly, fireless lanterns did little to calm my nerves.

"I knew we were going around in a circle," Gvar muttered only just loud enough for us to hear as if we'd not meant to.

Laros chimed in under his breath to Paylos, "Told you I recognized where we were."

I made a point to glare at each one of my men, especially Gvar, "Quiet. Or are you that eager to gain extra sentry duty?" Secretly, however, I was thankful for their contribution to this farce.

Lord Atarah threw a hand up in the air and growled, "Shut up with the theatrics. *You're* the one leading us in circles. You *insisted* on going this way when I said we needed to go left. Stop wasting my time." He turned around in the muck, his oiled duster hitting me in the shins from the sheer force of his movements and splattering some undesirable liquid onto my own coat.

"Right, because a noble who spends his time holed up in his study reading poetry and eating cakes would know his way around the sewers," I spat back in a very poor lapse in judgement. This man was getting on my nerves more and more by the day. He was just another source of stress—clearly trying to figure out what I was really up to so he could report me to Ovok and get all the credit for it. He knew there was something going on, and after learning how he'd hung his own parents out to dry—literally hung—I worried who Ovok would believe more.

I knew I should apologize and try to save face but, at this point, I was so stressed that all I cared about was leaving this forsaken death trap of stench.

Fortunately, Atarah did little more than give me a confused and rather annoyed expression before reluctantly retracing our steps. The grumbling among both our parties was also growing more evident, as everyone was understandably fed up with the putrid tunnels and soft, squishy ground that I really didn't want to think any more about.

It was disgusting down here. How in Baeno did anyone survive in this? Somehow, I couldn't picture anyone hiding down here long term, and if not for the mysterious figure I'd only barely had us avoid, I would think perhaps they were pulling my leg just to keep me from betraying them.

We finally arrived back where Atarah had wanted to take the left, and again down another mysterious, dark passageway we went, the eerie splash of the sludge against our waterproof boots the only thing breaking the silence.

I handed my lantern back to Gvar and had him walk alongside me as I maneuvered my inner coat pocket to take the maps of the tunnels back out. Constant scribblings to try and rectify the changes in the sewer system were already jotted down, and I drew another question mark with a circle around it to signify this part might have now been a loop. What those sorts of things really meant was places we needed to avoid if possible.

"That's it. We are going to get lost again. We need to head to the surface and regroup…. I need to adjust this map…again," Atarah announced, and no one argued.

Well, except me, because I was obligated to argue. "Lord Kovo demands results. We cannot continue to leave without answers—or are you so eager to invoke his wrath?"

"No, I'm just sick of having a Bethynese captain, who can't even find his own left foot, insists on navigating and acting like a child. Here I thought you were supposed to be disciplined." The sneer in both his tone and expression was enough to leave me wishing I could give him a taste of what a Bethynese soldier would face for such open disrespect.

"Fine, we can go up," I gritted my teeth, tired of his insults. "I will be informing Lord Kovo just who wanted to leave first if he asks, so be warned."

"Oh, be my guest. I'd love to explain to him just how *helpful* you've been face-to-face." He swung around again and marched off in the mire of the sewers, leading us to the closest sewer exit. Paylos and one of Atarah's men quickly located the ladder, and in a few minutes, we were out in the bright midafternoon sun, many of us quickly taking off the duster jackets we'd been wearing in the sewers.

"Move along!" I called vehemently to the small group of city-goers who had stopped to stare, and it worked much better than I'd been worried it would. We'd been jumped once after exiting already. Part of the reason we'd brought a larger party this time—my own men numbering twelve not including Atarah's mercenaries.

Quickly I read the street sign and realized we were in the lowest part of the northeast sector of the city. My head hurt from the fumes of the sewers, and the contrast of the light of the surface from the gloom below wasn't exactly helping.

"Let's get out of the streets," I barked the order, not waiting for Lord Atarah's permission before leading us through the wide streets of Alkemar. A few rocks came pelting from a group that quickly ran off into a side alley, and I didn't bother sending any of my soldiers after them. It was likely a trap to lead them away. We'd wizened up to those. It was another good excuse to not have to keep up the act of enforcing Ovok or Skayla's hand. I couldn't help but notice General Reth really didn't seem to be trying hard enough to keep the riots down, either. Where were *his* patrols? I shuddered as I remembered the imminent arrival of Grand General Brahj, and the threat of executions.

I hoped Yelsi and the others I'd left back at the palace had found *something* about Skayla when I returned. That was the goal; that's what Atlys had said we needed. But then what? How would it stop us from running out of time or finding The Underground? Somehow, I had a feeling there wasn't a plan for that, and I wondered if I was really about to be the scapegoat. Was there a plan at all? Was I just being a good little scapegoat? Jaythos surely wouldn't let that happen...but did he know?

This was not helping my nerves.

At last, we arrived back at the palace, fortunate to have avoided another riot for the day. The streets had been quieter since yesterday but only comparatively.

"I will draw up another map with the new adjustments," Atarah announced as soon as the courtyard gates closed behind us. "I shall send it to you shortly. Next time, I think it prudent that I take the lead. It seems you have the directions of a deranged mongoose."

I gave him a hard glare. "Weren't you the one that set us off chasing our tails this morning and lost us three hours by leading us too far west in the sewers?"

"Me? Never." He looked way too pleased with himself, giving me the sudden urge to wring his filthy little neck.

Jaw clenched and hands itching to give this pathetic elitist a taste of my anger, I said, "Might I remind you it will be both our heads if we don't start working together."

The way he looked off in some mockery of pondering made me want to scream.

"But you're such close friends with Lord Kovo, I would think you wouldn't be concerned? Or are you two in a bit of a spot?" he asked, contempt dripping like fat from a fine cut of steak.

"I would be more concerned for your own neck, if I were you." I tried to force calmness.

The smile that formed on his miserable face was slow and way too satisfied as he replied, "Yes. We do want our necks intact. Wearing a lot of high collars recently, Captain?" He turned around. "We'll see how long until he realizes I'm a better choice." Before I could think of a reply, he twirled his hand and had his soldiers follow him to where their horses had been left. He would return to his nice, posh estate while I was stuck here smelling like week-old slime and re-examining why I was even doing this.

"Captain, just give the order...no one has to know." Gvar came up beside me.

I gave some slightly strangled noise as I walked towards the palace doors, readjusting my collar to hide the yellowing bruise. I needed to talk to Jay. I needed to see him.... Was I going to get Gvar and the others killed? Were we all still just pawns?

"Captain?" Gvar sounded concerned, and unfortunately, I didn't really have any reassurance to give him.

"I need to think. And I need to find Yelsi," I murmured, making my way up the steps.

They didn't deserve this. Yelsi had been a farmer...Gvar a leather worker. Laros and Assin were best friends since childhood and had always planned on running a forge together. Paylos just wanted to settle down and get married.... All of my men were eager for anything but bloodshed. We'd been promised—once the war was over, the Council of Generals would reinstate the two-year conscription and we would be free to have a life. At least, what little life those in Bethyn were allowed to have.

And now, over eight years later, I had somehow kept them all alive just to be fodder for a rebellion that couldn't care less about anyone with Bethynese blood.

I was so wrapped up in my thoughts that I hardly realized I'd not only entered the palace, but made it back to my study, Gvar still quietly by my side.

Not until we were safe behind the study's shut door did he dare ask, "Is everything alright, Captain?"

I couldn't lie—I refused. "This was a mistake. What were we thinking, Gvar?"

The man's lips pressed tightly together, a determination behind his eyes that I wish I could mirror. "Jaythos trusted them; and they saved him. We were thinking that maybe if we proved that we weren't some…that we never wanted this either, things would be different."

Sitting down at my desk, I found myself burying my head in my hands, unheeding of the unsanitary grime still on them. "But is it too late for that?" I'd long ago become the thing I'd never wanted to be: the perfect soldier for the Council of Generals.

"Captain, with all due respect, it's a bit late to be second-guessing." Gvar sounded just a little nervous, now. "And we'll show them all we aren't what the Council has made us. As I've told you, I'm hearing discontent from soldiers. Everyone is tired of doing their dirty work, and I…I don't care what this costs us, at this point. I haven't felt so free in a long time. I'm done just surviving and justifying anything to do so."

"You're right. I'm sorry," I replied but didn't move. He was right; I couldn't go back to being what I was simply pretending to be now. I couldn't just fall in line anymore—but would anyone really have our back? No one had cared before. Or had they? Had that been more lies we were fed? Jaythos had found friends. But Jaythos had gotten out before…before the alliance with Skayla.

"Even General Reth's remaining soldiers seem unsatisfied," he added.

It was true. I'd been able to catch up with Feren—the general's right-hand man—and he had actually let slip how little he was looking forward to Grand General Brahj's arrival. Most soldiers were wisely afraid of him, but those under General Reth's command, in particular, hated him. Most likely because the two generals loathed each other; the grand general seeing General Reth's approach to leadership as weak instead of strategic. When people talked about what they thought all Bethynese soldiers were like, they were thinking of people like the grand general.

"Just be careful, Gvar. I know Feren and the others are easier to talk to, but they are still dangerous," I said at last, worrying my friend might get too bold with his attempts at feeling out the loyalties of others. "Reth's command is full of extremely intelligent and loyal soldiers."

"And you were one of them," he immediately pointed out. "And they keep talking about how much they liked you and are glad you didn't die in the avalanche in Rugo."

The knock on the door concluded any further conversation on the subject.

"Enter." I straightened instantly, making brief eye contact with a still-concerned Gvar before the door opened to reveal Yelsi.

"Captain." He put a hand to his chest and gave a quick nod. "We finally have—oh. Oh, you smell. Sir…have you not bathed yet?" he asked between chokes.

"Shut up and give your report." I let him shrivel under my glare, and yet his smirk didn't completely disappear. Those under my command—the ones who had joined me in this ridiculous decision of treason—had slowly become more lax in their behavior when we were alone. To be honest...I didn't hate it. Maybe Gvar was right; we were more free. Was I really starting to see why Jaythos had been so stubborn in Rugo?

"Lairn and I, uh, well. We found her, sir," Yelsi sputtered back on topic, clearing his throat after one last choke.

I stood up quickly, clutching the edge of my desk. "You what?"

THE LAST ESMER

CHAPTER XI: Havirax is the Worst...as Usual

<u>Ovok:</u>

"You had better not be trifling with me, Havirax," I said coolly as the man stood in my room, fiddling clumsily with The Living Stone and the ancient-looking box he was trying to shove it into.

His hands were shaking.

Good. Let him sweat—

"Me? Trifle with you? Never." He gave a nervous laugh and muttered something else under his breath as the stone slipped in his hands.

I came swiftly forward, grabbing the precious, glowing stone and shoving Havirax out of the way. "Do you even know how to do this, or are you still playing the grifter?" We didn't have time, and what Havirax lacked in intelligence he *also* lacked in skill. The only reason I'd helped him cheat his brother of the title of The Merchant was because he was easily used. Grenedil had too many morals for that, and I needed access to the ancient artifacts The Merchants possessed.

This box was one of them. While I was no Merchant, I had walked these worlds long enough to figure out how many things worked, and with a few swift motions, I was able to find a dial on the box that grew it in size proportionately. I slipped The Living Stone in with ease.

"Remind me again how you are of any use to me?" I asked coyly as I shut the box and turned the latch so it was securely inside. Then I turned the dial the other way, and it shrunk until it was nothing but the size of a pendant, glowing a faint green from the power it held inside.

Havirax handed me a chain with an indignant expression. "I was the one that got you this. Don't forget that."

Ckaknimaen giggled, and I couldn't help but find the statement amusing, myself.

I didn't say a word as I grabbed the chain and fastened the pendant to it. A moment later I had The Living Stone as a necklace hanging around my neck, sliding neatly under my shirt and away from view. I was pleased that the green glow was faint enough not to show through my clothing.

"Is that useful though when you don't even understand how to work half of these things?" I squared my shoulders and looked the man up and down. A pathetic worm. He'd almost been more trouble than he was worth. "Did you find something to locate a portal yet?"

Havirax looked anywhere but where I was. "I, uh. No, I don't have that one."

"But you know where it is?" I asked in a measured tone, knowing he was being vague on purpose.

"I mean...not exactly, no."

I could kill the simpleton. Make him scream. He tests us too much—

I didn't say a word, only staring unblinkingly at Havirax, knowing he would cave.

It took even less time than I'd expected. "Grenedil. He, uh, he took it. A while ago. When I was last on Eatris. Before we all left—he wanted to see if he could find your replacement, see—"

I smiled, and he stammered to a halt. "So you waited twelve years to tell me that?" My replacement. The one supposedly half-elf and half-human. As if there was anyone who could actually fit the role of guarding Eatris, let alone someone with that heritage. I had been the only reason that planet hadn't cannibalized itself, and without me, the Elves would have wiped out all Humans long ago. It was still hard to believe there was a child running around on Eatris that held that mixture of blood after the second Elvish War I'd been involved in settling.

Not that it was that pressing at the moment, compared to Havirax's apparent blunder. "I have been *waiting* for you to deliver the backdoor access to me, and I was under the impression you could actually follow through."

"No…no, I was busy getting those stupid blueprints put together for you. Do you realize how hard it was getting all the Maras' notes for the portal machines figured out?"

More useless excuses—

"Yes, and they didn't even work," I retorted, still unable to completely drop the reminder of that stupid notion that we would be replaced. That we *should* be replaced. Or rather, that we should have existed at all; the TetraWorlds needed a leash, not protectors.

"That's because Cyl was keeping it shut!"

Ack! Cyl—

Honestly, I wasn't sure whether the mental recoiling was Ckaknimaen or me, this time. Every time Cyl's name was uttered, it left a bad taste in the air.

But I didn't let it show. Instead, I raised an eyebrow, and Havirax instantly shrunk back, continuing with his pathetic attempts at logic. "Listen, we left Grenedil back on Eatris, so there's no chance of getting it now unless he was somehow the one that got through during the fight in the ravine you told me about...but I was figuring that was Cyl. Besides, he'd just be *with* the portal now, so isn't it easier to just find the portal?"

"Yes. So easy." I walked forward, then suddenly grabbed his collar and shoved him against the nearest wall. Ckaknimaen's delight echoed in my mind, almost as maddening as Skayla's laughs had been. "You are going to help me find that portal, or I am going to feed you to Dyress. Piece. By. Piece." I didn't have time anymore. I was close...*so* close. Yet things were falling apart just as quickly, and the idea of Cyl being here was already enough to make my blood boil. The coward. I wanted to rip him limb from limb. I hoped he knew just how responsible he was for all this—that he realized the blood of all those in this world was just as much on his hands as it was mine.

Stop complaining. Their pain tasted so good—

I shuddered at the sword's contempt even as I knew that, knowing Cyl, he didn't care.

Nobody cares. That's the problem. Nobody ever cares—

I released Havirax and gave a cold smile as he tumbled to the floor. "Now, if you want to continue to be useful to me, you are going to find that portal. I felt it open. It has to be somewhere in the northeastern part of the city." The Living Stone could sense it to a degree, but it wasn't giving an accurate enough pulse, and there was no way on this planet I would give such a thing to Havirax. There had also been the matter of the sudden presence of Eatrisian Gifting—one that was loud enough for any Myrandi to easily hear. But it had also dimmed soon after its arrival and left me more puzzled. Cyl held no Gifting—no Myrandi could. So had he brought someone with him? Whoever it was, they were yet another thing standing in my way. And, by the initial wave of energy I had felt, a very dangerous thing.

"Follow the captain, Kearn. He's the youngest of the captains and under General Reth. I sense he has not been completely honest with me. If you can figure out what he's doing—and if such knowledge helps me get the portal—then I'll let you stay here and enjoy your stolen manor and dead man's clothes," I addressed Havirax at last.

He got up hesitantly, brushing himself off and giving that nervous smirk. "Of course. Anything for you, my lord. Just point the way and I will be on it like a…a…."

"Just get on it," I growled. I didn't have time for this. But we were close. So close, Rhioa.

Where are you hiding, Cyl, you coward.

Estasia:

"We are running out of time to move out." I stood in Atlys's parlor, arms folded as I mirrored the lord's deep frown. He'd just finished explaining about Ovok's meeting with everyone and what had come of it. It explained the uptick in sewer patrols.

"Yes. And your little Bethynese captain is running out of time as well. Unless you are intending to leave him to die." His face twisted in disgust.

I sighed, "Yeah, no, that's not an option. If the captain's brother didn't kill us first, I certainly know who would." Sven would never let us play dirty like that, let alone Darby or Baey. Honestly, I could only think of one person that *would* be for the idea, and that only made me hate the option even more. I never wanted to associate any decision with that Cyl. There was still something he was hiding, but he was very tight-lipped about any of his past—other than the fact he had once been friends with Ovok, and that Ovok had forced his way through Cyl to get to Baeno, leaving him for dead.

"I still haven't heard from my runners to the west, so are we going to proceed under the pretense of using the ravine?" Atlys asked, looking as displeased as I felt.

I gave a stiff shrug. "I suppose so. Might as well try and move forward with some logistics. Can you discreetly look into digging a well? It would be easier than having to risk going into the woods for the creek every time. We need to try and keep everyone together. Wouldn't want anyone running into some patrol in the forest."

Atlys nodded. "A well wouldn't be easy to dig there. But I can look into getting the supplies for such a feat and putting it on the invisible airship you gave me. But getting any supplies is extremely risky right now, what with the rations being halted."

Yet another complication. Atlys usually sent us food once a month, and we were lucky in that he had just dropped off this month's supplies right before Ovok had ordered a halt. Still, that only meant we had a little more time, even with the other stores he'd kept secretly in case of such a scenario. "Fine, do what you can. You should also look at getting supplies for infrastructure. People will need shelter."

"The problem is not merely the supplies for the buildings, but the tools needed. The amount you would need would not go missing easily, and I know the tools you have in the sewers are crude and not really meant to build something to last the elements," Atlys pointed out, rubbing his forehead.

So many problems. How were we going to pull this off?

"And that is still assuming we get the people there at all," he added.

He wasn't wrong. "Yes, Cyl refuses to let us use the stupid portal to do so. Theoretically, we could have everyone evacuated in moments, but he said under no circumstances will he be opening it again, and Grenedil said he can't force it open with Cyl there to protect it. So that's out."

Atlys sighed, staring at the mantelpiece covered in layers of dust and mildew. "We will have to make do with the airship and Sven, then. Ovok smells something is up, and right now he suspects the captain, but I am starting to wonder if I might not be next. Lord Atarah is not helping the situation. As it is, I am having a hard time slipping any supplies through, as I'm not even supposed to be supplying the city. Unloading any shipments right now makes me look suspicious, and I only have so much in reserves."

I swallowed hard. I'd never expected Eugene to turn into such a power-hungry monster. Atlys had explained how he was trying to pin things on Kearn already. Guess we'd all changed. But if I ever saw him again…I really wasn't sure what I would do.

"Sir," a boy ran in from the hallway, gasping for breath as he said, "A message for you."

Atlys snatched the letter from the boy's hand and gave him a coin in return, sending him off before turning back to me. "It's from Illan. It must be important if he didn't wait for the next time I saw him."

Concern crept in, feeling that paranoia at the amount of people I was putting my faith in over this. I didn't like having so many loose threads.

Breaking the seal, Atlys quickly read it over, looking increasingly perplexed as he did so and only leaving me to grow more impatient.

"He says the captain has information for us…. But…he won't give it to anyone except his brother." Atlys walked over and handed me the letter.

I wanted to groan even as I read over the remarkably short letter.

To whom it may concern,

This is a direct transcription from our mole. I have already burned the original letter.

"I have information regarding the person you've been after, but if you want anything further, I need to talk to my brother. Kovo is growing more temperamental and impatient, and now has a house guest referred to as Havirax."

Idiot. I sighed, throwing the note back to Atlys so he could burn it.

"I guess I'll be going to see Sven, then." He was in the mansion, where Jaythos also was. I guess if anything, at least it wouldn't track anything back to The Underground. Just where Sven was hiding, if anything went wrong….

"Didn't expect to see you here," Marion commented as she let me in through the tunnel doorway, eyes clearly asking what was wrong even though her words remained casual. I had no intention of revealing anything more to the near stranger, even if she'd saved Jaythos and the others back in Rugo.

"Is Jaythos in any condition to move?" I asked bluntly as the door behind me closed.

"He would say so, at least." Marion looked on guard. "Is it Kearn?"

I gave no reply, only turning down the hall and to the living room.

"Estasia!" Baey's wings washed brighter from the darker shade of brown they'd been before she'd noticed my presence, but then quickly dimmed as her enthusiasm also gave way to concern. "Is everything alright?"

I looked at the other three in the room: Sven, Grenedil, and Astra. "Everything is fine," I replied simply. Nothing was wrong enough to risk talking in front of so many extra pairs of ears. "I just want to check up on Jaythos."

Baey's eyes narrowed, but she said nothing. She'd turned into a sharp little Birdie.

"And to check in on how you're doing." I turned my attention on Sven, who was sitting in a chair looking his usual impassive self. The intensity of the golden eyes was still not something I was used to, however. Better than those ghostly, colorless ones, but unnerving nonetheless. Alenor had guessed it had something to do with Skayla's hold on his memories being completely broken when he'd destroyed her amulet.

"I'm fine." He made a small, dismissive motion with his hand.

I just rolled my eyes. "Sure you are. So why the company?" I didn't bother trying to drag it out of him, but neither could I pretend I believed him anymore.

He seemed a little taken aback but did not say anything—as usual—instead letting Baey explain her presence.

"Grenedil and I had an update on the portal situation. Astra's family is safe from this Tyron, and so are we. Cyl says he went to Kryso."

"Kryso?" I frowned.

Baey seemed to have some understanding of what that was. Wings twitching and turning a shade of red, she said, "Alenor said that was…" the faltering was followed by a brief glance at Sven.

"It's where my father was from." He finished the sentence with a forced air of casualness.

Baey swallowed. "Yes. The third world."

I really didn't care how many worlds there were, right now. As long as more trouble wasn't coming to this one. "Great." I folded my arms and looked at Grenedil. "But shouldn't you be with Cyl? Is…*anyone* keeping track of him?"

Grenedil looked like a sad, pathetic puppy. "He doesn't listen to me anyway." He threw a discreet glance Astra's way.

It was Baey that gave the more reassuring, "Alenor and Darby have it under control."

"I should get back then." I sighed. Alenor was strangely off-balance around the stupid Drogan guard, and Darby had enough on her plate.

Sven didn't look up at me as he asked, "Why are you here?" The way he said that…did he think I was checking in like some babysitter on him?

"Oh, trust me, I wouldn't be here if I didn't have to be." I laughed dryly. "I have to check in on Jaythos, like I said. But…" Turning to Grenedil, I asked, "While I'm here…what did you say your brother's name was?"

Confused, Grenedil nonetheless replied, "Havirax."

That's what I'd thought. "Well, apparently, he's Ovok's guest. Is that going to be a problem for us?"

"Wait…what?" Grenedil jumped to his feet. "Ovok's caught him? I—"

"—No," I butted in, not exactly trying to be polite. "He is a *guest*." I was becoming increasingly concerned by Grenedil's track record in judging people's character, and I couldn't help but give a side eye in Astra's direction.

"He…what?" Grenedil's bafflement was predictable, if not frustrating. "But he…he…."

"Right now, I need you to tell me how much of a problem that's going to be for us, not how surprising it is." I fought to keep my patience, pretending I didn't see the way Baey was quietly pleading with me to be more gentle.

Grenedil's shoulders sagged, and his voice was hollow as he replied, "Quite a decent one. He has The Merchant's satchel, which holds a few of the relics from across the three worlds and the fourth realm—The Maze. Only he can see the satchel and only he can use it, but if he's…helping Ovok, then that could cause trouble. The only saving grace is that Havirax has no clue what any of the relics are or how they work, and since Ovok cannot see the bag or use it himself, he has to rely on Havirax being able to identify objects and their uses…which is likely frustrating for him, if I know my brother."

"Well, apparently, you didn't know him that well, seeing who he's working for," I grumbled. Ignoring his hurt expression, I asked, "So then can we steal this bag back?"

"No," Grenedil sighed. "It can only be willingly given from Merchant to Merchant, and Havirax had already refused to give it to me after he tricked the last Merchant into thinking he was me."

Raising an eyebrow, I couldn't help but comment, "And that didn't give you any clues that maybe he wasn't exactly the best person?" "Listen, I knew he wasn't great, but I didn't think he would do something like work for Ovok!" he shouted, exasperated. "I just thought he was jealous of me. I didn't...I guess it makes more sense now. I guess I'm just an idiot for thinking the best of family."

"We have all been there." Sven surprised me by stepping in, but admittedly, he was right. Even I had placed trust in the wrong people before, but it still didn't exactly help the fact that this meant we could be dealing with a host more problems than before.

"Do you know any of the things that are in the bag?" Baey asked with a lot more tact than I possessed.

Pinching the bridge of his nose, Grenedil sat back down, hunched over in defeat. "There's no way to know for sure. Countless things in there could be an issue: Things that make you invisible, things that can heal you, things that hold sentience similar to the Myrandi Blades, things that can contain—" He put his face in his hands, groaning, "—that can contain enormous amounts of power, meaning things that could help Ovok control or use The Living Stone."

"That's great." I threw my hands up in the air. "Just great."

"How long has he been The Merchant?" Baey's calm was jarring.

Grenedil did not look up. "Close to twenty-four years?"

"Then clearly, he's had plenty of time to go through the bag. Meaning there has to be a limit to what is useful for Ovok, seeing as he seems to have mostly been handling things himself here over the years," she pointed out. "Is there anything with the power of something like Moira's watch, Grenedil?"

He shook his head. "Relics of that level usually require you to be the original owner, or at least have a strong disposition to Gifting—which Ovok does not have. He may have access to some now that he possesses The Living Stone, but nothing that controls anything like time or reality."

"So then, if we can get Moira back soon, we still have a better ally than he does."

I couldn't help but wince, still thinking of my conversation with Darby. I would make sure to share my concerns with Baey, but privately. "I suppose that will have to do for now." I sighed. "Grenedil, if you can remember *anything* specific that is in that bag, I need you to inform me immediately."

"I can write a list before we leave."

Running my hand over my face, I tried my best to remain calm. "That would be great. I won't be here long, so if you could get that started, I would appreciate it."

"Are you going back to The Underground today, then?" Baey asked. "Syvil wants to come back with us, and Grenedil needs to return...."

"Yes." I waved a hand as I turned back to the hall. "We can divide and conquer. Probably a good idea considering the increased patrols. I'll be using the streets, so I can take Grenedil." It would be good for me to judge him a little better. I still couldn't believe how someone could have such bad intuition with people. Astra had better not continue this streak. Sven was fiercely protective of the child, and Baey had already repeatedly vouched for her...but I was skeptical. If not for the clear fact she was intensely afraid of hurting people—and that Cyl was against her—I would be a little less fond of her presence here.

"Can you take Syvil, as well?" Baey pressed. "Then I can use the tunnels. The patrols really are everywhere, but I'd prefer using the sewers to topside." She sounded...embarrassed.

I couldn't help but turn back around and give her a very pointed look. She should have thought about that before bringing Grenedil here. And...why *had* she brought him, again? "Fine." I turned back and left to go up the stairs.

Somehow, I got the feeling Baey had been trying to get Grenedil away from Cyl. As nice a thought as it was, I didn't like her habit for empathy affecting safety like that. I'd learned to let her go and trust that connection with others most of the time, but sometimes...I still had my doubts. And Grenedil's apparent habit for picking bad friends was not helping. The last thing I'd needed was knowing Ovok had a bag of magical objects at his disposal.

"Jaythos?" I knocked on the door and almost instantly found myself face-to-face with Maeko.

"I need to talk to him. About Kearn."

Maeko's dark expression did not change as he let me in. He had been even less prone to talking since they'd returned from Rugo. In fact, Baey had said he hardly left Jaythos's side or the room.

The only thing he'd really done was ask after Tanner, apparently.

I walked in and found Jaythos standing, rather awkwardly. I wondered if he was *actually* doing the exercises Baey had given him.

"Is Kearn alright?" He looked only a little unsteady, any pain he felt well-hidden behind that stoic Bethynese glare.

I waved a hand. "He's fine, for now. He found Skayla." I usually wasn't so willing to share that information, but if the secret wasn't safe with the very brother who had begged for Kearn's life, then I truly was at a loss. Besides, Jaythos needed to know what was at stake here and understand just how reckless his brother was being with this stupid demand. "But he will not tell us where she is. He says he'll only tell you."

The concern in Jaythos's brow was nearly imperceptible, and I might have missed it altogether if not for his next statement. "He's in trouble."

I tilted my head. "So I should be worried?"

Jaythos looked at Maeko, then back at me. "I don't know. But he doesn't trust you. He must be afraid something is going to happen…to him." I couldn't tell if the wince was from his healing wound or because of his brother. Granted, the brother had caused the stab wound….

"You are not well. I can go." Maeko intruded upon the conversation.

"No," Jaythos snapped, hand drawing close to his chest as he seemed to stifle a cough. "I'm feeling much better. Kearn won't tell anyone except me. It wouldn't be a trap—but he is afraid of something.

He wants me to make sure he's safe, that's why he wants me. I'm sure of it."

"Well, whatever it is, I don't have time for these games. Are you well enough to meet?" Should I even have bothered to ask? Clearly, whether he was or he wasn't, Jaythos had already decided he was coming.

"Yes. When and where?" Jaythos asked, clearing his throat.

I hoped he was *actually* up to this. "I will come get you. It won't be far, seeing as we are definitely not going to bring you into the sewers. Just be ready—rest and build up your strength so you aren't dead weight."

Jaythos nodded. "I'll be ready."

"And you," I addressed Maeko. "You'll come with me to help with Jaythos. Don't get in the way." I had kept my interactions with everyone from Valdon to a minimum, especially Maeko. I didn't care how sorry he was, he'd had his chance and had decided to put his anger at The GhostMaker's uncontrollable actions over logic and every evidence Sven had only wanted to help. I didn't have time for petty.

"We'll be ready," Jaythos repeated.

"Good. I will get you soon." I turned and left the room, taking a deep breath as I started down the stairs just in time to hear a shout come from where the others were.

"I did it! It works!"

It was Baey.

CHAPTER XII: Time to Spare

<u>Sven:</u>

I felt bad for Grenedil. If nothing else, I could understand the betrayal that had washed over him. I'd felt the same way when Skayla had turned, and understood people not being who you thought they were. I understood feeling like you were stupid for ever trusting them. I understood feeling responsible for the fact that very powerful objects now lay in the hands of the enemy.

"Here you go," Baey said as she handed Grenedil some paper and a writing pen. She'd briefly left to find something for him to use.

"So there's no way for anyone to get the bag, then?" I asked.

Grenedil shook his head, still looking defeated. "No. The bag has been passed down for centuries. If there was a way around it, someone would have stolen it by now. Which, at least, means Ovok cannot steal it from him." He returned to his task, writing a few more strange titles on the paper in front of him.

"Why don't you try your hand at the watch again, darlin'?" I suggested to Baey, figuring Grenedil would appreciate being left in peace to write. "You can stay and practice as long as you like. Unless you really need to get back to The Underground." I wasn't sure how helpful I really would be, but maybe I could at least be encouraging.

Her wings gave a brief flick, and a stray feather floated down to the ground. "Yeah, maybe I should. I guess Grenedil and I don't have to leave right away." She frowned, one hand going to the watch around her neck.

"Don't try so hard," I gave a small smile of encouragement. "No need to be so serious. Just connect with it—you always do that well with people."

A little of her stiffness faded. "I just...don't want to feel helpless, I guess."

"Then maybe let it help you," I prodded gently. I could only hope my suggestions would be actually helpful, but even if they weren't, I had faith in Baey.

With a frown, Baey gave an "Alright...." Then she took a deep breath and closed her eyes. "Just accept it..." she murmured to herself.

I knew she would get it. If anyone could, it would be her. After all, she'd first discovered she could use my ring all on her own, before I'd ever been around to tell her how to do it.

"I did it! It worked!" Her exclamation was as sudden as her change to wide-eyed amazement.

I felt a strange sense of excitement wash over even me. "That was fast."

She was grinning, now. "I mean. Technically not. I just...I was able to get all the way back here. You'd been coaching me for about fifteen minutes, actually."

"Wait—as in...you used the watch?" Grenedil jumped up from where he was writing, having been so engrossed in his task he had no longer been paying attention.

"Took you long enough, Birdie." Estasia's unexpected entrance startled me—I'd been too distracted with Baey's apparent victory.

Beaming, and wings now bright and alert, Baey turned to Estasia without so much as flinching, which made sense if she'd come back from fifteen minutes in the future—where Estasia had already entered the room.

"It was much easier than before," Baey threw a small smile my way.

I just shook my head, still gripping the arm of my chair. "I knew you would get it." This meant Moira might come home. The reality of that made my chest hurt.

There was a moment where everyone looked at me, and I realized I'd whispered the words. Slowly, I let go of the armrest.

"I have to get back—I need to tell Darby and Alenor." Baey's eyes were alight as they stared at me. "We're going to get Moira back. Sven, we're going to get your sister."

Yes. And I couldn't dare to believe it yet. Very little had gone my way in the past decade. "Then we'll go with the same plan?" I asked, still trying to process everything that had just happened.

"Correct," Estasia interjected. "And the sooner the better for all of us. We could use the advantage of time." She looked a strange mixture of relieved and somehow apprehensive. I couldn't quite explain it. Then she looked at me. "You'll still need to remain here, though, as discussed."

"Of course," was all I said. I knew I needed to make sure Astra's signature remained hidden from Ovok, but I so desperately wanted to be the one to go with Mum and Baey—the one to help get Moira back. And then since my memories had returned, I'd yearned for that even more. The memory of Moira's note in my hand when I'd found out she'd left to face Skayla alone—the last correspondence with her before her disappearance—was branded in my mind and so were the thoughts that had run through my head at the time. That feeling of helplessness and the relentless second-guessing of whether or not me being there would have stopped it from happening. Part of me wondered if I would have been left behind even if Astra wasn't a factor. I felt too much like a liability. After all, I only ever seemed to make things worse. First as The GhostMaker, now by tearing up and reordering reality on a whim.

"Is there anything else I should know before I leave?" Estasia asked, and I wondered how long I'd faded out of the conversation. I needed to stop this pathetic self-pitying.

"Actually, yes," I said, turning to Astra, having a difficult time concentrating on anything besides the hope of seeing Moira alive and well again. "Tanner was caught up in a memory yesterday. It was about Ovok's daughter—Rhioa. And Astra knows of her as well. She is apparently alive."

Estasia frowned. "But isn't that…didn't Syvil and all the other Drogans say that was the reason Ovok even came here? Because she died?"

"She's alive. That's why Tyron was trying to get off of my world. To find her and Ovok." Astra actually inserted herself into the conversation, speaking for the first time in a while.

"Perhaps she is only barely alive. Being struck by the Miadoris is what was supposed to have killed her, so perhaps it only brought her close to death. Ovok may be keeping her alive but is unable to save her. That could…be why Ovok wants The Living Stone," Grenedil mused aloud from where he was still writing the list. "The Myrandi are a lot more resilient on Baeno than on Eatris because of the power sources. The

Living Stone is meant to heal…. I don't know how Ovok kept her alive for so long, but if she needs healing beyond reasonable means, that must be why he wants it. He must be keeping her in The Maze, somehow."

"Well, I'm not sure it makes me feel better that maybe all this destruction was because he just wanted some help healing someone." Estasia waved her hands in the air. "But it doesn't really change anything, other than cementing that he wants to get off-world. With The Living Stone." She turned to Baey, and something unspoken passed between them. "I'll show you out, Baey. Best not wait any longer—the sooner you get back to The Underground, the sooner we can hopefully get ahead of this."

The mess we got in for family…I didn't know how to feel. About anything, anymore.

Little was said after Baey left. Estasia only stayed the hour in uneasy silence—going over the various things on the list Grenedil had made and debating which Havirax would likely be able to use. Then she, too, left, with a quiet Syvil and a reluctant Grenedil.

The clock chimed the evening hour, and the sound of the small model train coming to life filtered through the house.

"I want to help." Astra's tone had a surprising amount of conviction to it.

I turned from where I was now standing by the mantlepiece, unsuccessfully attempting to read her expression and better understand exactly what she meant. But, as always, it was enigmatic.

"They said Moira is your sister and you're trying to get her back. And Ovok…" She frowned deeply. "If this has to do with Rhioa, and if there has been no evidence of her here as Grenedil says, then Ovok may be pursuing all of you for the same reason Tyron is pursuing me: to get to Rhioa. So I want to help," she repeated her statement with somehow even more conviction than before.

"Alright," I said slowly, trying to give myself time to figure out how exactly she even *could* help. Seeing as I was already well-established at making things worse, I might not be the best person to ask how to be of assistance. "Well, your power does seem quite extensive." Uncontrolled but extensive. And seeing what mine had done to the city, was it really a wise idea to have her experiment with hers? I had been able to keep hers contained and hidden, but was it worth prodding?

"It has done me little good so far," she murmured, looking back out the window. "I don't have much to offer in strategy or fighting. You would have been better off with Louko or my brother here instead of me. But I can make a good bit of bait or distraction—especially if you're trying to lead off any Myrandi."

"Louko," I repeated the name. "Is he your friend?" I tried to steer away from the whole "bait" idea, knowing better than to try and directly confront it. It was better, for now, to redirect, no matter how horrified the notion made me.

Even from here, I could see the way her breath caught. At last, she replied, "Yes. He's a good friend." The way she said that made me feel like she didn't feel she deserved him as one.

"He's lucky to have you." With that, I had made up my mind. "Come with me." Stretching and readjusting my weathered coat, I turned to leave the room for the hallway.

Astra followed, silent even with the questions lingering behind those strange, blue eyes.

"You wanted to help. So let's see what you can do." Was this a bad idea? Maybe. But was it any worse than when I had practiced alone in the mansion's back tunnel? Definitely not. And it was separate from the sewers so we didn't need to worry about being discovered.

Soon enough, we were in the tunnel, the door closing behind us and leaving only the light from the bioluminescent lanterns that lined either side of the long hallway.

"This has enough room to spar," I said simply as I rubbed the pommel of my new sword. Mum had made one for me after I'd given Baey my old one, and I appreciated it. But now wasn't the time to get distracted—now I needed to help Astra. I quickly put the small, invisible sphere around us to separate us from true reality should anything happen.

"Are you certain this is a good idea?" Nervousness pervaded Astra's usually impassive expression.

I unsheathed my sword. "You had said you wanted to help. Let me see for myself how you fight."

Was that…red in her cheeks? "I think using me as a distraction would go better."

I didn't bother hiding my disgust. "Use you as bait? What would I say to Louko?" The thought that this child could think such a thing…. I wondered if it meant she'd been used like that all her life, or if she was just *that* desperate to help.

"He'd know I got myself into it," she murmured before asking, "Do you have a sword I could borrow?"

"Hold out your hand."

She did so, and I waved my own in some magical-looking gesture to match the illusion of a sword appearing in her hand. As I'd told Baey, such gestures were meaningless, but I felt it was less likely to startle Astra than a sword just materializing in her hand with no explanation.

She tested it, giving a few swings that showed me she was at least a little more familiar with weapons than she was suggesting. I didn't believe her to be intentionally *hiding* her abilities. It looked more like Baey and the lack of confidence she'd once had. Only, this seemed more complicated.

"The sword has no risk of harming either of us." I passed my own hand through my sword to demonstrate, altering reality just so that it would be permeable. "So don't worry. This is how I practice with Baey all the time. It's completely safe. Are you ready?"

Again, like when she'd first seen the model train earlier, I saw a brief spark of curiosity, and she had to pass her own hand through the blade I'd conjured up for her. But unlike every other time when she'd quickly stowed away her emotion, the curiosity remained as she nodded, taking on a nice, solid starting stance.

So we began.

It started slowly; Astra clearly hesitant. She threw a few strokes, doubt as clear in her face as it was in the light blows she dealt, but it was hard to tell if she distrusted me or herself.

"It's alright. Don't hold back," I encouraged as I gave a swing of my own blade.

She took a deep breath, and I saw it; that moment where one lets their mind go and lets instinct take over instead. Her hesitation left, replaced with something both quick and startlingly aggressive. It wasn't hard to tell she'd fought for her life before.

More than once.

Our blades met, and she kept good balance despite her small stature, twisting out of our lock before I could overpower her. This time I attacked, feeling for her technique as I tested the waters. It was…odd. I couldn't quite put my finger on it, but her style was always changing. Unpredictable and yet clearly not untrained.

Sometimes she put in a move or two that I would only have expected from someone of the highest blade mastery, but then the way she would follow through after such an attack was as if not even she knew it. It didn't strike me so much as blind luck as much as it did instinct, but instinct that conflicted with itself. Almost like different personalities clashing.

I disarmed her at last, puzzled as I reached out an arm to help her up. "You're quite good, you know," I said after seeing the lines of frustration in her brow.

She just brushed herself off. "You're going easy on me."

"I mean, yes." I didn't bother lying. "But I go easy on everyone. And I'm trying to get a sense of what you know." I drew my lips in a thin line as I tried to formulate how to ask about her form. Or rather, forms.

Something flashed in those blue eyes as she seemed to catch onto what I wanted to ask. "That might be difficult. Sometimes I don't know what is me and what is…" She shook her head. "It's complicated." She again took a ready stance.

I mimicked her, and again we began to fight. "I can do complicated," I replied as I caught her blade in mine once more, moving quickly around her to see how she would react to me getting behind her guard so soon.

There was another huff of frustration—and, I noted carefully, a very brief pulse of her energy—but she quickly reassessed, countering me in a manner that caught me off guard. Another highly skilled move that was not followed up on.

"I was once like your friend, Tanner. The one mind I'm still connected to is…he…he is a very good swordsman." The reply came out as a growl as she focused.

Suddenly, it all began to make sense. The instantaneous reactions were imprints of the other person…. Why did I have a feeling it was this Tyron she had mentioned before?

We went another three strokes before I disarmed her again. She was silent as she took her blade once more, body stiff.

"Loosen your shoulders. It will help you follow through with your movements." I saw the way she took my instruction. She grew instantly more rigid before forcing her shoulders into submission. But her eyes said something else.

I recognized that look too well: She was internalizing the critique as proof of her inadequacy.

"Again?" I asked instead of addressing the change, carefully contemplating my next move. There were several things going on—several things Astra's behavior had already told me, and the more I saw, the more I could relate. I understood the fear of failure as you remembered every friend you had been too slow to save. Seeing it now in someone so young, I burned to help.

Astra didn't say a word, completely shut down as she got ready for our next round.

At first, I tried to back off a little in this round, but it was clear she was too clever for that—the crease in her brow deepening with her dark demeanor.

So I leaned into it a bit more, trying to work out what exactly to do next after once again disarming her.

"Why don't we take a break?" I sheathed my own blade and waved my hand so hers would disappear from where it had landed a little way from us.

She didn't say a word, eyeing the hand I offered her. Tentatively, she accepted it to stand.

"Have you ever incorporated your abilities into fighting?" I asked, going over and leaning against the wall.

She crossed her arms, remaining standing where she was. "No. It was always too dangerous."

"If I might ask," I began, trying to tread lightly. "What are they, exactly? Your abilities?" I understood little beyond it being a very raw and active source of energy, and she had not said much other than that she was dangerous. While I had needed no further information before to keep us safe, I was curious, wondering if perhaps it wasn't all bad like she seemed to think.

"I…I guess I don't really know…." She trailed off. "I can't consistently control them, so it doesn't really matter."

Tilting my head, I watched her intently as I measured my next words. "But if you know what they are, perhaps I could help."

"Plenty of people have tried. My father—" She closed her eyes, breath catching. "We were having lessons. It was working…before Louko was captured. Before Keeshiff died." There was fear in her voice, and fear in the air. That was it, wasn't it? Her power seemed intrinsically linked with her emotions, much like Baey with her wings. The fear that had exploded when she arrived had been the trigger before, and then again when we were fighting.

But I was distracted by the names. Keeshiff…I remembered her choking out the fact that this person had died to Grenedil. "I see." I wished I was better with words, somehow able to comfort her. I realized that perhaps the best way was to keep discussing what we had been talking of before. "So what were you doing in those lessons?"

"Simple things." Astra took another shaky breath, seeming to collect herself. "The way Gifting works on my world is like…an energy source. You can do things like heal people and transport to different places, it just takes up energy. My father was trying to help me control the ability to transport from one place to another. And then through that…" she winced again, some memory flashing to the forefront for a moment before she hid it away. "We discovered I could control The Door."

Right. Grenedil had said she could use the portal after Cyl had allowed it—and that Cyl had cut her off from it for the time being, apparently.

"So your Gift is healing and transporting? Is everyone's the same in your world?" I asked, straying away from The Door part of it and the undoubtedly painful reminder of how she'd gotten here.

Astra's brow furrowed. "I, uh, it depends. I've done other things before. It seems certain people are more skilled in certain aspects. My brother has done things like create illusions, or start fires, or make shields. But it depends on race, too. Even though my brother can do all those things, he isn't a Bandilarian, so he can't use Gifting to change shape completely. Is it not that way here?"

"No, not here." I rubbed the pommel of my sword. "It doesn't depend on race. Some people just have the ability to interact with The Living Stone, and others don't."

"Living Stone?" Astra asked, seeming to recognize the title from the conversations between me and the others earlier.

"It's the power source of our world—the heart of The Creator, given to us millennia ago when reality was crumbling. It's the thing Ovok has stolen from us. It saved Baeno but also bestowed Gifts on some people. No one has ever figured out how it chooses who gets the abilities and who doesn't, but it does seem somewhat hereditary, as both my siblings were given Gifts as well as me." I got halfway through my explanation before realizing how strange it was to remember things so easily. I'd fought with my mind for so long now that it felt foreign for it to obey me without objection.

"So then, your Living Stone is what the Miadoris on our world is, to a degree," Astra mused aloud. "But for us, the Miadoris is in every person—whether Gifted or not. That's how I've ended up…in other people's heads before. I was struck by the Miadoris as a child. Usually direct contact kills people, but I guess being half Elf and half Human had something to do with it, according to others."

My eyes widened a little. "Elves exist in your world?"

She just shrugged. "Yes. Do you not have any here?"

I shook my head, amused by how casually she seemed to take this news.

"Is there anyone like Baey on your world?" I asked suddenly, curiosity getting the better of me with all the different races she was mentioning. I wondered if perhaps Baey wouldn't be so desperately alone. One of the many things now swimming around in my head was the reminder Skayla had massacred all her people; all the Esmers, just to get at Moira and me.

Frowning, Astra replied, "I don't know, sorry. I've never met any, but there are a lot of things I haven't seen in my world."

It was an interesting statement. I wondered what this Eatris was like. Was it as shrouded in mystery as Astra, and that was why she knew so little? Or had she simply not had the opportunity to learn about her world—much like Baey with ours?

Then I remembered what the whole point of talking had been. "So this Miadoris. It kills those who directly touch it, but it lives inside of everyone?"

"That is how it seems."

"Then," I crossed my arms, putting all the pieces together. "Is it simply defending itself? The only times I've seen or felt it react in you is when you are afraid."

She gave little reaction, but her gaze dropped to the floor. "I suppose that would make sense, yes." Her tone was listless. "I am not very good at controlling my emotions."

"On the contrary, I think you do much better than most people I see," I replied. "But somehow I don't think that is the solution." She was beginning to make more sense, and I couldn't help but feel a sense of loss for this child. "A raging river cannot be kept back forever."

Astra looked a bit confused, and it was a welcome change from the darkness that had surrounded her.

I even found myself smiling a little at it. I suppose my words had not exactly been clear. "You can try and tame a river—try and stop it with a dam and hope it doesn't break loose. Or you can use it to turn mills and grind wheat and create a way of life. Emotions are like the water. You can try and stuff them down or hold them back, and…" I sighed, my own emotions reminding me of how I failed to deal with them. "…and eventually they will overflow and win out. Or you can learn to go with them, and something good might come of it. Something great, even. I have—a sister."

I sat down, taking a deep breath as I allowed myself to relive this in full for the first time. "Skayla. She could see inside other people's heads—hear their thoughts and even influence them. Her powers grew and I watched her stuff it down. I watched her bury the emotions and live in the fear of what would happen if she couldn't control her powers." I looked away from Astra, closing my eyes as I remembered the nights talking with Skayla. The galas and events where I'd see her struggling to keep her shell from cracking. "And then, when it finally came out…it came out all at once. I still don't know what happened, but I wonder if maybe she hadn't isolated herself from me—if maybe I'd talked to her or if she'd let go of some of the weight on her shoulders—what would have happened instead. Something in her cracked, and the water all came out at once." I hadn't realized how much I'd spoken until I had to clear my throat from it.

"You sound like a very good brother." Astra's voice was quiet. "If she saw your thoughts, then she must have known you wanted to help. I…I'm sorry she chose not to accept it."

I had to stop from gagging. Oh yes. She had seen my thoughts. With a shudder, I tried to manage a smile, not wanting to discourage Astra. "Thank you. But the point is…maybe we can finish the training your father started…maybe you can stop hiding it like my sister did. It's not fear that destroys us, but rather what we do with it. I'd like to help you face yours."

"If you think it would help," she said at last, clearly not believing it. But that was alright for now. Perhaps I could help her believe it. If I could do that, maybe there was a point to me having woken up after all.

CHAPTER XIII: A Tale of Two Sisters

Baey:

I had done it. I'd actually done it. It had been so strange, jumping back so that the last few minutes had never happened—realizing that they never *would* happen. Part of me was ecstatic, the other part full of a dread left behind by the conversation I'd had with Estasia before leaving. She'd been the one to lead me out, and it hadn't been to give me a nice send off. Of course not. It had been so she could quietly share this newest troubling information:

"Don't tell Sven, but you need to be careful of Moira. Darby said she could get controlling. Don't let her have the watch until we're sure she will help us, alright?"

Controlling. I'd felt that desperate need in the watch, but it had been out of a place of fear—a place of helplessness that I understood, and maybe that's what scared me a little. Sven said to be myself, but what if that led to something others didn't like?

I stowed the thought away for now, focusing instead on getting through the sewers, but this time with a new ally.

The watch.

I had not been going too long when I heard the echoes of a patrol up ahead, but instead of trying to hide, I simply grabbed hold of the pendant around my neck and stopped fighting the feelings it brought with it. I accepted the helplessness and asked instead to be helped.

Again, the watch complied. It was an instantaneous change I still wasn't used to. No show, no elaborate visuals. I just…was suddenly back to where I had been a few minutes before, further up the tunnels and now able to divert my path in order to avoid the patrol. It was all just so…simple. Moira had always been touted as the most powerful of the three siblings, so it was odd to see how her power worked when compared to Skayla's or Sven's. With Sven, well, one could see the way he had displaced reality, and Skayla left behind her violet eyes. But Moira? It was untraceable.

And maybe…maybe that's why Estasia and Darby were so worried.

The rest of my journey through the tunnels was fairly unremarkable, with the exception of being forced to retrace my steps twice more because I had made a wrong turn. It was an odd thing that my body also returned to whatever state it had been at the time I returned to as well, meaning that although I had definitely spent much longer trudging through the sewers, my legs were no more tired than usual, even though my mind reminded me of how much longer the day was already feeling. It was such a strange mental dissonance.

I wasn't sure I could get used to it.

After a detour to get the required note to Illan for Estasia's meeting, I found myself at last back in The Underground. I took to the air to fly over to Alenor's forge, saving some time—an odd thought with the power I now possessed—and also allowing my wings a good stretch.

"I did it!" I announced as I landed inside the forge, coming through the gaping hole where the ceiling should have been.

Alenor was hammering away at something. She didn't hear me, so I walked forward and called louder to be heard over the noise.

A little startled, Alenor nearly dropped her hammer as she whirled around to face me, eyes widening as she processed what I'd just said.

"We're ready. I can do it," I said with conviction, smiling at the way Alenor seemed to come more alive. "We can go get Moira."

All in a moment, Alenor grabbed hold of both my arms, and I was launched into the air as she twirled me around in excitement. "I knew you could do it!"

I couldn't help but bask a little in the warmth, laughing even as some of my own feathers flew in my mouth and nearly choked me. Alenor put me hastily down and gave a rushed apology before quickly turning down the fires of her forge.

"We must go at once to Darby—we could leave tonight, even." The excitement buzzed in the air even more than the smell of ash and smoke from the forge.

"Is Estasia back yet? I wasn't sure if she made it before me?" I had to remind myself that I hadn't actually spent nearly as much time in the sewers as my mind wanted me to believe, but even so, Estasia had the advantage of being able to go more directly through the city. That being said, she hadn't left when I did.

Alenor's brow furrowed. "No, is she returning soon?"

I nodded as I helped her cool down the forge and get ready to leave. "Yes, but I don't think they're late yet. She took along Syvil and Grenedil, so it might be a little while yet." I paused and looked over to where Alenor took what looked like some sort of weapon—a small knife or something, it was hard to tell with it only having the tang and no proper handle yet. But what caught my attention was the green glow from the gem in the center of the blade. "I, uh, what are you making?"

The smile she gave was sly. "Just something for you. I still don't know if it will work. I'll let you know when it is finished."

Was that the rest of the shard from The Living Stone?

"So, to Darby? And then the plan, correct?" Alenor asked as she wiped her hands on the towel that hung by the apron she had just taken off.

I again clutched the watch around my neck. "Yes. If you're ready."

She threw the apron haphazardly on a nearby stool. "Very."

We made our way through the streets with little issue, but I found myself lingering on the drawn faces that occupied them. People who could, at any moment, be put in the line of fire if Ovok found us.

Estasia and Atlys needed to figure something out soon.

Before long, we stood in the tent, Darby welcoming us with her usual smile.

"We're ready to head for the ravine. I can control the watch." I cut to the point, eager to get going and admittedly wanting to see Darby's reaction for myself—to see what Estasia was talking about.

And there it was. I'd hoped Estasia was simply being her paranoid self, but I knew in my heart it was not so much paranoia as it was intuition. Darby's face flashed concern—and apprehension?—before she masked it behind a smile.

"Thackeray will be back shortly—we can have horses ready for tonight and you can leave for the ravine." Darby rolled up a map and handed it to me. "This is the patrol schedule as best as we've been able to predict. No one has been at the site for weeks though, so once you get clear enough of the city, you should be fine. Ferrick!"

The guard popped his head inside.

"Send for Thackeray. Tell him we're ready to ride tonight."

I rode the horse but not because I wanted to. I would have much rather felt the wind in my wings than have them struggle to stay awkwardly tucked close around another animal. The fear of having them somehow get tangled up between its legs was a fear I would never shake, but we needed the extra horse for Moira.

The night wind rushed against my face, still pretty warm and pleasant. Alenor, Thackeray, and I had been able to get away from the city with little issue; and I hadn't even had to use the watch. It was weird: Half of me was still afraid to, and the other half of me itched to use it whenever possible. I couldn't tell how much of it was me and how much of it was coming from the relic, but it left me wondering again about Estasia's warning and what kind of person Moira would turn out to be.

It wasn't long before the sun peeked above the trees, and only a little longer before we stood in front of the ravine, the horses having been tied back in the shelter of the trees.

Barely a word had been spoken between us, not that Thackeray had ever really been prone to conversation as it was. But what was really keeping the silence, perhaps, was the twisted ground in front of us; the carnage left from Sven's confrontation with Skayla and our escape. Half-formed buildings lay both out of the ground and in it, like reality itself had been displaced and then incorrectly reordered, much worse than it had been in The Underground and even Alkemar, with pieces of debris hanging suspended in the air, floating unnaturally.

"Alright. Well, let's get to it, then." Alenor took a step towards the ravine's edge, being the first to break the spell this deserted place had set over us.

"I'll keep watch from up here," Thackeray confirmed the plan we had set, but I appreciated the reminder. I'd seen enough harm from lack of communication.

Both Alenor and I nodded, and I grabbed hold of Alenor under her arms and flew us both down to the bottom of the ravine, clumsily landing and barely keeping her and me from tumbling over. I really hoped Syvil could help me with my flying some more. I'd been trying to get better at carrying people, but I still couldn't manage to land.

"You alright?" I asked as I brushed myself off.

Doing the same, Alenor gave a strained smile and a quick nod, instead asking, "Can you feel her?"

I closed my eyes, trying to listen to the watch. I...yes, I could feel Moira, painfully so. I felt the watch reaching out to her and I followed it, reaching out with my mind and hoping to pull her out so we could see her.

236

"Mother? Mother what are you—Father. He—help!"

I snapped my eyes open to see the ghostlike figure of Moira, flickering in and out of focus as she stood in front of us. Just as Alenor reached out for her, however, Moira blinked out of existence.

I forced myself to ignore Alenor's desperation, and instead reached out again with the watch. I was in control…. I could change how things were. I felt drawn forward, something pulling at my soul and urging my mind forward. I almost didn't register my feet moving until I brushed past Alenor, or at least what I guessed was her—my eyes were closed. They were closed because…because I could see *it*. I could see this place as it had been over a decade ago, and I had to go where the watch had been broken. There was a crack—a crack I could perhaps slip inside. That was how Moira was able to materialize, I was sure of it.

I dared not open my eyes, afraid the clear mental image would vanish and I would lose the connection to it. I had to stay in control—I needed to get inside the crack. Everything in front of my mind's eye was clouded and shifting; the rocks, the ground…but one thing stood out, cracked like glass shining brightly, like some ugly scar of light.

I reached my hand forward, not even daring to breathe as I saw my own hand reaching forward to touch it. I could almost forget my eyes were closed.

A strange sensation rippled up my arm and through me as my hand came into contact with the splintered rip in the fabric of time, and for a moment, it felt as if my entire body was being bent and contorted into fitting through the small tear.

"Who are you?" The voice echoed around me as I caught my breath.

I leaned over, gasping for breath and trying to settle my trembling body. I found myself staring at my feet, for there was no ground beneath it, only a misty white light. "I—I—" I swallowed bile as I quickly straightened, finding myself face-to-face with Moira.

It was then I realized my eyes were no longer closed, because they were wide in a mixture of confusion and panic.

Calm down, Baey. You're in control, I repeated to myself, hand going to the watch around my neck as I took several shallow breaths.

"I'm Baey. I'm here to save you." I should have thought more about what I was going to say, because I really hated how that sounded coming out of my mouth. Estasia probably would have choked…choked or laughed at me.

Moira—who looked very much like a real person now and nothing like a ghost—just stared, eyes glued to where I grasped the watch.

Her watch.

"How did you—it doesn't matter. Give me the watch. I need to get us out of here. Please." She reached out for it, and I shrugged back.

"That might break the connection and leave me stranded with you or gone. Let me get you out of here first, and your mother and Sven can explain everything." I felt like I was doing a horrible job of not sounding incredibly suspicious.

"Mother? Sven? Where are they?" She again took a step closer, desperation etched deeply in every line of her face.

I couldn't help but think how much younger she looked than I had expected her to. It had been hard to make out when she'd been so hazy and out of focus as that ghost, but now I realized she looked early twenties, maybe even younger than Estasia, but certainly younger than Sven.

Snap out of it.

"Try and take my hand." I extended it out, afraid that, at any moment, the strange world in front of me would disappear, and Moira with me.

Moira hardly even hesitated, grabbing my hand like a lifeline.

I closed my eyes again, trying to see the tear that had been there only a moment before.

"Just go back to where you last remember—there's no tear, you fixed it when you entered the Eternalis," Moira said, still sounding panicked. "Just go back."

I gritted my teeth and opened my eyes to her terror-filled gaze, trying to keep my composure. I needed to breathe. I needed to be in control.... I thought back to the moment before I closed my eyes and found myself recalling it with startling clarity. I could remember how every strand of Alenor's hair lay on her head; every thought that had gone through my head.

Go there. I'm in control.

I blinked, and there we were, standing before a panicked Alenor who had just watched her daughter disappear before her eyes.

Someone let go of my hand.

"M-m-mother?" Moira stumbled forward, dropping to her knees.

Alenor stood there, frozen for a moment as tears trickled down her cheek. Then she rushed forward, wrapping her child in an engulfing embrace as they cried together.

Reunited at last.

Kearn:

Gvar was right, it really was a little too late to be second-guessing, but I'd just never been this terrified and unsure of myself, or at least, not in a long while.

"We are almost out of time, Captain, and you're telling me you are going to be unable to accompany me tonight?" Atarah stood in front of his desk, already dressed in his usual sewer-going attire.

"Well, I am sure you will have a much easier time navigating the sewers without me, Lord Atarah. At least, according to you." I kept my hands folded neatly behind my back as I held his stare.

He matched my composure. "I suppose this is true." He threw a hand up and waved me away. "Do what you want. If Lord Kovo's little house guest asks me where you've been, I will all too happily explain."

Havirax, that stupid lackey who was lurking about the palace, snooping where he didn't belong. We'd been on high alert since he'd appeared, and I could only hope he hadn't seen Yelsi when he'd checked the secret spot behind the brick for a response to my last note.

"Oh, he will understand when I give my reasons," I smiled brittlely, hoping the man wouldn't catch my bluff. I was trying to get him to think I was investigating him, but in truth, I worried more by the hour that he was all too aware of what a good job *he* was doing of straining my already shaky relationship with Ovok.

Lord Atarah's expression flickered away from the smugness, eyes narrowing to hide the hint of worry I was sure I'd seen. "Don't cross me."

"I do not play games of deceit, Lord Atarah." I instinctively defended myself, still displeased with his very obvious blanket judgment of my people. Then I remembered I was, in fact, playing a very dangerous game of lies right now.

"Yes, I suppose that's true. Your kind don't bother hiding your sins in the dark, do you?" The response was cold.

As much as I bristled at the remark, this man was way too powerful to antagonize any further. But while I had met plenty of nobles with poor opinions on the Bethynese, it didn't make their hypocrisy any easier to live with.

"Well, at least we do not pretend to be what we are not." I tried to keep the edge out of my reply, but decided it was best to cut off any further conversation before I lost my head too much. "Good day, Lord Atarah. And good luck in the sewers."

With that, I turned on my heels and exited the room and his house, resisting the urge to tell him what I really thought of him and all his ambition and greed.

I didn't dare collect myself until I was on the street again, freed from the halls of the insufferably pristine mansion. The one Lord Atarah had been gifted for selling out his own kin. For the way he and the rest of the world despised Bethynese, I found it utterly hilarious how they had been so quick to turn against each other. Say what you would, but we weren't traitors.

I winced. Well. Usually not. It wasn't the same…. I didn't care about money. Only my brother.

"Sir?" Yelsi snapped to attention, awaiting the next part of our mission. I still worried he'd been followed after picking up the note this morning, but Paylos and Lairn had been diligently on the lookout.

"Yes." I gave Yelsi a short nod and went to mount the horse he had been watching, waiting for him to mount his own before we took off into the streets.

We were to meet in an old warehouse—one that belonged to none other than Atarah. I had guessed this was a play by Lord Atlys to make it seem like I was investigating the ignorant tool of a noble.

It was dangerous to be out in Alkemar so close to evening if you were in Bethynese uniform, so we had both chosen to wear plain overcoats. Thankfully, this was a temporarily acceptable move, allowed by Grand General Brahj.

Right. Because he had arrived this afternoon. I sighed, frustrated at the early arrival and knowing I really didn't have much time left. The executions would be starting soon, and I didn't know what I'd do if I had to participate. Already there was friction between his men and General Reth's, but that was expected. They had…very different ways of getting things done, and the grand general had always hated General Reth's nuanced approach.

After about an hour of riding around to make sure we didn't have anyone tailing us, Yelsi and I headed for the warehouse, which was closed down for apparent repairs. I took one of our lanterns and left Yelsi to guard the horses outside, quietly slipping in through a door that was already unlocked. I hoped that was because of Atlys and his lackeys and not because this was a trap.

The interior of the place made it clear it was meant for airship maintenance and assembly, with enormous parts littering the space—many still in their labeled shipment boxes. The darkness engulfed the light of my lantern, leaving me feeling more exposed than ever.

"Kearn?" The voice split the air and my nerves, immediate recognition of who it belonged to drowning out the alarm bells in my head. I turned around to see two shadowy figures under one of the awnings of the second story walkway.

"Jay?" I whispered, coming a step closer and wishing I could reach out a hand.

And then there he was, stepping into my light with an evident limp. The woman—I remembered her as the one who had been disguised as an inspector when we'd first docked the airship—came with him, offering an arm for support. But Jay didn't take it—of course he wouldn't.

"Are you alright?" His voice was weaker than from before his injury, but still stronger than the last time I'd heard it. Stronger, and full of worry.

I managed a nod, unable to look away from the pale face of my brother. It was the whole reason I was in this mess…and the only reason I was still alive. "For now," I choked out. "But I don't know how long that will last."

The worry in Jay's eyes deepened. It was strange the way he didn't try to hide it, and it almost made *me* want to hide, knowing I was causing it. "You need to get out of there, Kearn. Tell us where Skayla is and we'll keep you safe."

"I—but how are you going to get her out?" I asked.

The woman standing beside Jay huffed. "That would be something we could perhaps answer if you gave us the information."

Right. I hadn't dared even to write it down, afraid that Havirax was going to search my pockets somehow when I wasn't looking and find what I'd been up to. "She was moved. That's how we found her. She had been in the lowest part of the dungeon—apparently, she was being watched by soldiers from General Reth, who was the one overseeing that ravine outside the city until...whatever happened there. But Ovok had her moved to the west wing. She's on the top floor and third room down. And then Grand General Brahj arrived today and had his personal guard take over, as most of General Reth's top soldiers had been killed by..." I didn't know how to feel, trailing off. Killed by The GhostMaker during the battle at the ravine a few months ago. He was on their side now, which was good for them...but that meant more Bethynese soldiers would die. People I'd known. People who had accepted me. But then again, I'd watched Jay's friend be killed right in front of him by Ovok. We all just kept killing each other, didn't we?

Jaythos looked troubled. "Has...has there been any sign of others being as discontented as the rest of your group was?"

I pressed my lips tightly together, letting a tense shrug escape before I replied, "It's hard to tell. General Reth might be behaving oddly, in all honesty, but I'm not quite sure why. Those left under his command have been close with my soldiers, as we have spent time in the same unit before. I do know Gvar said there have been murmurs. I don't know how long that will last with Grand General Brahj in the city now, though. You know he's a brute and…Ovok has put him in charge of putting down riots by executing any who participate."

There was a moment of uneasy silence.

"You need to tread carefully, Captain," the woman said. "Your behavior won't go unnoticed for long."

"Yes. Well, I think that Lord Atarah is doing a plenty good job sowing doubt about me. I am supposed to find your hiding spot with him before the end of the week." I looked from the woman back to Jay, who understood what that would mean quite clearly.

He turned to the woman. "He needs to pull out *now*."

"No!" What had overcome me? I pretended like I didn't know. Like I wasn't suddenly desperate to prove to Jay I could be like him—that I could repay what he'd done for me. "I will see it through."

They both stared at me.

"Yelsi caught the whispers of the guards. Skayla is full-blown catatonic. Her relic or whatever has been completely destroyed and she has no power. Ovok clearly still wants her alive, though; otherwise she'd be dead, so what if he is trying to use The Living Stone to help her return to full power? Tell me what you want with her, and I'll do it. Then pull me out. But I need to know pulling out means safety. I need to know you'll actually have the back of some soulless Bethynese soldiers." I glared at the woman. "Because I'm very aware that's all we are to most. Despite the fact that everyone bowed to Skayla in their own way."

The silence stretched on for a long while, my brother's jaw working back and forth and the woman standing motionless beside him. She was impossible to read.

"So why?" The question filtered through the air. "Give me a reason to keep you safe—besides your brother. Why am I wrong to doubt you?"

"Because it was about survival. No one in Bethyn has done anything but that for a long time. We didn't want to be on anyone's side, but the Council of Generals decided for us. Better to have the illusion of a choice and keep some semblance of dignity." I took a deep breath. "But my brother almost got killed trying to save me. I don't want to see that again. So let me ask you something…" I looked away for a moment, trying to calm the emotions boiling inside. "Am I simply your puppet? Or are we allies? Are you going to do your best to protect my soldiers and me, or are you going to leave us to die like Ovok did back in the mountain?"

The woman laughed dryly. "Even if I wanted to, my friends would never let me. You're stuck with us, and I don't intend on *anyone* getting caught. We're not friends, and I have no desire to pretend to be. But you've proved your motives, and for that, I will return the favor."

I didn't miss the way Jaythos looked surprised, raising an eyebrow as he glanced at the woman with some form of amusement.

She did not return any humor. "If you're intent on staying, then I'll give you a location to find in the sewers. It's somewhere that was evacuated by one of our spies a while ago. It used to be a smaller hideout of sorts. That might help buy you some time and Ovok's favor while we organize an extraction plan for you. We're going to have you kill Skayla, and then we are going to get you out of there. Don't make me regret this."

CHAPTER XIV: License to Kill

Estasia:

It was settled. Kearn was to get us the guard schedule for Skayla's door, and then we would contact him with the official extraction plan. In the meantime, I'd given the Bethynese captain the location of Temorn's old evacuated hideout to hopefully buy him some time and credibility. I just needed one last thing.

Sven's permission for something.

"You will take care of him, right?" I was still not used to this Jaythos, the one that wore so much more of his heart on his sleeve. Not that I'd known him very well before, but he had definitely changed.

Perhaps we all had.

"Of course I will, I'm not a monster," I rolled my eyes as we stood in the vestibule of Alenor's manor. "Just stay here, and I'll handle the rest." Even if I was trying to figure out if The Underground would cooperate having Kearn and his soldiers hiding with them down there. They seemed hardly able to tolerate Sven as it was, but there were too many under Kearn's command to fit in this manor, crowded as it already was. He'd said he had about twenty still under his command that had survived the mountain collapse in Rugo. "And remember, everything that has gone wrong has gone wrong because I wasn't there. So forgive me if I find your lack of trust a little insulting," I added just as Marion entered the foyer.

"Went that well?" she asked, eyebrow arched.

Jaythos went for the stairs. "Where's Maeko?" he pretended as if he hadn't heard the question.

"With Tanner." Marion sounded a bit displeased.

Jaythos disappeared upstairs without another word. Marion, meanwhile, turned back to me. We didn't know each other too well, but she had done well caring for our allies. My...friends? I didn't care for Maeko—and I hardly knew Tanner—but Jaythos had been the first to accept Sven, and the only one to seem to understand his position. Perhaps we didn't know each other well, but out of everyone from Valdon, Jaythos was the one I would actually expect to have my back.

"Thank you for getting him back safely." Strangely enough, it was Marion who spoke, even though the words sounded as if they could have come from my mouth.

Not that "thank you" was ever my style.

I shrugged. "He was a pain, trust me. He seems to have recovered well, though." I dipped my head in acknowledgement.

Her mouth, meanwhile, tilted upwards in a smile. "Yes. Baey has also been very helpful in getting him to cooperate."

I waited a moment for her to ask what had happened at the meeting, but no prying came. I wondered if she just expected to hear it all from Jaythos later, and I decided that out of all our new acquaintances, she was the least likely to give anything away. After what I'd heard, I was seriously beginning to think the two Drogan allies we'd acquired along the way were more reliable than the human ones.

"Jaythos can fill you in later," I settled for the reply, then asked, "Where's Sven?"

Marion motioned with her head to the door behind her. "In the usual room, though he and Astra did do a bit of training in Alenor's tunnel earlier. Make of that what you will, but I did not sense any of her Gifting. Sven did successfully hide it, if that's what they were training with."

I relaxed but only a little. Marion had been the one to update me as regularly as possible on the threat of Ovok being able to find Astra. From what Marion said, Sven hid Astra's Gifting well, and most of Syvil's sensitivity was due to the recent trauma of dying.

"I'm going to go check on Jaythos and make sure you didn't cause him to strain anything. Let me know if there is anything else I should know." With that, Marion headed for the stairs.

I let the silence hang before turning towards the next hurdle: Getting Sven's blessing in assassinating his sister....

The sitting room was quiet, but with these two, quiet was not uncommon.

"You two put funerals to shame," I commented as I entered to find Sven in his usual chair and Astra by the window.

What I didn't expect from Sven was the visual reaction of...humor? I probably only caught it because even just the slight narrowing of his eyes was enough to change his usual troubled expression.

"Have you even been to a funeral before?" he asked, skeptical. More unexpected emotions.

"No. No, I have not." I smiled slyly, trying to play into the seemingly good mood he was in. Maybe he was finally starting to recover.

Was that? A laugh? Or was it just a cough? It was so quick I couldn't tell. But then, as all things did with Sven, the mood passed quickly, and he sobered, asking, "So how did it go?"

With all his memories back, I'd rather expected there to be a bigger shift in his personality. Like he would be magically more like the great Watcher with the charming smile I always used to hear about. I hadn't expected him to stay so much the same: gentle but weary. Well, at least, mostly the same. It was nice to see a bit more humor and life finally creeping in. Too bad I was about to undo some of that. The guilt nagged at me, no matter how I tried to ignore it.

I realized how late it was, and that it was pretty odd that both Sven and Astra were still up. He'd been waiting for me, hadn't he? With a sigh, I resigned myself to the fate of what this conversation would bring.

"We know where she is." I knew it didn't make much of a difference, but I didn't want to say her name. I didn't want to have to make this any more personal for him.

He waited in silence, and I was all too aware of not just his eyes on me, but the strange girl's as well. I didn't like saying things in front of Astra, so I decided not to explain anything about the details of the meeting. Instead, I stuck to the one thing I needed his approval for.

"We want to kill her."

"Do you have a plan?" Somehow, the eye contact was more unnerving than the way he usually avoided it. I didn't think I'd ever get used to those golden eyes. Somehow, they were almost as unnerving as Skayla's violet ones.

"Yes," I answered, feeling uncomfortable in a way only Sven could make me. "Just finishing the extraction side of things."

"Alright."

"Just like that?" I found myself suddenly…indignant.

"You don't need my permission, Estasia. But if you want it, you have it completely. I've failed to kill her three times now. I don't know what you expected me to say," he answered flatly.

Somehow, even with the realization of how silly this all sounded, I only grew more indignant. "But—but I'm about to order your sister *killed*, Sven. Don't you care?"

"Do you need my permission, Estasia?" His simple question only fed my frustration.

"What? No, I'm going to do it anyway. I just thought you would be upset." I crossed my arms, frowning at him and wishing he'd show something other than this weird sympathy.

But the sad smile was so much worse. "If you need my permission, you have it. I can take responsibility."

My face twisted up in a blend of disbelief and anger. "Would you stop it?" I threw up my hand. "I don't need you to take responsibility for anything, you idiot. I just wanted to make sure you were alright with me *murdering* your sister. Clearly you are, so I don't know what I was worried about."

"But you're not."

I froze. "What?"

Again, that stupid look that made me want to throttle him…or fix everything so he could smile and be *happy* for once.

251

"Have you ever killed anyone, Estasia?"

"I..." I couldn't find the words, my mouth stuck half-open as I desperately tried to run from the realization. "Stop it. Just stop it."

He looked away. Then, staring at the mantelpiece, he said, "It's alright."

"Look, you imbecile, I'm not even going to be the one killing her. I'm just g-giving the o-order," The unexpected sputtering was enough to make me want to scream. "Just stop it, alright?!"

The silence that filled the room was unsettling, and I hated it almost as much as Sven's earlier eye contact.

Almost.

"I'm sorry, Estasia. You shouldn't have to do this." He looked again in my general direction, but not in the eyes. "It shouldn't be your responsibility in the first place. But you have my permission. You aren't making the decision alone. It's alright."

"No. It's not." I clenched my fists. "Nothing about the last fifteen years of my life has been alright, and somehow, I'm choosing this moment to cave? I've wanted that woman dead and in the ground for half my life. Now I'm trying to find an excuse to be able to say it was someone else's idea when I don't even have to do the stupid thing myself." Why did my chest feel so tight?

"I'd be more worried if it didn't bother you."

I wasn't expecting that to almost break me, but it did. I could only be thankful instead for the sudden reminder that Astra was also in the room, and I didn't feel like giving away any more free emotion to a stranger than I already had. I straightened my shoulders, unable to resist throwing a cynical look her way. I rather wished I hadn't, either, finding a very similar expression on her face to what Sven's wore.

"Look. Just stop it with the sympathy. Congratulations, I'm not happy about it, but I'll be happier once the witch is dead. I'm glad you don't have a problem with it, and I'll let you know as soon as it's followed through." I crossed my arms once again. "I don't need your pity."

"It's not pity, Estasia." Sven's tone was even as he replied. "It's empathy."

I swallowed hard. "Yeah. I know. I'm sorry."

Bowing his head, Sven asked, "So was there anything else you needed?"

I wanted to say more, but I wasn't really sure how to form the words. Instead, I decided to be thankful for the opportunity to change the subject, and taking a deep breath, I turned to Astra. "Marion said you two were practicing in the tunnels?"

"Yes," Sven replied simply.

I narrowed my eyes. "Any reason?" Not that I was complaining. Sven needed the distraction.

"To help." It was Astra who replied. "I'm not sure I will be much use, but I would like to try."

"Alright, good. Can you control that power of yours?" I asked. "Because that would help a lot."

Astra winced.

"Give me a few days. I think she'll be just fine," Sven interjected with a confidence he rarely showed.

I couldn't help but smile at it. "Good. Because after we get Skayla out of the way, Ovok is the next step."

Sven:

"Alright, let's try this," I said as I closed the tunnel door behind us. I hadn't gotten much sleep last night after Estasia's visit—which had already been far into the evening as it was—and I was having trouble focusing on anything between awaiting news about Moira and, now, news of Skayla's death.

"Are you certain you can contain it?" The small voice asked.

"I doubt it would be worse than when you first arrived," I said, waving my hand as I set us in our own little space of reality. I added a little visual illusion for Astra's sake, making the dome visible and everything outside its perimeters blacked out so she could see the detachment from the actual world around us. It seemed to work, her shoulders dropping a little.

Rolling both my shoulders and trying to push every other problem out of my head, I announced, "Alright. So I think we should try and figure out exactly what it is your ability does."

"I don't know." Astra's reply was quiet. "The only thing I have consistently done with it is cause destruction."

"But you said you are able to heal as well? How does that work?" I pressed, finding it best to keep her mind moving…like mine.

"I'm not even trained in that, either. My father says I'm not even supposed to do it—I could have killed Louko. It takes a great understanding of how the body is put together and how it works, he says. I probably only knew enough because of…Tyron."

Aware of the tender subject, I carefully asked, "He was a healer?"

She nodded, but I saw the way she swallowed. I didn't need to know any more.

"So then, you need to understand how something works in order to fix it," I mused aloud, struck by how similar to my Gift this sounded.

"For healing, at least," Astra replied. "I don't really know how anything else works."

"If I were to hazard a guess, it has to be something along those lines. At least on our world, Gifting is like a strength or talent. It makes sense together…. You said the source that gave you your power is in everyone on your planet? Like a life source? Then your power might have something to do with manipulating…life? Or matter? You can still use it off-world, so it does not seem like you are only manipulating this power source, itself. It must give you a natural connection to things around you. You…you caused my coat to catch fire when you arrived. Are you able to create fire?"

"According to Ven, I do that often…" There was a ghost of amusement in the comment that faded quickly.

I tilted my head. "Who?"

Cheeks flushing a little, Astra mumbled, "Louko's uncle. He…he is a little like your friend Estasia."

"I see. Well, let's see if you can make some of that fire, ah?" I asked, trying to find a balance of listening without letting her get stuck in a pit of her own thoughts.

Concern etched her brow. "But I might catch you on fire again."

"Oh, don't worry about that." I clicked my fingers and my coat caught fire at the edges, only for me to wave a hand and make it disappear moments later. "I am quite safe. The perks of bending reality. In this small, controlled area, it is very easy for me to control what happens, because it will all go back to how it was before when we are done here."

Still looking uncertain, Astra let out an "Alright," and looked down at her hands. Concentration slowly overtook her, and a good five minutes passed by before she sighed and said, "I don't…really know how. I've not really done it on purpose before."

If nothing else, this forced me to let every other thought go, focusing only on how to help Astra. It eased the guilt and the anxiety of waiting to hear about my sisters. "Try and focus the energy inside of you—I feel it, at least, so I'm sure you can as well. For me, picturing how something acts and behaves helps. Maybe try and think of the way fire is made— the energy and heat created by the splintering of flint and steel."

Astra didn't say a word, only frowning and looking back at her hands. Another few minutes came and went, and then suddenly, flames burst from her palm, sputtering to life as embers jumped across the floor and over to me.

Eyes wide, Astra stepped back, startled, only feeding the flame and causing it to explode even more, leaping from her hand and beginning to engulf the room.

I instantly put it out, and we were left blinking and readjusting to the dim light in absence of the roaring flame.

Astra's hands were trembling. "I-I'm sorry. That's what happens—it's always too much, too strong. I can't control it."

"It's alright. You did great, Astra. I told you; you won't hurt me. See? I'm fine." I spun around to prove it.

She did not appear very convinced.

"I don't want to hurt you." The whisper was so full of anguish, it hurt.

"Astra," I bent over a little to be more at her eye level. "I swear on my life. I won't let you hurt anyone. Do you trust me?"

"I…" Her eyes darted away and back to me. "I believe you think you can."

"I think that, perhaps, is some of your problem," I said gently. "I can't be the only one thinking that. The only times my Gift has gotten out of control is in those moments where my anger…or fear…were greater than my sense of control. You are so afraid of what might happen that it just keeps happening, Astra. Remember the water. Control does not come from suppression. It comes from following the path of the river instead of fighting against it. You cannot change where it runs, only use it in its path. You need to trust the path of the river, and trust the ones helping you through it. I understand the stakes are usually too high for you to take the risk and try anything else. But this place," I motioned to the dome surrounding us in the tunnel, "is meant to be the one place you *can* take risks. Watch—I'll show you." I took another step back. "Stay exactly where you are."

After I was sure she understood and was at least a little calmer, I pointed to the floor, allowing a large crack to slowly spread until it separated her and myself. It widened, plunging down into the darkness of oblivion, similarly to how I'd shown Baey my powers. Then I raised both my hands and brought them forcefully down, causing the ceiling and walls within our dome to crack and crumble, suddenly melting away like ash in the breeze. All around us was not darkness, but a shapeless green light, the crack below our feet now gone and replaced with nothing. For a moment, I remembered just how much damage I had caused in the last battle with Skayla, and I was forced to take my own advice. I had to allow the river to run. I had to just…let everything else go. Astra needed this, and maybe I did, too. I looked over at her to find her eyes wide with wonder, and then with a click of my fingers, the protective dome disappeared, and everything returned to its original state.

"See? It will all come back whenever I lower the dome. I swear it."

She didn't say a word, instead looking around in awe at the tunnel, untouched and still very much in its original state.

"Are you ready to try again?" I asked.

Slowly, she turned back around and swallowed hard. "Alright."

I clicked my fingers again, and the dome reappeared, once more setting us away from everything else.

Astra closed her eyes and opened her palms, breathing deep and steady. The fire reappeared much quicker this attempt, and again, Astra jumped a bit in instinctual fear. With it, the fire blazed, but this time…this time she stopped herself, and I couldn't help but smile. For a long while, she just watched the fire dancing on her hand until it slowly shrunk down to the size and intensity of a candle's flame.

"There you go," I whispered. "Just like that."

She continued to watch, fascinated as she let the fire flicker, then weave through her fingers and along her wrist. She was controlling it.

"Good, Astra."

"I…" Her brow furrowed. "I can feel its energy. You're right…it…it mirrors mine, I think. It's almost…like when I heal. When I feel every muscle in a person's body and every…" she trailed off, and the flame vaporized into nothing. Her eyes were almost bright. But it faded quicker than the fire had.

"Are you alright?" I dared ask, recognizing the guilt in the expression.

"I always learn too late." She winced. "Maybe if I hadn't been afraid, Keeshiff would…." Her voice trailed off into a faint echo that ran through the tunnel.

"I understand. You were close to him?" I asked. The pain in her words and expression had been so clear I almost felt them as my own. Perhaps because I struggled with it myself.

"Yes. His brother is…Louko. My best friend." There was a deep, shaking breath as she folded her hands in front of her, looking down at them. "He was some of the only family Louko had left. Louko was captured, and we had to split up to try and get him back. Keeshiff went to the frontlines." She gave a taut shrug. "There was a spy. I sent a warning, but I should have gone myself. Keeshiff walked right into an ambush." Her voice was thick when she finished, "They said he didn't die right away. If…if I had just gotten there sooner, maybe Louko would still have his brother. But I didn't."

It all sounded so familiar. But it was not time for me. "It sounds like you did all you could, Astra. Keeshiff wouldn't want you to continue to suffer. Not when he isn't anymore." If only I could take my own advice. The very thing I was telling Astra to do now was the same thing I'd been fighting with myself.

Astra's eyes welled with tears as she looked up at me. "But how can you know that? What if it's not like that—what if he's still scared and never gets to know that his brother is safe?"

I took a deep breath, facing what I had been willfully ignoring since I'd woken up. "Because I've been there. And it's peaceful, the end. He's alright now."

Her gaze was fixed on mine, expression nearly desperate. "You've been there? And you're certain?"

"Yes." In all honesty, I still didn't understand the voice that had sent me back. I hadn't really been much use since returning. "But apparently someone thought I was better off alive." I was veering off my goal. "It was a peace I could never completely explain."

Astra seemed to absorb this slowly. She finally looked away, one hand returning to her wrist. "Did you want to stay there?" she asked quietly.

I gave a strange, half-hearted laugh; I didn't completely understand. "Honestly...yes."

"Why did you come back, then?" She looked around the dim tunnel. "Why trade peace for all of this?"

I struggled to stay in control of the emotions this conversation brought up. "Part of me knew I didn't deserve it. Not yet. But part of me thought my friends still needed me." Even if it had turned out that bit wasn't true.

"And of course, there was the usual ominous, ethereal voice telling me it wasn't my time yet." I smiled ruefully.

Astra only looked more sad. "*Thought* your friends needed you?"

I waved my hand dismissively, realizing I'd let myself slip. "Don't mind my complaints."

Uncertainty returned to Astra's face. Then it faded. "I have not been here long, but it has been long enough to see how your friends all look to you. And if you were willing to give up that peace for them, I understand why. They all seem to know why you are still needed here."

It seemed more like I needed them. But it wasn't the time for me—I should have been more careful with my words. I attempted a nod that would hopefully look more convincing than it felt. "Well, hopefully my purpose will include helping to get you home." Maybe then I could fool myself into thinking I had any use besides death.

Astra did not appear convinced. "Perhaps your friends don't need a purpose from you. Perhaps they just need *you*. If you, as you say, do not deserve to die, doesn't that mean you deserve to live?"

"That is the trick, isn't it?" I shook my head and grimaced. It was a possibility I was more terrified of than anything. It meant letting go of so much. "I suppose we'll find out after this."

Her gaze dropped to the floor. "I suppose we will," she murmured.

Both of us stood there in silence, too afraid to be hopeful of such a thing, but neither willing to deny the possibility. I realized now that she was wondering just as much about herself as she had been on my behalf. Perhaps, if it would help her to live, I could try it. More and more, I found myself invested in this child. Whatever happened, she needed to get home alive.

Astra started rubbing the scars at her wrists, then seemed to realize what she was doing and stopped, looking back at me. "Sorry. I did not mean to overstep. Should we try again?"

I felt a twinge of guilt at how I'd managed to get *her* so worried, but—for the first time—chose to ignore it, realizing it would only make her feel worse. "You never have to apologize to me, Astra," I replied evenly, working to keep my tone light after such a heavy conversation. "Perhaps we can experiment, too. You said you can feel every muscle in a person's body...can you do the same with inanimate objects? It must be the energy that creates an image for you of how it is made."

Astra squared her shoulders and said, "Let's try it."

We were at it for at least another two hours before I decided it was time to take a break, but Astra's confidence had seemed to grow exponentially in that time. We had deduced that her Gift definitely revolved around energy and the ability to manipulate it, and that because of it, that meant her emotions often caused a direct reaction with the energy around her and the fight-or-flight instinct.

We were getting places, and it was nice to see any emotion besides fear on the girl's face. I wondered if maybe our conversation had also helped.

The rest of the afternoon, however, was spent in relative quiet. As usual, no one from upstairs really wandered down, and I was stuck feeling torn between two worries: One, that Baey would not be able to save Moira; and two, that killing Skayla was either the wrong move or a trap.

"I'm sorry about your sister," Astra offered suddenly. The sun had gone down, and we were both sitting idly, waiting for a good reason to brave going to bed.

I found myself unsure of how to reply. "She…is complicated," I said at last. I'd almost forgotten Astra had been present during the conversation with Estasia.

Astra nodded slowly. "Complicated," she echoed quietly. "It's always harder when it's the ones we loved."

"Yes, yes, it is." I shook my head, not having expected her reply. "Makes it difficult to know how to feel about it, doesn't it?" Running a hand over my face, I tried desperately to clear my head, wondering if perhaps I should make myself some tea.

Astra pulled her gaze from the darkened window, brow furrowed in apparent uncertainty. "How do you feel about it?"

There she went again, turning things to me and trying to help. I had a feeling the least I could do for now was give her something in return after all she'd been giving. "I'm not sure. Skayla…I told you a little of her the other day, if you remember. Her ability was similar to Tanner's, but instead of memories, she could see right into your mind as it was in the moment—and without touching you. And then, it turns out, she could control you as well. She used it to do some…awful things. Things I still can't forgive myself for doing." I swallowed hard.

Sorrow settled over Astra's expression like a deep shadow. "You cannot forgive yourself, even though it was not you?"

I winced. "I…it was, to a degree. She took my mind and played with me like I was some toy. I was able to break out eventually, just not soon enough. If I was able to get away eventually, it just means perhaps I was able to all along." I paused, realizing how much I sounded like Astra from earlier, desperately explaining how she should have been able to save her friend. "I suppose you aren't the only one wondering about the 'soon enoughs'."

Astra was studying me closely, blue eyes full of painful understanding. Long seconds ticked away on the mantel clock before she asked, "Do you think it's our fault? All the ones we lost?"

"I—" Something broke a little inside me, and I found myself blinking my now watering eyes. "It shouldn't be." It felt so strange, the conflict that bled out from inside of me. I wanted to tell her it wasn't her fault, but the way she had lumped us together proved it would be impossible to convince her of such if I didn't also believe it, myself. "Maybe I've wanted it to be my fault because having no control over all of it sounds so much more terrifying." I was looking out into nothing as I processed it. "Maybe we both are just too afraid to let the river lead us. We want to believe we can tell it what to do. Maybe we just don't want to believe these sorts of things can happen to good people, and so convince ourselves that we just…we just can't be good."

"So it's all for nothing, then?" Astra's voice wavered. "All the pain and grief and…. If it wasn't our fault, then there was no reason for it at all…then it means nothing?"

I frowned, desperately trying to process this all. "I…I think it means it's not our responsibility. Maybe it's only for nothing if we let it consume us."

Astra looked back out the window. "I'm not sure that I know how to keep it from doing so," she admitted softly.

"I don't know either," I whispered back. I thought of Darby and Baey, how they kept trying to reach me—to convince me I was worth anything more than what Skayla had tried to make me. "Perhaps we start by listening to the ones who keep trying to tell us otherwise."

We sat in silence after that, both ruminating on it all. I was scared. Scared to think half of what I'd said was actually true. Scared to think of what might come next. But there was that small part of me that hoped maybe there was more than just the overwhelming guilt and weight of memories. If not for my sake, then at least for whatever Astra had endured. I understood now why Grenedil had so easily come to trust her, and I promised myself that no matter what, we would get her back to her family.

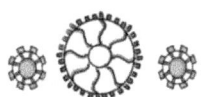

I vaguely remembered going to bed, but quite vividly remembered being awoken the next day by the intense knocking on the door. The excited voice filtering through was Baey. "Sven! Sven, we got Moira!"

THE LAST ESMER

CHAPTER XV: Save One, Kill the Other...Right?

Baey:

The door swung open and caused me to tumble forward in a flurry of feathers, only barely catching myself from falling on top of a wide-eyed Sven.

"She's at The Underground now. We can go see her whenever you're ready."

Soon, we weren't the only ones in the hallway; Jaythos, Maeko, and Tanner were all peeking out of their respective rooms.

But Astra had been first, jumping into the hallway in a quiet panic that I'd felt guilty for causing.

"Is she alright?" Sven asked breathlessly.

I ended up giving a very ambiguous head motion instead of a nod. "She's very confused, but physically fine from what we can tell. I thought you'd want to see her as soon as you could."

He looked down the hall to Astra and said, "Get ready. We're leaving."

"Is that..." Maeko frowned, crossing his arms.

"She's fine," Sven and I replied at the same time, and I couldn't help but smile a bit.

"I...don't really have anything," Astra murmured. "I'm ready now."

Then Tanner intruded upon the conversation, looking a little more with it than he had the other day. "Moira? You...she's back?"

I kept the smile as genuine as I could, trying to hide the worry for his fragile state and wondering what might trigger it. "She's safe, yes."

There was a dark expression that settled on his face following the remark. "Be careful," came the cryptic response. That definitely wasn't helping the dread already planted in my mind.

"Alright. If you both do exactly as I say, we'll be there in no time." I tapped the glass lens of the watch around my neck and gave what I hoped was a confident-looking smile, wings twitching in excitement as I turned around and led them down the stairs.

"I came over as soon as we got back. I know it's early but I didn't think you would mind," I said as I opened the doorway to the tunnel.

"Thank you." Sven, again, sounded breathless, undoubtedly anxious to see his sister after what, twelve years? I hadn't done the math.

Both he and Astra were quiet as I led them through the tunnels, needing to backtrack a few times, as usual. But having just gone down to get them, I still had a pretty good grasp on where all the patrols were, and so didn't have to use the watch too much. It had gotten so much easier to use, at least for the small windows of time I needed it for. I wondered how far back one could go, but at the same time, I was terrified of even trying something like that. I didn't want to go back and have to try and retrace my steps exactly—what if I messed something up that caused something even worse to happen? And what if I then couldn't get back to the same point in time to try and fix it?

No. I was fine sticking to just a few minutes.

At last, we arrived to The Underground, and I hoped Sven was too preoccupied with getting to his sister to catch the usual glares. It seemed that a lot of people were even more sour at him after the whole splicing reality incident from the portal.

"Sven!" Darby was waiting outside the tent, cheeks flushed as she caught sight of us. "I'm glad you made it. She's inside." She offered a smile that didn't seem completely genuine, and I remembered why. Estasia and Darby's warning had not been forgotten.

"Darby." Sven gave a small tilt of his head and some semblance of a smile before dipping inside the tent. There was also something else behind his eyes, but I couldn't quite make out what.

"Should I…." Astra shifted her weight awkwardly from one foot to the other.

"I'll stay outside with you." I smiled. "If anything happens, I can just go back and fix it. Don't worry."

Astra nodded, folding her hands and waiting patiently with me. In all honesty, I had hoped to go in and make sure the reunion went well, but Alenor was in there, and Darby had ducked in after Sven. That was the most important.

I turned back to Astra. "He hasn't seen her in…a long time." I was so relieved. Relieved I had actually come through for him and given him a little piece of his life back—of his family back.

A look of sympathy passed over Astra's face, but she remained quiet. I couldn't imagine being with so many strangers without even one familiar face—well, except Grenedil, who she hardly saw.

Estasia came barreling into view, then, skidding to a halt in front of me and trying to catch her breath. "Sorry. I had to relay something to Atlys this morning—she's here?"

"Yes. Everything…alright?" I asked, noting the worn expression behind Estasia's usually bright eyes, and the rigidness in her shoulders.

"Yes. Planning." The way she said that meant she was *not* fine. Planning meant…had they found Skayla? I knew better than to ask more, knowing Estasia wasn't about to share everything in the middle of camp.

"Alright. Well, she's inside. Still looks…twenty-ish, which is unsettling." I turned the subject back to the present problem. "Don't worry, I'll keep the watch safe with me."

I got a thankful nod from Estasia, and then all three of us were waiting outside, awkwardly silent, although I saw the wary looks Estasia threw at Astra, and the way Astra always caught them.

What a hypervigilant, trusting bunch we were.

Alenor popped outside, looking at me. "Baey—she seems to be catching on quite quickly. She was wondering if she could have her watch. I wasn't sure if that was a good idea, but said I'd ask."

Alarm bells went off pretty quickly in my brain, but I tried to keep my doubt discrete. "I don't know that it's a good idea right now. What with her still recovering."

"Right. I think she's just…a little scared after losing it got her stuck out there," Alenor replied, clearly troubled.

"You go talk. I'll stay with the tag-along." Estasia motioned to the tent.

I looked at Astra. "Will you be alright?"

Astra's uncertainty didn't exactly sell it, but her firm nod was enough to free me from waiting outside. I was beginning to feel a bit anxious at the way Moira had so quickly asked for the watch, and Estasia's pressing for me to go implied that maybe she was, too. I suddenly didn't want Moira alone without me, and yet I couldn't quite put a finger on why. I blamed Estasia for feeding doubt in my mind, but if that doubt had come from Darby...then wasn't it warranted? She'd known Moira for years, after all.

I stepped inside.

"I can't believe you haven't changed..." Sven marveled as he stared at his sister like a lost puppy. "Did time even...pass?"

Moira looked much less overwhelmed than when I'd last seen her, now sitting straight and poised in the chair and making eye contact with ease. I could still see the panic in the edge of every glance, but it was much better hidden as she got her bearings. The Maras were quite a resilient family, I had to give them that.

"I...yes and no. I knew time was passing, but it didn't feel like...years." Her voice faltered, but then she caught sight of me.

"Have you had any breakfast?" Sven asked. "You must be hungry."

"N-not yet," Moira turned her head and looked over at me. "Do you think...do you think I could have it back now? I just...I don't want to get lost again. I couldn't save..." Her gaze fell, and Alenor put a comforting hand on her shoulder.

I bit my lip, suspicion rising. Perhaps it was just the way Sven had wanted nothing to do with his ring after he'd come back, that having her so eagerly reach for it felt odd. Or maybe I needed to trust my gut. "I don't think that's a good idea right now."

"Do you think I could get some breakfast?" she asked suddenly instead, instantly dropping the subject. Alenor's hand was no longer on her shoulder.

"Yes, of course. You must be starving. I…" Sven looked around and addressed Darby sheepishly. "Might not be the best person to fetch it, though."

It was rather odd the way he acted as if it hadn't been his idea about breakfast in the first place.

"I'll go get some. You catch up." Darby ducked out of the room.

"So then…everyone else is dead?" Moira asked, her voice as fragile as Sven's smile could be.

And speaking of Sven… "Yes. As…as far as we know. Except for Darby and Thackeray. And Atlys."

"I…" Her eyes looked wet, and suspicion or not, I found myself broken for her. Just like Sven, all her friends were dead. While she'd at least had the blessing not to watch it, she instead was cursed to have a Gift that made you feel as though everything could be fixed.

"I'm sorry, darlin'." Alenor wrapped her daughter in a fierce hug, whispering. "But we're still here. And you're here now."

Moira cried into Alenor's shoulder, and Sven was left to quietly put a hand on his sister to try and help comfort her, but as always, I saw the guilt he so poorly hid. Maybe it was just me, but something about it seemed different this time. He didn't withdraw with the guilt—instead reaching forward for his sister.

Part of me wished to leave them, but the other half of me warned against it, a feeling I could neither justify nor shake.

At last, however, Moira quieted and once more squared her shoulders, asking, "So then…if this is all that's left, how are we trying to get it back?"

"A question I think Estasia and Darby are best equipped to answer," I interjected, again not wishing to share more information than necessary. Why was I less willing to share with Sven's sister than I was the stranger Astra who had shown up? Hopefully good instincts.

Sven looked up, and for a moment, appeared a little like he was going to argue, but instead nodded. "Yes. They're the ones mostly in charge. Them and Baey."

Moira locked eyes with me, having already been introduced on the ride back to Alkemar. She already knew I was the last of my kind, and she already knew I could control her watch. I hadn't explained that I could also use Sven's ring, and so she didn't have much to go on. For now, I wanted to keep it that way.

"Yes, though I have been out of the loop for a day or two with the journey to the ravine, and all," I admitted, again thinking of Estasia's uncharacteristically strained composure. I wanted to ask about her meeting with Kearn so badly.

That's when Darby re-entered, looking flustered as she said, "Cyl is poking his nose into things again," as she handed Moira a bowl of soup and placed a cup of water on a nearby table.

"Cyl?" Moira cocked her head, fingering the handle of her spoon like it was some unknowable object. Slowly, she lifted it, blew on the fairly warm looking liquid, and took a sip.

Darby and I, meanwhile, exchanged looks. I let her take the lead on this one, seeing as she was the one that had shared the original doubt in regards to Moira.

"That portal the Drogans came through all those years ago. He was the one that closed it behind them and kept it closed. He wasn't able to help us, but he had enough strength to keep Ovok from leaving to get more help. Supposedly," she added the last bit with a bit of a huff.

Again, Moira looked confused. "Supposedly?"

Darby nodded. "We don't know him very well. He only recently showed himself when the portal was disrupted."

At this, recognition seemed to dawn in Moira's eyes. "Yes. Yes, I saw it happen." She looked at Sven, eyes widening. "I saw you protect Mother...and...change things. I just couldn't get through the crack to help, and then...I always found it hard to remember the things that I would see when in the Eternalis."

I frowned. "You'd mentioned that before. The Eternalis?"

Moira bit her lip, looking a bit guarded. "It's just...what I call the space I was in."

I had begun to feel like she was reticent of sharing any of her Gifting with me, or how it worked. Unlike Sven, who had instantly jumped head first into trying to help me master it.

That being said, it had already been used against her once, by Skayla, so perhaps the doubt was a little more understandable.

They continued to talk, but Darby quietly took me aside, drawing me closer to the entrance of the tent where I could now just vaguely hear muffled arguments from Estasia and Cyl.

"I think maybe you should go out there. Cyl isn't happy about Astra or Sven being here," she whispered.

I needed no further encouragement, discreetly slipping out without anyone else even noticing.

I was greeted with a red-faced Estasia, a pale, yet almost angry looking Astra, and—as usual—a very irritated Cyl. I assumed that meant Grenedil was now the only one watching the portal. Funny how Cyl's concern over it fluctuated depending on whether he felt the need to control the rest of us more.

"Can we please take this away from the entrance?" I asked, patience for this Myrandi long since frayed.

Everyone stopped, and I motioned with a hand for us to "shoo."

For once, no one argued, and we stepped a bit away from the tent.

"I have Astra under control, Cyl. I have the watch, nothing has happened, and if something does, I will go back. What could possibly be the issue?" My wings stood stiff behind me, towering above my head in an attempt to look bigger.

"You have no way of knowing what she might be activating by being so close to The Doorway, and we might not know until it's too late. We saw how volatile she is already. And for some reason, you entrusted her to the man who turned this city inside out on a whim. Forgive me if I am a little skeptical."

"You are not here to give orders, Cyl," I hissed. "You are here to guard the portal. That's all you seem to care about, and that's all *we* care about you doing. And, might I add, it's the job you seem to be failing at doing right now—I assume you've once more given Grenedil the dirty work? Sven is more than capable of controlling both himself and Astra, and frankly, the fact Astra hasn't blown you up already speaks to the fact that I think she has a *little* more self-control than you give her credit for."

I heard a snort come from Astra and realized how bright her blue eyes were shining. I also noted the clenched fists, and hoped that Astra would continue to prove she could stay in control. I really didn't want to swallow my words, and I really didn't want to go back in time. Somehow, doing it to change the outcome with people I knew made me...uneasy. I didn't want to feel like I was using them.

"All it takes is one time, little one." Cyl's voice edged on a growl. "I've seen what mistakes can do to worlds. We're still living in the one the Maras made."

The hair on my back bristled, as did my feathers. I hated how he always called me that. "Your opinion is noted and duly ignored. Neither Astra nor Sven will be staying, and neither of them was planning on going by the precious portal. Sven has done a very good job masking Astra's Gifting—which is what I thought you were so worried about to begin with. The other Myrandi *I've* talked to claim they can't even hear her Gifting anymore. So please, enlighten me. Are you just afraid she's going to try and go back to the home you ripped her from?"

"Please stop. Both of you," Astra's voice held a quiet and unexpected authority. She turned to Cyl. "If you are worried about me destroying everything, then you are wasting your effort; Sven contained me before and can do so again if necessary. And yes, I want to go home. But even if you offered me the chance to do so this very moment, I would not take it. My family is safe—these people are not. I will not try to leave here so long as my leaving could harm them, or while I may yet have help to offer.

You have my word." Astra's eyes narrowed, her voice growing sharper. "And for someone who preaches of what one mistake can cost, you seem quick to forget that you were the one that brought me here in the first place. So stop pointing fingers when it doesn't help anyone: It only makes you look worse."

Estasia's smirk was impossible to miss, and I honestly was fighting my own at the way Cyl went silent.

"Forgive me for being careful," was all he said before turning around and leaving.

"I really hate that one." Estasia spat into the ground then turned to Astra. "Sven said he was training you? The minute you can control The Door, honestly, I would take you over that prick any day."

I gave a snort. "And that is saying something, because she hates new people."

"Shut up, Birdie."

Astra looked all too serious. "I didn't have much success at using The Door back on my world. But maybe Sven could help figure it out. I just...don't want to draw attention to anyone." She looked around, concern in all her movements as her eyes rested on some of the people moving in and out of tents in the distance.

"And that is why I would take you over Cyl," Estasia commented dryly. "Because he doesn't seem to care that much about the people. He just doesn't want Ovok to get the portal." She gave me a look that I immediately understood.

Cyl was a means to an end; the less that was shared with him, the better. Funny how Estasia cared so much about so many lives when once, not so very long ago, she had been pretty callous herself.

I liked this Estasia much better.

Kearn:

Get in, kill her, and get out. I repeated the words to myself as I calmly walked up the stairs to the next story. What if the sleeping draft hadn't worked? I had been told by Atlys the guards would be unconscious by the time I got there and, for some unknowable reason, I was deciding to trust him.

Night had fallen only about an hour ago, leaving shadows to dance against the bioluminescent lanterns lighting the passageways of the palace.

Hopefully Yelsi and the others were already gone, just as ordered. Vresh and Paylos had argued a bit about having to split up and leave at different times, but we couldn't risk leaving together. If all went as planned, Vresh would lead a group out on patrol to disappear, and then Gvar and the others I'd ordered to go with Lord Atarah tonight would vanish in the tunnels, given various coordinates by Atlys to lead them presumably to safety in the sewers.

That left just me.

At last, I came to the top of the stairs, faced with the empty hallway. Well, empty save the one guarded door.

I didn't breathe a sigh of relief at the slumped figures sitting in front of it, and as I walked over, I couldn't ignore the impulse to lean over and check their pulses.

Still strong. They were just asleep. But what would happen to them when they were discovered to have failed? Would the drugging fall on them or the kitchens downstairs?

There wasn't any time to think about it, so I grabbed hold of the keys on the one man's belt and quickly set it in the lock of the door. It creaked open with minimal objection, and I entered into a dimly lit, almost empty room. Two bioluminescent lanterns hung on adjacent walls, casting ghostly shadows on the table, chair, and a bed up against the one wall.

But I wasn't looking at any of the furniture, rather the person occupying it. The chair, to be exact.

She wasn't at all what I had expected. True, Yelsi had said she was catatonic, though I really hadn't been sure I believed it. That being said, the ghostly violet eyes were the only scrap of color on her pale, deflated frame; her hair falling loose around sallow cheeks; and an empty stare penetrating the gloom of the room better than any light.

She looked empty and strangely sad. Gone was the madwoman and her crazed laugh, leaving something far more terrifying in her wake: a ghost.

I drew my blade, the sound causing her to actually flinch—the first sign of life besides her barely audible breaths.

She blinked, staring at the sword with no expression. "Make it quick," she whispered with a voice that of someone who had forgotten how to speak.

I swallowed hard, the hair on the back of my neck standing up. Somehow…she was still incredibly creepy.

I hesitated, wondering if this was some sort of trap. Why didn't she fight? Or better yet…what had she meant? Did she…did she *want* to die?

Best not to think of it. Just do it and get out of here. I shook my head and raised my weapon, taking a deep breath as I tried to calculate the quickest way to kill this once-terrible figure who sat as a shadow before me now. The rumors were true; her mind had to have been broken.

That's when the door burst open, revealing two Bethynese soldiers that must have been unlucky enough to have seen the unconscious guards.

"What in the—" The words froze half-finished in the mouth of whoever had burst into the room behind me, and I swung around to find about three of Grand General Brahj's soldiers all standing as still as statues.

Make it quick. The words echoed in my head, but they weren't mine. I shook my head and turned around again to see Skayla still sitting in the chair. Was that…a tear?

Please.

"Are you—did you stop them?" I motioned back at the still-frozen guards. Their eyes were not violet, yet the only sign of life was breathing.

Skayla nodded slowly.

"Why?" I gripped my sword in both hands, my own breathing growing rapid as something began warring within me. I felt sincerity in the thought she shared. Make it quick. It hadn't been trying to convince me, rather just pleading for me to follow through. She…she genuinely wanted me to kill her, didn't she?

280

He wants me alive. The thought again floated in my head, and I shook violently.

"Stop. Talk out loud, witch." I raised my sword to her.

No reply.

It was then that I began to wonder if perhaps it took a great deal more effort for her to speak out loud than in my mind. What was I *doing*? I had to kill her! I had orders—

Orders. Is that all it was again? Was I just going to go kill for another master?

"I cannot keep them," Skayla's words were drawn out and slow as she referred to the frozen soldiers.

"He wants you alive for something?" I asked.

"To be...what I was..." There were images of her—of the Skayla I was very acquainted with. And then...then there was something else. A mirror. A deal...it ran from my mind, almost as if she hadn't meant to show me that part.

"You're coming with me." In that moment, I made my decision. I was still not completely sure what I'd seen, but this was not the same Skayla. Whether she'd put herself under her own spell by accident or something else, I wasn't about to give her the death she wanted.

She didn't budge, but I didn't wait for her to, grabbing her by the arm and yanking her with me into the hall. It was empty, but I knew it wouldn't be for now.

Stop!

I did, actually, for a moment. And then it vanished, and she was looking at me wide-eyed.

Quickly, I repeated the words Atlys had written out for me. *Hear but don't speak, know but don't read. Stand fast, stand strong.*

The icy feeling in my head and the sudden urge to stab the woman with a sword faded. Well, the former thing did, at least.

"Do that again and...I...well, I won't kill you, because clearly that's what you want," I sputtered angrily, panic gripping me for a moment as I realized just how stupid I was being. But she didn't have her relic, and I had already been instructed how to help avoid a MindHold—had she turned out to still be able to.

"Captain Kearn? What are you—"

None other than General Reth stood framed in the hallway, his group of six bodyguards lined behind them.

"Now would be a great time to do the mind thing," I growled when nothing happened, and realized whatever I had done must have temporarily dazed Skayla. That, or she had taken my threat very seriously. That's when I heard a noise from the door only a breath behind us.

Nothing left to do and not about to wait around to try and best Feren or the others I had once served closely beside, I pulled Skayla down the stairs, immediately pursued by the shouts and heavy boots of my superior and his soldiers.

The alarm would go off any moment, and with it, any hope of getting out. My horse was just outside the palace wall. All we had to do was get there...but would we have time to climb down the rope Atlys had said would be set out?

Panic was setting in deeper by the moment as I dragged a dazed Skayla down the halls with me, desperately trying to put enough space between us.

"Slow them down!" I yelled.

"Trying," came the deathlike whisper. *It hurts. My head.*

"Stop *doing* that!" I growled as we turned sharply down another hallway. The noise behind us stopped and with it the yelling.

But only for a few minutes, soon resuming, albeit much further away.

I put my back into it, not caring that Skayla was hardly still on her feet as she tumbled after me. There it was—the window. And tied to it, the rope promised by Atlys.

I shoved Skayla in front of me. "Climb down to the horse *now!*"

Can't...

I suddenly realized perhaps it wasn't wise to let the lady with a death wish climb out of a window. I shoved her aside and grabbed the rope, tying a quick, makeshift harness around her waist and ending it in a bowline knot. I didn't like the way her whole body was shaking.

"Climb out the window *now*. I'll drop you down slowly."

Thankfully, she didn't argue again, shakily framing herself in the window and looking down a moment before haphazardly dropping down, the rope going taut, and I tried to lower her down without going too quickly.

"Hurry and untie yourself!" I called down as I heard the voices coming closer. I needed the rope slack enough that I could get myself down.

As soon as the rope went slack, I launched myself at it, a mere millisecond before I was confronted by Reth and his soldiers.

I tried as quickly as I could to correct my wild swinging by the rope and climb down, but not quick enough. One of the soldiers—I recognized it as Telar—peered over, growled something unintelligible, and cut the rope as someone else shouted, "Wait!"

In some stupid, desperate attempt to keep from splitting my head open, I tried to land on my feet, flailing and not quite directing my fall.

There was a sickening crunch as my left leg landed straight on the ground, and a pain I had never experienced before exploded up my leg and through my body as I crumpled to the ground in a scream.

My vision went black, pulse roaring in my ears. I felt something or someone next to me, and they grabbed my belt. Then something squeezed tightly around my leg, and a desperate thought pierced my pain-clouded mind as I grabbed at my leg. It was wet. Wet with blood?

Stand up.

I couldn't tell if it was Skayla or my own survival instinct, but I did, biting back a scream and using what I hoped was Skayla's shoulder for support.

The horse.

It was a blur, but I was sure I mounted, someone climbing up behind me. How I actually did it...I wasn't sure, and the excruciating pain as my leg dangled on one side of the horse was enough to almost make me pass out.

Where. Where do I take you?

I couldn't force my lips to move, only allowing the thoughts to flow and hoping Skayla could understand them.

Blackness overtook me after that, but the pain never left.

CHAPTER XVI: After All, Who Needs Two Legs

Estasia:

I waited quietly in the living room with Sven, Astra, Jaythos, and Maeko. It was a bit more crowded in here than usual, but there was still plenty of room. I just didn't really like all the people. Maybe it was because of the strange sense of vulnerability I was wrestling with. As much as I'd tried to brush it off, Sven had been right: I was ordering an assassination—a murder. It had never been what I'd signed up for, and yet I didn't regret it. It was just harder than I expected.

The bell rang.

Kearn.

I leapt to my feet along with Sven and Astra, but while the latter two stayed in place, I ran into the hall and straight for the tunnel door, using the peephole to confirm it was indeed Kearn.

I wasn't prepared for the face that was on the other side of the door.

"Sven!" I yelled, unable to hide the panic this time.

Images of Kearn falling penetrated my mind and the horrible twisted leg. The blood froze in my veins.

Get out of my head!

Sven was beside me in an instant, an open look of worry as his hand rested at the sword by his side.

"Skayla," I whispered, suddenly unable to form words properly. "She…Skayla." I pointed to the door, and Sven wasted no time in looking for himself.

He's dying. Help.

"Get out of my head!" I yelled aloud, clapping both hands over my ears. I had almost forgotten how much I hated the idea of anyone rummaging around in there.

"...She...I can...explain..." This time the faint voice was audible, barely filtering through the door: Kearn. "Let us in...."

"No!" Sven's sword was drawn now, looking at me with an open panic I had never experienced in his eyes before.

It was a panic I was desperately trying to swallow myself.

"What's going on?" I turned to find not only Jaythos in the hall but Marion as well.

"Skayla. She's at the door—I—"

"She claims Kearn is hurt." Sven's voice made even me afraid.

"We can't let her in, Sven. We have to—"

"He's dying!" The voice was Skayla's this time, sounding genuinely frightened and extremely strained from effort.

Jaythos stepped forward, a look of terror mixing in with determination on his face. "Open the door. Sven can cut her down before she makes the threshold."

I turned to Sven, who gripped the hilt of his blade, and gave a sharp nod.

"Wait!" The voice was Tanner's, unexpectedly strong. "Let me test them. Kearn...he's not dumb." He looked at Jaythos then me. "Is there proof Kearn is actually there?"

"It seems as if he is injured. She's holding him up." Sven's voice was flat, his other hand hovering over the lock as if he was about to open the door himself.

"Tell Kearn to put his hand through the door. If they try and force their way in, kill her. But Kearn has to have a good reason."

I opened my mouth to argue, knowing there was no time to mess with the possibility of letting that madwoman in here. But then…then…she had been in our heads—my head—but not tried to sway us. I felt no persuasion. Something wasn't right. I didn't feel her anymore in my head, and couldn't she have easily forced me to open the door if she was trying anything? What had Kearn gotten himself into?

"Fine. Sven, stand ready," I ordered, stepping back so that Tanner could come up to the door.

"No—Tanner, this is the last thing you—"

"Stop. I'm doing it." Tanner cut off Marion's argument.

Looking to me, he nodded and came forward.

"We're opening the door. Kearn, put your hand through and let Tanner have it," Sven called.

It was a tense affair, the door unlocking and cracking open and a weak, pale, bloody hand sliding through. Tanner grabbed the hand and took a sharp breath, going paler than he already was and then going very still.

Suddenly, he gasped, pulling his hand away and whispering, "Let them in. It's not a trick—she saved him. Quick."

The look of desperation from Sven was hard to bear.

"Open it!" Tanner screamed, this time.

Sven jerked the door open with a stiff, lifeless motion, and both Skayla and Kearn tumbled inside, Kearn falling to the floor as Skayla failed to catch him.

There was blood on her frilled white shirt, but when I looked down at Kearn's leg, I almost vomited.

I heard someone stumble backward behind me, and only vaguely wondered who had been unable to take the sight.

"Quick—grab him and bring him into the living room!" It was Marion, leaping into action. Maeko was soon beside her, lifting the groaning Kearn between the two of them.

"Don't...touch her. I went through...a lot of trouble to get her...alive...." The words came between a mixture of gasps, what was left of Kearn's leg dragging along the floor in what had to be excruciating pain.

I had seen plenty of unsavory sights, but this was enough to make me want to pass out.

I stayed behind in the hall as they dragged Kearn as gently as possible into the next room, catching a glimpse of Jaythos—who seemed to have been the one to have half-fainted before—desperately limping behind them.

I'm sorry.

The thought filtered through my head along with a disjointed mess of...horrible scenes.

Before I knew it, Sven had slammed Skayla up against the wall, sword to her throat. "Do not *ever* try that again. If I hear your venomous whispers in my head again, I *will* kill you. Slowly. Piece by piece, just like you did to me. Is that understood?"

This was the moment I realized I'd never actually seen Sven mad. It was truly terrifying. So terrifying in fact, that I believed every word of his threat.

Skayla choked, hanging limply in his grip as she was forced to make eye contact with him.

"Stop! She can't properly communicate. Let her go—Sven, she didn't mean to." Tanner, who I hadn't seen this involved since he'd returned from Rugo, pushed me aside and grabbed at Sven's arm, unsuccessful in his attempts to pull him off of Skayla.

There was an agonizing moment of nothing before Sven let Skayla collapse to the ground. It was odd the way she did it like some ragdoll, unable to properly catch herself and so ending up as a disorganized mass of person on the floor. Every movement she made seemed more like a puppet than a person, and I wanted to shrink back at the way she gathered herself and sat huddled against the wall.

"I don't care what you saw," Sven spat, glaring death at his sister.

"Sven, if we kill her now, then Kearn was injured and maybe killed for nothing." Tanner put himself between the siblings, arms stretched out and life back in his gaze at last. "Something else is going on."

There was a scream from the other room, and everyone except Skayla jumped. Why couldn't I make myself move? Why did I feel so frozen, staring at what was left of that woman huddled in the corner with those violet eyes?

"I'm going to reach into her memories," Tanner announced with no warning, a look of calm determination. It was enough to bring me back to what was going on.

"What are you thinking? Your mind is barely holding on by a thread, you idiot. You can't—" I was cut off by the blatant disregard for what I was saying as Tanner swung his hand over to Skayla and grabbed her arm.

I pulled him away when his eyes began rolling back in his sockets, even when Skayla didn't flinch.

"Is he alright?" Sven asked, having helped separate Tanner from Skayla, and now using his own body to keep them that way.

"I'm fine..." Tanner grumbled, putting a hand to his head and scooting quickly away from me.

It was then that I realized I had always been *so* careful never to touch him. Stupid Skayla making me act impulsively. This had not gone to plan. This had *so* not gone to plan.

"You are *not* fine," I growled as I watched the kid tremble feverishly from head to foot.

I barely registered someone run behind us and into the kitchen for something.

Tanner laughed weakly. "Still not as bad as Ovok's head. That...so many years...so many...."

I shook his shoulder, trying to avoid any skin contact and hoping that would be enough to stop him seeing in my head. "Snap out of it, kid."

With a shudder, Tanner closed his eyes, wrapping his arms around his knees. "She had put herself in a MindHold. That's what happened.

I—" another shudder— "No fear. That's what she wanted. That's what drove her crazy." Then he looked up at Sven. "And you broke it when you destroyed her relic."

"Why?" Sven asked, tone still rigid.

Tanner fumbled for words, saying some things under his breath as he continued to rock back and forth. "She wanted to save my daughter."

I raised an eyebrow. "I'm…sorry?"

With a shake of his head, Tanner repeated, "My daughter—wait. No. Ovok's. She wanted to help Ovok's daughter and she was afraid. I…was afraid Moira wouldn't agree and would spin back time so I wouldn't even know I told her. I just wanted to help…I'm sorry I just…." Another gasp, and Tanner once more squeezed his eyes shut, hands going over his ears. "She isn't going to hurt us," he murmured.

Ovok's daughter…Rhioa. I remembered Baey mentioning Tanner's earlier outburst on the subject, and Astra's explanation that she was still alive. But…was that what this was all about?

I looked back at the motionless Skayla, staring at nothing with a blank expression. It was almost as if she wasn't even here. Again, someone rushed from behind us, back into the living room. But my attention was on Tanner and Skayla right now.

"If you kill her now, Kearn's sacrifice is meaningless. I *wanted* him to kill me and he didn't. Why didn't he just do it and get out of here…why did he…." Tanner devolved into unintelligible mumbling.

None of us replied to this. All I knew was that I couldn't leave Sven alone with Skayla, and I had no idea what I was now supposed to do with her. If Sven made another move to kill her, I wouldn't stop him, but unless he did, I would try and see about keeping her alive until at least Kearn could sort this out.

If he lived. Bile rose in my throat as I thought of his pulverized leg. "And Kearn. How did that happen?" I asked Tanner.

"Fell. Was…" Tanner shuddered. "I don't want to remember that."

"Don't," Sven spoke for the first time in a while. "Just breathe for a while, Tanner. It's okay. You don't need to keep looking."

Swallowing hard, Tanner gave a slight nod, eyes remaining closed.

Then Sven looked at me. "Now what?" Gone was the gentleness he had just used to address Tanner and back was the acrid tone.

I remembered my promise to him—that he would never have to see Skayla again. "I…I don't know. But if she just wants to die, I don't want to up and give that to her." I looked over to Skayla, who I could almost forget *was* alive with how she was acting. Or well, not acting.

Sven did not move, sword still out and pointed in his sister's direction. I didn't want to tell him to lower it.

"Sven, I-I'm sorry." The words came out without my permission. "This was not how it was supposed to go."

"This isn't on you." His voice was low, back to staring at Skayla. "Can you walk?" It took me a second to realize he was asking Skayla. "And don't you answer in my head."

Skayla didn't respond.

Sven kicked her one leg, albeit gently. "Get up."

Deciding it was best to intervene at least a little, I went over, heart beating as I carefully moved the tip of Sven's blade away. I grabbed

Skayla by the arm and dragged her to her feet. It was rather like handling a corpse, making me feel very, very uncomfortable.

At last she stood, breathing shallowly and staring at Sven.

"Stop that," Sven lifted the blade again, and Skayla looked away.

I had no desire to get in the middle of this, but I felt it would be a bad idea to leave Sven alone with her. Honestly, I didn't want *anyone* alone with Skayla. "Let's bring her into one of the interior bedrooms." No windows or way out—besides the door—would allow for Sven to at least get out of the room.

We made our way up the stairs, Skayla walking limply between us. At last, we got her into the smallest room we could find, and Sven quickly put his hand to the outside of the door, creating a lock out of thin air. He handed me a key without a word.

The reality bending thing was still not something I was used to.

"Sven, I—"

"It's not your fault. Stop apologizing. I'll stay here. You check on Tanner and Kearn. Make sure Astra is alright." The bitterness was hard to swallow, even if it wasn't pointed at me.

"Alright. I'll figure this mess out," I promised, even though it seemed my promises weren't something I could follow through on. "Just don't go in there. Stay outside—she can't do anything."

"I have no intention of stepping any closer to her than I have to," he answered flatly.

"Right." Still wishing I could stay, I retreated down the stairs and went to kneel by Tanner, who was still sitting on the floor.

"I...I don't want Kearn to die," he whispered.

"I'm sure he'll be fine." I really...*really* wasn't, but I didn't think saying that would help. "Let's go back to your room? I'll make sure you get updated as soon as I can, but someone might trip on you here." I did my best to sound comforting.

Tanner didn't reply, but got up, still hugging himself.

I went to follow him up the stairs, but he turned abruptly. "No. Go check on Kearn. Please."

"Alright." A little part of me was worried he'd get lost going back to his room by the looks of him, but I honestly needed to see Kearn.

Taking one final deep breath, I crossed into the living room and found myself immediately running into the kitchen to find a bucket, unprepared for what I had seen. Just barely finding the rubbish bin in time, I threw up my dinner.

After taking a few deep breaths in through the nose and then finding some water to rinse away the foul taste in my mouth, I returned to the room, at least knowing now what I was going to see.

For it appeared...Marion had just amputated Kearn's leg.

Sven:

I couldn't bring myself to sheathe my sword. I just stood there in the hallway, grasping the hilt like it was the one thing keeping me here. That voice in my head...I didn't care what it had been saying, I never wanted to hear it again. I didn't want to see what it had shown me. I didn't care if she was sorry. After my conversations with Astra, I'd slowly grown to accept that perhaps...this hadn't all been my fault. Perhaps it really was hers. And now, to have the person who'd made me do all those horrible things—who had mentally tortured me for a decade and made me murder all those I loved—sitting right on the other side of this door, I didn't know if I could control myself. I didn't know if I could even believe she was *sorry*, or even forgive her if she really was.

I whipped around at the sound of footsteps, only to see Tanner climb the last stair at the other side of the hall.

I remembered what he had said. She'd put herself in a MindHold? How did we know she wasn't manipulating his memories? Logically, I knew it didn't make sense. She didn't have her armlet, and she was clearly in bad shape. Skayla had been many things but never a liar. Even as crazed and sadistic as she'd become, she'd always tell you exactly what horrible thing she was going to do—or make you do.

I shuddered, finding myself in a staring match with the boy at the end of the hall. I wanted to ask him what he'd meant, but I didn't want to press—not when it was clear his own mind was hanging by a thread.

Breathe. I jolted at the word, finding myself paranoid over whose voice I was hearing. But it was my own, this time. I was trying to breathe...trying to relax. Trying to stop myself from going in that room and tearing Skayla apart for killing Da...for making me kill everyone else.

"I...I'm sorry." Tanner had come up to me, looking from the door to my still-exposed blade.

I swallowed. "Are you alright?"

His lips drew tightly together. "We'll both lie. Let's not pretend otherwise." The words were dull.

"I don't feel like lying," I said quietly, my fury abating a little in the presence of this poor kid. I remembered he'd just looked in Skayla's head. That meant seeing all she'd done. "I'm still weighing murder," I added bluntly then asked, "So are you alright?"

Tanner just kind of stared at me, blinking a few times. Then he looked away, back to where his room was. "I don't know. I don't know who I am, but I do know everyone in my head is definitely not."

I let out a pent-up breath, shoulders dropping in defeat. "I think I would be more surprised if someone said they *were* alright."

"I...I'm not saying you need to forgive her. I don't want you to think that," Tanner croaked. "I just...I don't think we should kill her. Kearn. He felt that maybe she could be important to keep alive, and I think Skayla might have use, still."

I was amazed this kid was still speaking after what he'd seen. "She's dangerous."

"She's broken. I don't think she can hurt anyone else." Tanner's reply was so confident.

But I'm broken, too. I wasn't sure what I even meant by that, but I just knew I couldn't see her again. I didn't want to look in those violet eyes— the ones that had laughed at me as they ordered me to do unspeakable horrors and had controlled me.

"You said...she was in a MindHold. How does that even work?" I asked at last, looking at the hand that held my sword.

"Well, not exactly a MindHold, I suppose. She just...manipulated herself. I—she—didn't want to be afraid anymore. She didn't want anything to get in the way of what she thought she had to do. But then I

296

guess…it meant she wasn't afraid of *anything*. Nothing held stakes or permanence and it sort of…spiraled."

"And she did this for Ovok?" Who she'd known, what, a few months at the time? Why?

"She…she wanted to help someone. Ovok—" His eyes went wide— "I remember now. Why he needs The Living Stone. He wanted to save his daughter, Rhioa. She's dying. The Living Stone could save her, and Skayla was going to bring him to it. Only—" Tanner flinched, bringing his hand to his head and groaning. I went to reach forward, but he shrugged me away. "She didn't know he was going to bring it off-world." The boy's breathing grew rapid, and his eyes shut.

I instantly put away my weapon. "Tanner, it's alright, stop searching. You don't need to look for any more information." Tanner had already mentioned much of this, but Skayla trying to help was new.

"But—" he looked at me now with a frightening, esoteric expression. "That's all I'm good for. Information."

Forgotten was the nightmare behind the door. Now, all that mattered was this child. "No. I don't care about the information. I am more afraid about the kid in front of me acting like his mind is melting. Tanner— Tanner—" I gently grabbed one arm, forcing him to stay in the present. "You've seen her head. You know I cared about her. I don't know you well, and I'm sorry for that, but I still don't want to lose you like I lost her. No amount of information is worth that price. Understand?" I had been torn in so many directions, and because of it, all this time I'd missed Tanner. I had hardly visited him when we were in the manor—all because I was afraid of what Astra might trigger or get triggered by. And before that…when we were fleeing Kaedovarna, I had missed the signs. The signs of a soul too burdened by the lives of others, just like Skayla once had been.

Slowly, Tanner dropped his arms, a few tears running down his cheeks as he slowly nodded. "Alright."

"Alright?" I repeated back to him, holding eye contact.

He nodded. "I think Estasia's right…. I need…I should sleep."

I did not try and fake a smile. This kid didn't need that. I just patted his shoulder. "Alright. Please, Tanner, actually rest."

"I will," he answered sincerely. Slowly, he collected himself, and I watched as he walked back down the hall and disappeared into his room, leaving me once more alone in the hall. Once more, I was faced with the door that stood between me and the person who'd turned me into what I was. But was I that? Was I really that monster, or had that always just been Skayla?

The commotion from downstairs continued, but it was mostly lost on me as I collapsed against the wall, sinking down to the floor and putting my head in both hands.

Alone, fractured, and faced with an impossible dilemma, I found myself quietly weeping. I didn't want to process the information Tanner had given me—I didn't want to think about how Skayla had both been completely responsible for her actions and yet…not. I didn't want to think about how I felt a mixture of uncontainable rage and a broken sort of sympathy. I didn't want to unpack all of this. I had nothing left in me to try.

But then I remembered the promise I'd made myself: to try and not let this consume me. To maybe try and live. And so, I did not allow myself to stay like this for long, picking myself up off the floor and straightening my coat. Even if it was hard to forget who was on the other side of this door behind me.

Those eyes…that voice.

I heard footsteps in the hall downstairs, and soon, someone was climbing the stairs. It was Estasia, looking pale.

"Is he…alright?" I eked out the question as she came down pretty quickly, closer to my end of the hall.

She gave me a look that made me think he definitely wasn't. Then she replied, "He's still alive, thanks to Astra and Marion. I'm getting a room ready for him. Are you alright?"

"Astra?" I had…I had *completely* forgotten about her! What was wrong with me? It always felt as if I forgot someone or something, even *with* my memories back. I was desperately worried I would let one of them down.

Estasia gave a quick nod as she put a hand on the latch of a nearby empty guest room. "Her healing…she was able to help. And she controlled herself very well. Said your lessons helped." With that she disappeared into the room, leaving the door open. The light she'd activated inside flooded out into the hallway, as did the noise of her preparing the bed. She came out to quickly grab some more blankets from the closet down the hall, then went back into the room without another word.

I just felt stuck, knowing I shouldn't have left Astra, and yet now unable to leave Skayla. Skayla. She was in the room right behind me, supposedly harmless but still very much alive. With a deep breath, I renewed with force the shield around Astra's presence, hoping her power's presence had not leaked out in my lapse of concentration.

At last, Estasia exited the room and addressed me again, "And Tanner went to bed, right?"

"Yes…eventually." I rubbed the pommel of my sword. "He said…Skayla had accidentally put her own mind in a MindHold, of sorts. What if he's right, and that's what made her go insane? And that it makes sense that it's gone with the breaking of her relic?"

She gave a frown. "I still don't know if I believe that."

But maybe I did. Still, I would be lying if I said I wasn't eager to change the subject. "Are they bringing Kearn up?"

"Yes, they're just…" She shuddered. "Making sure he's stable enough to move."

My eyes narrowed. "Are you—"

"I'm fine, don't you of all people ask me that. Just focus on—" she waved her hand in the air. "Just don't worry about me. I'll sort this out. Somehow."

Yes, somehow. We both knew it was a problem that wasn't really "sortable."

Any further conversation was cut off by quick footsteps, and we were soon joined by none other than Astra, breathless and visibly strained. Was she…limping? I stepped forward, unsure what had happened.

"Is that the room he's going to be in?" she asked Estasia.

"Yes—are you alright?" Estasia stepped out of the way.

Astra grunted what seemed to have been meant as a reply and went to enter the room.

I couldn't help but say, "Astra—you're limping." It seemed nothing short of blatant observations would make her acknowledge it.

"I just...was helping downstairs. I'll be back." She entered the room, and a blue flash briefly illuminated the hallway from the room. I felt the surge of energy; it was measured, not out of control or emotional like I'd felt in previous instances of Astra using her abilities.

Estasia's brow furrowed as she looked inside, and she turned to say something, unable to finish whatever thought was forming as the blue flash again exploded. Estasia looked back into the room and ran inside. Meanwhile, I was distracted by several more sets of footsteps running up the stairs, and soon Marion, Maeko, and Jaythos were filing into the room.

I wanted so badly to enter, worried for Astra and for what was going on inside, but I was stuck guarding this stupid door, wondering if my fate was about to once more be tied to staying by Skayla's side day and night.

I didn't want to think about that. I really...I *really* didn't want to think about that possibility.

"Alright, get out! Everyone except you—and Astra, go get some *rest*." Marion's shrill orders pierced through the open doorway, and soon everyone except for Jaythos and Marion came out, looking about as lost as I felt.

Astra was last to wander into the hallway, swaying and looking generally terrible.

"Maeko, guard that door, would you?" Estasia ordered as she jabbed a finger in my direction, interrupting me from asking Astra what she'd done.

"I—I don't think that's a good—"

"I'm not letting you stay there. Let Maeko take over," Estasia cut me off in a way that proved arguing was futile.

Yet I was doing just that, opening my mouth in an attempt to list every single reason no one else could be watching Skayla.

"Shut up, Sven! I'm not letting you do that to yourself!" Estasia shouted much louder than I could have ever expected.

I just…sort of stared, unsure what to do. I was paralyzed, unable to move and unable to really process any of this.

"Maeko, get over there and take his place, and if you have to physically carry him away, do it," Estasia growled, arms folded as she stared me down. "Tanner checked Skayla and said she wasn't a threat, but don't go inside or anything unless Marion or I say otherwise."

Numb, I stepped away as Maeko came over. "She's right, Skinny. I will help." I could barely register the lack of hostility in his voice before Estasia continued to bark commands.

"Sven, you get some sleep. *And* you—" she diverted her attention to Astra. "Get some sleep as well. You both look like you have the plague, and if either of you try and show your faces before tomorrow afternoon, I will personally ban you from seeing anyone. Is that understood?"

Neither of us spoke, only nodding.

"Good. Now go."

Astra and I both walked down the hall back to our separate rooms, a great pressure building in my chest that felt like it might just be the death of me. But I still noticed Astra's limp, and quietly asked, "What happened?"

"I…was trying to help him. Sometimes I get sore afterwards," she whispered.

It was then that I realized that her limp matched the leg that Kearn had injured. Had she…had she seriously taken on the pain herself? Could she transfer that sort of energy? I felt sick at the thought, and yet I knew the last thing Astra wanted right now was to be prodded…because that was the last thing *I* wanted as well.

I would definitely be addressing this tomorrow, though.

"I'm sorry," I replied instead as we stopped in front of her door. "Thank you for helping."

She looked at me as if she wanted to say something else, then looked back down to where the others were. "You too," she said simply before slipping inside.

I finished the trek back to my own room, closing the door behind me and sinking to the floor. I had no intention of sleeping. Too many nightmares would follow me if I did that now. But then again…they already had found me, hadn't they? For now she was just down the hall.

CHAPTER XVII: The Trap is Set

<u>Ovok:</u>

"Did you find them?" I asked, hands folded behind my back as I faced away from Havirax for my own sanity. Everything was hanging by a thread. I needed to get off-world. I had to get to Rhioa—had to get off this cursed prison of a planet and make this bloodbath all worth it.

"I found who Kearn was working with," Havirax replied.

—So he let them get away? Pathetic. They're all pathetic, just like you—

My fists clenched. "So you didn't follow them into the sewers?"

"I tried—but it was dark and...rather unpleasant. But he isn't working with Lord Atarah, after all." I could hear Havirax shriveling up.

I had thought Atarah was helping him—I'd been almost sure of it. The unnatural hunger to rise to the top after being in the holding camps had raised alarm bells. Perhaps once again I'd overestimated the morality of those on Baeno.

"Then who is it?" I asked, staring out into the afternoon light of the window and debating when I could get rid of Havirax. He was doing a poor job of continuing to be useful to me, as it was. I'd given him all the bait he'd needed, and still, he hadn't brought the portal to me.

"Atlys, my lord."

—Ha! That worm? This'll be fun—

I turned around, intrigued and also a little doubtful. "And how are we sure?" Unlike Atarah, Atlys had everything to lose. He thought his family was still in the holding camp, didn't he? Or had he figured out they were dead? I wasn't thinking clearly these days—how could I be so careless to overlook such possibilities? Perhaps Ckaknimaen was doing more to crowd my brain than even I wanted to admit.

—Well, that's not very nice, is it. After all I've done for you—

I shuddered. Yes, after all it had done…all the blood it had made me shed.

"While those idiots spooked Kearn and made it impossible for me to follow, I was able to catch who had left the horse and rope out. It's a servant from the kitchens. He passed a note to Atlys, who was due in the palace earlier this morning to hand in the shipping reports. Meanwhile, Atarah was in the sewers all last night. So while he is incompetent, perhaps, I think Kearn was the one leading him astray all last week."

I raised an eyebrow, looking down at Havirax with a cool smile. "A bold claim, coming from one whose uses are also so few."

Swallowing hard, Havirax asked, "Should I bring in the servant?"

"No. I will get Atlys myself. No one is to touch the servant. We can't let anyone else know Atlys is missing. He's the one that must have been supplying the rebels with food and necessities. He must have had a store already put aside in case of a situation like this, where rations were being watched. Of course." I didn't trust anyone to bring in the noble without attention. Clearly, I was the only one that could get anything done competently. I ignored Ckaknimaen's ironic giggling at the thought. "Monitor the servant, but under no circumstances is he to realize Atlys is gone. Three days—can you manage that?"

"Yes, sir, three days. Of course."

I knew that was most likely all we had. Any longer, and we risked further correspondence needed between Lord Atlys and the rebels. Fortunately for us, it seemed Atlys had already made contact. This meant no one would miss him for at least a day or so, and hopefully that was all I needed.

I could be quite persuasive—

I withheld another shudder at the thought as it crept into my mind like poison. I hated this sword.

And yet, you know you need me. I'm the only thing with a backbone. Coward—

I forced myself to ignore the whispers, instead turning to Havirax. "Get out of my sight, but keep me updated. I am not to be disturbed. Have General Reth and Grand General Brahj keep looking for Kearn, and don't let up on the tunnels."

"Uh, my lord…it seems General Reth is being…well, he isn't happy about Kearn's switch in loyalties. He's pulling what's left of his garrison back."

What? I didn't have time for this. Everything was crumbling. "Just get out of my sight and tell Brahj to deal with it *and* his insubordinations," I ordered.

Havirax was all too happy to leave, and I was again alone. I clutched the small pendant around my neck, feeling the pulse of The Living Stone run through my veins.

"I'm sorry, Rhy," I whispered, shuddering as I prepared for what I was about to do. One more casualty. I was so close; I couldn't turn back now and make this all for nothing.

I pitied Atlys.

—*Finally. I get my fun.*

Baey:

Making sure Kearn's soldiers made it to The Underground had been a chore. They had been ordered to split up into groups, Thackeray, Alenor, and I taking a few each. I'd had to spin back time half a dozen times for us to get it right, but at last, we'd successfully gotten them through.

Then had come the tricky part; getting them into The Underground without a riot. We'd quickly had them discard their Bethynese armor, changing them into clothes Atlys had provided, and then had them posted to Thackeray as new recruits.

I thought it was silly. First, Sven, now this. They'd clearly proven themselves, yet still the people seemed to turn up their nose if help didn't come from the right place. What exactly was going to happen when they had to rebuild the city next to people who had been in MindHolds? Oh, but that was fine, because they had just been faceless victims. Sven had been unlucky in being The GhostMaker, and the Bethynese had always been hated. Those being treated in The Underground and recovering their memories hadn't even been able to fight as hard against the MindHold as Sven, but somehow, he was the one being punished for it.

"Estasia is due this afternoon. She isn't late, yet," I reassured Darby as we waited together in the tent.

Rubbing her forehead, Darby sat down again in her seat after having gotten up for the thousandth time in response to some mundane sound outside. "I know, I know. I just feel like something is going to go wrong—what if Skayla—"

"Her armlet was completely shattered, and Kearn doesn't know where The Underground is." I felt like we'd gone through this a few times already...but I understood her anxiety. Perhaps I was calmer simply because of the watch, but so far, I hadn't been able to go back any more than an hour or so. That being said, I couldn't tell if it was because I couldn't or *wouldn't*. Something about going further back scared me—things unraveling so far as to never have happened. I didn't want people forgetting their decisions.

"Of course," Darby sighed, leaning back against her chair.

Alenor was with Moira back in the forge, and Grenedil was keeping Cyl at the portal, leaving only the two of us to wait for Estasia. I couldn't help but feel bad for Grenedil and perhaps a little guilty. He seemed so isolated, and if Cyl was someone he'd considered a friend...he must not have had very many friends.

And then Syvil was still resting, insisting we would work more on my flying this evening, if everything else went to plan.

"Lady Darbeshay," A guard entered, nodding to me and then Darby. "Estasia is waiting outside."

Darby jumped to her feet. "Let her in," she said quickly.

I didn't move, hoping that by staying calm, I would perhaps help Darby remain so as well. She was usually so collected, but Skayla hit home for a lot of people. Hopefully we were rid of her now.

"So we have a problem," Estasia announced immediately upon entering.

Well, that wasn't a good start.

In an uncharacteristic show of stress, Estasia put both hands on her head, pulling her hair in some mesh of anxiety and frustration. "So Skayla isn't dead. She's currently being held at the manor. Kearn, in some idiotic move, decided *not* to kill her, but escape with her...and in the process completely ruined his leg in a fall and forced Marion to amputate it last night. We're not sure if he's going to make it, but Astra is apparently quite skilled in healing, and Sven had been giving her lessons in controlling her ability, so she was able to help heal Kearn enough to theoretically prevent him from dying. So then Sven threw Skayla up against a wall and Tanner looked in her head and almost had another meltdown, and I left Maeko in charge of guarding the door where Skayla is and told Sven I'd kill him if he tries to go anywhere near her room."

She then took a deep breath, looking at me before continuing. "Tanner claims Skayla had put some form of MindHold on herself and that's what made her go insane all those years ago. He said Ovok asked her to help get him to The Living Stone so he could save his daughter— the one Astra already said was still alive—and Skayla was too afraid to tell Moira but she wanted to be able to help him, so she did something to take away all fear and it just completely took away any impulse control...but Ovok is trying to get to the portal so he can leave with The

Living Stone. And it's all to save this stupid daughter." She paused a moment, looking back and forth between us and dropping her arms in apparent surrender. "So I have a former psychopath locked up in the manor after promising Sven I'd never make him set eyes on her again, and if we kill Skayla now we'd completely throw Kearn's choice out the window, and Tanner thinks she could still be useful and claims she is completely harmless…and she *did* save Kearn…any ideas?"

I blinked. "I…what?" I struggled to process. Skayla…she'd let *Skayla* into the same house as Sven?!

"Skayla is alive, I don't know what to do about it, and your little friend whose mind has been slowly turning into a puddle is insisting she's cooperative." She threw up her hands again for emphasis.

"Is Sven *alright?*" Darby asked what we were both thinking. I'd told her before about the whole Rhioa thing, but we hadn't known about it being the cause of Skayla's fall.

"What do *you* think?" Estasia was openly distressed. "Of course he's not alright. The only thing I can think of is to send him and Astra back here—Astra seems in much better control now and, as Baey told Cyl, Sven's been able to successfully hide her Gifting or whatever that problem was."

"Yeah…maybe that's a good idea. If you saw her use her Gifting and can confirm it was under control, I don't want Sven in the same house as that woman," I said, flicking my wings to try and relieve some of the stress. "Is Tanner really sure Skayla isn't still working for Ovok? That this isn't a trap?"

"If it was, then she'd be here by now—and you would have gone back in time already to stop this from happening, right?" Estasia turned to me. "I realized the fact you didn't go back to stop us yesterday means we're probably fine."

I bit my lip. I hadn't tried to go back that far before, but I had a feeling I could if I wanted to. She was probably right? And if Skayla had been playing a game, Tanner surely would have seen it. No one to date had ever been able to hide memories from him. Unlike Skayla, his Gift wasn't based on will. It just read your experiences, whether you wanted them read or not.

"Okay. Well then, I'm going back to get Sven and Astra. We need to deal with Cyl, though. He's not going to like that," I replied, drumming my fingers against my leg.

"I couldn't care less what he thinks," Estasia spat. "But we need to figure out what to do with Skayla."

"What does Sven want?" This time it was Darby, voice tense.

Running a hand over her face, Estasia said, "Well, when I asked the first time, he wanted her dead. But then we both agreed we couldn't just kill her now after Kearn lost his leg to bring her to us."

A sigh passed between all three of us.

"Then we have to keep her in the manor. I want to talk to Sven and see if I can figure out what he actually wants." Darby closed her eyes for a long while before opening them again. "If Skayla really did fall prey to her own power, then to a degree she is a victim...but by choice. She should have known the dangers of such a monumentally stupid move…but no one in The Underground can know of this. We *cannot* speak her name."

"Agreed," I said.

"As it is, the timeline for the evacuation of The Underground needs to be put into full gear. Atlys's search to the west wasn't fruitful, so we're stuck with the portal site, and I think we need to prepare for that. This won't go unnoticed for much longer—as soon as the initial searches die down, you need to go and talk to Atlys." Darby addressed Estasia. "But we need to wait a few days…it's too risky now."

"I suppose we can just use that time to try and brainstorm how in Baeno we'll move everyone." Estasia's response was riddled with the stress we all felt.

Wings straightening as I arched my back, I prepared for the other issues at hand. ""I'll leave immediately. Estasia? Do you mind dealing with Cyl while Darby prepares a place for Sven and Astra?"

"Fine. But if that lizard starts yelling at me, I don't care who he is, I'm about ready to punch that smug little face," Estasia growled.

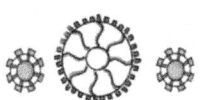

Sven was the one who let me inside, looking wound so tightly he could spring at any moment.

"I heard what happened," I murmured as he closed the door behind me. I couldn't help but take note of the blood stains all over the floor, trailing down into the living room. It was clear someone had tried to clean the floor a little bit, but somehow, I got the feeling they were more concerned about other things.

I heard the little steam train chugging along on its track somewhere in the house, but other than that it was quiet.

Sven's jaw visibly tightened, but he said nothing, hand just gripping the pommel of his sword like a lifeline.

I knew the only way to break through and get him to say anything. "How are Tanner and Astra?"

"Astra is still sleeping. Tanner is in the living room," he replied. Had he been guarding the tunnel entrance the whole time? It would explain why he'd been so quick to open the door.

I took a step towards the living room, and he did not follow. "Are you coming?"

He stared at me, tension rippling through every muscle. "We don't know if they were followed."

"Come with me, Sven. No one is coming. I'll make sure of it." I tapped the glass on the watch.

This did little to change his mood, but he followed this time when I went towards the living room. Yeah, there was no way he was staying here.

Tanner was in Sven's usual chair, anxiously tapping his fingers on the arm of the seat.

"Tanner, how's your head?" I asked, pulling up a seat on a stool—much easier to navigate my wings around compared to the sofa.

He actually looked at me with something like recognition. "Still here, I think."

I attempted a smile as I replied, "That's good. Estasia told me what happened. I didn't realize you were *that* much of a moron."

He shrugged, fingers ceasing their anxious drum beat as he searched me intently. "Are you going to kill her?"

I looked back at Sven, who was as emotionless as a brick at the doorway. "How sure are you that she's not spying?" I asked Tanner.

"Very. She...her memories began weaving with Ovok's and I'm remembering more of his now. I..." He put a hand to his head and winced. "I just have...a horrible headache."

Concern grew with every moment. "That is not convincing me you're alright."

The smile he flashed back wasn't his. I couldn't explain how I knew, but I just did. It didn't match the rest of him. "Oh, I'll be fine. Always am."

"Tanner, stop it," I whispered. This was worse than when he'd been unresponsive.

The fingers once more began their terrible drumming. "I need to talk to her."

I choked. "What? No, you do *not*."

"I need to help her—I need...I need her to help me." His fingers closed around the armrest. "Marion and I haven't gotten much of anywhere with—Skayla won't hurt anyone else."

"You can't know that." Sven's voice creaked into existence. "She's hurt plenty of people already, and I don't think she's the one you should be asking for help."

"I won't let anyone get hurt, Sven. In the meantime, you and Astra are coming back to The Underground with me. Tanner—" I stared long and hard. "Don't do anything without Marion's permission. I'm going upstairs. You two get ready."

"I need to stay here." Sven's argument was unexpected. "Something could happen."

I stood up and stretched my wings, trying to hide the worry that felt like it would burst at any moment. "I will assess Skayla myself. If Tanner is right, then there is nothing she will do. Trust me."

I didn't like the anguish bleeding through Sven's facade. "Baey—"

"Please," I begged softly. "Trust me. I know. I won't let anything happen, Sven."

He swallowed hard, saying nothing. Then, after an agonizing moment, he stood aside, eyes falling to the ground.

"Thank you," I whispered. Then, a bit louder, I said, "I'll be back down in a few minutes," and left the room.

My heart felt heavier than ever as I climbed the stairs, the weight of it only abating with the anxiety reminding me I was going to have to come face-to-face with Skayla, the woman who'd continually ruined my life. The one who'd taken Sven, who'd killed my family and all my kind, who'd killed countless friends from Valdon…and if Tanner *was* right, then she was not fully to blame. Still to blame in some capacity but perhaps not fully.

Maeko was guarding a door further down the hall than the open door I stopped at, and I briefly nodded to him, knowing that's where I was going next.

He gave a small sign of acknowledgement, but looked about as lively as Sven had when I'd arrived.

I went through the open door where I found Jaythos sitting by a bed, hand clasped around his brother's. Kearn was laying under a heap of bedding, pale face holding the telling lines of stress from the surgery last night.

"How is he?" I asked, addressing Marion, who was standing nearby putting some medicine away.

"Alive. The shock when he wakes will tell us a lot. No infection so far—Astra saw to that," Marion replied.

"And him?" I pointed the question towards Jaythos.

Marion grimaced, giving a tense shrug. "We are waiting for Kearn to wake up."

I wished I could give Jaythos more comfort, but I knew the only one who could do that was Maeko, and he was still guarding the hall.

Right.

"I need to see Skayla," I whispered after coming closer to Marion.

Her mouth drew in an even tighter line than it already had been, if that was possible. "I don't know what that idiot was thinking," she murmured.

Honestly, neither did I. Only two people did: Kearn and Tanner.

"I'm going to assess her for myself and see if she's worth the risk."

"Don't touch her," Jaythos growled from where he was sitting, not moving a muscle even as he proved he'd been listening the whole time. "If Kearn wanted her alive, he had a reason. Don't touch her."

"I have no intention of it," I replied calmly, the irony of Jaythos defending Skayla was not lost on me. "I assume she is who Maeko is guarding?" I returned my attention to Marion.

"Yes. She doesn't seem to be able to physically talk very well. Don't be surprised if she tries to communicate…mentally. That's what set Sven off so badly."

I winced. Ah, yes, I could see that going downhill very quickly. "Thank you," I said. I resisted the urge to try and say something to Jaythos, instead leaving and going up to Maeko.

"She has not moved," he reported, stepping aside and unlocking the door. "Be careful, little Baey."

Somehow the nickname didn't bother me so much anymore. "I always am," I reassured, opening the latch and stepping inside.

Skayla was sitting on the edge of the small bed, legs hanging limply off the side as she stared into nothing.

"Skayla. Do you remember me?" I asked, remaining outwardly calm even as my pulse quickened.

An image flashed in my mind—of me swooping in and rescuing Sven in Hytat.

With a shudder, I said, "A simple nod or shake of the head would be sufficient."

Sorry. The word was said simultaneously out loud and in my mind, even as Skayla's face remained blank.

It was unnerving.

"Why did you save Kearn?" I asked, remembering what Estasia had said about what Tanner had learned.

Again, another memory began flashing inside my mind; of him falling and me—well, Skayla—quickly using his belt for a tourniquet. The image vanished quickly.

"Sorry."

"Why?" I repeated the question, resisting the urge to put a hand completely around the watch. If I had to go back in time, I wasn't making Moira's mistake.

"He...was being...stupid." The words were slow and drawn out. "Wasn't listening."

Kill me. The words rang in my head quickly. She'd told him to hurry and kill her.

"Why did you want him to?" I gave up trying to make her talk aloud, realizing I would probably get better answers if she answered mentally, despite how unnerving it was. I felt no influence, and as long as it lined up with what Tanner said, I would be alright. Besides, I still remembered how Sven had coached us on how to resist a MindHold, and Skayla didn't hold the same power when she'd had her armlet.

Several horrible visions of the Skayla I knew well popped up in my head, not disappearing quickly enough. *I didn't want to be that again.* The words seemed to echo in my mind.

I was a fool.

The next few minutes were spent with her providing the same information Tanner had given us. That she had used a mirror to turn her mind against herself—to rid herself of fear so that she could help Ovok. As Grenedil had suspected, it was all to get The Living Stone for Rhioa.

At last, I was safely on the other side of the door, trying to catch my breath after the mentally exhausting back and forth.

Maeko stared at me, concern in his eyes.

"I'm alright. She...she is harmless. Just don't...don't let Tanner in here unless Marion lets him," I pleaded.

He nodded, brow furrowing even though he remained silent.

I took another deep breath, preparing to go downstairs and get Sven out of here. Hopefully, this would all pay off...hopefully, Tanner was right; Skayla would be useful.

CHAPTER XVIII: I Seek Help from a Madwoman

Tanner:

I squeeze my eyes shut, wishing to block out the roar of people's thoughts tormenting me. Go away…please, go away. I just want some peace and quiet. No more noise.

"Skayla?" I feel Sven's hands on mine, and slowly, he lowers them away from my ears. Not that it was helping anyway.

"I want it to stop," I whimper, already hearing his own thoughts mingling with everyone else's. He wants to help, he's worried. He's…he's calming me. In his head, he's calming me. He knows I'm there.

"Why don't we go somewhere far away from people? I could use a hike." He smiles at me, bringing me to my feet. The commotion around me continues, but I let him lead me back into the streets. I already know where he is taking me…I can see it in his mind. I wish for once it could be a surprise, but the way he's picturing it so clearly is almost calming. The waterfall…the birds chirping…I let him lead me there.

"Sven, maybe you should stay behind," I suggest, already hearing the confusion rattling in his mind. Moira is beside me. I feel so…guilty. I want to tell Sven, but Moira has already shown me what will happen if we include him. He wouldn't understand. He wouldn't like the way we rerun scenarios until they're perfect. He would claim free will and that we're just

manipulating everyone. But it's to protect them—why can't he understand that?

Sven looks only half as crestfallen as his thoughts. He wonders why we don't talk like we used to. He wonders why we don't value his input. He thinks maybe we're right, and he isn't on the same level as us.

I force myself out of his head, already feeling as if I've violated his privacy. I don't like rifling in his head, because he wouldn't like it...not if he knew how much I keep from him.

I feel so...torn. Ovok says if we use The Living Stone, then we can save his daughter. I can't ever get a proper read on his mind—not easily. It is both terrifying and oddly refreshing. But I don't know what to do. I have one chance at this; no Moira to spin back time if I approach anyone wrong. But Mum and Da...they've moved The Living Stone. It's made me so...angry. Angry that they would do such a thing without telling us—as if they were afraid of us. I don't know where it is, and I know no one will tell me. They're all too afraid of the Myrandi. Too afraid of what they don't understand.

Too afraid, just like they're afraid of me. I've read their minds. It makes me strangely desperate to help Ovok and make a difference for someone who, perhaps, feels as alone as I do. As burdened as I do.

Maybe he's right. It's time to stop being afraid.

I snapped my eyes open, breathing heavily as I tried to remember what I was doing. The mirror...the—

"No, stop it," I mumbled with a shake of my head. I'd been searching for something…in my memories. Wait, were they mine? No. Someone else's. Skayla's. But they'd felt so much like my own head.

I looked around the room I was in, familiarity bleeding from a thousand different thoughts that weren't mine.

No. Not thoughts. Memories. I wasn't a mind reader. I wasn't Skayla.

My head hurt…so much. Everything hurt, honestly. Every move I made reminded me of something else—some injury, some traumatic event. I didn't want to think of any of them long enough to determine if they were my memories.

I got up from my chair, alone after Baey had left with the others. That's right. She'd told me not to talk to Skayla alone, so I'd sat down and decided to try and see if Skayla had any way of coping with her abilities. But my head was so jumbled, sometimes it didn't like me looking for things.

I went up the stairs slowly, the memories of this building whispering unbidden to me. Years of solitude quietly weeping. All alone. I'd hated every moment of it, and yet I'd forced myself to be useful. I hated hiding, even if I knew it was the best way to keep The Living Stone safe.

Not me. Alenor.

I wandered over to where Maeko was guarding the door to Skayla, looking up at him blankly. "I need to speak with her."

There was something like sympathy in his expression, and it just made me angry, but I couldn't quite remember why.

"Talk to Marion."

"I don't want to talk to Marion. I want to talk to Skayla," I growled.

Maeko just shook his head.

"Fine." I spun around and headed for the open door where Kearn was being kept, surprised I even remembered that. Marion was checking over Kearn's stump. I suddenly keeled over, gripping my knee with the unwelcome memory of it crunching on the solid ground.

"Tanner, what are you doing in here?" Marion's concern filtered through the pain. I took several deep breaths, trying to remind myself the pain wasn't real.

Finally, it faded. "I need to talk to Skayla." Whether desperation or pure obsession at this point, I was still thankful for being able to remember what I wanted.

Marion's frown deepened. "I don't think that's what you need. Stay there, let me finish this." She turned back to Kearn's leg, finishing up the new bandaging.

"I need to. She—she might be able to help. Nothing we're doing is helping my head, and it hurts…Marion, it hurts so much," I pleaded, almost breaking down in tears from the overwhelming pressure building inside of my mind.

"Alright." The voice was right next to me, and I realized only upon opening my eyes that they had squeezed shut on their own. "But I'm going in with you—Jaythos?"

I heard a grunt of acknowledgement from beside Kearn's bed.

"You know where to find me if anything happens. Just yell for Maeko," Marion ordered as she steered me into the hall. "Alright, let's go."

I…honestly had not thought she would agree so easily. Or at all. Was I really that bad?

You know the answer to that.

We stopped in front of Maeko. Marion took the lead. "Alright, Maeko. Thank you for keeping watch. We're going to go in just for a minute or two."

I tried to avoid Maeko's scrutinizing gaze as we crossed into the room.

Skayla's blank stare was something I understood, more than I wanted to admit. I wondered if she'd moved at all, and suddenly wondered if she'd had any water.

A picture of some water on a nearby table floating into my head, and I turned to see just that on the small table to my left.

She was in my head. Did she remember me from the other day, or was she just in such a state that she didn't really care who came in to see her?

More images floated up in my mind. Of last night…but…not just then. Of older reports detailing Lord Emarian having a wielder of mind abilities. I suddenly wondered if this was Skayla sharing thoughts with me, or if it was just me and my thousands of identities.

It's me.

"If you both could try talking out loud, I would prefer it," Marion's voice broke the deep concentration I had fallen into.

I'll try.

"Tanner." The name escaped Skayla's lips in some unnatural collection of sound. It was like someone was speaking who had no idea how to properly put the sounds together, but was desperately trying to imitate a human's voice.

It was a little creepy.

Sorry.

"Yes, that's right," I answered aloud, finding myself fairly unbothered by the intrusive thoughts from Skayla. Maybe because there were always about a hundred others floating around in here.

Speaking of…they were quieter than usual. I felt almost like myself. Or well, just less like other people.

"Are you doing that?" I asked, knowing she knew what I was talking about, if she still was in my head.

She gave a strange head motion, almost like a shrug but without any movement from the shoulders.

Marion leaned over and whispered, "What is she doing?"

"Just…my head is quieter," I replied, knowing it would be a bad idea not to keep Marion in the loop. They still saw Skayla as very dangerous, even if I knew otherwise. The level of empathy I found myself having was almost frightening, especially when also faced with the memories of people like Sven.

Sven. The name echoed. *I hurt him.* A few quick images burned in my mind but were swiftly pulled away. *I hurt everyone.*

The sorrow pressed against my chest, even after I felt her withdraw. I didn't need her to tell me, I already felt the weight of her actions. I felt everyone's regret. Hers, Sven's, Marion's, Jaythos's…they all stayed with me.

"You want…help," Skayla commented, again with that unnatural tone.

Not wanted…needed. I needed help, and I was so desperate that I was willing to gamble with her for it.

What makes you think I can? Look at me. Look at what I became. You're already close enough to it without my help.

I scoffed, working my jaw back and forth as I searched for the words. "And yet you've quieted my head for now."

Not really. I simply found you.

Something inside me shifted as I processed the words. She…she found *me?* I was still in there? "What do you mean?"

"You," she repeated out loud. *I wanted to talk to you, so I found you.*

"How? How do *I* find me?" I asked, desperation nearly strangling me.

Skayla winced, the first outward reaction to anything. "I…don't know. You are different." *We are similar but not the same.*

"Please, you have to help me," I begged, ignoring the hand Marion put on my shoulder.

Skayla's face actually twisted in some show of anguish. "You've seen…my help." *I'll just turn you into a monster, too. No. Kill me. Leave.* A torrent of frightening memories plunged into my mind, all focused on Skayla and what she had done.

But I just stared at her, refusing to be driven away by fearmongering. She'd need to try harder than that, or did she really not realize this was already my life? Reliving everyone's nightmares every day.

I thought I saw a tear in her eye.

"No one can help. I'm going to turn into what you were if nothing changes, and I've already exhausted all my other options. So it's you or no one, Skayla. Make Kearn's sacrifice worth it, or watch me turn into you: It's your choice."

<u>Sven:</u>

Baey had suggested Astra and I sit in on her lesson with Syvil, saying it would help us to relax after the events of the last day. However, I knew it was just because she wanted to keep both Astra and me as far from the main grounds of The Underground as possible.

I felt crushed, *her* voice still echoing in my head. Paranoia tore away at me piece by piece as I found myself constantly mulling over what might be going on at the manor. Had Skayla simply been waiting for me to leave? Would she use Tanner?

"Are you…alright?" Astra asked hesitantly, having been sitting next to me on one of the large empty crates we were using to observe Baey's flying exercises.

I saw the way Baey kept looking back, as if trying to find out if I was paying attention—trying to see if I was distracted. I didn't have the energy to pretend I was.

"Better than you, perhaps. You could have died," I replied to Astra. We hadn't had a chance to discuss what she'd done for Kearn, and then I had been so wrapped up in myself I hadn't asked about it. She hadn't spoken a word since last night.

"Tyron's memories showed me how," she murmured. "I was careful."

My fists clenched. "No. You weren't. You did something—you took the pain, didn't you? Took the energy from it and transferred it to yourself. I saw the limp. Didn't you say something about healing being dangerous before?"

There was a long silence in which Syvil's gentle instructions filtered over to where we sat.

Then Astra said, "It was worth the risk."

"No," I replied flatly. "It wasn't. What would happen to your family? I've used too much Gifting before—that's how I almost never woke up, Astra. That's how I got *that* far. It's always worth the risk until it isn't…until you don't come back, and I really don't want to tell your family you aren't coming home. I don't want to tell Louko."

There was another silence as Astra's shoulders drooped, the only motion from her otherwise unnaturally still frame. "I didn't know what else to do." Her blue eyes were fixed on the ground and her hands gripped the edge of the crate. "The healing of my world causes pain. His injuries were…were so extensive, and he had lost so much blood already. I was afraid he would be too weak and would go into shock if I did not try to carry some of it for him. I have practice with pain." She gave a terse shrug. "I don't even know if it matters. I don't even know if he'll live. But if he does, I…" Her eyes met mine before returning to the floor. She seemed to bite back whatever she'd intended to say, instead mumbling, "I don't know. Never mind. I did not mean to add to your burdens, and I'm sorry for that."

I knew what she'd been about to say. She thought if she could save Kearn, maybe it would repay being too late for her other friend. "It's alright. I understand. Just please, don't do that again." I knew she would. I knew she would because too much of what she said sounded like me.

The way she wouldn't look at me confirmed my fears. "You did the same for me, didn't you?" she said quietly. "Stepped in, put yourself at risk to contain me. Sure, you saved the others, too. But you didn't know me—why not kill me? It would have been easier. And it would have meant far less risk for you."

I didn't respond, forcing myself to just watch Baey as she returned to the ground and shared a few words with Syvil. I didn't know what else to do—I couldn't tell Astra she was wrong, because she wasn't.

"You are worth no less than I am," Astra went on, picking up her head. "And even if I had gone too far, it would not have been your fault."

Maybe. Maybe it would have been Skayla's instead. "Just please, try and be more careful," I pleaded.

Astra let out a pent-up breath. "I will. I'm sorry."

Any thought of further conversation was put to rest as Baey and Syvil walked back over to us, both looking energized. It was nice to see Syvil acting a bit more like himself, and it seemed the flying lesson had helped.

"You're getting better," I commented to Baey, trying to put myself back together. But I just couldn't stop thinking of Skayla.

"She is," Syvil's voice was still quiet but held pride. "She'll outmaneuver even a sparrow in no time."

Baey's wings blushed along with the rest of her. "I doubt that. But I do feel less...clumsy."

"Yes. You are indeed less like a chicken strapped to a glider."

I coughed to hide the chuckle that escaped at the image, ignoring Baey's pretend anger. Meanwhile, Syvil looked reasonably proud of himself for the analogy.

"Thank you for letting me be of use." He sobered, bowing his head. "At least I can help you fly."

I could hear the sorrow in that last bit. I couldn't even fathom what it must be like to lose one's wings—and then to endure the torture of watching others fly.

"I should be the one thanking you," Baey replied.

He took a sheepish step back, giving the clear message that any further discussion on the subject would make him uncomfortable. Whether because of embarrassment or the bittersweet reminder of the loss of his wings, I felt it was fair to him to drop it.

Baey also apparently caught on, turning to me. "Do you think maybe we could spar? I've missed it." Her wings flicked in anticipation, color morphing into a dark bronze. "I've been trying to practice without you, but it's not the same."

I knew what she was doing, but I still nodded. I would have been lying if I'd said I hadn't missed the little ball of feathers, and maybe it would do me good.

I gathered myself up and gave a shrug to Astra before taking out my blade. "Do you need me to alter yours, or can you do it on your own, now?" I asked Baey.

She blushed. "I can't do anything more than illusions. I think...maybe that's the limit. And even then, I need to be close to the ring." As she spoke, she unsheathed her blade and tapped it against the ground.

Somehow the blade didn't seem so haunted with her as its owner. "So if you could...."

I waved an idle hand and on her last tap, her hand went through. "Are you sure? It took me a while to master anything more than illusions."

Taking a defensive stance, Baey replied, "Yes. I don't know how to explain it, but...I can feel a block. Like reaching a boundary."

I made the first move, the clash of our blades ringing in the air. There was a calmness to Baey that had definitely not been there the last time we had fought, and I realized the last time was...well, a while ago.

"Interesting," I grunted as Baey pressed forward, but as I released tension in an attempt to cause her to lose her balance, she used her wings to twist around and make a play for my legs. "You've definitely gotten better."

Her feathers puffed at this, clearly way too pleased with herself, and I took the opportunity to get around her guard, almost landing a stroke that would have ended the match.

Her concentration returned very quickly, and I couldn't help but smile as I said, "I guess I just need to compliment you in order to win now."

"Oh hush," her growl was anything but hostile, and the flush in her cheeks and wings told me all I had to know.

The match lasted a solid minute before I disarmed her, and as I helped her up, I couldn't stop the proud smile fighting through my other fears and worries. "You can definitely hold your own now. Well done." I looked back at Astra. "Maybe you two should do a match. Baey could definitely use another skilled partner other than me. It's good to get used to different opponents."

Both Astra and Baey stiffened, the former looked rather worried about the idea while the latter seemed more afraid to show her excitement at the possibility.

Syvil chuckled from where he sat, prompting Baey to become temporarily distracted before turning her attention to Astra. "I wouldn't mind," she said hesitantly. "If you want."

"Um," Astra's cheeks were red and her hand twisted around her other wrist. "I wouldn't mind either, but I'm not terribly good."

I couldn't help but raise an eyebrow, then turn to Baey. "She's lying. Good luck." I waved a hand as I turned back around and headed over to take a seat next to Syvil.

Astra slowly got up, looking at me and hesitantly putting out her hand.

Right. She still didn't have a weapon. Perhaps that could be changed, now that she'd proven herself both as an ally and able to control her abilities.

A sword appeared in her hand, and she gave a thankful nod before turning back to Baey.

I wondered what was more shocking to me, the fact that Baey was actually quite tall and I somehow hadn't noticed just *how* much she'd grown until now, or the fact that Astra was incredibly short. Either way, they were quite a contrasting pair as they faced off.

The first round was a quick one, Astra coming out the victor. Baey did not have the sort of field experience I was sure Astra had, especially when it came to fighting someone skilled who wasn't me. But by the third round, it was a little more evenly matched, and Baey was able to get around Astra's guard and secure a win. That just meant Astra was even more ferocious the next round, and Baey was caught a bit off guard by it. I was satisfied to see how she quickly adjusted, though, and while Astra won that round, Baey won the following one.

"Alright, I think that's enough," I interjected as they stood there, Baey panting and Astra looking a bit tired herself. Baey had, after all, already exerted herself plenty before this.

"That was great!" She was beaming as she extended her hand.

Astra looked at it a moment, blinking in apparent confusion before offering Baey her sword.

"Oh uh," Baey blushed, wings fluffing out again. "You, uh, you shake it. It's like…I don't know, a sign of respect?"

Now it was Astra's cheeks that burned, and she took back the sword and offered her hand, shaking it awkwardly with Baey's.

"Sorry."

Baey stretched out her wings and just smiled. "Oh, I'm the one who should apologize. I guess I just forgot you weren't from here for a minute. So what do you do when you finish a match?" she asked.

Syvil muttered something about stabbing people in the back on Eatris, and I remembered that his exit from that world hadn't exactly been a genial one.

"I, uh, I don't know, I guess." Astra shrugged.

"Well, now you can confuse everyone on your planet by trying to get them to shake hands," Baey laughed.

A hesitant smile made its way onto Astra's face. "I'm sure it would throw Louko for a loop."

With a tilt of her head, Baey asked, "Who's Louko?"

334

I caught the way Astra hid the regret in her eyes as she quickly said, "He's my friend, and a much better swordsman than me." A far away expression took over as she, surprisingly, went on, "He's always curious about new things and places. I think he'd be fascinated with everything here."

Baey's smile did not waver as she said, "I'd love to meet him. Though I think I'm a little afraid of him already if he's better than you."

Astra blushed. "I'm sure he'd love to meet you all. And he would be very grateful for how you have treated me."

It was nice to see Astra engaging in conversation, no matter how small. Baey tended to bring people out of their shells, and it seemed this girl from a strange world was no exception.

I let them babble on, Baey doing most of the talking and Syvil chiming in once or twice to ask about the Myrandi. I wondered how long it would be until Astra could go home—how long it would be until we were able to get The Living Stone back from Ovok, if ever. I was so used to things going wrong, but somehow it didn't make it easier when they did. More than ever, I was desperate for us to win; desperate to get some rest from all of this death and horror. Hopefully, with the watch fixed and Moira back, we could.

But why did I still only feel apprehension?

CHAPTER XIX: The Problem with Family

Estasia:

"So they settled in alright?" Darby asked. We'd placed Sven and Astra in the same area as Kearn's soldiers. Away from the general public and their judgemental stares.

I gave a tense shrug. "As much as can be expected. I think Baey is going to update us this morning on how they are. She took care of them last night." I hadn't argued. Sven didn't need me right now. Baey was a much gentler hand, and he needed gentle. It would have been better if Darby had been able to be there, but we'd been a little busy trying to calm Cyl down.

That had been a bigger issue than we'd thought.

"Oh, so you haven't talked to them this morning?" Darby looked a bit crestfallen.

She'd tried to hide the fact that she'd really wanted Sven back in The Underground, but she hadn't exactly done a great job of it. "No. I came straight here. It's best not to catch Sven unawares in the morning, and they both could use the sleep anyway."

Darby took a sip from her mug, staring at its contents way longer than she had to. "Yes, of course. Did you check in with Grenedil yet?"

"Not yet," I replied with a huff, poring over the map of the sewers that lay on the table in an attempt to hide my own discomfort. "That's my next stop. I just wanted to make sure no one had been stupid enough to ignore orders."

"No. As we discussed with Baey before she left, no one is allowed in or out. Sounds like it would have been impossible for Baey and the others to even get back if not for the watch and Sven's ring. Everyone is scared enough about the fallout to stay put. Some people know how to follow orders." The corner of her mouth twitched.

I traced the map, following what I judged would be the most exposed portion of the sewers and the most obvious for the patrols to be able to find us, if they got past the illusion around the entrance. Once this blew over a bit, we would move the civilians here to the ravine, using the invisible airship from Hytat to fly them over. It would take multiple trips to get everyone there, and even with it being an invisible ship, we didn't want to risk a Drogan flying into it, so it was better to wait for nightfall to launch. With over nine hundred people in The Underground, that would take at least four trips, and we could only make a max of two trips a night, meaning it would take two nights to even move everyone out there. I'd really been hoping we would find a better place, but it seemed the ravine would have to do.

"Hopefully Atlys will at least be able to utilize the next few days to move supplies to the ravine and dig a well," I mused aloud. Atlys's scouts had returned just before we'd executed our ill-fated plan regarding Skayla, cementing that there were no better places to hide to the west. Then in his letter from Illan the morning following Kearn's disaster of an escape, he had confirmed that we would be going forward with the contingency plan we'd set if things had gone awry. "We just have to hope the invisibility of the airship would be enough." The patrols were getting too close here, and I already feared what could come of this. It wouldn't have been a problem if that idiot Bethynese captain had just killed Skayla instead of taking her, but now they were after something. Before, they would just have been looking for a murderer. Now they knew for sure he'd been working with us.

That moron.

The tent flap opened to reveal Baey, looking bright and more refreshed than she had any right to be.

"Morning." She gave me and Darby a smile.

"Well, hello there, Birdie," I murmured as I turned back to the map, feigning disinterest and letting Darby be the one to ask after Sven.

I didn't have to wait long. "How are they?" Darby asked.

"Better than I feared. We even did a bit of sparring last night after they arrived. Sven is going to visit Moira with Astra. I'm going to keep an eye on them—make sure no one tries to make trouble."

"And by no one, we mean mostly Cyl," I decided to point out the obvious, because he was the real person that needed babysitting, not Astra.

There was a collective sigh as the room's mood lowered a few more notches from its already pretty dreary atmosphere.

"Should I check on him first?" Baey asked. "I keep worrying he'll try and do something irrational about Astra, seeing as he was worried Astra's presence could trigger the portal."

With a groan, I replied, "Oh I'll check on him, don't worry. I just wanted to know how Sven was."

Oh wait, I hadn't meant to admit that part out loud. Funny enough, it didn't bother me as much as I'd expected it to.

Baey's smile, however, did.

"Shut up, Birdie." I glowered at the girl. "Alright, I'm out of here. Wish me luck with that dolt of a doorkeeper."

"Good luck," Darby called after me.

My mood grew fouler with every step I took closer to the portal, and by the time I was let through the barricade by the guard, I was in no mood to hear the bickering between Grenedil and Cyl.

In Grenedil's defense, he sounded about as perturbed as I did, albeit more on the drained side of frustration and less on the side of ripping Cyl a new one.

"Nothing has happened. If I didn't know better, I'd say you just don't like the fact that you aren't the only one that controls The Door." I could hear the sleeplessness in Grenedil's voice before I even caught a glimpse of the dark rings below his eyes. I was more surprised by him having a backbone.

Cyl, however, looked as poised and collected as ever, sitting straighter than a pole on his seat by the portal machine, a patronizing expression on his face as he towered over at Grenedil. "When she brings Ovok right to us, you'll regret your words, child."

"Out of the two of you, he is not the one I would be calling a child," I said with a humorless smirk, crossing my arms and glaring at Cyl a moment before turning to Grenedil. "Has anything happened with the portal?"

"Not yet, but it's only a matter of time." Cyl was the one who replied.

"I wasn't asking you." I continued to look pointedly at the fraying Grenedil.

He didn't exactly seem thankful for the attention, either, dismay instead washing over him. "Nothing. Cyl's worried what might happen if she has another episode."

I decided now was time to deign Cyl with some attention, turning to him and saying, "Seeing as she helped heal someone and made the journey here without incident, I do not think we have to fear for another episode. Sven has it completely under control."

Cyl said nothing immediately, but he didn't have to. I still remembered his terse comment regarding Sven the other day. The comment about him being a loose cannon, just one breakdown away from turning everyone inside out.

I resisted the urge to shiver, wondering if that was even something Sven could do. But I knew Sven, and I knew he would do anything to protect us and all the innocent people in this city. Cyl, on the other hand.... I was seriously beginning to wonder if he cared about anything besides this stupid portal.

"So then, why are you here?" Cyl spat out the question.

We had not exactly told Cyl about Skayla, just that Kearn had been wounded and had acquired a trail which now meant there was to be no travel in and out of The Underground. I also had no intention of informing him, already worried word of Skayla might somehow get out among the people of The Underground.

"I'm here to make sure you didn't do anything stupid," I replied, matching his tone.

His eyes narrowed. "I'm not the one you have to worry about, child."

I hated how he called us that. "And yet you're the only one here that is actively stirring up unnecessary trouble, *Cyl*."

"Actually, from what I hear through the city, I'm not the only one 'stirring up trouble'," expression brittle.

"Cyl, please just stop," Grenedil begged. "They've survived this long, leave them alone. All you want is Ovok stopped—so let them stop him their way."

Cyl just cocked his head in an uncomfortably reptilian way. "They've not been surviving. They've been losing. I'd hoped perhaps Baeno had enough backbone to keep themselves alive while I was unable to help, but it seems they had about as much backbone as Kassander."

"More backbone than you," I threw back, not sure who this Kassander was, and honestly not caring. "But I'm not here to argue with you. Because unlike you, I have better things to do." I threw a small, sympathetic look at Grenedil before returning to Cyl. "Like trying to figure out why Ovok's daughter Rhioa was worth all this destruction." I wanted to watch Cyl's reaction—to catch him off guard. I'd gotten him sufficiently riled up, now I wanted to see if it was enough to lower his guard.

And…well, something happened. Something in his eyes I couldn't immediately figure out. It was recognition but not just of Rhioa's name. I again wondered what he was hiding, something in my gut reminding me just why I didn't trust this Drogan.

I had really wanted Cyl to actually *say* something, but alas nothing ever went fully my way. I continued anyway. "*Grenedil* had been right with his hunch. All this time, Ovok didn't care about destroying the world.

He just cared about getting The Living Stone for what he needed. What do you know of his daughter?"

I watched Cyl measure his next move carefully, but he kept that mightier-than-thou attitude and stood up to turn away, purposefully masking his face so that I couldn't read it. "Daughter*s*. He has two. One was left on Eatris to keep his secret empire as functioning as possible. Both are elite assassins, helping Ovok keep Astra's world firmly under his control without anyone even knowing. Trained by Ovok's monster of a wife, Dyress, before she disappeared. You don't want to meet them, trust me."

"Dyress?" I asked, allowing a small diversion in the topic.

Cyl stiffened. "Yes. She's the one that killed Ovok's father, got him on the Myrandi throne, and gave him the Myrandi blade, Ckaknimaen. But even she was too much of a rabid dog for his taste. Everyone assumed he killed her about a century ago after she went after Kassander, a friend of mine and once a friend of Ovok."

Kassander? The one he'd just insulted Baeno with? Somehow, I got the feeling I wasn't missing out on much by not being Cyl's friend, if that's how he talked about his friends.

"So *can* The Living Stone save Rhioa?" I asked, turning the conversation back to the daughter. And that's when I saw it, the slightest bit of tension in his shoulders at Rhioa's name.

"Who knows. If Ovok thinks so, it's likely. Although since the incident with Rhioa, I wouldn't exactly call him rational. It might just be that it was the only thing he could rationalize would work, and so was willing to take the gamble." Cyl's tone had even more of an edge to it. "But trust me, if he leaves Baeno with it, your world will slowly begin to fade away, just as it did before The Living Stone was born."

Sven and Alenor had explained to me some of the legends of old. About how the world would slowly tear itself apart without The Living Stone to anchor it. We definitely wanted to avoid that.

"It sounds like gambling innocent lives might be something you and Ovok have in common. I'm starting to see why you were friends," I smiled smugly, proud of how clearly this made him angry. Cyl's stare bored into me, and for a minute, I thought maybe he would turn into his Dragon form and incinerate me with that acid-like fire of his. It seemed he really hated being compared to Ovok, huh?

"You would be gambling with even more lives if I let you use the portal, *child*." The words were venomous.

I decided that was enough poking. Getting him any angrier might cause him to actually turn more… Dragon. That, or it would give poor, horrified Grenedil a heart attack. But I'd found something—a small, nearly imperceptible chip in this ancient Guardian's armor. The question was, how could I pry it out so it was open to examine?

Baey:

I had asked Sven and Alenor to wait for me before telling Moira about Skayla, uneasy about the thought that she would be told any important information without me present. Now, just outside of Alenor's forge, I hesitated, hearing the conversation filtering through and feeling guilty over the doubt.

Alenor was chattering away, explaining the various things she was doing around the forge as Sven assisted, or so I gathered by the sound of her occasional request for him to fetch an item. Moira, in the meantime, would chime in with a suggestion or question. It sounded like…a real family.

Taking a deep breath, I entered, knowing the facade of serenity was about to be shattered.

"Baey—fantastic, come on in," Alenor's eyes were alight with the fire from her forge as she beckoned me in.

I didn't want to ruin this, but they'd planned to tell Moira. Still, I would let Alenor and Sven take the lead.

Inside, Moira and Astra sat on a pair of stools in one end of the forge, while Alenor and Sven were in the workshop portion of the forge, working on shutting down the fires. I didn't miss how tense Astra looked, eyeing every tool that hung against the walls.

Alenor's smile was wide, something I didn't expect after the whole Skayla problem. "I have something for you." As she spoke, she went over to a table and took hold of a long, intricately carved staff bound with leather near the center for grip. Coming out of the tip was a long, narrow spearhead—the thing I'd seen Alenor working on just the other day—with three feathers that I realized had to have been mine tied at the base of the blade, and in the center of the blade glowed a green stone, its glow penetrating through my skin and into my very soul. It…called to me.

"It's your relic," Alenor said as if she was holding something very sacred. "Sven was able to help me with the finishing touches." She turned to her son, who was standing quietly nearby. Beckoning to him, she had him take staff. "Why don't you give it to her?"

I felt strangely stuck in place, confusion and longing washing away any memory of what I had originally come here for. Slowly, Sven came up, offering the spear to me with an intense gaze.

"It's time you had your own, darlin'," he said, the simple words causing a wave of foreign emotions to wash over me.

Almost shaking, I slowly reached forward and took hold of the spear, a flurry of energy coursing through my body. All at once, I felt...a sense of completion. It was a strange bond, the way the spear instantly felt a part of me, and me, a part of it. I gripped it hard, heart beating quickly as I looked back to Sven and Alenor.

"Now, take this and put it around your waist—" she handed me some sort of utility belt. "There is a small button on the staff of the spear. If you press it down and hit the butt against the ground, it will collapse and you can store it in the holster." She pointed out the small, carefully hidden button. "Go ahead and give it a go."

I obeyed, fascinated as the staff of the spear folded in on itself until it was like a knife with a handle. There had been no visible seams—no way to tell it could do such a thing. Alenor was a genius.

"And it's quite strong. Don't worry about it collapsing on you during a fight." Alenor folded her arms, admiring her handiwork with no small amount of pride. "And to make it full length again, just give it a good shake as you press the button."

I obeyed, and just like that, it stretched out to full length, nothing to show it was so easily compactable.

But another question was busy tickling my curiosity. "So, uh, what does it do?"

Alenor laughed. "I don't know."

"Try using my Gift, Baey," Sven encouraged gently. "I think it might channel your empathic abilities for Gifting so you don't need, say, a relic."

I was still in shock, overwhelmed by emotion as I continued to stare at the spear. But then, I looked up at Alenor, holding out my other hand and thinking of a flower, of how much I wished I could give her something in return.

Almost immediately, a bright red rose appeared in my hand. Alenor's smile widened.

The rose wrinkled away into nothing, and I actually laughed a little. "I...wait," I frowned, turning around and facing Moira and Astra. As excited as I was, I did note a strange look of apprehension in Moira. I continued on, "But is it only people with relics...or do you think I could use anyone's Gift now?"

"A good question," Alenor purred. "Seems some experimentation is in order."

"Wait, you can now control anyone's Gift?" Moira's sudden intrusion into the moment was filled with apprehension. "Doesn't that sound a little dangerous?"

Caught up in the moment, I'd suddenly forgotten how I'd kept my ability to use Sven's ring a secret from Moira. Again, that gut feeling. I turned and faced her. "I'm not going to go mad with power, if that's what you're worried about."

"You say that, but why won't you return what's mine?"

Just like that, the whole atmosphere of the room changed.

"I'm...sorry?" My brow furrowed even as my gut twisted in a knot.

"I've already dealt with the betrayal of a sister—and I thought I knew her." Moira was shaking. "Forgive me if I have very little trust for you."

"Moira," Sven took a step forward, indignation dripping from his tone. "Baey *saved* you."

And that's when it happened. I blinked, and everything felt...strange. Sven had backed down for some reason, back in his place behind me, and Moira no longer looked hostile.

"And you're sure she can control it?" Moira asked, voice not nearly as confrontational as a moment before.

"Yes," Sven said with conviction, nothing betraying any hint of the argument that had just begun to unfold. "I would trust her with my life, Moira."

"Wait...wait, what? What about—" What was going on? I whipped my head from Moira to Sven and Alenor, confused by the lack of hostility. "She just...didn't you hear her?"

Sven's brow furrowed. "Baey? What are you talking about?"

I spun to face Moira. "What did you *do?*" I hissed, my free hand grasping the watch even as my other hand tightened around my new relic.

Again, I blinked, and I was suddenly facing Sven and Alenor again.

"I trust you will use the power wisely," Moira said meekly. "You seem like a good person."

"Stop!" I screamed, causing everyone to jump. This time I felt Moira try and spin back time and retry the scenario, and I thrust all my will into trying to stop it.

Surprisingly, it worked.

"Baey? What's going on?" It was Sven, whispering gently as if I was some bear and he was afraid of prodding me.

"She's spinning back time—why are you manipulating the conversation?" I glared at her. "How much have you been doing this?" Suddenly, I remembered that odd moment the other day, when she'd first asked for her watch and had gotten shot down. I'd thought it strange no one else had acted like it had happened, and I realized that's because…it never had. "You're doing this all just to get your watch back."

"What?" Alenor's voice was thin. "Baey, are you sure—"

"I am *positive*. I just relived the last minute and a half three times; I'm pretty confident." I glared hard at Moira, who was surprisingly glaring just as much back at me.

"I can't help you all without it! I won't be able to go back any further than I've had the watch, and the longer you don't give it back to me, the longer I can't undo anything!" Moira threw up her hands. "We saw what happened to the world without me to stop it—what do you think is going to happen? I already could have gone back and stopped that captain from saving Skayla if you'd just let me!"

"*How* did you know that?" Sven asked, vehement. "We haven't even told you that yet."

Moira's face went pale, and again, I felt her try and go back. Again, I fought it. This time, it was much more difficult.

"Oh *no,* don't you even!" I shouted, not missing the buzzing energy of Astra from her corner as she waited to see if she was needed. "How long have you been doing this?" And how had she been doing it without the watch? My guess was it was like Sven—she could turn back time a few minutes at a time without the watch. It would seem me having her relic allowed me to travel back with her and remember what had once happened. Or the spear. I wondered if there had been anything she'd spun back without me realizing it.

"Listen, I'm only trying to *help!*" Moira shouted back, standing up with both fists clenched.

"No!" I pounded my spear against the ground with the word, wings flaring out. "No, you're trying to *control* the situation. Just like I felt in the watch."

My head was spinning, wondering how in the world we were supposed to rein this in. If I wasn't around, I wouldn't be able to tell when time was turned back—what if she kept redoing the scenarios until we catered to her? What if she found a way to convince them?

"How long, Moira?" Sven sounded angry.

"I am trying to help, Sven, please listen."

"How long!?" he yelled, this time.

"I—"

I slammed the butt of my spear again on the ground. "It doesn't matter how long. She isn't allowed out of my sight, and as soon as we can get back to the manor, I'll use Tanner's Gift to see just how much she's hiding."

"I can detain her," Sven's tone was cold, but beneath it, I heard how broken he was. "Create a barrier she can't leave. I have long acquainted myself with the limitations of both my sisters."

"No—please, I swear I'm trying to help!" Moira cried. I felt her desperation, if only because she was now frantically trying to turn back time.

"Just stop her from turning back time, and once she's been in there for ten minutes, she'll be unable to escape without the watch," came Sven's empty instruction.

"Are you sure?" I couldn't help but ask.

"Yes. I knew her before she had the watch, and she was never able to go back more than ten minutes. And I made sure of it myself—I didn't just take her word for it."

I nodded, all of us ignoring Moira's pleas as a shimmering dome enveloped her, giving her enough space to sit and move around a little in the forge.

We waited ten minutes in anguished silence, Astra's buzzing energy the only tangible sign of anxiety.

"Enough time has lapsed," Sven announced, motionless as he stared in the direction of his sister.

There were angry tears in Alenor's eyes. "Can she hear us?" she asked.

"No," Sven replied.

"...so she was manipulating us?" Alenor's question was tortured.

It took all my strength to reply, "I...it seems so. I don't know—but she wanted her watch back, and she tried to sow doubt against me in order

to get it. When it didn't work…she just went back in time and tried again."
I had wanted so badly for my gut to be wrong, for Estasia to have been wrong.

But I was beginning to see why Estasia had trust issues, and I found myself wondering again just how far back this had gone. How long had Moira been subtly influencing even the smallest actions of those around her? That pulsing need for control that came from the watch grew in intensity, and I found myself unable to conjure any more words, just staring dumbly at Alenor and Sven.

I had just wanted to bring their family back; and instead, I'd exposed just how fractured it was.

Sven:

It was just my luck, wasn't it, that I'd have both sisters stabbing me in the back. I stood there in disbelief, wishing I wasn't so…unsurprised.

Was this really what it took to get me to see? I remembered all the times I'd been left behind for official summits and peace talks between the various nations and factions of Baeno. I remembered how astonished I'd been, at times, over how they'd gotten people to agree. I'd known Moira and Skayla both had used their abilities to help bring peace, but had it always been this much? Had Moira been manipulating me all those years, perhaps knowing how I would react and, therefore, spinning back time so I was unaware?

I felt like reality itself was crushing me, closing in like water in my lungs. Yet at this point, it didn't really change much. I didn't want to say I was used to it. No. I was *resigned* to it; resigned to knowing nothing was ever simple. Nothing ever went right.

"We can't clear her until we look in her memories," I said simply, putting a hand on my mother's shoulder as she fought to stay composed. She'd thought she was getting her family back. Instead, she just got to see how far each of her children had fallen.

"That will be several days, at least." Baey looked helpless, wings rippling from one color to another in dismay.

"And only if Marion deems Tanner well enough," I added, the image of the boy still too present in my mind. "And if he agrees. Please, don't push him."

Baey's wings twitched in some mixture of irritation and anxiousness, and she asked, "Will we be able to bring food to her in there?" she pointed to where Moira was being kept inside the small dome I'd created.

"Yes." I looked at Mum. "Are you alright?"

We stared at each other for a while before she whispered, "I will be. Just please…darlin', don't do anything stupid."

My heart broke a little as I remembered I already had. So many times. I was just trying desperately to make up for it now. Unable to speak, I gave a simple nod.

"We need to tell Darby and Estasia as soon as possible…" Baey murmured, wings now giving a more measured, repetitive flex.

"I'll tell her. You stay here." I didn't really process it was me who was speaking. "You need to make sure she doesn't try anything. The dome around her will stay intact without me here." Well, as long as I stayed in The Underground, that was. But I wasn't going to say anything about limitations in the presence of Moira, even if I knew she wasn't listening. One apparently couldn't be too careful around her. "Astra, can you also stay here in case?" I turned and asked the young redhead; she had admittedly been acting very on edge the whole time in the forge. I felt bad for asking her to stay, but if Moira did somehow get out, she was the most powerful one here along with Baey.

Astra nodded, determination in her eyes.

No one argued with me, and so I left, ignoring the venomous glances in the streets as I pushed my way to Darby and Thackeray's tent.

The guard let me in without hesitation, and I found myself face-to-face with a surprised Darby.

"We have a problem," I whispered, conscious of the fact we didn't really want anyone else knowing this—not even the guard outside, at the moment. The last thing we needed was for panic to ensue over this.

Darby drew close, waiting for me to explain further.

"Moira," I continued, voice still low. "She's not to be trusted."

The lack of shock on Darby's expression was…frustrating. Frustrating and a little crushing.

"What happened?"

I forced myself to go on, ignoring the way my chest squeezed itself. "She was spinning back time…trying to get the watch back. She apparently had, at one point, even gotten Mum and me to tell her about Kearn and Skayla, because she knew…and I definitely don't remember telling her." It hurt, knowing Moira would have had to seriously play with my state of mind in order to get that kind of information out early—and then…to have erased it from ever happening…I felt violated and used.

I hated feeling used.

"What?" Darby actually looked startled now, eyes widening. "Is she contained? How do you know?"

I recited the facts as coldly as possible, quickly explaining while Darby stood in patient silence. It didn't take long, but it felt like forever.

"Are you…alright?" Darby asked at last, eyes full of worry and pity.

"Yes, I'm fine," I hadn't meant to snap. "I'm…sorry. I'm just sorry."

For some reason, Darby did not recoil like I expected her to. "Well, you said you have contained Moira, and Baey is watching her, right? Maybe sit for a minute and collect yourself," she offered, pulling up a seat for me.

I took a step back, vehement as I replied, "No, the last thing I need to do is sit *down*. Maybe you should be a little more worried about me turning out to be as manipulative and self-serving as my siblings." The acute sensation of drowning again filled my lungs as they tried to force air down but instead only got nothing. "Nothing is going right—nothing is working. It just keeps getting worse and I'm so *sorry*."

Stepping forward, Darby put a slow, gentle hand on my shoulder, using her other hand to tip my chin up against my will and meet her gaze.

"Sven. It's not your full responsibility. I'm sorry I kept it from you…but I already didn't trust Moira," she said, regret showing. "I told Estasia, and we agreed Baey was to keep an eye on her. She'd always…unnerved me. I'm sorry, I should have told you."

I stepped away from her, unable to contain the anguish. "What?" Was I…was I blind? I remembered my own reasons for hiding my own true abilities from Moira, but…but I'd never thought that much of it. I'd always put it off as my own paranoia. "I…but she never would have done anything to hurt anyone. I didn't think either of them would have." I fought back the tears. "Have we always been the monsters?" I looked at Darby, the realization too much. Had I just always ignored it? Had we ever been on the right side? Had I…always been used by a sister?

"No—no, Sven, stop it." Darby grabbed my hand and pulled me forward into a hug that was so startling I was unable to even register it had happened. Though once I did…I couldn't bring myself to let go. I had no strength left to resist.

"Not monsters. Just people." She let go at last, putting both hands instead on my shoulders and trying to look me in the eye. I…couldn't. I just couldn't.

"I don't think Moira was malicious. I want to talk to her, myself. I think…I think we definitely should not trust her, but I think, perhaps…her power made her feel responsible to make everything go right. You said it yourself; she wanted the watch back because she wanted to fix everything." She sighed, not letting go of me. Part of me wanted her to, so that I could run. The other part of me desperately wished she would never let go. "I can understand where she's coming from, even if I don't agree with her. You did the right thing. You're not a monster, Sven, just a victim of other people's choices."

I thought back to my conversation with Astra, and as much as I wanted to pull away in this moment—to suffocate in this feeling of responsibility for my sisters, I suddenly wondered if maybe…I should listen to Darby. Maybe I finally wanted to believe her, because I didn't think I could continue to take this sense of failure.

Closing my eyes and taking a shuddering breath, I tried to process what she'd said, tried to believe her. I didn't know if I could, but at the very least, I felt less like screaming and more at terms with the horrible mess things had become. Or...apparently, the horrible mess that had always been.

"I'm sorry," I couldn't help but whisper again.

Darby reached up a hand and gently touched my cheek, a sad smile on her lips as she said, "Sven. You have nothing to apologize for. Please."

Grabbing her hand, I slowly pulled it away, but found myself unwilling to actually let go of it. It was warm and comforting...a lifeline. I had forgotten how much I'd missed her, locked away in the manor for the last few days.

"Thank you." I barely managed the words.

With a nod, she wrapped her hand more effectively around mine, releasing her other hand from my shoulder as we stared at each other for a while. "Now, why don't you sit for a little while? And then you can bring me to Moira, and we'll figure this out together. No more being the solution, Sven. Alright?"

I wasn't really in a place to process all that meant, but I trusted her. I let her help me sit, and for a while we said nothing, the silence for once comforting and not like a choke hold. I knew it was because of who shared it with me.

At last, however, there was no escaping what we needed to do, and I stood up, this time able to reach her eyes as I spoke. "We should go."

Coming over and entwining her hand in mine, she said, "Yes. We should."

I didn't pull away this time.

As we made our way back to the forge, the stares didn't bother me so much, and I wondered if they were less hostile because of Darby, or if I just cared less with her here beside me.

Either way, we reached the forge without so much as a heckle, and it was with great effort I let go of her hand.

Darby seemed equally as unwilling, but at last, we separated as we walked inside.

No one had really moved since I'd left, making me hope maybe I hadn't been gone as long as I feared. The only one that had really changed position was Mum, sitting in the far corner with a dark expression.

"She can hear us now," I announced to the room after allowing sound to perforate Moira's nearly invisible prison.

"Darbeshay, please listen—" Moira immediately leapt up from where she'd been sitting, only for Darby's hand to fly up in a motion that cut off the defense.

"I'm not letting you out," Darby said simply, shoulders squared and composure much calmer than either me or Mum. "No one person should be the judge of who gets to live and who gets to die—not even if the person being judged is your sister. We all agreed that Kearn's change of plan could prove useful, and we had no intention of needing anyone to go back and change what happened. I know the captain certainly wouldn't have wanted that, even if it was possible."

I couldn't help but remember how hesitant Baey had been when the suggestion *had* originally been brought up. It only made me more upset that Moira could so easily suggest undoing so many choices.

"You are all going to get yourselves *killed*. You have no idea what you're up against," Moira hissed, more desperate than fierce.

"With all due respect, Moira, I have been fighting and surviving for the past decade, even with you gone. I think perhaps you are the one more out of the loop. I know you trust no one, and that is unfortunately why I have never trusted you."

Darby paused, putting both hands behind her back. "So until you can prove that you're ready to work *with* us, and not use us, I think you're going to have to stay in there. And that includes not just proving you can work with me or your brother or your mother, but Baey as well." She turned around, acknowledging the young Esmer briefly before going back. "I would suggest you get on her good side by continuing to help her learn how to use your watch."

"Darby, you have no clue what I've seen. You can't leave me in here—I need to help." Moira pressed her hand against the barrier.

"No, Moira. You need to control. That's very different from helping." Darby turned to me and my mother, then took a deep breath, "I truly am sorry."

Chapter XX: Splice the Rope

<u>Tanner:</u>

Marion had, begrudgingly, continued to let me talk with Skayla. It was the only time I could really think clearly, the way she found my consciousness, quieting the other noise enough for me to actually have a thought for myself.

It wasn't perfect, but it was better.

Can you give memories to others? she asked, even as her face remained mostly impassive. It had been a day or so, and I realized that while her mind was mostly intact, there was a disconnect between her body and her. It had gotten less unsettling, but I hoped maybe continual interaction with her would help that.

"I apparently did it with Kearn, once, according to Marion. But we haven't been able to replicate it." Marion had insisted I reply outside of my head even with Skayla being able to read my reply. At first, it had been so that there was a level of accountability with her in the room, but today, she had trusted me to be in here alone, worried with how Kearn had not woken up yet. But I still answered aloud, hoping maybe it would help Skayla to remember to speak aloud as well.

That had come with less success.

I could do it. Give someone else thoughts that weren't theirs. Make them their own. Maybe you can do the same with memories.

I winced, not exactly about to give anyone else the crowded head I had.

With objects, not people. I felt a brief but potent wave of anguish and guilt. Skayla hadn't meant it about people, but she'd realized I would immediately come to that conclusion, given her track record.

Seeing as Marion had already suggested this, and I'd already *tried*, I felt a little disappointed by the suggestion, frowning as I half-heartedly fiddled with the stool I was sitting on, hoping maybe she would give a further example of *how* she did it.

Fortunately, she came through, images of splicing rope coming to mind. Putting two separate things and making them part of each other…so taking a foreign memory and fitting it into something it originally had nothing to do with. When Marion and I had tried, we'd always approached it by more of placing it *into* the object, rather than trying to bind the fiber of memory and object *together* as one. Hopefully Skayla was onto something….

I gripped under the edge of the stool, concentrating and allowing the paranoia I'd had of taking on more memories to wash away, instead I replaced it with intent. It would be to get rid of something instead of take it, for once. I kept the image of splicing rope in the front of my mind, along with one of Maeko's memories of Serafina. The one of her dying.

After a moment of frustration, I gave up, finding myself now only stuck with the stupid memories of those who had sat on this stupid stool. So much for Skayla having a new angle. This was about as useful as Marion and my attempts.

You have to want it.

I stared at Skayla. "You think I don't *want* to be rid of them? They're making me go insane. Quite literally, and I would have thought you'd understand that."

I felt pain. *I do. That's why I'm telling you. You have to want it.* More images—memories of her when young and afraid. Crying to Sven. Hating her Gift. Telling her parents she wished she could be normal. Then the opportunity arising when they were offered their relics. The ability to deny the relic. Then the hesitation—the realization that…that I didn't know how else to live anymore. That everything I knew of people came from my Gift. The fear of vulnerability and ignorance.

I shook my head, trying to steady my shallow breaths. "That's stupid," I muttered, ignoring the truth behind it. The truth that…well…none of what I knew about any of my friends came from things they'd told me. No one…no one *talked* to me, except Baey, and even then….

"I couldn't…live. Without knowing." Skayla's words came out in sluggish drawls. "I…wish I had."

Swallowing hard, I found myself realizing I had to accept that I didn't really have any connection with anyone—not even Baey—except for the ones I'd forged because of memories I'd stolen. I needed to give up control if I wanted to stay sane, and that could mean giving up…everyone.

But had I ever really had anyone if it was all fake like this? I'd always felt that way about those at Valdon but never Baey. Never Marion or Syvil. Would I lose them as friends?

I took another deep breath, again closing my eyes and reaching out into the memories of the stool, feeding it the memory of Serafina. The memory that I needed to let go of. That felt so necessary to know and understand Maeko. But it wasn't mine.

I thought again of the spliced rope, tying the memory into the seat and leaving it there until I couldn't actually remember what it was I'd been tying it to.

You did it. Skayla was…almost smiling. It was a little creepy, as if it was a smile painted on a face more than anything else, but it at least wasn't the crazy-looking smile she'd once sported.

The smile vanished quickly, and I had a feeling she'd seen the reaction in my head. I wasn't sure whether to feel bad about that or not.

If it is like a thought, then the memory will remain where you leave it, until you take it back.

The sudden temptation was much stronger than I wanted to admit to, but I knew I should leave it where it was—whatever memory it had been. However, that did help a little bit, and that meant that at least important memories—ones I'd taken from Ovok, for example—would be able to be stored and recovered when necessary. Because those ones were what was hurting my head the most, at the moment.

You could have died.

I looked aghast, thinking how I would have liked to have known that *before* trying her suggestion.

No. Not with the stool, dolt. I felt a small slice of humor before the guilt returned. *Ovok. He is older than a millennium. That mind could and should have killed you. Even I didn't consider it worth the risk to really penetrate that deeply. I had a hard enough time scratching the surface of it, as it was.*

"Oh," I murmured. "Well…at the time, I figured we were all going to die anyway, so…." I gave a grimace, wishing I could forget Sefen's cold body. I wondered if I could maybe use this same method to get rid of memories that were mine that I didn't want.

NO! The thought was so loud I put my hands over my ears. *Remember what using my Gift on myself did to me. Don't you dare.*

I blushed, embarrassed and a little sobered at the rebuke. I was, after all, trying to *avoid* becoming like her.

"Sorry…I won't." I wished the warning hadn't come with an overwhelming rush of memories that detailed just what atrocities Skayla committed. Yeah, those were definitely next on the list of things to get rid of.

We sat in silence for a little longer before I heard a faint commotion outside.

"Your injured friend," Skayla whispered, having clearly read not just my mind.

I got up, giving a quick nod of thanks and then leaving the room to find that Maeko was no longer at the door. I made sure to close it carefully, and then ran over to where Kearn's door was left ajar, the source of commotion coming from inside.

"Calm down, stay there. You're alright, breathe—Jaythos, get me that bottle and a handkerchief."

I was faster than the still-limping Jaythos, crossing the threshold of the room and grabbing the needed items. Kearn was wrestling feverishly against Marion and Maeko, leaving Jaythos to hover like a flustered mother worrying about her young.

"Tanner—fine, that's great, just pour a little bit of that into the handkerchief and give it to me." Marion's confusion was pushed away as Kearn struggled.

I immediately did as I was told and then deposited the now-damp handkerchief into her hand. She quickly stuffed it in Kearn's face, and he went almost instantly limp. Well, maybe not completely limp, but definitely a lot more docile.

"Is he alright?" Jaythos's open concern was not something I thought I would ever get used to.

"He's fine," Marion grumbled, standing up and arching her back. "It's just a mild sedative. He's going to hurt himself. Kearn—Kearn, can you hear me?" She all but shoved Maeko out of the way and went over to Kearn's head, opening wide an only half-open eyelid.

There was a groan.

"Good, now listen up—you try that again, and I'll have Maeko sit on you. You need to lie still and get better. I don't want to have to console a blubbering Jaythos if you kill yourself," she continued even as Jaythos hesitantly sat back down in his seat beside his brother, grabbing hold of Kearn's hand.

"You've lost a leg. Do you understand?" Marion asked gruffly. I winced, knowing that wasn't exactly how I'd want to be told. Then again, if it stopped Kearn from getting up….

Kearn's eyes fluttered open again, but I wasn't able to see much from where I was standing, now that Jaythos and Marion both blocked my path.

"Skayla?" Maeko grunted the one-word question as he came back my way, brow wrinkled with worry.

"She's fine."

"I should go." Maeko seemed to ignore what I'd said, putting a hand on my shoulder before leaving.

I swallowed hard, trying to keep myself from wondering what he was thinking. I needed to stay here, in *my* head.

"No—don't try that again." Marion's warning snapped me back to the scene playing out in front of me. It was an odd disconnect I'd grown used to; feeling as if I was simply watching more memories play out in my head and what was unfolding before my eyes wasn't *actually* happening here.

I tried to remember who I was watching this. I *wasn't* Jaythos...he was sitting over his brother, trying to calm him down.

"What—where's—"

"She's fine," I spoke up, not really understanding what I was talking about. I found all three staring at me, Kearn's eyes rather glazed over in half-conscious pain.

"You didn't kill...her?"

"What—you wanted us to?" Marion seemed about ready to throw her hands up in the air, but instead used them to push Kearn back down.

"No—no. I don't—"

"Calm down, Kearn. You're going to hurt yourself...more...." Jaythos squeezed his brother's hand.

"My leg..."

"I know. Just rest."

I felt out of place, watching this unfold like some unwelcome stranger. Eventually, Kearn drifted back to sleep and after another ten or so minutes, Marion left his bedside to come over to me.

"You alright?" she asked in a low voice.

I nodded, forcing myself to look away from the pair of brothers at the other end of the room. I wasn't fine; I didn't even know who I was. Or who *she* was.

"Is everything with Skayla…fine?"

Skayla. Marion's question helped ground me and helped me remember. There was hope. "Yes. We…we found a way to help me. I can put my memories into objects—get them out of my mind if they aren't mine. Like what you were saying—Skayla knew how to do it."

Marion grunted, expression softening. "Well, then I suppose that witch was good for something, after all. Is your head clearer, then?"

"Not yet…I only tried once. But I think if I take Ovok's out, it will help a lot." I fiddled with the hem of my shirt. "I just…need to put it into an object I can easily keep. In case…we need more information from his memories."

"Perhaps something on your person, then?" she suggested. "Something not easily lost."

"Maybe…almost like Sven's ring, or something," I frowned, immediately wondering why I'd suggested anything when I already had my armlet. What was I even suggesting again?

"Tanner?"

Who was I…I swallowed the panic.

"It's Marion. Let's get you something quick, hm?" The strange woman steered me out of the room—where were we?—and down the hall to another room, where she quickly began rifling through a few drawers.

"What...what's going on?" I shouldn't have asked this strange woman. Why did I keep trusting strangers? Why couldn't I remember who I was?

"This will do," the woman murmured, pulling out a broken compass from a small nightstand drawer and whirling around. "Tanner, focus. It's me, Marion. You're in Alenor's manor and we need to get those memories out of your head."

The compass—wait, I thought it should have been a watch, or was it still hiding in my pocket—no. That wasn't me. Sven. Sven had been...when he'd shown up to Valdon. But this wasn't Valdon, and I wasn't Sven.

Just breathe.

The compass was pressed into my hand along with, "Do whatever it was that Skayla taught you. Get some room in your head. Please, kid, just...hurry." She sounded...concerned. Someone was concerned for me?

The image of a spliced rope pierced through my muddled mind, and suddenly I remembered what Marion was talking about. Well, and that her name was Marion.

My fingers closed around the compass. I allowed myself to feel the memories attached to it, taking a deep breath as I was about to be sucked back into Ovok's fathomless mind. It was not a pleasant experience. Screams...so much screaming. And blood. And...feeling lost.

"He's insufferable!" I throw my hands in the air, pacing the room as Dyress listens quietly from her seat. "He just sits and watches the world tear itself apart. All he cares about is collecting his rare items."

"He only has one form left, though, doesn't he?" Dyress asks coolly.

Yes, he does, and I have kept it secret already. My father was supposed to step down as Lord of the Myrandi—that's what the law said after losing your first form. But he'd stayed, anyway.

"If he were to fall, would not you be put forth as his successor?"

I freeze, turning to face Dyress. "What? You're not suggesting—"

"Please. I would never dream of telling you to kill your father," She stands up, fingers brushing against the intricate yet dangerous looking blade that hangs at her side. "But maybe someone else would be willing to get some blood on their hands, if it was for the good of the Myrandi and Eatris. Your father has long been corrupted by power. I am suggesting justice for breaking Myrandi law."

Justice? My father is corrupt...but is justice truly his death?

"Or would you rather watch him cause more death by his corrupt complacency?"

Splice the rope. Don't think about it. Just splice the rope.

"What did you do?!" I stare at Dyress as she now stands over the bleeding body of my dear friend, Kassander. Not far away cower my two young children—my two daughters, looking bruised and terrified. And...chained up?!

370

Dyress just laughs. "Oh please, I'm so sick of your erratic morality."

"No," I snarl. "You have gone too far—step away from them."

Don't get lost in it...just splice the rope.

"You will keep my daughter safe?" I ask calmly, sizing up the human that has been so bold as to risk his life for my daughter's freedom. A freedom I should have granted long ago.

"With my very life," he answers. "Will you do the same for her sister?"

Eyes narrowing, I once more wonder at Tyron's gall. No one has spoken to me like this and lived. And yet, it hurts to know I have given reason to doubt I would care for Rhioa and Tirzah. No one knows. I've hidden my weakness too well, and yet in this moment, I am weak as I reply, "You underestimate what a father would do for his daughters."

Splice the rope. I gasped, not expecting the unpleasant sensation of things being drawn from my head and into the compass. When I'd tried this before, I was pretty sure I'd tried just one memory, not a whole person's mind. It hurt...so much.

But then.

"Tanner?" Marion put a hand on my shoulder and shook me gently. "Tanner, are you alright?"

I opened my eyes, smiling in relief as I whispered, "Yes," with more sincerity than I had used in a long time. I could finally be free. Already, my head felt so much better. I clutched the compass, giving a weak laugh. "I think I'm going to be alright."

Estasia:

It had been another two days since the Moira incident, and I was getting antsy. The tunnels were still crawling with people, but I wanted nothing more than to check in with Atlys and maybe see if Baey could use Tanner's Gift on that no-good Mara. So far, they were a perfect split of a family. I would die for half of them and I would love to kill the other half.

Well, apparently, I would love to chicken *out* of killing the other half, but the sentiment remained and I was still in a foul mood.

"Atlys already confirmed right after Captain Kearn's escape that we have gone to plan B. He knows we need to wait before contacting him. The silence is not just expected—it's needed." Thackeray voiced his uncertainty as he looked over some papers with Darby.

"Thay is right. We shouldn't risk it," Darby confirmed. "Lord Atarah and that general Brahj of Bethyn are both scouring the tunnels with a passion. Just wait until it's calm enough to safely make it through, and stick to what was agreed."

"But if I bring Baey, then we can just nix the plan if she says it doesn't work," I pointed out. I just...I had this bad feeling, and my instincts were rarely wrong.

Darby tapped the table. "Yes, but Baey is watching Moira, if you recall. Atlys knows we won't be making contact for a while."

"But Illan...I could talk to him." If I was being completely honest, I had already made up my mind about this. "No one would expect anyone sneaking back into the palace, anyway. And if they do, Baey can fix it—I trust Sven and Alenor can keep Moira in check for a few hours."

Neither Darby nor Thackeray looked particularly pleased, but it was the former that spoke. "I do not intend to use Sven as a constant guard for his two sisters. I think he's dealing with enough as it is."

For a moment, I faltered, unable to quench the little bit of guilt that had risen with Darby's comment. "Listen, I don't either. But I just…I have a bad feeling, and you know what, if everything goes fine, then maybe we just have Baey spin back an hour or two so that I never even left, and then Sven didn't have to watch Moira—with Sven's permission, of course," I added the last bit quickly, hating even the idea that either of them would think I wanted to go behind anyone's back with this. Ew. I left that to Moira.

"Thay?" Darby turned to her brother. "Perhaps I'm too close to this. What do you think?"

And that was why I actually found Darby competent. She knew when she had a biased opinion and reached out for others' advice. Her and her brother both were level-headed and probably two of the most competent people in our little rebellion. Which, I suppose wasn't saying *that* much, but they had done well surviving all these years, and for that I could respect them.

Running a hand through his hair, Thackeray replied, "Well, she hasn't been wrong yet." I was surprised by his change in tune. But perhaps like I had learned to trust them, they had also seen how valuable my instincts were in things. A wise decision, in my opinion.

"Fine." Darby sounded anything but pleased with this. "But ask Sven before you go. And make sure Baey is fine with it, too."

I gave a mock salute and said, "Certainly. Hopefully I'll be back before you know it."

Baey was easy to find, still guarding the moronic Mistress of Time. They'd moved her from the workshop back to the tent where she'd originally been staying, only a few paces from the command tent. We'd wanted to keep her close and secure—and away from prying eyes.

I announced myself before entering, finding Baey sitting cross-legged and wings spread out as she faced Moira. It seemed as though they might have been talking. I wondered if Moira had finally agreed to help her with learning the watch. That had been...a point of contention.

"Baey, a moment outside?" I got right to the point, knowing that Moira could hear us when in the tent. Sven had put that barrier so that stepping outside was enough to block out sound.

Instantly, she was up, tucking her wings close to her as she followed me outside the tent.

"Everything alright?"

I waved a hand. "For now. But how far back can you go, as of now?" I got to the point.

With a frown, she replied, "Well, I'm not completely sure. The longest I did in the tunnels was thirty minutes, like I told you. I think...I think I could do a good few hours, but I haven't tried." She sounded pretty confident.

That was enough for me. "Would you be willing to come with me to see if we can get to Illan?"

"Wait—" she leaned forward, even though we'd already been speaking quite discreetly. "With everything going on out there?"

"Yes." My answer was immediate. With every moment that passed, I grew more certain something was wrong. "I need to check in and I can't wait any longer. I was going to ask Sven if he'll wait with Moira. If he wants, we can even spin back time perhaps from before we leave so he doesn't even have to—only if he's fine with it, of course."

Baey bit her lip in thought. "You're really certain?"

I nodded. "Please. Something isn't right."

Taking in a deep breath, Baey seemed to give up, her wings rippling with a yellowish green, a much rarer lapse of discipline on her part. Her wings were usually able to stay relatively neutral, these days.

"Thank you," I answered, even though she hadn't actually said anything. "I'll go get Sven and be right back."

I didn't wait for her to say anything else, heading over to where Sven and Astra were staying—where the Bethynese soldiers were also set up—away from prying eyes.

Sven and Astra were entering the center of the ring of tents as I did the same, most likely having just gotten back from one of Astra's practice sessions. I was very much looking forward to the possibility of Astra being capable enough to handle things without Sven needing to be around, especially if that meant maybe taking Cyl off portal duty—and any sort of duty at all, for that matter.

"Sven, do you think…" I waited to finish my sentence until I fully caught up to them, leaning in close. "…you could watch Baey's guard post for a little?"

Concern was instantly evident in his face, and I was a little annoyed at the way Astra also frowned, clearly having heard us despite my low tone.

I carefully grabbed Sven's arm and pulled him a little off to the side, giving Astra another glance before continuing, "I need to check on something. I…I know you don't want to, and Baey can even make it so it doesn't technically happen, after we find out what we need to. But I…I *really* need to check on something. It's important. I'm sorry, I don't want to ask this of you."

Sven looked amused? Raising an eyebrow and asking, "Did you just apologize?"

"Oh, shut up." I narrowed my eyes, giving him a light punch in the arm that he flinched at, only making me feel even more guilty.

He sobered, smile fading away. "Of course. Astra and I can." He turned. "You up for a little guard duty?"

I almost hushed him, but realized it was vague enough that no one would understand. I still didn't exactly like that a bunch of Bethynese were just sitting here in our last safe haven.

"Alright," Astra's reply reminded me of the present task.

Sven turned to me. "Then we're all set. And…" He frowned. "Don't worry about turning back. I'll be just fine. It's not worth that sort of meddling."

I wanted to argue but knew it was no use. "We might still go for it, for other reasons," I went for that angle, instead. "If we get what I need and don't want to waste any time."

Sven nodded, "Alright. Just…be careful."

"Always am," I said with a mock salute.

"We can't get in there," Baey huffed as we took our very first step into the sewers.

I turned to her, taking a second to understand what must have happened. "Wait…really?"

"Yes…we've been trying for…what feels like hours. All the entrances are sealed and you got caught twice."

With a huff I declared, "I never get caught."

"Well, you did. Twice."

I crossed my arms, annoyance penetrating the determination I had felt only seconds ago. "I don't believe you," I said with narrowed eyes, trying to get the humor to mask my frustration.

Baey let out a half-hearted laugh, then said, "Should we try for Atlys? Maybe his house isn't being watched like the palace."

"Alright," I breathed out. "So we'll take the sewer exit on Venson Street?"

"Yes," Baey replied. The fact we were still discussing this plan had to mean it worked, right?

The way to the exit was extremely quick, though I guessed not for Baey, as she led us through with the precision of a sixth sense. After that came weaving through the city, her wings folding around her back and dragging the ground like a coat. She'd gotten incredibly good at the camouflage thing. As chaotic as the streets were, Baey knew exactly what side alleys and streets to take to avoid both the patrols and the crowds. Without her, even I wouldn't have been able to have made it through the city streets undetected. Not with them like this. Even as it was, we had several close calls.

At last, we arrived at Atlys's street, making our way around back and slipping in through the cellar window that was quite broken and left that way for us specifically.

Baey barely managed to squeeze through, muttering about her big wings and stupid small spaces.

It was quiet inside.

We made our way up to the main floor; Baey again giving the all clear.

Atlys was nowhere to be found.

Not the parlor, the cellar, the office...nowhere. I knew this didn't necessarily mean anything at all, but the hair was still standing up on the back of my neck, telling me something was very wrong.

"Estasia. Over here!" Baey called from the parlor, and I quickly made my way over, staring at the sealed letter covered in dust.

"Where'd you find that?" I asked quickly, snatching it from her and looking around as if we were being watched.

"Shoved up the chimney." She acted…unsurprised.

I didn't wait any longer, taking the fact Baey hadn't turned back time as a sign we weren't about to be ambushed. The seal was untraceable, and the handwriting on the inside a careful, nondescript print instead of cursive.

He's been discovered. I'm writing this two days after Captain Kearn's escape. Kovo plans to execute Atlys on the fifth day from when he was taken, which I assume is when they expect to have gotten any necessary information out of him. I noticed him gone the day after Kearn's escape. They claim he is overseeing a shipment to Eknemar. His employees seem to be already carrying out pre-existing orders in regards to his more underhanded activities with you, but Atlys himself is in Kovo's custody. Get out of The Underground before Kovo finds you. Hopefully you find this before it's too late.

This wasn't Illan—it was in Kaedovarnian, not our code. I could feel the color draining from my face.

"What is it?" Baey's voice held a concern that was definitely warranted.

"We need to get back *now*." This was bad. Very, very bad.

THE LAST ESMER

CHAPTER XXI: Not This Again

<u>Baey:</u>

"He's being executed tomorrow," I announced once again, gripping the edge of the table. We'd risked Moira being unattended in order to have everyone here. Nothing had happened so far in the hundred times I'd run through this scenario.

"How far can you go back?" Sven asked. Again. Only, he didn't know that.

"I…I don't know. It seems like I can't go back any more than a few hours—and Moira hasn't been very helpful. I…I've been trying for hours. I've only gotten back to when the letter was found—you've always had me practice. I've been trying this for…hours. Maybe a whole day." I was going crazy. I…really was going crazy. We'd been through this all before, and I couldn't get any further.

"Alright. Then we plan a rescue. Was that—"

"The letter is two days old. But executing Atlys could mean they know where The Underground is. Or it's a trap. Either way, it seems if we get stuck, I can only go a few hours back so we'd have to be quick." We were almost reaching the end of where I'd run this scenario to; I would start to not be able to go back as far. Not that it mattered, all that happened was us coming back, but it still filled me with a strange sense of paranoia.

"I can make it quick," Sven piped up, looking around the room. "I feel we know I'm the best bet. If Baey and I go, then we can run a perfect scenario and get him out." He turned to Cyl. "We won't be able to get all the civilians out with the ship fast enough. It would take several days. Could we use the portal for The Underground civilians and—"

"*Absolutely* not," Cyl cut him off, and I was glad this was the first time I'd gotten here because if I had to hear him speak so condescendingly to Sven ever again, I might punch him in the face. "If Ovok is close to the portal, sending an entire underground city through it will definitely alert him to its location. Do you *want* him to get free? There's more than just your world at stake. Astra has a whole world, too. And my world—your *father's* world!"

I found myself grinding my teeth together, annoyed at the way he seemed to care about people's family and worlds *now*. The hum of energy from nearby told me that while she remained quiet, Astra wasn't exactly pleased about this either.

"We aren't going to just sacrifice the city!" Darby shouted, staring Cyl down like a feral cat.

Cyl put his hands up in a defensive gesture. "I am not suggesting that, only a better solution."

"We need to get the people out by tomorrow, then." It was Alenor. She turned to Sven. "What if you and Baey worked together…if you tried to do what you did with us, but with a clear head? Do you think—"

"No," Sven whispered. "That would be a thousand times the scale of just a few of us. We saw what that would do." The statement was followed by a shudder.

"Okay, the ship. Estasia…if we got a few more airships, then Sven could cloak them and we could move more people? Could we steal some from Atlys's shipyard?" I tried to ignore Cyl as best as I could, focusing on a solution that didn't involve sacrificing the very people we were trying to save.

Estasia tapped her finger against her leg, looking over the map of the city laid out on the table in front of us. "No, we can't. This city is locked down tight right now—and if Atlys was captured, that would mean all of his assets are being carefully watched. The best idea we have is to do the *portal*," she said all too pointedly.

"Then I suggest you prepare yourself for the sacrifices that have to be made, because I am not opening that thing to a madman." Cyl's unwelcomed objections again pierced the air.

The very idea that he might be right frightened me. I didn't like the callousness of such an idea.

"I am *not* standing by and watching innocent refugees caught in the crossfire." Thackeray was the first to get over the quiet indignation that had overcome us all.

"Then maybe you need to—" Cyl's argument was cut off by the entire ground shaking.

And that's when the ceiling fell. A rock came crashing down, ripping through the tent ceiling and right into us.

It took me a moment to process that we weren't all pulverized, and when I opened my eyes, I saw the blue sphere surrounding everyone as the tent fell around us in ruins. But I also saw the horrible scene unfolding before us: fire. Fire, and a gaping hole in the ceiling of The Underground, from which an enormous Myrandi in Dragon form had just flown down— larger than any I had ever seen. Even larger than I had ever seen him before.

Ovok.

"Baey, go back, quickly!" Sven grabbed hold of my shoulders and shook me. "You need to go back *now*—" he was cut off as something slammed into Astra's forcefield. It was Ovok.

The forcefield crumbled, and Ovok's tail was mysteriously diverted from crushing all of us.

Concentrate. Go back, go—

I clutched the watch, but couldn't focus through the panic closing my throat. Someone pushed me to the side, and I realized it was Estasia, not Sven.

Sven was fighting Ovok, and so was Astra. They were going to get killed.

"We need to get out of here!" Estasia actually looked…scared. "Go back—*now!*"

"I'm *trying!*" I froze, as my eyes zeroed in on the still form of Thackeray as Alenor dragged Darby away.

Go back, go back, go back. I couldn't think. I felt the ground rumble beneath my feet as Sven used it to launch himself in the air, Ovok suddenly shifting from Dragon to Human just as who I guessed was Cyl did the exact opposite.

Astra's blue energy was everywhere, trying to hold Ovok down. But something green glowed from inside his shirt collar as his sword deflected it. How was his sword deflecting Gifting?

Everything was falling; everyone was screaming. It was like some sort of bad nightmare.

Go back. Go back.

"Go back!" I realized the words weren't just being said in my head. Estasia was still screaming them at me.

I clutched the watch around my neck even as my hand went for the spear collapsed in the sleeve of my belt. With a quick motion it opened to full size, and I tried to squeeze shut my eyes to go back.

But then I saw Sven get shoved out of the way by Astra just in time for her to get impaled.

"How far can you go back?" Sven asked, calmly.

Blood. My vision was still stained with blood. It took all my self-control not to shake as I got a grasp of my surroundings. I hadn't gone back that far. "We…we have to get everyone out *now*," I gasped. "Ovok's going to be here any second—Sven, Astra don't engage, let Cyl. We have to evacuate everyone—get out of the tent—it's going to collapse in just a few minutes."

Everyone stared at me, but no one argued.

"What do we need to do?" Alenor asked quickly.

"Sven, Astra, come with me. We need to stop the ceiling from collapsing in on itself. Quickly! Darby, Thackeray, Estasia, get everyone to the ocean exit. Cyl—do what you do and protect that stupid portal. Grenedil, make sure he does just that!"

We scrambled to action, Sven and Baey following me as we rushed out of the tent.

"Mum, get Moira—I dropped her prison!" was the last thing Sven yelled before we left.

"The ceiling!" I called as the ground began to rumble again. Astra, Sven, and I concentrated all our energy as the cracks formed and a few stalactites from the calcite-coated bricks broke loose, and they evaporated in a flurry of mist. Sven.

"I can't...whatever it is...it's really large—Baey, we can't—" Sven didn't get to finish his sentence as a giant Ovok broke through, a large green stone glowing from a necklace plate around his neck.

All we could do now was damage control, once more the screams piercing the air.

The rocks all evaporated, and this time no one was crushed, at least, but chaos still reigned.

Suddenly, two giant Dragon forms clashed in the air: Ovok and Cyl. But the latter was riddled with scars and clearly sluggish in comparison.

Even if I'd lived this before, I could no more process it than the first time.

"Astra, help evacuate! Baey. Drop me over him—*now!*" Sven grabbed my arm and used his Gift to push us high in the air before I could even spread my wings. Having a passenger was not exactly easy, but Syvil had been having me practice carrying others whilst doing maneuvers. We were over Ovok and Cyl just as Ovok's metal-coated claws ripped into Cyl's chest, sending blood everywhere.

"Now!" I dropped him, but just as he was heading right for Ovok's back, the giant Myrandi twisted his body and...vanished.

But not vanished. Before I could process it, Ovok was a person, falling through the air with Sven. Then a Dragon again, using his gigantic tail to fling him across the city.

I dove after him but was caught by Ovok's claw, trying to squeeze me.

"Where *is* it?!" Ovok's growl shook the cavern.

Go back, go back…but I couldn't—too much was going on. I couldn't breathe, I was being cho—Somehow, I had enough wherewithal to grab my knife from inside Ovok's death grip, jerking it as hard as I was able into the inside of his claw and actually getting him to loosen the grip *just* enough so I could quickly push out of it, my wings fighting against the pain as he'd almost crushed me.

A hand grabbed my ankle, yanking me down as I found myself face-to-face with a force much more terrifying than I'd ever experienced. The eyes were not like Skayla's—no. Ovok was perfectly sane. Sane and determined. Or was it desperate?

That's when I realized we were both falling. He had grabbed hold of my shoulder, getting ready to plunge his sword right through my chest.

With the most powerful beat of wings I could manage, I fought upwards, using the force of them to knock him off of me. I went spinning in the air, a giant whoosh knocking me off course and completely disorienting my flight pattern as, again, I was being shadowed by an enormous Dragon. I weaved between the giant claws, trying to keep between him. But the moment I got close and in his blind spot, he shifted back, clashing his blade against my spear's metal staff and knocking me off. One of his legs looped under my leg and he slammed the pommel of his blade against my knee cap even as we free fell.

I screamed. Oh no. I was about to die.

Just as his blade was about to rip through my chest, blue energy knocked him off of me, and something else caught me.

"Go back, quick, darlin'," Sven whispered in my ear as my vision blurred in pure agony. I saw someone launch in the air—Astra. Even with my darkened vision, I saw the form of Ovok growing and shrinking.

Agony. I couldn't think...only registering pain.

Then I saw Astra falling, unconscious as Ovok went after her just as he had me.

"Astra!" I tried to scream, forcing Sven to spin around and jolt my leg.

"It doesn't matter! Go back, we're all dead!" Sven yelled at me in a way that was uncharacteristic even as I felt him try and break Astra's fall. But he had no energy left. I could feel it. I realized he was shaking now and remembered how he'd been tossed by Ovok.

Go back. Go back. Go back. Tears streamed down my face as I desperately tried to focus above the screams...the fire...the pain.

"It's alright, darlin'. We're fine. Just remember when we're alright," Sven's whisper somehow filled me with just a small moment of calm. Just enough.

"How far can you go back?" Sven asked. Again. Only, he didn't know that.

The pain was gone, but the fear wasn't—the horrible truth wasn't. "I need to talk to Moira—" I didn't explain myself, I just ran out of the tent, too many horrible images of what had happened just moments before forever burned in my brain. But they hadn't happened. They hadn't…but why did they feel so real?

Maybe because they were about to happen again in only a few moments.

I burst into Moira's small tent. "How do I go back further—tell me, now."

"A bit anxious all of a sudden?" Moira's smile was brittle. "I wondered what it would take. How many times have you watched everyone die?"

"Shut up and tell me." My temper suddenly flared as I realized she'd been waiting for this—she wanted an 'I told you so,' didn't she?

She cocked her head, looking only a little bit sympathetic. "Maybe now I'm not so bad?"

"Stop it and tell me what I need to do, I can't go back more than a few hours at a time." And I apparently was too distracted right now to go back further than a few minutes…. I needed to get a grip.

"I told you." Her eyes were as cold as her tone. "I can't help you now. I warned you that you should have given my watch back—then I would have been able to leap back days. Now you're stuck."

"I don't need *you* to do it!" I threw up my hands. "*I* need to be able to do it—and you gloating over the fact that you can rub this in my face *really* doesn't endear me to your character, Skayla—oh, sorry. Moira. Wrong sister." The claw of panic in my chest didn't care if I was a little cruel at this moment. I needed her to help me, and she needed a wake-up call from her self-righteousness.

Moira's lips twitched, but she finally said, "You need to get into the Eternalis. Just like when you rescued me." At least she wasn't mincing words. "I'm guessing we don't have much time, do we?"

"No, and if you'd stopped wasting it before, I would already know how to go back further—"

"Wasting it? We have all the time in the world now." Moira was laughing. "Now you'll understand my pain a little—now maybe you won't act so all-knowing and pure with your high morals. Go back a few more times and see how you feel after watching everyone die over and over and over again—"

"Would you *stop* it!?" I screamed even as her words sunk deep. What if I couldn't save anyone? What if I was stuck in this loop because this stupid, *selfish* woman couldn't get past her own ego? Any second the rumbling would come, and death would begin again. It was so hard to focus.

"This is *not* my fault!" Moira shouted back.

The ground rumbled. It was starting.

I shut my eyes and forced myself to go back.

The smile on Moira's face wasn't exactly very friendly. "It seems we both can tell when the other goes back if we're in each other's presence."

I supposed that made sense. I didn't have time to bother with the information right now.

And of course, Moira couldn't help but continue to gloat. "I tried to tell you. Funny how, even with the watch, your foresight was horrible."

"If I had given you the watch, then you would have controlled us all like soulless dolls, and we wouldn't have known any better for it!" I shouted back, uncaring if others heard.

Moira's cheeks burned. "Better than being dead, don't you think?"

I just scoffed. "You're saying everyone being your puppets is better than being dead? Should I call you Skayla again for that philosophy? Or maybe she got it from you."

I didn't expect the little bit of horror that drained Moira's color. "It's not like that."

The ground rumbled, and everything started over.

With the way we just both stayed in the tent, you could almost feel like no time had passed at all. We were alone, stuck in a loop of eternity and doomed to live forever right at the cusp of the end of the world. With horror, I suddenly wondered if I would actually age if we just kept doing this…or if I could truly be stuck here forever, endlessly arguing with this woman who refused to help me save my friends—her own family.

Moira, however, seemed very unbothered by the prospect, preoccupied with calmly convincing me of her own virtue. "Skayla took away people's free will—she wants to control. I'm just trying to protect everyone."

I was shaking as I replied, "You really don't hear yourself, do you? Manipulating people is just a different way of robbing them of free will. The difference between you and Skayla is just one of you makes people think they still *do* have the ability to make choices. I've seen what playing god does to people. Sven can tell you: It's not pretty."

Moira let go of me but didn't sit back down. "Trust me. Maybe when you've seen your loved ones die a few more times, you'll understand."

I looked her right in the eyes as I replied, "I have grown up watching my loved ones die. I watched those in Valdon—where I lived—dwindle day-by-day in the face of a war I wasn't allowed to help fight in. I watched Sven save me and I couldn't help as he gave himself up to a living nightmare for eight years. I watched the one woman I saw as a mother betray her family and me to Skayla for a broken promise. Unlike you, I learned very early on that bloodshed happens and no matter how much we try—we can never stop all of it. Eventually, you either realize that…or become the very thing you're trying to stop." I thought of Namaya; how she was so desperate to stop us from dying that she joined Skayla. Suddenly, I understood. As I stared at Moira, I understood.

The ground began to shake.

I spun time back a few more minutes. Moira was now sitting, but her face was pale.

"I'm sorry," she whispered.

I gave no reaction, only saying, "I don't want your apology. I want you to make it right. And that starts with you helping me."

There was a long silence that felt meaningless in the face of this eternal moment.

And then, Moira spoke. "You need to do more than just go back. You need to reach the space between—the Eternalis. Do what you did to save me."

The hope was so strong as it rose in my chest that I thought I would faint for a moment. "But before, your presence is what drew me. Now I don't have anything to feel it," I explained as best as I could, trying to still my pounding heart.

Gone was her jeering and cutting remarks, at last. Now, I saw actual empathy in her gaze as she said, "It's still there. Just feel it without me. It's the space right before you jump. Think of it as the spindle which allows you to unravel the string of time back into how it was before."

It was getting so hard to breathe, this feeling of being stuck giving me the worst sort of claustrophobia I had ever experienced. I was stuck, suffocating and sinking as I watched my worst nightmare play out over and over again.

"Baey," Moira's tone was surprisingly sincere. "I know whatever you saw was horrible. But you have to learn to go back anyway—to let it not affect you. Otherwise, you could end up dead or trapped like I was. Only no one will be able to save you."

"Alright, let's try this. Find the spindle. Think of that space where you found me. How did it feel when you opened it?"

I focused, trying not to think of the rumbling that would happen in only a few short moments. Suddenly, it was easier to focus. Time meant very little now. I was stuck here, in this loop, able to try as long as I needed to. I didn't care if it took eternity…I wouldn't give up. I would live in this moment as many times as I needed to if it meant saving my friends.

And suddenly, I felt it. The turning spindle. I couldn't explain it, but I reached out in my head and took it, stopping it, and in a blink, I was surrounded by nothingness, just like when I'd gone to save Moira.

There was a moment of panic as I wondered if I would be able to figure out how to leave, but I reminded myself I had the watch…and I had forever.

It was hard to explain, but it felt different being in here than before. Without the focus on trying to get Moira out, I was more acutely aware of just how…clear my mind was. It was almost as if I was reliving the last few hours of my life right at this moment, there and yet here all at once.

Could I reach further back? I tried to think of yesterday, and strangely it came very, very clearly. I imagined it like the string, reaching out in my mind and grabbing hold of the memory.

I was still in the tent; Moira was calmly sipping a cup of water. Had I done it?

"Baey, a moment outside?" The voice…it was Estasia. She was outside the tent.

"You need to go back further," Moira murmured. "But this is what, almost half a day? The longest you've done, surely."

I nodded. "I…yes, I've done it—I was there. Do you think I can go back further?"

Moira gave a weak chuckle. "Yes, just…remember. Things will never happen the same way again. You've unraveled the string, and when you try and wrap it up again, the twine will be different. Nothing ever falls the same way twice."

Only some of that made sense….

"Baey? You alright?" Estasia's voice again called from outside.

"I'm going to talk to her—thank you," I said, the last bit sincere despite my disagreement with Moira's...methods.

Moira's brow furrowed. "Is this really far enough?"

"No. But I need Estasia's advice. And I could use talking to a friend." With that, I exited the tent.

The moment I set eyes on Estasia, I couldn't help it. I wrapped her in a fierce hug.

"I—woah, Birdie—uh...you...okay?"

Tears streamed down my face, but I didn't care. I kept squeezing my friend, taking this moment of solace knowing I was about to go back even further. "I...saw something horrible, Estasia. Ovok knows we're here. Atlys has been captured. He's being executed tomorrow. Someone left a note at the house warning us, but for all we know, it could have been Ovok and it was a trap, not a friend. It wasn't Illan, you'd said."

"I *knew* it," Estasia hissed, strangely calm about all of this. She slowly extracted me, her face burning as she said, "So then, how can we stop it?"

"I...Moira's helped me be able to go back further. But I don't know how far back I can go. I need to try more. I just...how far? What should I do?"

"Well, find out when Atlys gets caught, and we'll go from there. See if you can find who left that note. Then, as long as it isn't Ovok, we can find out. And maybe...maybe go to Tanner. See if there is anything he can tell us—maybe Skayla knows something."

I took a deep breath, trying to keep steady. "Okay. Okay, I'll try that."

"Are...are you alright?"

No. Not really. "I just…please don't die." I couldn't get the terrible sight of my dead friends out of my head. "Promise me…you'll be as careful as possible?"

"If you go back…I won't have promised that, you know," Estasia said with a smirk that only partially hid her concern.

"I know," I whispered. "But hearing it will still help."

I'd never seen such a soft look from Estasia. "Alright. I promise. Now go. See you soon, Birdie."

With that, I melted back into the Eternalis, determined to save my friends.

I had decided to keep Moira with me whenever I turned back time for more than a few hours at a time. I didn't want her forgetting any of the conversations we'd had, and she was, at last, being cooperative. I wasn't really sure how our connection worked, and if she even would forget anything should she not be in my immediate area, but I didn't feel like taking that chance.

First, I decided to track down whoever it was that had given us that note. It took a lot of trial and error, but at last, I was able to figure out when exactly they had gotten into Atlys's manor to place it. I'd explained myself a thousand times to everyone, but no matter how tiring it was, I was determined to continue to do so—to not stoop to secrecy like Moira. So far, everyone had agreed.

Now I sat in the parlor, the room dark and abandoned. Moira sat in the opposite corner, ordered to stay completely still unless I gave the word.

The stranger was coming tonight.

Outside, I heard the choruses of distant mutiny, a chilling echo that sounded too close to the chaos from that untold time in The Underground. The time no one but me would remember.

There was a noise, and I gripped my spear tighter, ready to pounce on whoever was coming through the front door.

The figure was tall, and seemed that of a man. However, he didn't appear the right build for Ovok—it was hard to tell.

Somehow, though, I got the feeling Ovok wouldn't have let me sneak up on him like this. At least, not the first try. The ease with which he had repeatedly dealt with us was something I wouldn't easily forget.

The figure looked around the room before entering properly, unable to see through my wings' camouflage.

Slowly, he inched closer to where I was standing by the chimney. Just a few more steps…two…one….

I lunged at the stranger, putting him in a choke hold as I stunned him with a blow from my wings. He fought with a decent amount of strength, but it was quite clear he was no warrior, struggling against my grip as I used my spearhead to press the blade against his face.

"Who are you?" I hissed.

No answer, only futile struggling.

"Listen, I'm the one you're leaving that note for. So who are you?" The struggling stopped, and he asked, "You're with The Underground?"

"Who. Are. You?"

"Let me go, and I'll tell you."

I decided…why not. I'd get to see what he'd do. If he jumped me now, he clearly couldn't be trusted. If he actually told me, then it would save some time—even though now I had…time to spare—and would prove himself to me a little bit. Not much. But it would be a start.

"Baey…" Moira's warning came from where she was now standing, ready to involve herself.

I didn't say a word, only gave a look that reminded her she was not here to give me advice on my plan. She was here for me to keep watch in case this mysterious messenger had brought backup, and to make sure if I needed more help with the watch.

She gave a short nod and remained quiet.

Slowly, I released my grip, and the stranger pulled away, brushing himself off and getting out a good coughing fit before clearing his throat.

The hostility in his eyes evaporated as he declared, "Ah! You're the Esmer, then. My name is Eugene. I'm a friend of Atlys."

Wait. No. "Eugene *Atarah?*" I gawked. "In no world are you our friend—you were actively trying to expose Kearn."

"Look, I didn't expect you all to use a Bethynese spy—they don't *do* that sort of thing. I was just trying to get Ovok off Atlys's back and keep the Bethynese from finding your stupid underground hideout."

"How do you know any of this?" I left out the part where Atlys had said he wasn't to be trusted. I wanted to know if…if somehow, Atlys had been lying to us. All this time.

"I'm answering quite a lot of questions for you." The displeasure was evident in his tone.

"And I'm being awfully patient by not skewering you," I retorted.

He decided it prudent to continue, "I decided it was best Atlys didn't know I'd figured out his little schemes. Easier to have plausible deniability. I'd known he was fighting back even before they released me from the holding camp. I hid a few paper trails here and there, framed some of his little mess ups on my parents so they got executed after things went wrong at the ravine." He waved his hand dismissively.

"And why exactly should I trust a man who gave up his own parents like that?" I didn't bother mincing words.

"Listen, I don't really have much time for this, but trust me, they weren't worth saving. It was them or Atlys, and I really preferred carrying out what Angeline would have wanted. Atlys was good, but he still made a few mistakes. No one cared about me. They all banked on me being too afraid of going back to the camps." Eugene's tone was sharp, reminding me a lot of how Estasia had been when we'd first met her.

That's when I remembered this meant Estasia might very possibly have to come face-to-face with Eugene. Oh dear. A problem for another time. "Who's Angeline?"

"Atlys's dead wife. But what's important is that you need to get Atlys out of there. I was able to figure out he was snatched yesterday—the day after the captain's little escape. He could have already given away your position—"

"He'd never do that," I replied, tone harsh at the accusation.

"Look, I know he would hold up a very long time, but you haven't been around Kovo the last few days. I wouldn't blame Atlys for caving."

I swallowed hard. "Alright. Fine. Do you know where he is?"

Eugene let out a tense sigh. "Somewhere close to Ovok. Not in the dungeons, that's for sure."

"Is there anything *else* you'd like to tell me?"

"No, not really. But I would very much like to know what you intend to do," he replied.

I simply said, "I don't know yet," and disappeared back into the Eternalis with Moira.

"I need to talk to Tanner," I addressed a very surprised Marion. "It's urgent." I'd left Moira in The Underground to avoid any encounters with Skayla.

"He is more than just a tool, you know," she said as she turned briskly around, motioning for me to follow. "And he's only just finally doing better, so if you do anything to change that, I will never forget it."

My wings burned with embarrassment. "I would not ask unless it was completely necessary. He's my friend," I replied. "And I'm only trying to save his life as well as everyone else's."

From what I'd gathered, the manor was also something that was discovered and raided during Ovok's attack on The Underground.

We arrived at the hall at the top of the stairs. "I think he's still with Skayla. Wait here."

My whole body stiffened. "What? By himself?" That was the *last* place Tanner needed to be; what was she thinking?!

Marion gave a long sigh. "She's helped him find out how to store memories. As broken as her mind is, she has, after all, proved to be useful. Tanner has been talking with her and I have made sure the appropriate precautions were in order."

"This is Skayla we're talking about, she should be nowhere near Tanner's head," I argued, forgetting for a moment the real reason I was here.

Calmly, Marion simply replied, "His head was already gone. There was very little more harm it could have done—and I would have liked to see you turn away his begging. Now I will return."

"Wait," I called after her, wings twitching as I made up my mind. "If he's already in with her, then maybe I'll just come too. Perhaps Skayla can answer some questions for me as well."

"Very well." Marion folded her hands behind her and then continued to lead me down the hall to where Maeko was guarding Skayla's door.

I couldn't manage a smile for Maeko today. Not with the dire situation going on. Not with the visions of death still too clear in front of me.

He let us in quietly, looking concerned.

There was Tanner, perched on a stool with bright eyes and a...a smile? He turned, the smile growing. "Baey! Didn't expect to see you." He hopped off his stool and came over, a completely different person than the one I'd seen before.

Perhaps I already forgave Marion for letting him near Skayla. "Tanner you—you're feeling better?" I asked even as my gaze wandered to the quiet figure sitting on the edge of the bed in the opposite corner of the room: Skayla. She looked just as limp and strangely lifeless as she had before, except that she was watching us now. No more dead-eye stares into nothing.

"Yes—we've been able to transfer memories into objects. I...feel much better."

You need something.

I shuddered as the whisper slunk into my brain, like some weird itch I couldn't scratch. I hated it.

"Did she say something? She's...she's still not very good at talking aloud." Tanner winced. "We're working on that."

"Yes..." Skayla's answer came out slowly. "Apologies."

Pressing my lips close together, I decided it was time to get to the point. Seeing Tanner so improved I had, just for a minute, forgotten that this most likely would never happen. Suddenly, I asked, "When did you start?"

"After you left. About two days ago."

"And so you've been better for that long?" I pressed.

Looking a bit confused, Tanner nodded. "Yes, mostly. And then better every day since."

"Good. Because I have to go back another day in time, and I don't want to...I don't want to make you go back like that."

Something bad— "Happened then?" Skayla's voice switched from my mind to her actually speaking in a way that left me disoriented.

402

"Yes. Ovok—he found out where we were." Once more, I didn't mind spilling this sort of information to her, seeing as this would never happen in the end. "He was able to capture one of our informants."

"What?" Tanner's eyes were wide. "Then why are you here?"

"Because I've been stuck going back in time. Over and over. Trying to find a way to fix it." I tried to keep my tone as even as possible as I explained.

An intense feeling of sympathy—of understanding—blew through my mind before quickly disappearing. I turned to Skayla. "He's going to take The Living Stone off-world. He's going to revive Rhioa. If there is *anything* either of you know—anything that can help us.…"

Images began to flash through my mind, like vivid memories playing out for me. Skayla's memories.

"He…just wants his daughter…back." The words were emotionless, a strange dissonance to the overwhelming feeling Skayla was pouring into my head.

"No," Tanner interjected. "Not…not anymore." I turned to find him holding a strange, broken compass in his hand. "No. He wants more than that. Now, he wants to get rid of the power sources on each of the worlds. After what Cyl did, he doesn't trust anyone."

My blood ran cold. "What? What do you mean, what Cyl did?" *"I had a friend, once. Cyl. He wasn't there when I needed him."* The memory of Ovok's words to Skayla popped into my head almost before I'd finished my sentence.

"He refused to help," Tanner replied, not realizing Skayla had already gone into my head. "He begged Cyl to take her to Baeno and get her

help. He'd sworn he would even step down as the Lord of the Myrandi—
that he wouldn't do a thing. He said he was done playing with people's
lives."

He was very good at spinning lies from truth.

"No," Tanner interjected once more, giving me the feeling Skayla had
spoken to both of our minds, this time. "Not this time. This time, he was
telling the truth. He didn't want any of this…he just wanted Rhioa to be
alright. And Cyl…well, he didn't care—said it was what Ovok deserved.
He said she wasn't worth saving."

"You don't say," I emphasized each word one-by-one. "How
interesting." And how convenient for Cyl to just leave all of that out. "So
then, is there anything else you can tell me that might help?"

Tanner frowned. "I could show you how he fights. Give you the
memories. Maybe that will give you a chance."

"Do it."

CHAPTER XXII: Let's Try This One More Time

Baey:

I stood there, gripping my spear in the midst of Alenor's forge. No matter how many times I tried, I couldn't go back further than this. I'd tried early on for what felt like years, always back to this point. We'd all theorized it was because of my relic—I could go back further than a day, but only up to when my spear was forged; up to when I was able to better channel my abilities.

"Baey? Are you alright?" Alenor was always the first one to ask when I didn't reply.

This would have to be it, then. Whatever move we made, it had to be done from here. I locked eyes with Moira, who nodded. She had become increasingly *less* irritating the more we'd gone through this.

"What's the matter, darlin'?" It was Sven this time.

I took a deep breath, looking between both of them before I said, "We need to meet with everyone. Atlys has been found out, and in a few more days, The Underground will be razed to the ground." No matter what we had done from this point on, Ovok came. We'd saved Atlys a handful of times, failed a handful of times…and found him too late. He was still alive as of now, but not in great shape. Eugene was right, I couldn't blame Atlys for giving in…not after what I'd seen. Regardless of what came after, Ovok always came, and sooner if we rescued Atlys—Grenedil had figured out that Havirax had an invisibility relic that allowed someone to follow us back.

405

"We don't have much time to get the plan going, but trust me, I will explain to everyone together." Turning to Astra, I couldn't help but add, "And for all that is good and kind in this forsaken world, would you *please* follow instructions?" I looked back to Sven, too many vivid memories of things that would hopefully never happen replaying over in my head. "And would you stop getting yourself killed, too?"

"Baey...what's going on?" Alenor whispered.

"Moira helped me figure out the watch," I gave a guarded expression in the direction of the other Mara. "I'll explain once everyone is in one place—quick, Sven, you and Darby go get Estasia. She's arguing with Cyl at the portal. But just...wait for the arguing to stop, she's getting important reads off of Cyl. Astra, you come with me and Moira— Alenor...Thackeray is down with the Bethynese soldiers. We meet at Darby's tent." There was a scramble of action as everyone obeyed, Moira being the only hesitant one when coming to follow Astra and me.

"Are you going to tell them?" Moira asked in a low voice as we quickly made our way through The Underground.

"I will give you the opportunity to," I replied shortly, taking note of Astra's attention. Moira was trying in vain to keep her from hearing us, but Astra had told me of her enhanced hearing—on one of my many replays—and that only left me amused at Moira's whispering.

"You can make this right and do things my way, or you can continue down the path that got you in this mess to begin with." The memories were still present—I had risked going to Tanner with Moira a few attempts ago—I'd needed to make sure Moira wouldn't have any more tricks up her sleeve. When I'd gotten what I needed, I'd made sure to go back so that Tanner would not actually have to add her memories to the list of ones he'd need to get rid of. I'd seen it all…Moira going back countless times, orchestrating and manipulating the world for a false sense of peace. Going back to keep Sven in the dark when he'd not approved. She'd manipulated Skayla into it, the two of them keeping the world in check. Moira had helped create the perfect storm for Skayla to crack; the rhetoric drilled into her head let loose with no bounds upon erasing fear. Maybe Moira wasn't the villain, but she wasn't the hero she'd thought she was either.

It wasn't long before everyone was gathered in Darby's tent, but it still wasn't soon enough.

I didn't wait any longer, immediately plunging into a shorter, more condensed version of what had gone on. "So, no matter what, Ovok gets in here and gets to the portal. Even when Grenedil was able to lead off Havirax, Ovok had already gotten the information from Atlys about our whereabouts. He moves faster when he knows we know he's coming. By the last round of attempts, we'd decided a few things: To evacuate starting today, get Atlys tonight, and trust Eugene Atarah." I watched Estasia carefully at this last part.

"What?" She looked like she'd seen a ghost.

"He was the one that told us Atlys was captured. It's a long story, and I think it's easier if he tells you, but he's the only way we're going to be able to evacuate everyone to an actual safe location—the ravine is not going to work. You and I must go find him as soon as this is done. The only way Atlys isn't found is if we hide him in Eugene's house. There's no time for further explanation—we *have* wasted too much time talking before. But after we get through this, I am happy to explain everything in as much detail as anyone wants. I'm not going to hide anything," I said pointedly, staring at Moira. She looked away. I had not betrayed her part of the story yet, giving her a little more time to be the one to tell it.

"We should rally as many people as possible to protect the portal," Cyl interjected. "Evacuation should be the last thing we worry about, right now."

"No," I didn't bother hiding the vehemence in my tone. He'd suggested this before, but I felt it important for this part to play out again. I was trying to meddle as little as I could in people's opinions of others, and I knew everyone hearing Cyl's true priorities was important.

"Not a chance," Sven replied, fists clenched. "It would be a bloodbath."

Darby quietly touched his arm.

"A few lives in exchange for keeping Ovok contained is a price we have to pay." Cyl's callous tone was like a hangnail. So…irritating. "They could buy us valuable time for a counter attack."

"What?" It was Grenedil, of course. He'd grown sick of all this, of Cyl. "Why don't we just use the portal instead to *transport* those people out of here and to safety? If Ovok knows where it is, then why bother hiding it?"

"Because then it will just get Ovok here a lot more quickly!" Cyl pounded his fist on the table, causing most everyone to jump—Moira and me the exception.

"And you're willing to kill hundreds of people for a few spare moments before he arrives?" Astra asked. It had become clear to me over the past hundred or so scenarios I'd lived through that if there was one thing Astra hated, it was innocents dying. Well, honestly, anyone dying. I'd grown to admire her, for as much as she'd left me pulling my feathers out trying to keep her and Sven alive, it had proven her character. I would trust her with not just my life, but the lives of my friends. At least one of Grenedil's acquaintances had panned out.

She'd already saved several of them a few times, whether she knew it or not.

"I refuse to use the portal for such a trivial matter. We need to either risk Sven moving it, or shut it down and seal it off completely." Cyl seemed unbothered by Astra, looking down at her like some insignificant animal. "You and Baey may be called as new Guards to replace the failures of your worlds, but I have been standing watch for hundreds of your lifetimes. Trust me: Ovok reaching The Door would cost far more than any death toll." I hated it, and it took all my discipline to stop from shouting back at him myself.

But I knew someone else was about to do that for me.

"I'm *sorry*," Grenedil spat. "Saving the lives of hundreds of people isn't a *trivial matter*, Cyl. Last time I checked, we were supposed to be watching over the worlds and protecting them, and I'm pretty sure the people down here with us are included in that."

"Enough!" Cyl shouted back. "Argue about it all you want; I will not do it! Blame Ovok for the blood—not me. I had *nothing* to do with it!"

And now, I felt I should jump in with the last bit of information I had on him. He had shown his motives, now I just needed everyone else to know. I'd made sure we had enough time for this bit. "Yes. You know, it's a funny thing, Cyl. You so conveniently forget to explain your part in all this." I tilted my head, staring hard at him. "I'll give you one chance to come clean before I tell them."

"Tell us what?" Sven asked, voice sharp.

"You know nothing, child. Don't threaten me." Cyl was so confident, wasn't he.

"Oh, I don't. But there's a friend of mine that took all of Ovok's memories, and I went to visit him a couple times when I went back to try and fix this. Funnier thing is…he knew you."

Cyl paled, and words could never describe just how satisfied his discomfort made me.

"He said Ovok came to you *begging* to go to Baeno and save Rhioa. He said he would give up everything if you just helped—that he wouldn't try anything. And you know what? He meant it. He had no intention of putting Baeno into this chaos, but hearing you, his last friend, turn away so callously from helping his daughter…you are the straw that broke the last bit of restraint. And now, because of you, Ovok intends to not just take The Living Stone, but find the source of every world and stop anyone from having any sort of power ever again. To stop anyone like you from getting a position of authority. The world is burning because you didn't deem a soul worth saving. So you are going to do exactly what we ask you to, or Astra will be the one using The Doorway. Understand?"

The anger radiating off of everyone in the room was palpable.

"I can lock you *all* out of it!" Cyl growled. "How dare you threaten me— there is no time for this *petty* squabbling—"

"Shut up!" I yelled. "You have cost *thousands* of lives. You've cost us all. If you want to be able to continue to purport your self-righteous image, then you will stand back and you *will* help evacuate the city. It's the least you can do after the way you abandoned Ovok and left us to clean up his mess. And if you decide not to help, then you can forget about us helping you fight Ovok. I care about the people stuck here because of your mistakes. Besides, I've been through this all a hundred times already, remember? Don't you think I've made sure we could use the portal even without your support? It's just *easier* if you cooperate."

It was not exactly a pleasant thing to see a Myrandi this angry. But I'd seen Ovok up close, and it was *much* worse than even Cyl's best glare.

He didn't say another word.

"Wonderful," I said with a sarcastic smile. "Now, let's hurry this up, we're running out of time. Estasia and I need to leave in thirty minutes if this is going to work."

Sven:

"We could give Moira the watch back, then, so she can help in trapping Ovok?" I suggested as we finished up the planning. This was all…very overwhelming, and there wasn't even time to process it.

Moira had been quiet the entire time, not even explaining much about her and Baey's training. Now she blushed, mouth half open as if she struggled to find any words.

"I…" she began at last, hand fiddling with some of her skirt. "I don't think I can be trusted with it."

No one said a word, but I noted the small look of approval from Baey.

"I can't promise my judgement would be the best," Moira went on. "I...I had a hand in making Skayla what she is today. I...she and I used to go back and change things without telling anyone. I told her it was the only way to keep people safe—I thought it was. Maybe it wasn't. But I'm only admitting this now because Baey will paint a much more frank picture of what I've been doing and how I've manipulated you all. I am sorry, but I cannot promise I won't do it again, given the opportunity."

I looked at Baey in disbelief. What? What did Moira mean?

Now, Baey spoke. "She would get information and then go back in time so no one knew she had it. That is the simplest I can explain—and only Skayla was privy to it. That's how they kept peace on Baeno for so long. That's why, without fear, Skayla immediately jumped off the cliff of peace meaning control over everyone."

I...what? The betrayal cut deeper than I could comprehend, but what was worse was that looking around...I saw a lot of faces lacking the shock I was experiencing. It was frustrating. Frustrating and a little crushing. Was it just *that* easy to pull the wool over my eyes? Was I...was I blind? I remembered my own reasons for hiding from Moira when we were younger, but...but I'd never thought that much of it. I'd always put it off as my own paranoia.

"You used...everyone?" My voice was hardly even a whisper.

Darby's hand went not on my shoulder this time but entwined in my hand. My attempt to pull away was pathetic really.

"I'm sorry, Sven." Moira looked away. "I thought it was the best way."

"The best way?" I couldn't believe the words coming out of her mouth. Then Darby squeezed my hand, and I was all too quickly reminded about the precarious situation. I turned back to Baey. "So then, is that it? You'll make the announcement, and then we'll start gathering people for the portal evacuation?" It took all of my will to stay on task. To stop from breaking at yet another betrayal from a sister. I felt…so used.

"Yes." Baey's wings were grey as she spoke. "And Estasia and I will leave for Lord Atarah to secure the agreement for us to evacuate there. We should get going."

With that, we were dismissed into our various assigned groups. Astra would be with Grenedil and Cyl—the only one truly capable of keeping an eye on the self-serving Drogan—while Alenor was paired with Moira, Thackeray with Syvil, and Darby with me.

But I barely made it three paces from the tent before Darby again grabbed my hand and spun me around. "Sven. Are you alright?"

"There's no time not to be," I replied tersely, going to turn once more. Baey would be addressing the city any moment now.

But a hand grabbed my face and, with a strange mixture of tenderness and force, turned me to look right in her eyes. "That doesn't mean you still can't acknowledge you aren't alright, Sven."

I swallowed hard. "I just…were we ever the good guys? Or were we always the monsters."

I didn't pull away as she caressed my cheek gently, then moved to my hand and grabbed it firmly. "Not monsters. Just people," she said with a gentle smile. "And your sisters' faults are not your responsibility."

I thought back to my conversation with Astra, and as much as I wanted to pull away in this moment—to drown in this feeling of responsibility for my sisters—I suddenly wondered if maybe…I should listen to Darby. Maybe I finally wanted to believe her, because I didn't think I could continue to take this sense of failure

Unsure what to say next, I found myself squeezing her hand back, desperate to keep the contact—the lifeline. "We should go," I whispered at last.

She nodded, but did not let go of my hand, leading me on so that we could prepare to evacuate the city-dwellers. If they would listen to me....

Only a few moments later, Baey's voice split the air, carrying unnaturally into every corner of The Underground. She was using my ring—accessing it through her own relic now and thus able to channel mine without possessing it. I wondered exactly how many times she'd gone through these scenarios, to be able to so thoroughly understand how her relic and Gift worked so well.

"People of The Underground, I am speaking to you on behalf of Darbeshay and Thackeray Ostinar. I am Baey Tihali Mornaro, the last Esmer, as many of you know. We have found a safer location for you, and need your assistance in moving quickly and quietly. Your complete cooperation is necessary. As long as you follow our instructions, everyone will remain safe. However, the only way we get through this is if we put aside our prejudices. Those who will help you include Sven Mara, as well as a few Bethynese soldiers who have been crucial in giving us information to keep all of you safe. They have risked life and limb on your behalf even when they knew they would get nothing but scorn in return. If we're going to get anywhere, we need to stop repeating the same mistakes. Just as fear drove Skayla to madness, fear will drive us apart. There are countless people who have sacrificed everything for you. And trust me when I say that we would not have let any of them here had we not been completely confident in their loyalties. So please, listen to them and follow their instructions. Stand fast, stand strong, and we'll see the daylight together."

"Well," Darby said with a brisk breath. "That's that, then."

We set to work, helping the occupants of the city in organizing their belongings and gathering by the portal, where Cyl and the others were. We were to wait three hours before actually sending anyone through, and we had to at least wait until Baey and Estasia returned and gave Cyl the coordinates, but it would take possibly longer to get everyone organized anyway. I was surprised at the lack of hostility while helping, and wondered how much of it was Darby's presence and how much of it might just be Baey's speech. Who knew, but it seemed even the Bethynese soldiers—who Thackeray had gone to fetch—were being treated civilly as they helped a nearby old woman with her things. Maybe everyone was just scared enough of dying.

Nothing particularly extraordinary happened in this time, except for what was expected with an attempt at organizing the chaos of moving hundreds of people to a small section of the city where we could then leave through a small portal.

Cyl looked...incredibly displeased, a huge contrast to Grenedil, who was now the one giving orders to Cyl and Astra regarding the portal.

"How long is left until we have to go through?" Darby asked Grenedil as the last of the people were finally gathered in the square. She had stuck close beside me, and strangely, I wasn't complaining. The plan was to move everyone into this apparently secret location Lord Atarah had. I was still very confused how one of the biggest thorns in our side from the surface was supposedly such a big part of this succeeding, but I trusted Baey.

Grenedil pulled a pocket watch from inside his coat pocket—he was full of gadgets and things that were difficult to find these days. "Still waiting for Baey, but she should return any moment."

I felt Darby squeeze my hand. "Are you going to be alright?"

Somehow, just her presence had been enough to chase everything away, and I'd been so focused on getting everyone to the square and the portal that I'd scarcely thought of anything else besides our task. Our task—and her hand in mine.

"Yes, thank you," I whispered back. Her brief, genuine smile was contagious.

"I should go check on the others," she whispered, giving one more squeeze of my hand and a confusing wink before disappearing into the crowd, leaving me a bit baffled.

Grenedil cleared his throat. "So once Baey gets back, all we need is the map coordinates and then we can start putting people through."

"I still would like it known—"

"Oh, shut up, Cyl. We know you don't care about saving anyone." I'd never seen Grenedil so antagonistic towards someone. Granted, I hardly knew him, but I was still pretty confident in betting it wasn't easy to get this sort of reaction out of him.

"Then I use The Door to go to a few places around the city, and after go to the manor to evacuate Marion, Maeko, Jaythos, and Kearn to Lord Atarah's manor. After that, I bring Tanner and…his companion…here. Is that correct?" Astra chimed in to confirm the plan, looking much different from the last time I'd seen her. She stood straight, eyes almost glowing in determination—or maybe it was the confidence of being more in control of her Gift. Or the anger at Cyl. Whatever the reason, I was glad we had her as an ally and not the other way around. As it was, she kept giving Cyl looks that would make me shrink into the nearest pit if they were directed at me.

"Yes," Grenedil replied to Astra. "Remember, only go three places, Baey said." At last, his nervousness betrayed him a little, rubbing his pocket watch anxiously.

Astra nodded.

"And then we can get you back home," he added, throwing a sideways glare at Cyl, who just gave a very unimpressive huff.

"Yes." Astra's reply was quiet, especially above the general noise of the people milling about, waiting for us to leave.

I really hoped Cyl hadn't lied about Astra's family being alright…. If he had, I might just accept that extra bit of blood on my hands. After everything she'd done, Astra deserved something in return.

The next few minutes passed without further conversation, everyone deciding to collectively ignore Cyl, who seemed very preoccupied with looking poised and in charge even though he now was so far from it. With Darby now gone, my mind returned more to the tumult of information trying to process itself: Cyl refusing to help Ovok, Moira and Skayla both having removed true free will in an attempt at peace…and Ovok coming here in just a few more hours. Baey said once we activated the portal, we would only have about an hour to get everyone out, because Ovok would sense the portal. Astra's use of The Door throughout the city would help provide a temporary distraction, but with Ovok already knowing where The Door's off-world entry was, he wouldn't waste time figuring out why someone was using it to go around the city. It was more to catch the attention of any other Myrandi, and ensure no one went to wherever we were sending the civilians.

"Alright, it's time." Baey's voice came very suddenly from right above us as she flew down. "Here are the coordinates." She handed a piece of paper to Cyl. "Open the portal."

Cyl let out a very loud, long sigh. "Stand back."

We already were standing pretty far back, having given the machine Mum had made quite a bit of space before the crowd, but I had a feeling Cyl was just trying to feel important, at this point.

A crackling blue light appeared, growing from an orb into an elongated oval, then warping into the shape of a door, the image of a forest clearing with some well-built cabins appearing through it. Silence fell on the crowd gathered as everyone caught sight of the mysterious portal—the one that had once brought the Myrandi here.

Cyl gave an over-important bow, stepping to the side. "As you wished, a portal for your foolish plans." However, I caught the little added, "Don't blame me when this goes wrong," that he murmured under his breath.

Baey stepped forward, "I'll go in first and explain the situation, then I'll come back for you and everyone."

She disappeared a moment into the blue haze, leaving us to wait awkwardly for about ten more minutes before she reappeared. "Alright. We can begin the evacuation."

It was much quicker than expected. Cyl grew the portal, and so quite a steady stream of people was able to make it through at a time. A few of Kearn's soldiers were the first to go through, and I soon understood Baey's reasoning for that. They were quick and organized, having already established an efficient system for carrying across supplies from The Underground and into this secret village-space. I didn't know much of where the other side of the portal led in terms of precise location, but I didn't need to. Baey had been very clear that there was no time for questions.

I was pleasantly surprised with how everyone was through the portal in far under the deadline Baey had given, and I was quite aware we had the Bethynese soldiers in part to thank for that.

"Now?" Alenor asked as we regrouped, The Door to The Underground just a few feet away, and Grenedil and Cyl guarding it.

"Now, you stay with the people." Baey landed and walked over to us, a newfound confidence in every movement. Not the sort of confidence that made you brave enough to stand up for yourself, but the sort of practical confidence from being in control of your every move. It was the sort of confidence a trained swordsman had, completely aware of how their body worked. I could see it in every motion Baey made. Gone was the awkward way she'd try to walk around her wings. Gone were the stumbling landings she was so prone to before. I knew I was now looking at someone who had lived for lifetimes—someone who had faced despair countless times, and who had taken that time to learn instead of be overcome by it. I wondered how many times she'd watched our attempts fail—how many times she'd seen us die—and, as I looked in her eyes, I saw another thing I had never seen before. A look I understood, and one I had hoped never to see in her. I knew I wasn't the only one with ghosts.

"You, Darby, Thackeray, Syvil, and Moira," Baey continued on. "Make sure to keep an eye out for patrols, and no matter what happens, do not leave. I will come with you to make sure you're settled in, and then I'll return to the others to get ready for Ovok."

No one argued, but I saw the worry in Mum's eyes.

"We need to leave now." Baey turned back to the portal.

"Please, be careful." Mum looked at all of us, fear all too evident. Fear I didn't blame her for.

I wrapped her in a fierce hug. "Don't worry, Mum. We'll come back."

She clung to me like her life depended on it, but at last managed to let go, wiping a tear from her face. "Thank you. Now go."

"I'm going to keep you to that," Darby interjected as she and the others prepared to head through the portal to whatever lay on the other side. "That you're coming back."

I nodded, making a promise to myself. We would *all* come back.

CHAPTER XXIII: Eugene Atarah

Estasia:

"You're *sure* he's helping?" I asked, too afraid to hope. If Baey said he'd help us hide everyone, that had to mean something, right? Or was it a matter of guilt-tripping? Were we going to use intimidation?

Baey sighed. "Yes. I think it's best if he explains. We have time—it will take a while for them to get all the people and supplies ready to move." Her wings turned dark.

"What?" I couldn't help but ask. "Don't do that—don't get all sad and not say anything."

We were almost to the tunnel entrance, so we didn't have much time before speaking wouldn't be an option. This only made me more desperate for answers; more…afraid in general. The idea of seeing Eugene face-to-face after all these years was something I had both burned for and dreaded the idea of. I knew he was different—from what I'd heard between Illan and Atlys, he couldn't be the same kind, compassionate kid I had known.

But what if he was? And why did that scare me more?

"I think it's best if you both talk…without me intervening too much, Estasia. I'm not meddling in this. It's important for him being able to work with us that I don't just go in ordering things. You have to do a lot of the talking."

I made a deeply displeased expression even though she couldn't see it. "Oh yes, going all noble on me again, are you, Birdie?"

She chuckled but said nothing. And just like that, we arrived at the city exit, and the time for conversation was over.

I only found my anxiety growing as we made our way through the tunnels and then quickly to the streets above. I hadn't felt this way in a very long time, and I hated it. It was…it was helplessness. The idea that I truly had no idea what was going to happen next. It didn't help that the sewers had been nearly impossible to wade through—even with Baey's ability to use the watch. The chaos of the streets was almost safer.

Finally, we arrived. Even as stressed as I was, I couldn't help but let out a snort in contempt as I stared at the gaudy mansion before me.

"*This?*" My smirk held little humor in it.

"Ring the bell, and tell them your real name," Baey instructed.

I choked. "What?"

"No one knows who you are. It will only hold meaning to him, and then we'll be let in undisturbed. Trust me." Baey's wings were perfectly camouflaged as a cloak around her, so dark you couldn't even see the feathers, meaning I couldn't even dream of deciphering what she was feeling right now: I could only trust her.

I settled for glaring at her and replying, "You better be glad I like you, Birdie," as I walked up the gigantic marble steps to pull on the doorbell.

The door opened and a butler blinked at me, took one look at my raggedy appearance, and turned up his nose.

"Just tell him Estasia is here," I grumbled. I was honestly surprised he hadn't slammed the door on me, but then I realized it was most likely because Eugene had quite a few smelly, raggedy-looking informants right now due to his searches in the sewers, which again made me very confused as to how this worked; hadn't he been the one who had sowed doubt about Kearn? Why was I doing this?

I resisted the urge to look back at Baey. That little bird better be thankful I had the faith in her to go through with this, given the slim information she was providing.

The doorman disappeared, but only briefly, opening the door wider and beckoning me inside. Baey was right behind me, and we were both shown inside.

"Follow me," the man said with a good dose of disdain. "And take your shoes off, if you would." He pointed to a mat by the door. "We don't need your *filth* dragging all over the carpets."

This was definitely not endearing me to Eugene. With a good dose of venomous stares in the doorman's direction, I obliged, and soon, we were escorted down the hall and a few doors down. Without another word, the man opened the door, and Baey and I stepped inside the room.

It was a large study, of course. Just like every other pompous noble's house: shelves filled to the brim with books that were only there to show status; an ornately carved desk that was way too big to be really necessary; and the pipes lining the bottom of the wall, showing off the access to fresh water whenever desired.

But nothing prepared me for the perfect peacock of a man that occupied the room, dressed in a full blue velvet suit, tailcoats falling pristinely behind him as his tall figure towered over us. His facial hair was groomed in a way no normal person would have time for, making him look every inch the sort of aristocrat I despised.

"E-Esa?" He was staring at me, disbelief open for everyone to see.

To be frank, I wasn't really sure what exactly came over me, but in that moment, all the anxiety and fear evaporated, leaving behind instead a deep anger. I marched right up to where he stood in front of his stupid desk and slapped him square across the face.

"What—" he fell backwards, catching himself on his pretty little desk as he rubbed his cheek.

"What in the *world*, Eugene! All this time I was feeling *sorry* for you, and you were really just living it up here! What a beautiful little prince you make, wrapped in all your pretty things as we all *starve* to death. Wow, what was I even worried about?" I laughed in disbelief, watching the shock from his face melt away and be replaced with apparent anger. Baey *had* to be joking. This porcelain doll was going to *help* us?!

I turned to her, but she remained quiet and unreadable in the corner.

"Oh, *sorry*," I turned back to Eugene and bowed. "Lord Atarah, I humbly beg your pardon."

"Excuse me?" The acrid tone was expected. "Last time *I* checked, I wasn't the one who turned over their best friend for a stupid cash reward, then disappeared until randomly showing up over a decade later to…assault and mock me?"

My cheeks flushed against my will, and I felt just a little bit of my confidence deflate. "First of all, that wasn't me, you imbecile. That was Temorn—and trust me, I made sure to ditch him the moment I found out. Second, I looked for you for weeks! And third…in what world does that excuse all *this* rubbish?!" I motioned wildly about the room. "Just fall in line with a tyrant without so much as a fight, huh? All too willing for a nice plush bed. Do you have any idea where I've slept the last twelve years?"

"I can very well imagine, thank you. Do not pretend to know me. Now, tell me why you're here before I kick you out myself. Unless you came here for no other reason than to slap me and make rash, ill-informed judgements?" He straightened his coat, grip much tighter on the fabric than it needed to be.

"Because unfortunately, someone told me that for some reason you actually want to help us, even if I am finding it incredibly hard to believe, at the moment," I said the last bit between my teeth, pointing not at this garish Lord Atarah but instead to Baey.

His eyes narrowed and his whole demeanor shifted unexpectedly. "You're working with Atlys, then?"

"Give me one reason to trust you with *any* such information," I challenged. He'd come to that conclusion all too quickly, meaning as much as I refused to admit it, clearly, he already knew about us. So Baey was, of course, probably right.

A dry, humorless smile plastered across his face as if his last bit of patience was slowly leaving his body, and he replied, "Because I am the one who leaked the information to Atlys about Angeline and Lyci's deaths."

I forced myself to keep my composure. No one knew about Atlys's dead wife and daughter. If anyone had, Atlys never would have kept his charade. "Excuse me?"

"How do you think Atlys found out? No information from those camps is ever released. The only way you know anything is if you're a guard there or an occupant." His voice was ice.

"You know they only let go of snitches," I retorted, matching his tone. "No one else leaves that place alive."

His face dropped, and he folded his hands neatly behind his back as he glared. "Do you really think *so* little of me? Or do you just remember so little? You want to know? *Fine.* I was released because they realized my parents didn't *care* what they did to me. You know what those holding camps are for, I assume? They put someone you love in there and threaten you with harming them if you don't cooperate. Funny how you forget I ran away from my parents because they couldn't have cared less about me. They only wanted me back because it looked bad for their status. But then Skayla took over and the only thing that mattered was power. Birthright and your children didn't matter anymore. So my parents started embezzling, stealing from Skayla's spoils. When the threats or actual harm to me didn't change anything, Skayla laughed it off and had me released."

He leaned in close and whispered, "I don't think I need to tell you about what happens in those camps, do I? I'm sure you've heard plenty of stories. They don't do it justice. The starving is one thing, but everything else…oh, that's a whole other story. The lucky ones die. Atlys's family was lucky." He pulled back. "But you know why they tried to run off? Because they knew Atlys would do anything for them—and that he would break under the choice of forsaking everything he believed in, or causing unimaginable suffering to those he loved. So they made the choice for him.

"When I started getting the consequences of my parents' actions, I thought…surely, they were rebelling against Skayla. That despite my opinions of them, at least they were doing the right thing. But no…they just didn't care what happened to me. And you know what I realized that day? No one cared about me. Not you, not Temorn, not my parents. And when Skayla released me, she told me *exactly* what my parents had been up to." That smile…it scared me. "She saw my bitterness and anger and thought it would turn me into a perfect little soldier. But I used that to keep an eye on Atlys and his…projects. Do you know how hard it was to frame my parents for that fiasco at the portal site?"

Atlys had told me of the camps—of how they'd locked away some of the nobility's loved ones and threatened horrible things if they went against Skayla. He'd mentioned Eugene had been let go from one about eight years ago, but he'd said he thought it was because Skayla realized the Atarahs actually *wanted* to help her—that they didn't care about anything, and I'd assumed he had been just as corrupt in order to be let go. Had Eugene really suffered through all that, all this time?

"But you are the *picture* of loyalty to Skayla! And what about Kearn? If you claim to be helping, why try and *find* The Underground and expose Kearn as a spy?" Even as I processed all of this horrible information, I grasped at straws; straws that could keep me angry.

"Because I didn't know that stupid captain was a spy! All I knew was he was horrible at playing politics and he was close to Kovo. I was *trying* to get attention away from Atlys, because Kovo clearly suspected him. Never would I have guessed a Bethynese captain was playing spy. And, for your information, I was trying to lead him away from The Underground—which yes, I know where it is—well, roughly, seeing as that whole sewer system was reordered. Why do you think there were never any good maps available for the sewers? Because I burned all except the old and useless ones, which I'd already turned over to Kearn." He scoffed, shaking his head in apparent disbelief.

"Look, Eugene, I didn't know." I found myself stumbling to reassess, sudden washes of sympathy eroding my indignation. "But can you blame me? How do you really expect me to believe you when you're all dressed up in *their* finery? Just look at your house! It looks like you've been groveling at Skayla and Ovok's feet. If you were so set on helping, why didn't you tell Atlys you were on our side and try and *help!*"

He tilted his head a little when I said Ovok's name, and I realized he still only knew him as Kovo, and Ovok simply as Skayla's pet. Nonetheless, he replied, "Because I couldn't risk *my* operation being discovered, Estasia. If I allowed myself to be tied to Atlys in any way, that risked other lives being put in danger. I've spent the last few years of my supposed freedom trying to smuggle as many people from those hellish camps to a safe haven, and if Atlys knew and then was found out for *his* little smuggling endeavors, then everyone I am trying to take care of would die, too. And they would face double the consequences as escapees from that place. I just didn't expect you to jump to such wild assumptions when I had only ever given you friendship. Silly me saw you here on behalf of Atlys and thought you'd actually changed and cared about anyone but yourself."

That hurt. "Hey. Who's here making judgements, again?" Fists clenched, I took a deep breath and said, "Congratulations, you've proved you aren't a groveling coward. I—" I stopped mid-sentence. What was I even saying? I didn't have a reason to be angry anymore, because I wasn't really angry at him. I was angry at myself—for so easily assuming the worst of him. I was upset that I had sooner believed Temorn was on our side than I had Eugene. "—I need your help, and I'm sorry, alright? I'm really, *really* sorry. I never would have let Temorn turn you over if I'd known that's what he was doing. You were my only real friend, and I lost you and stopped trying to find anyone else. We've both got our problems. But Atlys is in trouble, and Baey says you're the only one who can help."

He looked...stunned the moment my apology left my mouth, but then horrified at the mention of Atlys. There was no more time for us to squabble, and we both knew it.

"What do you need?" he asked without so much as a second of hesitation, and again, I found my anger further dissipate, replaced by something that hurt a lot more.

"You have land," Baey stepped in to explain. "We have Moira, the Mistress of Time. You and I have had this conversation before. We need to evacuate The Underground to a safe place, and the refugee camp you've been hiding in your parents' western territory holds enough for both your people as well as ours."

"I..." Eugene looked shocked, but not quite as shocked as I was at Baey just immediately admitting to being able to mess with time. "But how would you get there? It's days away."

"We have access to the portal the Drogans arrived through. If you give me a letter that will prove I'm working with you, I can present it to your people at the camp." It was strange how much older Baey seemed, now, as she spoke. "We have supplies that Atlys had already been stockpiling that we can move for you after we deal with Ovok, but that can be sorted later.

"I..." Eugene frowned, looking from me to Baey. "You have the Mistress of Time, you claim?"

In one smooth motion, Baey presented the watch from around her neck. "Yes. You and I have had many conversations. But I need you to trust me."

"Alright." The way in which Eugene simply...accepted it was unexpected. He took out a piece of paper from his desk and quickly began writing something on it. "And you'll save Atlys? I swore I would do everything I could to keep him safe—for his family."

Of course he had. Of course he was the same stupid Eugene who would do anything to help someone. The guilt I felt was frustratingly deserved.

"You have to get him tonight, while Ovok is occupied," Baey continued on. "Get past the Bethynese soldiers and you'll have a clear shot. Estasia will come with you to extract our other inside man."

"Ovok?" Eugene asked.

I waved a hand in the air. "Yes, yes, Lord Kovo is Ovok. Drogans have human forms. It's a long story."

He seemed to understand it wasn't important, which honestly was strangely refreshing after how many times those from Valdon had doubted me. Or maybe I just missed him more than I liked to admit, and it was nice to be able to work with him.

Oh great, I really was going soft.

"In regards to the Bethynese soldiers, I doubt that will be much trouble. Brahj has had his hands full trying to contain the mutineers after Reth abandoned his position. Kearn and his entire group turning traitor was a lot more divisive than expected. But I can get you in. No one knows your face, right?" he asked me.

I swallowed my surprise that there was an actual Bethynese mutiny, and instead nodded, turning to Baey. "You said Illan was being watched, but hadn't been taken in, correct?"

"Yes." Baey adjusted her spear, wings flicking occasionally almost like a cat's tail would as she addressed Eugene. "You need to be careful. He will be followed when you take him. It's Grenedil's brother, Havirax. We'll have Estasia lead him to Atlys's shipyard and I will have Grenedil waiting. He will contain the threat. Eugene—" Her casualness again just showed how many times she'd lived this.

Eugene, however, seemed confused by this, stumbling out an, "I...yes?"

"You need to leave with Atlys. Without Estasia. As long as she distracts Havirax, you will get in and out successfully. Providing you keep your wits about you." She raised an eyebrow.

Eugene said nothing, but a flicker of doubt washed over his face as his cynicism appeared to catch up with everything that had just passed between us.

Baey looked him dead in the eyes and simply said, "I have Moira's watch. I've lived this before. Trust me. I already trust you, seeing as you died trying to help us once."

I just stared at Eugene. Again, that sounded like the boy I had once known. I could see that one throwing his life away for a few strangers who barely trusted him.

Eugene accepted this fairly well, to my surprise, only looking a bit shocked before giving a small nod. "Alright. Then is there anything else Esa and I should know before we start?" he asked, using his signet ring to seal the letter he'd finished writing before handing it to Baey. The old nickname wasn't so awful to hear this time.

"Just the coordinates so I can give them to the ones running the portal," Baey said.

Eugene put up a finger, then scribbled something on a scrap of paper. "Here."

"Thank you," Baey said with a dip of her head. "If I may, I need to also write down the schedules of the guards and the best route—from what we have learned from previous attempts to free Atlys."

Eugene quickly gave her a pen and paper, and as she wrote, she explained the rest of the plan in more detail, giving us as much information as she could. With the amount of procedure that was going into this, I understood why she wanted it written out for us. Even with my close attention to everything she was saying, there was no way I would remember it. Some things relied on being within minutes of precision.

"There," at last Baey finished, handing me the paper full of things she had explained.

We spent a while going over the paper again and the route both Eugene and I would need to take, Baey's instructions, at times, startlingly detailed. At last, when she was sure we understood all the details, Baey announced. "Now I must check in and make sure those at the manor are ready, and then I have to get back to The Underground and help with the evacuation. Please be careful."

There was a weird pit in my stomach as I replied, "I think, seeing as who you're about to face, you're the one that needs to hear that more, Birdie."

Her smile didn't reach her eyes. That wasn't something that had ever happened before.

"I'll try." With that, she turned to Eugene. "Don't get her angry."

He gave an inelegant snort and replied, "I will."

I didn't realize I was glaring at him until the edge of his mouth twitched in a smile. I felt a distinct urge to punch him in the arm, and then realized I was still feeling intensely conflicted about this.

"I am sure you will," Baey replied. "I need to leave now. Take care of each other."

I wasn't good at goodbyes but still regretted saying nothing more before she left. I thought that maybe…maybe if I didn't say goodbye, then she wouldn't be able to leave forever.

After all, here was Eugene, gone for a decade after not saying goodbye. Though in all honesty, I wasn't sure what the result of all this would be. The truth of what had happened to him weighed on me more than I wished. We were so different now.

"You're still difficult to work with, aren't you?" Eugene asked dryly once we were alone.

Now I *did* punch him in the arm, not expecting him to flinch the way he did. "Oh, settle down, you little peacock."

"I can already tell this is going to be great…" he grumbled.

"Just stick to getting Atlys, and we'll be grand." I wiped a finger on his desk in a vain search for dust.

For a second, I thought maybe he really would, but then he asked suddenly, "So what's your angle, Esa?"

The question hurt, and part of me didn't want to think about why. "Listen, *Gene*, there's no angle. Just like there wasn't an angle with you, alright? They're friends, and if this is some elaborate ruse on *your* part, trust me when I say I will tear you to shreds for it." I looked at him. "Now, are we going to save Atlys or what?"

"Hm." Eugene watched me carefully, his hands still folded neatly behind his back. "Fine."

CHAPTER XXIV: Off We Go

Estasia:

We spent the next half hour going over the detailed plan Baey had imparted us with as many times as we could, determining we would need pocket watches to make sure nothing went awry. It was nice to be able to melt into the preparations for a while: No more questions or backhand remarks, just committing to the plan. It felt…odd, like some strange nostalgia. There was so much relief in knowing that he'd actually never intended on following Skayla or Ovok, but we were still changed. I couldn't stop thinking about the fact he'd been willing to kill his own parents. Gone was the naive wonder in his eyes, replaced by something much more callous and lonely. Something I could relate to.

At last, we finished preparations, and all there was to do now was wait for it to come closer to evening.

"I imagine you might like to get cleaned up a bit before you change into your disguise?" Eugene asked as he led me out of the study.

I wrinkled my nose, looking him up and down in all his gaudy finery. "Are you worried I might stain your furniture?" The words tumbled out without thinking.

"I was simply thinking you would be more comfortable—and cleaning up from the sewers would make you less conspicuous in the palace. Plus I've been down there enough to know you could easily get ill from not properly washing afterwards." His tone was the only thing that gave away his defensiveness, his face hiding it much better and his posture otherwise calm. It was practiced; I could recognize the signs of surviving with secrets in a world Skayla owned.

"Right," I said tersely. "I suppose a bath would be nice."

Eugene didn't say much else as he showed me to the washroom, where I spent the next twenty minutes cleaning up and getting in the slave disguise one of his staff brought up for me. I despised the uniform, repeatedly reminding myself I was no longer a slave and no longer bound to serve. It was just a disguise...and honestly, I found myself a bit silly for being so bothered. Even if this was still better than anything I had ever worn—the palace slaves seemed to have a little more presentation than those in the Kovian Fortress.

Still in an ill-temper, I went downstairs and down the hall to find the room Eugene had said we would wait in. It was a large sitting room, adorned with all sorts of nauseating baubles and fancy things meant to impress. I hated how unnecessarily large it was, as if designed to shove the owner's status down your throat.

"You know, Atlys lived in shambles," I commented as I sat in a nearby, perfectly upholstered chair.

Eugene was sitting across from me, a book in his hand as he sipped tea with the other. "Atlys could afford to look destitute. There's tea if you want it," he replied idly, setting his cup down and turning the page.

"You're infuriating," I grumbled.

"I doubt I am any more infuriating than Temorn—who you apparently are still fine working with." His eyes flitted up to me for a moment, hard and judgemental, before returning to his book. I was beginning to doubt he was actually reading it.

I tried not to give into my instinctual panic as I asked, "How did you know that?"

Turning the page, he simply replied, "I kept an eye on Atlys's movements, and I knew very well Temorn still ruled the sewers. My parents ignored his little syndicate because it wasn't worth dirtying their hands to go down there, and they didn't realize there was anything more than a few criminals taking refuge in the sewers. I knew Atlys used them to help with his smuggling and intelligence gathering. Temorn always had the self-preservation of a cockroach. I wasn't surprised he'd successfully evaded Skayla's attention, and when I convinced my parents to handle their affairs, I was able to help conceal Temorn's group."

I only relaxed a little, the explanation making enough sense. "Well, I would have you know that I work with Atlys, and do my best to avoid interacting with Temorn. He's not been much used anyway since the patrols in the sewers had increased."

There went the little doubtful eyebrow raise—the little prick. "So you slapped him, too?"

I gave a smug little smile. "In fact, I punched him square in the face. So hard he lost a few of his precious golden teeth."

I was, however, frustrated when I didn't get the reaction I was hoping for. No. Instead, Eugene simply turned the page of his book again.

"So, are you happy then?" I asked, crossing my arms.

Still no emotion on that stupid face of his, he took another sip of his tea. "Yes, yes, I am." The reply was empty.

He was infuriating. "Well?" I asked.

"Well, what?" He turned the page of his book.

"Would you put that thing down?" My fist came down on the chair much harder than I'd meant it to.

Slowly, Eugene placed his cup down and closed the book.

"You know, Atlys is still in there, *dying*, and you sitting here reading and having a great little afternoon tea is not endearing me to your character."

"I do not need to *be* endearing to you, Estasia. That is not required." He looked at me with a steely expression. "What is required is simply that we cooperate."

"You're right." I threw up my hands. "You don't need to be anything but civil. But somehow your lack of...of...*anything* makes it difficult to even cooperate with you. It makes you just another aristocrat, helping out just because it is convenient to your status."

Eyes narrowing ever so slightly, Eugene replied, "I can assure you; this is in no way benefiting my status. You should know that. Why should I care what you think of me? You're helping me free Atlys, are you not? That is all I require. Why does anything else matter?"

"Because we were friends, Gene!" I didn't care; I shouted. "And...and I wanted my friend back for *so* long. What Temorn did to you—*and* to me—destroyed any faith in people I had. But I would have done anything to get you back."

The tip of Eugene's mouth twitched upwards ever so slyly. "Aw. I knew you still cared about me."

"Why, you—" I launched myself at him, taking his book and hitting him in the arm with it.

But I would be lying if I didn't say hearing his laugh after so long wasn't nice.

"I told you; I wanted to know your angle. Glad to see it's not as callous as it once was." He looked up at me, earnestness having replaced the emotionless void he'd had there before. He stood up, putting both hands in his pockets like an embarrassed little child. "I missed you. But I didn't miss your pretended stoicism."

I gave him a good scowl as I replied, "You play the aristocratic jerk a little too well. Maybe I would have shown myself better if you'd tried a little more to be *nice*." Had I...seriously just gotten owned by my own trick?

He chuckled. "Yes, well, you weren't the only one who gave up trying to have friends after what happened."

"If Baey was here, she'd say some rubbish about that getting us nowhere and all that," I said with surprising conviction.

"I don't know, I survived." Eugene's reply was less than helpful.

I punched him in the arm. "Quit sounding so much like me, moron. You're supposed to be the optimistic one."

Rubbing his arm, Eugene said, "Am I? What happened to you? You're the one who always talked about everyone's bad intentions."

"It's a long story," I mumbled as I went back to my seat, plopping down and feeling more at ease.

Eugene also went back to his chair, albeit with a great deal more pomp and grace, sitting down and putting his book back on his lap. He reached for his tea. "Well, we do have time to spare...you could...tell me? Over some tea?" He pointed to the other cup beside his. "It's still quite warm."

Narrowing my eyes at the suspicious tea kettle and cup, I shook my head. "I'm good, thank you. Not really a porcelain kind of person."

"Very well. I suppose these next few hours will be quite awkward then," he commented as he opened his book again.

I remained calm, even despite the sudden urge to yank the stupid book out of his hand. "I just meant I didn't want tea, moron. And perhaps that I wasn't about to go spilling any of my story unless you go first."

He scoffed. "I already told you mine."

"You told me some of it, yes." I pressed, unsure how much of it was me wanting to hear the full story, and how much I was just trying to stall for time on giving up mine.

The book was placed on a nearby pedestal as Eugene began, "Fine. But you had better hold up your end and tell me everything."

Again wondering if I really wanted this, I nodded. "It's a deal. I'm bored enough for a good story."

His laugh was terse. "It isn't exactly a very good one. But I'll tell you nonetheless." Settling in his chair, he began, "You and Temorn abandoned me to my parents. We left Alkemar as soon as possible so that I'd be 'free of bad influences.' I was sent to the strictest boarding school in Patelayna. The Drogans arrived, Skayla conquered Patelayna, and I was taken during the siege of the city of Eknemar. I already told you about the holding camps." He stopped, waving dismissively.

I'd heard of the holding camps for a while, but part of me hadn't really believed them. At least, not until I'd met Atlys, and he'd proven he had, in fact, been under duress. Part of me wondered now if Skayla purposefully sowed doubt as to the camps' authenticity, in a way to get people to believe everyone was just simply going along with Skayla and not being forced.

"Believe me, there are plenty of nobles who joined just for the fun of it," Eugene went on, "Or were deemed too powerful or influential, and thus killed immediately. But Atlys's family was not either of those. There were some good people in that camp. There still are." He shuddered. "They do a good job of keeping you alive though, for the most part. Angeline and Lyci's cases were pretty rare." I didn't miss the way he faltered. "But you heard the rest already. I was released due to my parents' apathy. In all honesty, I wasn't in the camps for that long. Though I couldn't really tell for sure how much time had passed. All I know is I was released around eight years ago."

"And then just…decided to play the long game for revenge?" I asked, skeptical.

He shook his head. "Not revenge. I couldn't care less about my parents. I simply used them for my own gain. They were all too glad to slowly give me more and more run of their estate when it became clear I was very adept at elevating their favor with Skayla as well as their profit. I needed their land so I could hide those I was smuggling out of the camps—I had been able to carefully replace a few of the guards at the camps—there are, of course, more than one camp. After managing to get a few moles on the inside, we carefully began faking deaths of occupants. But it was more difficult with my parents alive. Besides, I was also trying to protect Atlys after Kovo—or Ovok, as it seems—was alerted to the presence of The Underground and demanded to know how it had gone unseen for so long. I'd been slowly adding incriminating evidence in my parents' book keeping so that Atlys's slipups would be pinned instead on them—in case of emergency. Turned out the contingency was good forethought, otherwise Atlys would have been executed after the ravine battle and not my parents. I may be petty, but I wouldn't just murder people for fun, as delightful as that may seem. No. I just. Decided seeing as no one cared what happened to me, I would use that to cater to what people already *expected* of me. But I didn't want anyone to feel as trapped as I had all my life. Skayla made the whole world suffocate under the pretense of order. I'd grown up under that same philosophy, and I didn't want anyone stuck in those forsaken camps. That is all, Esa."

I sat in silence, slowly digesting all of the information. I still remembered how he'd talked of his life before meeting us—the lack of identity, the emphasis on discipline, and not sullying his family name.

"And now it's your turn, Esa. What happened?" he asked, leaning forward in his seat.

I again crossed my arms, not exactly thrilled about this. But a strange part of me really, really wanted to tell him; wanted to make up for lost time and explain just how much had changed. "Well, after Temorn told me what he did, I went looking for you. But you'd already left Alkemar, so I settled with leaving his mother's gang and instead surviving on my own. Worked pretty well until Skayla took over the city. Then I got caught and carted off to be a slave." I didn't like remembering those years. They were a dark, frightening time. Alone. Not having any will to live besides the instinct for survival. "I got in trouble a few times. We were disposable, starving half the time and being worked to death the other half. I was shuffled around a few places, and then ended up in the Kovian fortress."

It all seemed so long ago now. "I got in a little *too* much trouble. Stole from the wrong person and it escalated all the way up to Skayla. She had her precious GhostMaker teach me a lesson. But he didn't." Shaking my head, I repeated, "He didn't. I'd never seen someone successfully fight a MindHold before, and something just...I don't know. Changed. If someone was willing to fight off something so impossible just to help me—no one important—maybe I should do the same. I started this underground network of slaves. We had our own code and everything— and because we always got moved around, soon, we were all over Baeno. Our plan was to somehow break The GhostMaker out. But we couldn't figure out how to break the MindHold permanently. Then as if by some miracle, he escaped on his own, and after a few more incidents, I end up saving him and bringing him to Baey and her friends...and I realize maybe there's more to life than surviving. Maybe I don't just want to simply survive anymore."

I paused again, looking down at my hands, now folded in my lap. "Then we came here, and I couldn't resist going to where I'd stashed my things—where I'd stashed the painting you made me. I thought you were dead and that I'd failed you, and I'd never get a second chance."

"You kept it?" he asked quietly.

"Oh, hush. It was like one of three things I owned." I had, after all, kept Temorn's knife as well. Granted, it had been for more practical reasons.

"I'm sorry." The words sounded so sincere. "That sounds horrible—what you went through. I'm glad you're alright."

I just rolled my eyes, giving a shrug as I replied, "If there's one thing I've learned, it's that we all have gone through it, the past twelve years. I don't see a point in comparing scars. Everyone has them."

"Yes, I suppose that's fair. I guess we've all just been in our own personal hells. Hopefully that changes." A shadow passed over his face. "Hopefully we get Atlys out alive."

The mood died even more, if that was possible, and I frowned. "Yes. Hopefully."

"I promised his family I would keep him safe. I don't want to break that promise now."

I looked up at Eugene, who appeared much more tired and worried than I remembered him looking before. "Well, I also made a promise to myself. To keep my friends safe. I trust Baey—her plan will work."

Eugene nodded, taking a deep breath before he said, "Well then, I suppose this will be a great trust exercise for us both, won't it?"

The stories died away, and soon we fell into silence, Eugene sipping his tea and reading his book, and me, mentally going over our plan a few more times.

At last, it was time to leave.

We didn't say a word as we left in the cheap carriage, trying to remain under the radar. The streets were almost hushed compared to usual:

Was it another calm before the storm? With it being close to sunset, I wouldn't be surprised. A few stones did hit the carriage—whether hitting us on accident or thrown at us on purpose—and I hoped Eugene wouldn't have any issues getting Atlys back to his manor.

I realized there weren't many Bethynese soldiers out tonight. Eugene had mentioned there being difficulties among the ranks—even if I found it hard to believe someone as high ranking as Reth would now commit insubordination.

We were let in at the main gate of the palace, and just as Baey's instructions had claimed, there were very few guards. It felt deserted, the atmosphere straining under it.

"This is it," Eugene announced. We'd be parting ways from here. "Good luck."

"Yeah. Same to you," I replied. I didn't even have to be overly worried about being discreet in my exit from the carriage, let alone wandering the halls and making my way down to the slaves' quarters. Arguments echoed among the palace corridors—arguments about loyalties and integrity. Arguments about whether to stay or leave like Kearn.

I couldn't believe my ears. Never would I have expected to hear any such words from a Bethynese soldier, let alone a whole host of them. Kearn had left a mark, it seemed, and I wondered if he even knew the sway he'd had among the soldiers. He'd never struck me as very charismatic, but then again Bethynese weren't exactly looking for charisma in their role models. I'd also never been able to pay much attention to the hierarchy of the Bethynese, outside of the Kovian Fortress.

At last, I found the slaves' quarters, and—after checking the time on my pocket watch—ignored the looks I got as I entered the men's section.

"What are you doing here?" Illan hissed as I found my way over to him.

"Getting you out of here. You've been compromised." I knew better than to physically force him out the door, lest one of the other slaves stepped in to help him, but I gave him a glare that hopefully proved my resolve.

The fear that showed itself in his eyes was unexpected. "Alright. I don't…I don't think we'll be missed. Some have already dared to make a run for it."

And he hadn't? Guilt rose as I wondered if it was because of my orders. That this little idiot had decided to stay in case there was further need of him. A brave fool.

"Let's just go," I murmured, extending a hand and hoping he would take it.

Thankfully, he did, and we were racing down the halls, quickly checking the time once or twice to make sure we were still on track with the plan. I could feel Illan's questions breathing down my neck—or maybe that was just his anxious panting—but dared not answer anything when I knew we were being followed. Somehow. I saw no one, but I knew better than to doubt Baey. She was obviously right—or I was losing my edge: It had to be Havirax using some invisibility relic. Otherwise, I would have definitely seen him.

We made our way down to the cellar where the sewer entrance was, and we wasted no time ducking down into it. Illan still quiet. I was just shocked at the ease with which we could move through the palace. It was…it was an odd feeling, knowing this cruel empire was finally falling. Everything Skayla had done was starting to come unraveled. But had it come too late?

We eventually made our way out of the sewers and into the dark streets, illuminated only by the few lights left unshattered by the angry groups of people now wreaking havoc in the streets. For the first time, I wondered how we would actually convince people we were the good guys…and how anyone would believe Atlys or, especially, Eugene.

"Where are we going?" Illan whispered in my ear, breaking his silence for the first time as we headed for the waterfront.

"Somewhere safe," I replied, again looking around the streets to try and catch who was following us. But still, I saw nothing—although it was pretty hard to tell with all the people in the streets now.

At last, we arrived at Atlys's warehouse.

Grenedil was not in my immediate sight, but unlike our invisible tail, I was still able to figure out where he was hiding.

"Now what?" Illan sounded tense, and honestly, I didn't blame him.

Now there was no point in secrecy, and I replied, "We've been tailed. I'm waiting for backup."

Hopefully, Grenedil would pull through. He'd been of marginal use so far, but Baey trusted him, and so I had to go with that.

And then I saw it, Grenedil leaping into what seemed like nothing but air, and grabbing hold of something. Well…nothing.

Grenedil:

I waited in the gloom of the warehouse, completely still. I had been worried Havirax might have access to Chaly's Bracers, but the only one who would be able to see him using them was me—which, according to Baey, had been our solution in the past. This whole situation left me wishing I could just scream. I'd been a fool to think Havirax stealing my right as The Merchant had been some isolated incident, and for once, trying to make the best of it by telling him how to serve in his post. It was becoming clearer by the moment that I'd been a fool in a lot of things…especially in thinking Cyl actually had anyone's best interests in mind.

I was so stupid.

And yet here I was, sitting by and watching as always. Still alone. For years, I'd been trying to find Cyl—thinking that despite his rough edges, he was the closest thing to a friend I had besides Mitheau, who I'd only barely reconnected with before leaving for this mess of a planet.

I hoped she was alright. Astra had said she was safe, at least, before she'd left.

Astra. How easily she seemed to form connections. The more I watched everyone, the more I realized just how…alone I was. My brother was helping Ovok, of all people. Then, as if that alone wasn't enough, the one person I'd looked to for mentorship was absolutely fine sacrificing hundreds of innocent people for his pride. I was left knowing I was nothing more than one person pathetically trying to make himself useful when the only thing that would have done so was given to his brother instead.

I wasn't The Merchant. I didn't have anything that could help. For the most part, I'd just gotten in the way, unable to even help Astra properly or stop Cyl from stranding her here.

Footsteps.

I refocused my attention and found the woman, Estasia, entering the large space with another stranger. I combed the area immediately, glad that apparently my hunch in some past attempt had been correct; even though I was not The Merchant, I still held some of the perks of it—including the ability to more easily see through a relic's disguise.

"Now what?" I heard the whisper from the man accompanying Estasia.

That's when I saw it; the strange, mirage-like effect in the blank space. I crept closer, completely silent as I made my way over to where he was watching Estasia. I had to act quickly before he moved and I lost track of him again.

Close enough at last and hoping I was still undetected, I launched myself on top of my invisible brother, grappling with him and desperately trying to find and grab hold of his arms—which was, admittedly, an extremely difficult thing to do when said brother was invisible.

"Get off me!" Havirax squealed as he landed a weak punch at my face. It was still enough to knock me backwards, but not before I managed to grab where his arm should have been upon hitting me. My hand came into contact with the leather bracers and I pulled him forward, wrapping my fingers as tightly as I could around his arm.

He was now on top of me, and with only a second to spare, I took hold of his arm with both my hands, yanking it as hard as I could. My brother let out a howl of pain, thrashing wildly and successfully punching me in the face as we tumbled across the floor.

But I stubbornly held on.

It was a strange thing, trying to rip open a leather bracer when you couldn't see it—let alone the arm it was attached to—but at last, I got the stupid thing to come loose. Suddenly, Havirax was revealed in all of his pathetic glory.

"You worthless *prat!*" he spat as he launched at my face.

Someone pulled him off of me, and I heard a sound akin to a shriek come from Havirax. I got my bearings just in time to see Estasia land a solid kick to his stomach, knife in her other hand.

I wasn't sure if I was relieved to see no blood on it.

"Stay down," Estasia growled the command.

Still in possession of the one arm bracer, I got up and brushed myself off, coming over and grabbing Havirax by the arm I'd so cruelly twisted only a little while before.

Spitting on the ground, he whined, "Oh, you always just have to come along and ruin it, don't you, Dilly?"

I squeezed the arm harder, and he squirmed. "Shut up. Don't you say another word unless it's to answer *my* questions. Where's the bag?" The Merchant's bag—the one that could never be stolen, only given freely to a new bearer.

"Ha, this again? Pathetic. You know, I might make a bad Merchant, but I think it's safe to say you'd be far worse with how you've turned out."

Havirax's sneer was ruined by a pathetic looking grimace, followed by yet another howl.

Estasia had apparently stepped on the hand that he was using to prop himself up.

"The bag." I had asked him for it once before, and he had refused, saying it was his chance to prove to me he could be just as good as I was. Foolishly, I'd believed him; believed all he'd wanted was to prove that he didn't have to live in my shadow.

I'd let him play into my ego, and thought maybe he would be something, and that I could make the best of the situation by helping him be The Merchant I'd hoped I would be.

"I'm not giving you anything, Dilly." The smugness returned. "You know how it works—I've given you my answer and I'm not changing it." The smirk hurt. He was right, of course. If I killed him—not that I would, even in my most desperate moment—then it would prevent The Merchant's bag from ever being able to be passed to me. It could only be given freely. Otherwise, certainly Ovok would have long since forced him to give it over. However, that's not exactly what I meant.

"Oh, I'm aware, but you are going to reach into that bag and you are going to find the jade handcuffs. They're pretty distinct."

"I'd like to see you make me." Havirax actually laughed his time, even through the grimaces.

Suddenly, Estasia grabbed him by the collar, forcing me to relinquish my grip on his arm as she pulled him up and against a nearby wooden support beam. "I know a rat when I see one," she said dangerously, putting the knife to his throat. "And you know what they all have in common?"

Havirax was too shocked to speak.

The blade pressed further against Havirax's throat, and I saw the faintest bit of blood, causing bile to rise to my throat. "They all squeal eventually." The smile that came with the statement was enough to make my blood run cold.

"F-fine. Here—" Havirax squirmed against Estasia's iron grip, his right hand going by his side and suddenly disappearing as if into some invisible bag—because that's exactly what was happening.

Estasia looked slightly confused—but took the handcuffs that suddenly appeared in my brother's hand.

"Let me put them on," I came forward again, ignoring the glare I was now receiving from Havirax. Estasia handed the cuffs to me without a word, and I wasted no time in securing them to my brother's wrists. It was a handy thing Havirax hadn't thrown these out or insisted he had no idea what I was talking about, as they would keep him from running off. I turned to Estasia. "He can't run now. You can let him go."

She didn't move, only looked skeptically.

"They tie the wearer to whoever put them on. He can't do anything I don't want him to." They were bound with a very twisted, old Eatrisian Gifting—something not dissimilar to what had created the Forest of Riddles. I was normally against using any relic that contained dark Gifting, but Havirax was an exception.

Though still sporting a doubtful expression, Estasia slowly released Havirax.

"According to the plan, now we blindfold him and get on our way." She pulled out some cloth from her pocket and tied it around Havirax. "You'd better be right about these cuffs."

For once, I was.

"Falling in line like a good little pet as usual, eh, Dilly?" Havirax's voice dripped scorn.

I clenched my fists. "No one cares what you think, Havirax."

"Aw, is that a backbone you're trying to grow? Did Cyl not turn out as warm and fuzzy as you remembered?" His mockery was cut off by Estasia kneeing him in the gut again.

She shrugged apologetically. "Sorry. He was getting obnoxious. Reminded me too much of someone."

Choking and gasping for air, Havirax gave little resistance as I grabbed him by his coat collar and started following Estasia out.

"Maybe you haven't changed so much, after all. Can't do the dirty work, but you're just fine with watching someone else do it," Havirax grumbled. "Would you have even cared what she would do to me?"

Before I could form any sort of reply, Estasia snapped back, "Oh please. Stop pretending you're anything but a spineless coward, and shut up before I give you to The GhostMaker."

"Yes. *Quiet.*" I put force into my words, knowing the cuffs would compel Havirax to obey my command.

Red-faced and silent, my brother could do nothing but walk with us as we left the warehouse.

As soon as we'd made it back to Eugene's manor, I asked for a private room where I ordered Havirax to begin making a list of things that were inside the bag—as I still was not allowed to see or access it. I had to take his word for what was in there, and hoped the handcuffs were powerful enough to keep him from lying.

So many things were missing. This was such a mess. There was hardly even anything helpful left in there, besides something that would help Astra with her Gifting—should she still need or want such a thing. I was optimistic her lessons with Sven had paid off.

Other than that, the most useful and dangerous items in here had been the cuffs, the bracers—which I had kept after relieving Havirax of them—and the tears of Fiondyn, which allowed whoever drank them to forever forget.

At last, I emerged from the room, knowing I should find out the status on Atlys—who Eugene had apparently returned with just before we'd gotten back.

I found Estasia outside of the room where Marion was working.

Her expression was grim. "He'll live, she said."

"Was it bad?" I didn't know why I bothered asking; her face said it all.

"I'm surprised he held out as long as he did."

I took an attempt at a deep breath, saying, "I should check on Havirax...." We had left him with Lord Atarah, for the time being, that way we could discuss things without worrying about him eavesdropping.

"Alright. Don't go anywhere, though. We have to stay here until…"

Suddenly, the ground shook, and we were forced to use the nearest wall for support.

"Until we find out who wins *that*," Estasia finished grimly.

Ovok's attack on The Underground had begun.

CHAPTER XXV: Scars

<u>Kearn:</u>

I found myself staring at where my leg *should* have been under the covers. Jay and the woman—Marion, I think her name was—had explained the whole series of events to me about half a dozen times, but I still didn't want to believe it. Vague nightmares crept in the shadows of my mind; ones of the excruciating pain and being held down. Memories I began to think might have been when I'd permanently parted ways with my leg. I decided it prudent not to look closer into those.

I was scarred now. Imperfect. I'd never be let back into Bethyn again—even if by some outlandish chance I was ever pardoned for my treason. I didn't even know if my own soldiers—my own friends—would ever look at me as anything but damaged goods. But Jay...he wasn't.

"How are you feeling?" my brother asked as he limped in. I found myself bitterly thinking how I would have been lucky just to have a limp. Perhaps this was the way I was meant to atone for almost killing him.

"Alright...everyone is still safe?" I asked for the hundredth time.

He nodded. "They'll be happy to see you."

My eyes fell again to where the empty spot lay on the bed. "Perhaps."

"You know, Baey says Alenor is going to make a leg for you. You'll be as good as new in no time."

"We both know I'm spoiled goods now, Jay," I said, making fists and wrinkling the sheets.

Jay was quiet for a moment. "I thought we weren't going to care what that cursed country thinks."

I just huffed, leaning back on the pillows that propped me up and refusing to reply further.

"No one you care about seems to think it matters. The only thing they asked was if you were alive."

"But I'm no *use* to them anymore!" I cried. "My one job—the one thing I promised was to keep them safe, and now—"

"—And now you have kept them safe. Helped them get free of Bethyn. And it's time I try and keep you safe for once, Kearn." My brother's voice was so quiet, yet somehow more than enough to get me to shut up. "You may be an imbecile, but losing a leg doesn't make you anything but brave."

I frowned, looked up from the sheets covering my lap to stare at him. It had been drilled into me for so long that scars meant failure. I wanted to believe that maybe they meant something else instead—that maybe Jay was right.

Before I could figure out how to reply, we were both distracted by a commotion outside the door, and before Jay could go to open it, Marion came bursting in with a bag.

"We're leaving. Astra's going to transport us to a safe haven—Atlys was compromised," she announced as she shoved the medical supplies by the bed into the knapsack. "You stay here with your brother. Astra will be here in a little while."

I sat up straighter, ignoring the pain that shot down my leg as I did so. Atlys? Was he alright?

"What about Skayla?" I couldn't help but blurt out the question. If I was going to be maimed like this for life, I wanted to know if it had been for nothing. Even if I still wasn't really sure what it *had* been for.

"She and Tanner are going to The Underground—they'll stay in a small outlet tunnel until things are secure. I need to go get things ready," Marion replied before exiting the room in a rush.

"Well, this seems grand," Jay muttered under his breath, rubbing the back of his neck.

I wasn't sure exactly how much time had passed, but it had to have been close to half an hour. I didn't really feel up to making conversation with Jay, instead finding it hard not to stare constantly at the stump under the blankets where my leg abruptly ended.

Marion, at last, returned to the room, this time followed by a small, redheaded child. The girl smiled hesitantly at me. She seemed vaguely familiar....

Another man followed them in: Maeko.

"Alright, that's everyone, Astra," Marion announced, coming back over to where I was on the bed. "Maeko, bring over the wheelchair."

It was then I noticed Maeko had some sort of folded device with him, and a few clicking gears later, a strange chair with wheels opened up.

"Maeko needs to transfer you over to the chair. Try and stay as still as you can, alright?" Marion explained as the Rugonian man came over.

Jay looked about as uncomfortable as I did with this arrangement, murmuring, "Be careful, Maeko."

Sufficient to say, the transfer of me from bed to chair was an unpleasant experience, and I thought my jaw might break with how hard I found myself clenching it.

But at last I was sitting, feeling somehow more exposed than ever as I sat like some pathetic old man in this strange, moving chair.

"Alright, Astra, ready to go," Marion said with a nod in the girl's direction.

A strange light enveloped us—and I thought I saw a sort of illuminated door frame—and we were suddenly standing in the middle of a very different house. A house…I recognized.

"What…are we doing in Lord Atarah's manor?" I asked, apprehensive as I gripped the armrests of the wheelchair.

"Unfortunately, it would seem we're on the same side, Captain." I recognized the voice before I even recognized his face. "If it's any consolation, I feel quite bad about the leg." Lord Atarah looked down at the now much more exposed stump.

I wanted to disappear, feeling my cheeks flush.

"What is going on?" I hissed, looking to Jay and his friends.

Of course, the stupid aristocrat answered instead of my brother. "It seems you weren't the only one pretending to be Ovok's lapdog. I can explain better, but you don't look very well—why don't you get settled in a room? I can have my physicians look after you."

"Marion is just fine, thank you," I replied tartly, finding the idea of having to be exposed to any more ridicule from strangers unpleasant.

"Very well." Lord Atarah dipped his head. "I can only hope your recovery is quick, as I think the famed rebel captain is going to need his strength if he wants to help lead the rest of the Bethynese traitors."

I scowled. "Yes. All twenty of them." Friends that might not even want to see me like this.

Lord Atarah laughed. "Oh, no. Quite a few more. It seems even I underestimated your influence among the Bethynese army. Reth has effectively abandoned his post. I think, regardless of who wins this fight tonight, you're going to have quite a fun little uprising on your hands." With that, he said a few quiet words to Marion and left.

But I was struck dumb, feeling oddly detached as I was wheeled to a room and given a bed. Never in even my most unrealistic dreams had I imagined anyone from Bethyn turning to rebellion. And now…Reth? I thought of the doubt I'd seen in his eyes whenever he'd addressed me. What did this mean? I found myself staring, voiceless, at my brother, and we held the same look. The one that maybe…maybe one day, we could go home after all.

And maybe it would actually be a home.

Ovok:

It was time. No more waiting.

—*Could we not have tasted his blood a little longer?* Ckaknimaen's whispers were getting tiresome.

This whole thing was getting tiresome.

Atlys had been stronger than expected, but nobles weren't a breed meant to withstand anything except a cushioned life, no matter how much they tried to deny the fact. I swallowed the foul taste in my mouth even as Ckaknimaen tried to revel in it.

Such a distasteful affair. I weaved undetected through the city of chaos, making my way to the area that I had felt the surge of the portal come from. I had been able to narrow down the area between the few things I'd thus far bled from Atlys, as well as my own deductions around the previous portal opening that I'd sensed.

At last, I arrived at the cliffside Atlys had admitted using to smuggle food out of the city. He hadn't said it, but I knew it wasn't just smuggling *out*. The Underground was here, beneath the cliff, I was sure of it. Originally, I had planned to continue to push Atlys and be sure before making such a mess of the hillside, but with the activation of the portal, I knew I had no time. They were leaving—and I could not chance them moving the portal again like last time. Part of me hoped there had been some successful evacuation, however. There had already been so much more death than intended—I hadn't wanted this.

Oh Rhy, I didn't want this at all. I swear. I'm sorry. It didn't matter now. Nothing that could have been mattered, and I knew I wasn't the only one to blame.

I wouldn't waste time on a discreet entrance, knowing it would just mean the possibility of raising their alarms. This needed to be quick; I needed to get in, get through that stupid doorway, and find Rhioa. I had to make this all worth it.

—But more than just Rhioa, now, Ckaknimaen whispered. *We know what you want.*

The blade's influence had become hard to disentangle from my own thoughts over the years, but every once in a while, it stepped too far. Because in the end, we still wanted very, very different things. It would act like it had won in making me the monster, but it still wouldn't get the chaos its twisted edge craved.

I rolled my shoulders and unsheathed the sword, gripping it hard against the screams that echoed in its memory. The way it strained at its leash like a wild dog was disgusting, and yet too often, I indulged it.

I shifted from Human to Dragon; the transformation took one practiced moment and the Myrandi Blade shifted and melted into my claws as I went from man to beast. I grew, knowing it would take an astounding size to be able to break through the earth and into the secret hiding place where they kept my daughter from me.

Launching myself into the air, I climbed, each wing stroke reminding me of my resolve. Each stroke bringing me closer to Rhy and saving her, and closer to what would become my long-term goal. Desperation clutched my gut, but I had lived with that long enough.

I dove down, head bowed and claws out. I hardly processed hitting the ground, the whole world shaking as I tore through and into the hollow cave below.

But then something happened that I did not expect. Instantly, I felt something pierce my neck, albeit very shallowly considering my current size and the Myrandi's resistance to many of Baeno's weapons. Jerking away, I instantly shifted back to human as I fell, twisting my body so that I could see what had attacked.

That's when the other Myrandi slammed into me. I barely had time to shift back to Dragon form as Cyl's jaws tried to swallow me whole, and I almost immediately found myself in a lock with the one person in all the TetraWorlds I would gladly tear limb from limb.

We clawed a moment in the air, but he was still clearly the lesser skilled, especially after our last fight had left him so crippled. Fury launched itself in the form of acidic fire as I spewed it at Cyl. I wanted him to scream—to feel even a fraction of the torment he had abandoned me with.

In my anger, I almost forgot Cyl was plunging me down towards the ground. Just in time, I was able to get on top of him, using him to break our fall as we collided with the floor. Rubble went everywhere, but I didn't care. Cyl was here—that meant I had been right; The Doorway was here somewhere. I could feel it.

—*Kill him, kill him! Let's see the color of his cowardly blood.*

For once, I couldn't agree more. More than anything, I wanted to watch him bleed. Suddenly, something threw me to the side, and just as I was about to fly up again, I found myself pinned under some invisible force.

It was…it was Eatrisian Gifting. So I had not been imagining that shift all those days ago. Cyl had brought an Eatrisian.

I felt the roar in my ears now, even as The Living Stone around my chest protected me from becoming completely incapacitated from the massive exposure to that cursed world's power.

The invisible barrier mixed with the way everything around us seemed to be crumbling. The world itself seemed to bend around us, and The Living Stone pulsed in response to what I guessed was Sven Mara's abilities. But something wasn't right. How had they known I was coming? I shifted again to my human form, using Ckaknimaen and The Living Stone to combat whatever forcefield had trapped me on the ground. Just as I was beginning to move, another figure slammed into me from above.

Sven.

I found myself locked eye-to-eye with the human who had made my life surprisingly difficult these last few years.

I dodged to the side as he adeptly swung his own blade at me, a skilled swordsman for his kind. What was more worrisome for me, however, was the very apparent use of, not illusions, reality. I felt him trying to will Ckaknimaen into useless ribbons. It was a combination of the sword's own powerful Gifting and my possession of The Living Stone that kept the blade from being undone.

The ground opened up beneath me, and I fell, already shifting back to Dragon form as the ground began to close around me. But just before it could, I saw something.

The Esmer. She was hovering above, shouting directions as the glint of green came from the spear she held.

With all the will I could muster, I shot my wings up, breaking through the earth closing around me and using the strength of The Living Stone to fight up against the Eatrisian forcefield still binding me to the ground. I grew. Bigger and bigger, trying to break free, and even as I did, my eye caught something glint from around the Esmer's neck.

A watch, fallen from its hiding place beneath her shirt, now swinging around her neck in plain view. All in a moment, it clicked. They had been too organized; too sure of how I would react.

I knew I had seconds to destroy the watch before she realized her mistake and went back to correct it. Because that's what it was—a mistake. I put all my force into a leap and launched into the air, my tail just barely able to swing up around and almost hit her. In her attempts to avoid it, she came close enough for me to grab her leg as I switched back to a human before another wave of Gifting tried to bring me back to the ground. I let it, dragging her down with me so that I landed right on top of the Esmer. Immediately, I grabbed the watch around her neck with one hand and turned into a Dragon once more in order to crush it in my hand. This time, I would make sure the relic was pulverized.

"No!"

It was too late. I couldn't help but smile coldly as I shifted back to human and stood up, opening the palm of my hand so that the shards of gold and glass sprinkled onto the ground. "Let's make this fight a little more fair, shall we?" I snarled. "Now give me what I want, and I won't kill you."

"Ovok! *Stop* this!" Cyl's draconic shout split the air as he appeared through the chaos and launched right at me, a move I easily worked around between a quick shift in form and back. I let Ckaknimaen taste a little blood as its steel tongue traced Cyl's side as he flew by.

I looked back at the Esmer. "You shouldn't have played sides with him. He'll only let your friends die, little one."

"I think you've killed enough of those already," the girl spat back, resolve in her eyes as she thrust her weapon at me.

I ducked calmly out of the way. "Yes, I am sorry about that." But it was too late now; there was nowhere to go but deeper into the sea of blood that Cyl had pushed me into. There was nothing left but to either drink or drown now.

It was clear they no longer had the upper hand. Gone was the unrelenting flurry of attacks. Gone was the impossible precision and timing. Sure, the chaos was still plenty distracting, especially between the Eatrisian Gifting and Sven Mara's confusing abilities. But now I had the upper hand. I had Ckaknimaen; I had The Living Stone; and I had spent hundreds of years mastering the art of transformation. With the strength of The Living Stone pulsing around my chest, I was able to fight against the Gifting of the others. I had not expected Eatrisian Gifting to be present, but now that these fools had lost the element of surprise and the ability to know my next move, I knew it was only a matter of time before I got around their guard. Just a few more tortured minutes, and it would all be worth it. I could see the portal, guarded now by Skayla's irritating younger brother—who had retreated to it upon the Esmer's orders—and the small, redheaded Eatrisian.

I was done playing games.

The Esmer girl had done a fair job at catching me off guard—but no matter how many times she had gone back in time to try and control this battle, it was still insufficient. She needed a few more lifetimes to catch up, though her attempts now at matching my stride in close combat were admirable as she went to block one of my moves.

I began to transform, shifting back to Human mid-change just as she'd launched into the air to prepare in fighting a very large Myrandi. Too late she realized her mistake, and as she dove down, I focused in on her left wing, rolling to the side just in time for the ground beneath me to turn into an armlike-appendage and hold me down, thanks to Sven. Barely, I avoided it and held to my target: the Esmer diving towards me. I leapt from the ground and mentally apologized for the agony I was about to inflict on the naive child even as my blade screamed for her blood.

I felt the pulse of Eatrisian Gifting hit me, but I'd expected that, allowing it to pull me down—but not before I ducked out of the way of her spearhead and grabbed hold of the staff, pulling her down with me as Ckaknimaen stood poised, catching her wing through as we both fell to the ground.

The girl screamed, and I closed my eyes, quickly tearing Ckaknimaen away from its prey and releasing the blade from her impaled wing. I shifted to Dragon form as Cyl plunged at me, but the old fool had no tact in combat. So now without his precious little Esmer to keep us from a longer engagement, I shifted back to a Human and plunged my sword into his shoulder.

Kill him. A little to the left.

I refused the blade's request. No. I wanted Cyl to watch everything burn. He had destroyed my world—my Rhioa—I would destroy what he held dear. I would make him see just how much he'd failed to do the very thing he'd refused me for. That pathetic excuse of greater good—the greater good that turned a blind eye to the suffering of those it deemed unworthy.

468

Rhy was worthy.

I felt the world around me begin to change—even as I didn't see it—and knew Sven was trying once more to contain me within one of his tricks. But even as I once more shifted to Dragon and launched from Cyl's plummeting body, I allowed The Living Stone around my neck to break the seal. His powers were indeed impressive, but they were a mere taste of the source; the source that was now mine to command, and it was clear he was beginning to tire.

I landed on the ground in front of him and the redhead, once more Human; sword drawn and just barely scraping the ground as it hungered for more victims. I couldn't help but smile a little at the sound of Cyl's labored groans, not far off. He was the only one I didn't mind suffering.

"I'm leaving *now*," I demanded even as I was forced to bring Ckaknimaen up to deflect a blast of fire from the redheaded girl.

"No. You're not, Ovok."

Everything stopped for a moment. I turned around to find Skayla standing there, looking more miserable than even I had last seen her.

I hadn't really expected for them to keep her alive.

Gripping Ckaknimaen, I turned back to Sven and the redhead, who looked about to start another wave of attacks.

"I said *NO!*"

Suddenly, my ears were ringing—no. Not my ears. My mind.

Even she couldn't be *that* stupid. I swung back around. "Get out of my head, you lunatic!" I shouted, intending to run her through.

Except...my feet. They wouldn't move. And Ckaknimaen was laughing. Laughing at me. Laughing at….

469

"I said. You aren't…going…anywhere." Each word that came from Skayla was labored, like it took every ounce of strength to eke them into existence. Only now I realized she wasn't *just* speaking them. They were in my head, echoing around my brain. Blood trickled from her nose.

"Stop it!" I shouted, but now I couldn't tell if I'd even said the words out loud. My hand—the one with Ckaknimaen—began inching forward. "You don't have the strength for *this*," I hissed. It didn't make sense. Somehow…somehow all her years of tapping into the watch's power had to have let her still use The Living Stone.

—*It is time for your blood, now. What fun.* It laughed at me as I moved against my will.

No! Skayla had tried to get in my mind before—had tried and failed. I fought against it, trying to use The Living Stone's pulse to combat her power. But…it wasn't working. Not like it had with Sven.

Because unlike him, Skayla had learned to draw power from other relics. She had used the broken watch for a decade, and unlike Sven…she knew me. As much as I had tried to protect against it, she knew me.

Panic took over as it grew more and more difficult to fight against the pull of her persuasion. *Just let go—let the blade have it.* I couldn't even tell what was Ckaknimaen anymore and what was Skayla, everything in my head was a blur. Everything except the image of Rhy, laying there helpless, waiting for me to come find her—to save her from the fate I'd let her walk right into. My own child, trapped between death and life because I'd foolishly let her go. Foolishly trusted someone else to take care of her.

That's when I realized…my hand….Ckaknimaen…Skayla….

I couldn't breathe. The blade's handle protruded from my chest as everything exploded in pain. All I heard now was the laughter of Ckaknimaen.

And Skayla, as her voice echoed in my fading mind. "Your turn to be afraid."

CHAPTER XXVI: One Last Look in the Mirror

<u>**Sven:**</u>

I couldn't immediately register what was going on as I stared at the form of Ovok, crumpling to the ground with his own sword impaled through his chest. But that wasn't who I ran to.

Skayla crumbled to the ground soon after, violet eyes staring out into nothingness even as I caught her—barely keeping her head from smashing against the cold cavern floor. Not that it mattered. I couldn't see her breathing.

In that moment, I didn't understand what I was feeling or why. Were the tears running down my cheeks relief? Was the pain in my chest because of the life wasted? Or was the strange acceptance because of the peaceful expression on my sister's otherwise blank face. Gone was the madwoman I'd known or the broken shell I'd been trying to avoid. In this moment, the only person I saw was my sister; the sister I'd loved and grown up with. I knew she wasn't going to wake up—she'd conquered a mind that would have killed her even *with* her relic. But there had been no hope for her here, and she was now able to do something…something I knew I couldn't.

Rest. Accept the peace I'd chosen to wake up from.

I realized suddenly Astra was standing over me, looking down at the body in my arms with a conflicted expression. I knew she was about to ask if she should try her Gifting on Skayla. Just barely, I shook my head, whispering, "This is better…she's at peace now. I know she is."

"It—it vanished!" The confused call forced me back into the moment around me, but I didn't let go of Skayla's limp, lifeless body.

It had been Cyl who'd spoken out from over where Ovok had been. I assumed he meant Ovok's body, except wouldn't he have expected that to happen? That had always been what happened when a Drogan died, in my experience.

"What do you mean? Is The Living Stone there?" Baey called out as she dragged herself over to where Cyl was; where Ovok's body *had* been. Blood dripped from her wing, but she briefly met my eyes.

I was about to ask her if she was alright when Cyl cut in with a blunt, "No. Only his blade."

I turned around, wide-eyed as I stared at Cyl. What…what did he mean? We'd all seen the glowing green coming from around his chest. How was it *not* there?

Baey's staggering intensified in an attempt at a run, and Astra quickly went over and helped her regain balance after she almost fell. "What do you mean, it's not there? It has to be! How's the sword still there? Where did he go…." The panic in her tone helped break the spell I was under. I suddenly realized the implication.

"He must have…he must have bound it to himself, somehow. Whatever held the stone kept it with him. Naturally, Grenedil didn't seem to think that would be among The Merchant's possessions." Cyl's tone was flat. "If I were to guess…he's going to reappear by one of his daughters, and my money's on Rhioa."

My chest tightened. "Wait. Where is *she*?"

"In The Maze. The world between worlds. My theory is the Amaranthine Axis."

Held up by Astra, Baey looked from Cyl to me, frantic as she asked, "Then…The Living Stone…it's off-world? W-what does this mean?"

The hatred that had been on Cyl's expression faded to something far more serious as he replied, "Nothing good."

With The Living Stone gone, there wasn't much ability to rest or collect ourselves. It was only a matter of time before the world began to revert to the shattered state it had been in before The Creator had bestowed The Living Stone upon Baeno; reality would fade away into shadow and chaos. But that meant…leaving. And not everyone could go.

Astra had insisted on healing Baey's wounds and fortunately, I had not acquired any serious ones from my engagement with Ovok or protecting the portal. It had been settled that using the Eatrisian Gifting on Cyl would do more harm than good, and so he was given more conventional aid.

I didn't have long to decide what to do with Skayla's body, but I knew I shouldn't do it alone. I asked Astra if she could fetch my mother and Moira, and soon all three of us were standing on the cliffside, the ocean waves lapping at the base of the rocks as I held Skayla's body, now wrapped in a dark cloth I had conjured with my Gift.

No one said a word. Moira was stiff and angry, but Mum…she was sad. I didn't know what I was. As I released her body and used my Gifting to carry her into the air and slowly down into the ocean, I tried to understand the feelings warring inside of me. I just…watched as her body glided unnaturally across the waters. She had been so much to me: a friend, my closest sibling, my nightmare. She had caused so much death and yet, so had I.

Swallowing hard, I manipulated the waves to bring her under, disappearing forever from my sight. There was an odd sense of final camaraderie as I watched the body of the person who had caused me so much pain disappear forever. The conflict in me evaporated as I was left not with the image of her wicked smile, but instead, the eyes so full of regret when Kearn had brought her back that night.

I would hold onto that memory.

"Thank you." Mum took my hand, squeezing it as she, too, watched her daughter fade into the water.

Moira did not say a word, but I understood.

As much as I found it difficult to move, we had to get back to the others, who were hopefully already formulating our next move.

Not much was said between us except for the decision to head through the portal to where everyone else had evacuated to. We needed a plan, and I knew the plan would involve leaving to find Ovok. Only…it would mean more than leaving just a city or country.

Soon, everyone was cramped into a small cabin that had been provided for us. I was confused at the village we had found ourselves in, but there was no time for questions. All I knew was Lord Atarah had apparently come through in spades.

Darby, Thackeray, Grenedil, and Estasia had all been fetched by Baey and Astra, and we huddled around the small space with various grim expressions.

Grenedil was the one speaking at the moment. "I had no idea he had the Box of Aldari. I didn't know it was in the satchel...I'm sorry. My recollection of what was in there was incomplete, but I should have thought of it. It's supposed to be unable to fall from the neck of whoever wears it but...I wouldn't have imagined it meant it would go *with* Ovok after his first death." He pounded his fist into his open palm. "Cyl's right...he likely reappeared by Rhioa, and Havirax confirmed she's not on Baeno. She was kept in the Amaranthine Axis, supposedly."

"Then we go there?" I asked.

"No," Grenedil shook his head wildly. "That place is a trap of time. Its nickname is The Cage. Time does not move in there in the sense that you will not age, but merely stepping inside for a few minutes causes hundreds of years to pass."

"It's the center of The Maze—the center between the worlds," Cyl interjected. "Ovok won't stay there for long, I imagine. He has a device that lets him inside it without missing any time from the outside worlds. But there was only ever one made, and it was for the Lord of the Myrandi. Who is currently...Ovok."

"Then what are we supposed to do?" I looked to Baey, knowing she no longer had the answers. Part of me was relieved that cursed watch was gone, after all we'd learned about Moira's corruption. "Do we have any idea what Ovok's next move is?"

"I think I do." Tanner spoke for the first time. He hadn't said much, but he didn't seem so confused or lost anymore. He grabbed something inside his pocket, looking faraway for a moment before taking a deep breath. "He wants the source of Gifting from all the worlds. He wants to get rid of it."

"What?" Cyl exclaimed incredulously. "That's ridiculous. Why?"

The hatred with which Tanner looked Cyl in the eye was something even I couldn't match. There was still a little Ovok in him yet. "Because he has decided power corrupts absolutely. He wants it gone, because even his friends let it change them."

Cyl just glared back at the boy, not saying a word.

Tanner continued, "I don't understand how, but he knows how to combine them—return them to the original form they were in before The Creator gave them to the worlds."

"So what would this mean?" Estasia asked, crossing her arms. "Because it doesn't sound like he wants to destroy them. What would it mean for Baeno?"

Cyl sighed. "If he somehow managed this…it could mean chaos. No more Gifting—the worlds did exist before the gifts of The Creator, but they eventually failed. That's why pieces of Himself were given to each world to keep them alive. Baeno began crumbling out of existence and reality…Kryso lived in darkness…Eatris was a dead planet where life began withering away. It could mean countless deaths and chaos."

"So then, some of us have to leave and stop Ovok," Estasia said matter-of-factly. "And obviously two of those have to be Baey and Sven."

Everyone sort of looked at her.

478

"Well, someone has to go stop him, and with Skayla and Ovok gone, I think enough of us can manage taking back this mess of a world—half the Bethynese have already abandoned post as it is. You beat Ovok once, so Baey and Sven should go because they're the strongest. Astra should go because she needs to go home, Cyl and Grenedil should go because they're the only ones who know their way around that Maze thing you keep talking about. Tanner needs to go because he's the only one that's been in Ovok's head, and Alenor should go because she has the knowledge of The Living Stone," Estasia continued on, giving no time for anyone else to speak as she went down a list that, honestly, I couldn't argue with.

"As for those that need to stay…Marion and Syvil need to help us deal with the Myrandi problem. Many of them were in a MindHold and I've already discussed with Marion while at Eugene's. She said without Ovok, those that had been loyal to him wouldn't even know what to do. And I…" For the first time, she faltered, looking the most open I'd ever seen her as she faced both Baey and me. "I have to stay. I need to help Eugene and Darby. I don't want you nobles mucking things up a second time," she laughed, addressing Thackeray and Darby at this. Her expression turned earnest as she turned back to look at me and Baey. "So I can't go with you this time."

"Alright," Baey replied, voice quiet. "You're right."

"It's settled, then?" Estasia looked around the room. No one argued. "Then let's say our goodbyes, because you shouldn't waste any more time than necessary."

"I'll have your supplies packed," Thackeray announced, leaving the tent. I was a little confused when Darby quickly left with him, and for some reason, I was also…disappointed? I wondered if I'd get to say goodbye.

"Take care of Mum, will you?" Moira asked, speaking for the first time.

I turned my attention back to my remaining sister. "I will," I promised, wishing I could say something else. I could tell by the look in her eyes she was just as conflicted.

"Oh, please." Mum came up, elbowing me as she said, "I think we all know who will need more looking after with the way he goes about getting in trouble."

It felt odd, joking after having just buried Skayla.

"Don't go dying again, alright?" I was surprised to see Estasia come over to me, looking strangely emotional. "I'm not there to drag you out of the holes you get into."

I winced. "Right."

"Oh, come on." She punched me in the shoulder. "I was kidding. Just…take care of Birdie, huh? I know you'll have each other's backs."

Swallowing hard, I gave a nod. "Don't worry."

Rolling her eyes, she replied, "I always do. That's what's kept me alive so far."

I couldn't help but give a small smile at the comment, but then turned back towards the exit of the tent. I…I wanted to say goodbye to Darby. The longer she was gone, the more I realized I had to.

"I'll go see how the supplies are coming," I said quickly before making a pass for the exit.

I didn't get three paces away from the tent before Darby ran into me.

"Oh, sorry—Sven!" She stopped in the middle of an apology. In fact, she also stopped trying to use my hand to help her back up, instead grabbing it much harder as she added, "Just who I needed to see."

Any words I had were stuck in my throat, and I realized I hadn't really been sure what I was even going to say to her in the first place.

Fortunately, she kept talking. "Look, I talked it over with Thackeray and…and I'm coming with you."

I couldn't explain the feeling that washed over me, other than lightheadedness. "W…what?"

"Last time you left, you didn't come back for a decade and you…" She looked up at me, eyes so full and earnest as she squeezed my hand harder. I realized I was squeezing back. "I know Baey has your back…I know she's more than capable of keeping you safe. But I don't want you to be alone. I can't handle you disappearing again—and if you can't come back, then…at least I'll be there, too."

"I…Darby, I can't ask you—"

"—Sven look—I care about you. A lot. It's alright if you don't return it—I know at the very least, you probably can't return it right now. It's a little selfish, but I need you probably more than you need me, and I'm…I'm coming. Even if just as your friend, I'm coming." She stuttered to a halt, panic all too evident as she seemed to register what she'd said.

I couldn't find words. All I found myself whispering was, "I don't want to be a burden." But there was so much more I wanted to say, if only I could find out how to say it.

She released one of my hands—to my despair—and gently touched my face. "You've never been a burden, Sven. Know that."

Closing my eyes a moment, I whispered, "Darby I...I don't think I know myself enough yet to know what I want." I was surprised by how I was choking back unexpected tears. "I don't think I can give you anything right now. I can't...I can't even—"

"It's alright," she laughed through her own tears. "I'm not asking you to be anything. I'm just telling you: I'm not going to let you be alone. And if you just want that as a friend, then I will always be here as a friend. I just want you to live and be happy."

"I'm trying to want that too," I whispered.

Her smile did something to me. I couldn't breathe, but it wasn't because of panic.

"Good," she said. "Because you deserve to be."

"I just...there is so much I've done—to you. To your brother. To—" I looked away.

"I never saw you in any of those moments. I only saw your sister's eyes, Sven. And now I only see you, and I want you to be able to see yourself again like I see you."

It was hard to speak, but I managed, "I'm trying. I think...I think I really am now."

Slowly, she took her hand back from my cheek. "Good. That's all I want, Sven."

"I want to tell you that I..." I winced, turning away for a moment. "I just don't know myself enough, yet. I don't know where the guilt stops and I begin."

Her smile was so beautiful and genuine. "And that's alright. It is enough for me to be here for you as a friend."

My breath caught, and I found it hard to speak through the lump in my throat. "I think…I think I need that. I miss my friends. All of them. And I've really liked having you back."

She took my hand, squeezing it hard, then pulled me in for a fierce embrace that I didn't fight against. "And I missed you. We'll get The Living Stone back. Together. I won't let you be alone again."

I didn't fight. For once, I didn't question anything, I just allowed myself to repeat what she'd said over and over in my head. *I won't let you be alone again.*

Baey:

"You alright, Birdie?"

I stood there in the tent, still trying to process…everything. My failure. The fact was that even despite going back thousands of times, I'd still messed it up, and this time I couldn't fix it.

"I need you to come," I said quietly. "You're always the one with the good ideas."

Estasia snorted. "I mean, yes, but you weren't half bad yourself with this whole mess."

"No—this wasn't just me. Half the plan was you or Darby or Eugene. I…let Ovok grab the watch. I could have gone back otherwise—I could have fixed it so—"

"Listen." She grabbed my shoulders, pulling me so that I was forced to make eye contact. "No one died—" she stopped a moment and then added, "—no one important died. None of your *friends* died, right? And

483

from what you told me, we all died various horrible deaths before. Atlys is going to make it. I have a feeling he's going to be quite pleased with sporting an eyepatch, and Sven and Astra are in one piece. That's because of you. So no. You don't need me." With a shake of her head, she murmured, "I trust you, Baey. Just don't let it get to your head."

"But what if I—"

"—Listen, most of us only get one try to get things right. So you'll just have to be good with that like everyone else." She smiled, punching me gently in the shoulder and then ruffling my hair. "But come back, alright?"

Swallowing hard, I nodded. "I will. Promise."

"Good."

There wasn't much time to waste on more goodbyes. The last surprise was Darby insisting on coming with us—to Estasia's slight chagrin. But then Thackeray had announced the supplies were ready, and it was time. Soon, we were alone in the abandoned Underground, the group of us all looking pretty grim as we waited for Cyl to open The Doorway into this Maze. Havirax was, unfortunately, coming with us, bound to Grenedil. He was the only access Grenedil had to The Merchant's Satchel, after all.

I noted Ovok's blade—the one that had so wickedly whispered when it had pierced my wing—was with Astra, just as Grenedil had insisted upon. There had been another pretty big argument about it, but Astra had said she'd dealt with plenty of voices before from the Miadoris—whatever that meant—and it had finally been agreed to let her take it. I still did not completely understand how these Myrandi blades worked, but Grenedil had said its tongue was too potent to even think of giving it to Cyl. I still didn't know how I felt about putting that sort of burden on anyone, but I didn't want us leaving it here, either.

"So I think…we should head to my brother first," Astra spoke up. "If Ovok is after the sources of each world…then that's where he might be off to next."

Cyl sighed. "And where on Eatris is that?"

"Cithan." Astra's fists clenched. "Where Ovok's other daughter, Tirzah, helped us put the Miadoris."

The bright rectangular door appeared in front of Cyl, illuminating the space and reminding me again of the gravitas of this decision. My failure was leading us further away from home than I ever could have anticipated.

"To the city of the Elves, then," Cyl announced, motioning for us to follow.

Yes. Hopefully our next stop wouldn't be the end of worlds.

EPILOGUE:

Ovok:

I gasped, suddenly standing in the dim lantern light of a strange place. Panic erupted as I frantically felt my chest, the memory of Ckaknimaen's wicked teeth all too clear. But I was looking for something else—something more—

My fist closed around the small box hanging from my neck, and I found myself unable to breathe. I'd hoped that the binding would last past a death, but there had been no way to confirm it.

Death. I was now down a life. That witch had killed me.

I heard the gentle breaths of someone nearby, and turning, realized all at once where I was.

There she laid, so vulnerable, clinging to life in its last moments here in the Amaranthine Axis. My Rhy. I'd appeared next to her, of course. Of that I was not surprised.

I stumbled over, taking The Living Stone from around my neck and pressing it to her forehead. "Please. Please, Rhy, you need to wake up." *I have done terrible, terrible things for this. Please don't make this for nothing.*

Her breathing deepened and her eyes flickered open, revealing those cursed, unnaturally blue eyes that came only from the Miadoris' touch. The same eyes that Eatrisian stranger on Baeno had possessed.

I swallowed hard, feeling suddenly lightheaded. A relief deeper than I'd ever experienced spread through my whole body, and all I could do was whisper, "Rhy."

"...Father...?"

I gripped The Living Stone hard as I retracted it from her head. I watched my daughter slowly come into full consciousness, and suddenly wondered how long it would be until she'd find out what I'd done.

And what I was about to do.

THE END

...FOR NOW

Next book in the *A Daughter's Ransom* series:

OPERATION LIFT

Victoria is the worst...

...which wouldn't be so bad, except that she's married to Xander's dad—the king of the most powerful nation on Kryso. Convinced that Victoria is secretly using his dad, and with no one who believes him, Xander is determined to find proof. But what he uncovers is much bigger than he bargained for.

When a mysterious off-worlder stumbles through a portal, it sets off a chain of events that turns Xander's world upside-down. With secrets and betrayals at every turn, how will he ever get back to his dad? And what happens when the only person he can trust can't even remember his own name?

About the *A Daughter's Ransom* series:

The TetraWorlds live in ignorance of each other's existence...

One fallen behind in a Medieval time of fantastic and dangerous creatures, another fallen asleep in the comfort of their Victorian age, and the last torn apart by its own Modern innovation. When a dark threat rises up against them—one so quiet that none know to stop it, a Guard from each world must be called to protect their planet's source. But what will happen when these worlds entwine?

About the author:

NIAMH SCHMID:

Born in Clifton Park New York, Niamh is (unfortunately) a human being. She would much rather be off in some pretend world battling an ogre or taming a rabid pegasus, but instead is currently engaging in completing a bachelor's in Piano Performance. In her spare time she cares for her two mini ponies (or monsters), Freddie and Taffie, as well as her Dorkie (dachshund/yorkie mix) Tobie. She also loves to compose, collect stamps, and dabble in being a very mediocre artist.